CW00622002

WHEN THE FIVE MOONS RISE

WHEN THE FIVE MOONS RISE

Jack Vance

DISCARD

UNDERWOOD-MILLER
Novato, California
Lancaster, Pennsylvania
1992

FAIRMONT BRANCH LIBRARY
4330 FAIRMONT PKWY.
PASADENA, TX 77504

WHEN THE FIVE MOONS RISE
ISBN 0-88733-145-9

Copyright © 1992 by Jack Vance
Original jacket art copyright © 1992 by Vincent DiFate

An Underwood-Miller book by arrangement with the author and the trade publisher, Tor Books. No part of this book may be reproduced in any form or by any electronic or mechanical means including information storage and retrieval systems without explicit permission from the author, except by a reviewer who may quote brief passages. For information address the publisher: Underwood-Miller, Inc., 708 Westover Drive, Lancaster, PA 17601.

Jacket typography by Arnie Fenner
Book design: Underwood-Miller
Printed in the United States of America
All Rights Reserved

FIRST EDITION

Library of Congress Cataloging-in-Publication Data
Vance, Jack, 1916–
    When the five moons rise / by Jack Vance. — 1st ed.
    252p. 24cm. —
    ISBN 0-88733-145-9 (hardcover) : $29.95
    1. Science fiction, American. I. Title.
PS3572.A424W44   1992
813'.54—dc20
                                    92-18617
                                        CIP

Contents

WHEN THE FIVE MOONS RISE

NOISE

Captain Hess placed a notebook on the desk and hauled a chair up under his sturdy buttocks. Pointing to the notebook, he said, "That's the property of your man Evans. He left it aboard the ship."

Galispell asked in faint surprise, "There was nothing else? No letter?"

"No, sir, not a thing. That notebook was all he had when we picked him up."

Galispell rubbed his fingers along the scarred fibers of the cover. "Understandable, I suppose." He flipped back the cover. "Hmmmm."

Hess asked tentatively, "What's been your opinion of Evans? Rather a strange chap?"

"Howard Evans? No, not at all. He's been a very valuable man to us. Why do you ask?"

Hess frowned, searching for the precise picture of Evans's behavior. "I considered him erratic, or maybe emotional."

Galispell was genuinely startled. "Howard Evans?"

Hess's eyes went to the notebook. "I took the liberty of looking through his log, and...well—."

"And you took the impression he was...strange."

"Maybe everything he writes is true," said Hess stubbornly. "But I've been poking into odd corners of space all my life and I've never seen anything like it."

"Peculiar situation," said Galispell in a neutral voice. He looked into the notebook.

1

II

Journal of Howard Charles Evans

I commence this journal without pessimism but certainly without optimism. I feel as if I have already died once. My time in the lifeboat was at least a foretaste of death. I flew on and on through the ark, and a coffin could be only slightly more cramped. The stars were above, below, ahead, astern. I have no clock, and I put no duration to my drifting. It was more than a week, it was less than a year.

So much for space, the lifeboat, the stars. There are not too many pages in this journal. I will need them all to chronicle my life on this world which, rising up under me, gave me life.

There is much to tell and many ways in the telling. There is myself, my own response to this rather dramatic situation. But lacking the knack for tracing the contortions of my psyche, I will try to detail events as objectively as possible.

I landed the lifeboat on as favorable a spot as I had opportunity to select. I tested the atmosphere, temperature, pressure, and biology; then I ventured outside. I rigged an antenna and dispatched my first SOS.

Shelter is no problem; the lifeboat serves me as a bed, and if necessary, a refuge. From sheer boredom later on I may fell a few of these trees and build a house. But I will wait; there is no urgency.

A stream of pure water trickles past the lifeboat; I have abundant concentrated food. As soon as the hydroponic tanks begin to produce, there will be fresh fruits and vegetables and yeast proteins.

Survival seems no particular problem.

The sun is a ball of dark crimson, and casts hardly more light than the full moon of Earth. The lifeboat rests on a meadow of thick black-green creeper, very pleasant underfoot. A hundred yards distant in the direction I shall call south lies a lake of inky water, and the meadow slopes smoothly down to the water's edge. Tall sprays of rather pallid vegetation—I had best use the word "trees"—bound the meadow on either side.

Behind is a hillside, which possibly continues into a range of mountains; I can't be sure. This dim red light makes vision uncertain after the first few hundred feet.

The total effect is one of haunted desolation and peace. I would enjoy the beauty of the situation if it were not for the uncertainties of the future.

The breeze drifts across the lake, smelling pleasantly fragrant, and it carries a whisper of sound from off the waves. I have assembled the hydroponic tanks and set out cultures of yeast. I shall never starve or die of thirst. The lake is smooth and inviting; perhaps in time I will build a little boat. The water is warm, but I dare not swim. What could be more terrible than to be seized from below and dragged under?

There is probably no basis for my misgivings. I have seen no animal life of any kind: no birds, fish, insects, crustacea. The world is one of absolute quiet, except for the whispering breeze.

The scarlet sun hangs in the sky, remaining in place during many of my sleeps. I see it is slowly westering; after this long day how long and how monotonous will be the night!

I have sent off four SOS sequences; somewhere a monitor station must catch them.

A machete is my only weapon, and I have been reluctant to venture far from the lifeboat. Today (if I may use the word) I took my courage in my hands and started around the lake. The trees are rather like birches, tall and supple. I think the bark and leaves would shine a clear silver in light other than this wine-colored gloom. Along the lakeshore they stand in a line, almost as if long ago they had been planted by a wandering gardener. The tall branches sway in the breeze, glinting scarlet with purple overtones, a strange and wonderful picture which I am alone to see.

I have heard it said that enjoyment of beauty is magnified by the presence of others: that a mysterious rapport comes into play to reveal subtleties which a single mind is unable to grasp. Certainly as I walked along the avenue of trees with the lake and the scarlet sun behind, I would have been grateful for companionship—but I believe that something of peace, the sense of walking in an ancient, abandoned garden, would be lost.

The lake is shaped like an hourglass; at the narrow waist I could look across and see the squat shape of the lifeboat. I sat down under a bush, which continually nodded red and black flowers in front of me.

Mist fibrils drifted across the lake and the wind made low musical sounds.

I rose to my feet, continued around the lake.

I passed through forests and glades and came once more to my lifeboat.

I went to tend my hydroponic tanks, and I think the yeast had been disturbed, prodded at curiously.

The dark red sun is sinking. Every day—it must be clear that I use "day" as the interval between my sleeps—finds it lower in the sky. Night is almost upon me, long night. How shall I spend my time in the dark?

I have no gauge other than my mind, but the breeze seems colder. It brings long, mournful chords to my ears, very sad, very sweet. Mist-wraiths go fleeting across the meadow.

Wan stars already show themselves, ghost-lamps without significance.

I have been considering the slope behind my meadow; tomorrow I think I will make the ascent.

I have plotted the position of every article I possess. I will be gone some hours; if a visitor meddles with my goods—I will know his presence for certain.

The sun is low, the air pinches at my cheeks. I must hurry if I wish to return while light still shows me the landscape. I picture myself lost; I see myself wandering the face of this world, groping for my precious lifeboat, my tanks, my meadow.

Anxiety, curiosity, obstinacy all spurring me, I set off up the slope at a half-trot.

Becoming winded almost at once, I slowed my pace. The turf of the lakeshore had disappeared; I was walking on bare rock and lichen. Below me the meadow became a patch, my lifeboat a gleaming spindle. I watched for a moment. Nothing stirred anywhere in my range of vision.

I continued up the slope and finally breasted the ridge. A vast valley fell off below me. Far away a range of great mountains stood into the dark sky. The wine-colored light slanting in from the west lit the prominences, the frontal bluffs, left the valleys in gloom: an alternate sequence of red and black beginning far in the west, continuing past, far to the east.

I looked down behind me, down to my own meadow, and was hard put to find it in the fading light. There it was, and there the lake, a sprawling hourglass. Beyond was dark forest, then a strip of old rose savanna, then a dark strip of woodland, then laminae of colorings to the horizon.

The sun touched the edge of the mountains, and with what seemed almost a sudden lurch, fell half below the horizon. I turned downslope; a terrible thing to be lost in the dark. My eye fell upon a white object, a hundred yards along the ridge. I walked nearer. Gradually it assumed form: a thimble, a cone, a pyramid—a cairn of white rocks.

A cairn, certainly. I stood looking down on it.

I turned, looked over my shoulder. Nothing in view. O looked down to the meadow. Swift shapes? I strained through the gathering murk. Nothing.

I tore at the cairn, threw rocks aside. What was below?

Nothing.

In the ground a faintly marked rectangle three feet long was perceptible. I stood back. No power I knew of could induce me to dig into that soil.

The sun was disappearing. Already at the south and north the afterglow began, lees of wine: the sun moved with astounding rapidity; what manner of sun was this, dawdling at the meridian, plunging below the horizon?

I turned downslope, but darkness came faster. The scarlet sun was gone; in the west was the sad sketch of departed flame. I stumbled, I fell. I looked into the east. A marvelous zodiacal light was forming, a strengthening blue triangle.

I watched, from my hands and knees. A cusp of bright blue lifted into the sky. A moment later a flood of sapphire washed the landscape. A new sun of intense indigo rose into the sky.

The world was the same and yet different; where my eyes had been accustomed to red and red subcolors, now I saw the intricate cycle of blue.

When I returned to my meadow the breeze carried a new sound: bright chords that my mind could almost form into melody. For a moment I so amused myself, and thought to see dance-motion in the wisps of vapor which for the last few days had been noticeable over my meadow.

In what I call a peculiar frame of mind I crawled into the lifeboat and went to sleep.

I crawled out of the lifeboat into an electric world. I listened. Surely that was music—faint whispers drifting in on the wind like a fragrance.

I went down to the lake, as blue as a ball of that cobalt dye so aptly known as bluing.

The music came louder; I could catch snatches of melody—sprightly, quick-step phrases. I put my hands to my ears; if I were experiencing hallucinations, the music would continue. The sound diminished, but did not fade entirely; my test was not definitive. But I felt sure it was real. And where music was there must be musicians...I ran forward, shouted, "Hello!"

"Hello!" came the echo from across the lake.

The music faded a moment, as cricket chorus quiets when disturbed, then gradually I could hear it again—distant music, "horns of elf-land faintly blowing."

It went completely out of perception. I was left standing in the blue light, alone on my meadow.

I washed my face, returned to the lifeboat, sent out another set of SOS signals.

Possibly the blue day is shorter than the red day; with no clock I can't be sure. But with my new fascination in the music and its source, the blue day seems to pass swifter.

Never have I caught sight of the musicians. Is the sound generated by the trees, by diaphanous insects crouching out of my vision?

One day I glanced across the lake, and—wonder of wonders!—a gay town spread along the opposite shore. After a first dumbfounded gaze, I ran down to the water's edge, stared as if it were the most precious sight of my life.

Pale silk swayed and rippled: pavilions, tents, fantastic edifices.... Who inhabited these places? I waded knee-deep into the lake, and thought to see flitting shapes.

I ran like a madman around the shore. Plants with pale blue blossoms succumbed to my feet; I left the trail of an elephant through a patch of delicate reeds.

And when I came panting to the shore opposite my meadow, what was there? Nothing.

The city had vanished like a dream. I sat down on a rock. Music came clear for an instant, as if a door had momentarily opened.

I jumped to my feet. Nothing to be seen. I looked back across the lake. There—on my meadow—a host of gauzy shapes moved like May flies over a still pond.

When I returned, my meadow was vacant. The shore across the lake was bare.

So goes the blue day; and now there is amazement to my life. Whence comes the music? Who and what are these flitting shapes, never quite real but never entirely out of mind? Four times an hour I press a hand to my forehead, fearing the symptoms of a mind turning in on itself.... If music actually exists on this world, actually vibrates the air, why should it come to my ears as Earth music? These chords I hear might be struck on familiar instruments; the harmonies are not at all alien.... And these pale plasmic wisps that I forever seem to catch from the corner of my eye: the style is that of gay and playful humanity. The tempo of their movement is the tempo of the music.

So goes the blue day. Blue air, blue-black turf, ultramarine water, and the bright blue star bent to the west.... How long have I lived on this planet? I have broadcast the SOS sequence until now the batteries hiss with exhaustion; soon there will be an end to power. Food, water are no problem for me, but what use is a lifetime of exile on a world of blue and red?

The blue day is at its close. I would like to mount the slope and watch the blue sun's passing—but the remembrance of the red sunset still provokes a queasiness in my stomach. So I will watch from my meadow, and then, if there is darkness, I will crawl into the lifeboat like a bear into a cave, and wait the coming of light.

The blue day goes. The sapphire sun wanders into the western forest, the sky glooms to blue-black, the stars show like unfamiliar home-places.

For some time now I have heard no music; perhaps it has been so all-present that I neglect it.

The blue star is gone, the air chills. I think that deep night is on me indeed.... I hear a throb of sound, I turn my head. The east glows pale pearl. A silver globe floats up into the night: a great ball six times the diameter of Earth's full moon. Is this a sun, a satellite, a burnt-out star? What a freak of cosmology I have chanced upon!

The silver sun—I must call it a sun, although it casts a cool satin light—moves in an aureole like an oyster shell. Once again the color of the planet changes. The lake glistens like quicksilver, the trees are hammered metal.... The silver star passes over a high wrack of clouds, and the music seems to burst forth as if somewhere someone flung wide curtains.

I wander down to the lake. Across on the opposite shore once more I see the town. It seems clearer, more substantial; I note details that shimmered away to vagueness before—a wide terrace beside the lake, spiral columns, a row of urns. The silhouette is, I think, the same as when I saw it under the blue sun: silken tents, shimmering, reflecting cusps of light; pillars of carved stone, lucent as milk-glass; fantastic fixtures of no obvious purpose.... Barges drift along the quicksilver lake like moths, great sails bellying, the rigging a mesh of cobweb. Nodules of light hang on the stays, along the masts.... On sudden thought, I turn, look up to my own meadow. I see a row of booths as at an old-time fair, a circle of pale stone set in the turf, a host of filmy shapes.

Step by step I edge toward my lifeboat. The music waxes. I peer at one of the shapes, but the outlines waver. It moves to the emotion of the music—or does the motion of the shape generate the music?

I run forward, shouting. One of the shapes slips past me, and I look into a blur where a face might be. I come to a halt, panting hard; I stand on the marble circle. I stamp; it rings solid. I walk toward the booths, they seem to display complex things of pale cloth and dim metal—but as I look my eyes mist over as with tears. The music goes far, far away, my meadow lies bare and quiet. My feet press into silver-black turf; in the sky hangs the silver-black star.

I am sitting with my back to the lifeboat, staring across the lake, which is still as a mirror. I have arrived at a set of theories.

My primary proposition is that I am sane—a necessary article of faith; why bother even to speculate otherwise? So—events occurring outside my own mind cause everything I have seen and heard. But—note this!—these sights and sounds do not obey the laws of science; in many respects they seem particularly subjective.

It must be, I tell myself, that both objectivity and subjectivity enter into the situation. I receive impressions which my brain finds unfamiliar, and so translates to the concept most closely related. By this theory the inhabitants of this world are constantly close; I move unknowingly through their palaces and arcades; they dance incessantly around me. As my mind gains sensitivity, I verge upon rapport with their way of life and I see them. More exactly, I sense something which creates an image in the visual region of my brain. Their emotions, the pattern of their life sets up a kind of vibration which sounds in my brain as music.... The reality of these creatures I am sure I will never know. They are diaphane, I am flesh; they live in a world of spirit, I plod the turf with my heavy feet.

These last days I have neglected to broadcast the SOS. Small lack; the batteries are about done.

The silver sun is at the zenith, and leans westward. What comes next? Back to the red sun? Or darkness? Certainly this is no ordinary planetary system; the course of this world along its orbit must resemble one of the pre-Copernican epicycles.

I believe that my brain is gradually tuning into phase with this world, reaching a new high level of sensitivity. If my theory is correct, the *elan-vital* of the native beings expresses itself in my brain as music. On Earth we would perhaps use the word "telepathy." So I am practicing, concentrating, opening my consciousness wide to these new perceptions. Ocean mariners know a trick of never looking directly at a far light lest it strike the eyes' blind spot. I am using a similar device of never staring directly at one of the gauzy beings. I allow the image to establish itself, build itself up, and by this technique they appear quite definitely human. I sometimes think I can glimpse the features. The women are like sylphs, achingly beautiful; the men—I have not seen one in detail, but their carriage, their form is familiar.

The music is always part of the background, just as rustling of leaves is part of a forest. The mood of these creatures seems to change with their sun, so I hear music to suit. The red sun gave them passionate melancholy, the blue sun merriment. Under the silver star they are delicate, imaginative, wistful.

The silver day is on the wane. Today I sat beside the lake with the trees a screen of filigree, watching the moth-barges drift back and forth. What is their function? Can life such as this be translated in terms of economies, ecology, sociology? I doubt it. The word intelligence may not even enter the picture; is not our brain a peculiarly anthropoid characteristic, and is not intelligence a function of our peculiarly anthropoid brain?...A portly barge sways near, with swampglobes in the rigging, and I forget my hypotheses. I can never know the truth, and it is perfectly possible that these creatures are no more aware of me than I originally was aware of them.

Time goes by; I return to the lifeboat. A young woman-shape whirls past. I pause, peer into her face; she tilts her head, her eyes burn into mine as she passes.... I try an SOS—listlessly, because I suspect the batteries to be dank and dead.

And indeed they are.

The silver star is like an enormous Christmas tree bauble, round and glistening. It floats low, and once more I stand irresolute, half expecting night.

The star falls; the forest receives it. The sky dulls, and night has come.

I face the east, my back pressed to the hull of my lifeboat. Nothing.

I have no conception of the passage of time. Darkness, timelessness.

Somewhere clocks turn minute hands, second hands, hour hands—I stand staring into the night, perhaps as slow as a sandstone statue, perhaps as feverish as a salamander.

In the darkness there is a peculiar cessation of sound. The music has dwindled; down through a series of wistful chords, a forlorn last cry....

A glow in the east, a green glow, spreading. Up rises a magnificent green sphere, the essence of all green, the tincture of emeralds, deep as the sea.

A throb of sound; rhythmical, strong music, swinging and veering.

The green light floods the planet, and I prepare for the green day.

I am almost one with the natives. I wander among their pavilions, I pause by their booths to ponder their stuffs and wares; silken medallions, spangles and circlets of woven metal, cups of fluff and iridescent puff, puddles of color and wafts of light-shot gauze. There are chains of green glass; captive butterflies; spheres which seem to hold all the heavens, all the clouds, all the stars.

And to all sides of me go the flicker and flit of the dream-people. The men are all vague, but familiar; the women turn me smiles of ineffable provocation. But I will drive myself mad with temptations; what I see is no more than the formulation of my own brain, an interpretation.... And this is tragedy, for there is one creature so unutterably lovely that whenever I see the shape that is she my throat aches and I run forward, to peer into her eyes that are not eyes....

Today I clasped my arms around her, expecting yielding wisp. Surprisingly, there was the feel of supple flesh. I kissed her, cheek, chin, mouth. Such a look of perplexity on the face as I have never seen; heaven knows what strange act the creature thought me to be performing.

She went her way, but the music is strong and triumphant: the voice of cornets, the resonant bass below.

A man comes past; something in his stride, his posture, plucks at my memory. I step forward; I will gaze into his face, I will plumb the vagueness.

He whirls past like a figure on a carousel; he wears flapping ribbons of silk and pompons of spangled satin. I pound after him, I plant myself in his path. He strides past with a side-glance, and I stare into the rigid face.

It is my own face.

He wears my face, he walks with my stride. He is I.

Already is the green day gone?

The green sun goes, and the music takes on depth. No cessation now; there is preparation, imminence.... What is that other sound? A far spasm of something growling and clashing like a broken gear box.

It fades out.

The green sun goes down in a sky like a peacock's tail. The music is slow, exalted.

The west fades, the east glows. The music goes toward the east, to the great bands of rose, yellow, orange, lavender. Cloud-flecks burst into flame. A golden glow consumes the sky.

The music takes on volume. Up rises the new sun—a gorgeous golden ball. The music swells into a paean of light, fulfillment, regeneration.... Hark! A second time the harsh sound grates across the music.

Into the sky, across the sun, drifts the shape of a spaceship. It hovers over my meadow, the landing jets come down like plumes.

The ship lands.

I hear the mutter of voices—men's voices.

The music is vanished; the marble carvings, the tinsel booths, the wonderful silken cities are gone.

III

Galispell rubbed his chin.

Captain Hess asked anxiously, "What do you think of it?"

Galispell looked for a long moment out the window. "What happened after you picked him up? Did you see any of these phenomena he talks about?"

"Not a thing." Captain Hess shook his big round head. "Sure, the system was a fantastic gaggle of dark stars and fluorescent planets and burnt-out old suns; maybe all these things played hob with his mind. He didn't seem too overjoyed to see us, that's a fact—just stood there, staring at us as if we were trespassers. 'We got your SOS,' I told him. 'Jump aboard, wrap yourself around a good meal!' He came walking forward as if his feet were dead.

"Well, to make a long story short, he finally came aboard. We loaded on his lifeboat and took off.

"During the voyage back he had nothing to do with anybody—just kept to himself, walking up and down the promenade.

"He had a habit of putting his hands to his head; one time I asked him if he was sick, if he wanted the medic to look him over. He said no, there was nothing wrong with him. That's about all I know of the man.

"We made Sun, and came down toward Earth. Personally, I didn't see what happened because I was on the bridge, but this is what they tell me:

"As Earth got bigger and bigger Evans began to act more restless than usual, wincing and turning his head back and forth. When we were about a thousand miles out, he gave a kind of furious jump.

"'The noise!' he yelled. 'The horrible *noise!*'" And with that he ran astern, jumped into his lifeboat, cast off, and they tell me disappeared back the way we came.

"And that's all I got to tell you, Mr. Galispell. It's too bad, after our taking all that trouble to get him, Evans decided to pull up stakes—but that's the way it goes."

"He took off back along your course?"

"That's right. If you're wanting to ask, could he have made the planet where we found him, the answer is, not likely."

"But there's a chance?

"Oh, sure," said Captain Hess. "There's a chance.

DUST OF FAR SUNS

I

Henry Belt came limping into the conference room, mounted the dais, settled himself at the desk. He looked once around the room: a swift bright glance which, focusing nowhere, treated the eight young men who faced him to an almost insulting disinterest. He reached in his pocket, brought forth a pencil and a flat red book, which he placed on the desk. The eight young men watched in absolute silence. They were much alike: healthy, clean, smart, their expressions identically alert and wary. Each had heard legends of Henry Belt, each had formed his private plans and private determinations.

Henry Belt seemed a man of a different species. His face was broad, flat, roped with cartilage and muscle, with skin the color and texture of bacon rind. Coarse white grizzle covered his scalp, his eyes were crafty slits, his nose a misshapen lump. His shoulders were massive, his legs short and gnarled.

"First of all," said Henry Belt, with a gap-toothed grin, "I'll make it clear that I don't expect you to like me. If you do I'll be surprised and displeased. It will mean that I haven't pushed you hard enough."

He leaned back in his chair, surveyed the silent group. "You've heard stories about me. Why haven't they kicked me out of the service? Incorrigible, arrogant, dangerous Henry Belt. Drunken Henry Belt. (The last of course is slander. Henry Belt has never been drunk in his life.) Why do they tolerate me? For one simple reason: out of necessity. No one wants to take on this kind of job. Only a man like Henry Belt can stand up to it:

13

year after year in space, with nothing to look at but a half-dozen round-faced young scrubs. He takes them out, he brings them back. Not all of them, and not all of those who come back are spacemen today. But they'll all cross the street when they see him coming. Henry Belt? you say. They'll turn pale or go red. None of them will smile. Some of them are high-placed now. They could kick me loose if they chose. Ask them why they don't. Henry Belt is a terror, they'll tell you. He's wicked, he's a tyrant. Cruel as an axe, fickle as a woman. But a voyage with Henry Belt blows the foam off the beer. He's ruined many a man, he's killed a few, but those that come out of it are proud to say, I trained with Henry Belt!

"Another thing you may hear: Henry Belt has luck. But don't pay any heed. Luck runs out. You'll be my thirteenth class, and that's unlucky. I've taken out seventy-two young sprats, no different from yourselves; I've come back twelve times: which is partly Henry Belt and partly luck. The voyages average about two years long: how can a man stand it? There's only one who could: Henry Belt. I've got more space-time than any man alive, and now I'll tell you a secret: this is my last time out. I'm starting to wake up at night to strange visions. After this class I'll quit. I hope you lads aren't superstitious. A white-eyed woman told me that I'd die in space. She told me other things and they've all come true. We'll get to know each other well. And you'll be wondering on what basis I make my recommendations. Am I objective and fair? Do I put aside personal animosity? Naturally there won't be any friendship. Well, here's my system. I keep a red book. Here it is. I'll put your names down right now. You, sir?"

"I'm Cadet Lewis Lynch, sir."

"You?"

"Edward Culpepper, sir."

"Marcus Verona, sir."

"Vidal Weske, sir."

"Marvin McGrath, sir."

"Barry Ostrander, sir."

"Clyde von Gluck, sir."

"Joseph Sutton, sir."

Henry Belt wrote the names in the red book. "This is the system. When you do something to annoy me, I mark you down demerits. At the end of the voyage I total these demerits, add a few here and there for luck, and am so guided. I'm sure nothing could be clearer than this. What annoys me? Ah, that's a question which is hard to answer. If you talk too much: demerits. If you're surly and taciturn: demerits. If you slouch and laze and dog the dirty work: demerits. If you're overzealous and forever scuttling about: demerits. Obsequiousness: demerits. Truculence: demerits. If you sing and whistle: demerits. If you're a stolid bloody bore:

demerits. You can see that the line is hard to draw. Here's a hint which can save you many marks. I don't like gossip, especially when it concerns myself. I'm a sensitive man, and I open my red book fast when I think I'm being insulted." Henry Belt once more leaned back in his chair. "Any questions?"

No one spoke.

Henry Belt nodded. "Wise. Best not to flaunt your ignorance so early in the game. In response to the thought passing through each of your skulls, I do not think of myself as God. But you may do so, if you choose. And this—" he held up the red book "—you may regard as the Syncretic Compendium. Very well. Any questions?"

"Yes, sir," said Culpepper.

"Speak, sir."

"Any objection to alcoholic beverages aboard ship, sir?"

"For the cadets, yes indeed. I concede that the water must be carried in any event, that the organic compounds present may be reconstituted, but unluckily the bottles weigh far too much."

"I understand, sir."

Henry Belt rose to his feet. "One last word. Have I mentioned that I run a tight ship? When I say jump, I expect every one of you to jump. This is dangerous work, of course. I don't guarantee your safety. Far from it, especially since we are assigned to old 25, which should have been broken up long ago. There are eight of you present. Only six cadets will make the voyage. Before the week is over I will make the appropriate notifications. Any more questions?…Very well, then. Cheerio." Limping on his thin legs as if his feet hurt, Henry Belt departed into the back passage.

For a moment or two there was silence. Then von Gluck said in a soft voice, "My gracious."

"He's a tyrannical lunatic," grumbled Weske. "I've never heard anything like it! Megalomania!"

"Easy," said Culpepper. "Remember, no gossiping."

"Bah!" muttered McGrath. "This is a free country. I'll damn well say what I like."

Weske rose to his feet. "A wonder somebody hasn't killed him."

"I wouldn't want to try it," said Culpepper. "He looks tough." He made a gesture, stood up, brow furrowed in thought. Then he went to look along the passageway into which Henry Belt had made his departure. There, pressed to the wall, stood Henry Belt. "Yes, sir," said Culpepper suavely. "I forgot to inquire when you wanted us to convene again."

Henry Belt returned to the rostrum. "Now is as good a time as any." He took his seat, opened his red book. "You, Mr. von Gluck, made the remark, 'My gracious' in an offensive tone of voice. One demerit. You, Mr. Weske, employed the terms 'tyrannical lunatic' and 'megalomania' in reference to myself. Three demerits. Mr. McGrath, you observed that freedom of speech is the official doctrine of this country. It is a theory which right now we have no time to explore, but I believe that the statement in its present context carries an overtone of insubordination. One demerit, Mr. Culpepper, your imperturbable complacence irritates me. I prefer that you display more uncertainty, or even uneasiness."

"Sorry, sir."

"However, you took occasion to remind your colleagues of my rule, and so I will not mark you down."

"Thank you, sir."

Henry Belt leaned back in the chair, stared at the ceiling. "Listen closely, as I do not care to repeat myself. Take notes if you wish. Topic: Solar Sails, Theory and Practice thereof. Material with which you should already be familiar, but which I will repeat in order to avoid ambiguity.

"First, why bother with the sail, when nuclear-jet ships are faster, more dependable, more direct, safer, and easier to navigate? The answer is three-fold. First, a sail is not a bad way to move heavy cargo slowly but cheaply through space. Secondly, the range of the sail is unlimited, since we employ the mechanical pressure of light for thrust, and therefore need carry neither propulsive machinery, material to be ejected, nor energy source. The solar sail is much lighter than its nuclear-powered counter-part, and may carry a larger complement of men in a larger hull. Thirdly, to train a man for space there is no better instrument than the handling of a sail. The computer naturally calculates sail cant and plots the course; in fact, without the computer we'd be dead ducks. Nevertheless the control of a sail provides working familiarity with the cosmic elementals: light, gravity, mass, space.

"There are two types of sails: pure and composite. The first relies on solar energy exclusively, the second carries a secondary power source. We have been assigned Number 25, which is the first sort. It consists of a hull, a large parabolic reflector which serves as radar and radio antenna, as well as reflector for the power generator; and the sail itself. The pressure of radiation, of course, is extremely slight—on the order of an ounce per acre at this distance from the sun. Neces-sarily the sail must be extremely large and extremely light. We use a fluoro-siliconic film a tenth of a mil in gauge, fogged with lithium to the state of opacity. I believe the layer of lithium is about a thousand two hundred molecules thick. Such a foil weighs about four tons to the square mile. It is fitted to a hoop of thin-walled tubing, from which mono-crystalline iron cords lead to the hull.

"We try to achieve a weight factor of six tons to the square mile, which produces an acceleration of between g/100 and g/1000 depending on proximity to the sun, angle of cant, circumsolar orbital speed, reflectivity of surface. These accelerations seem minute, but calculation shows them to be cumulatively enormous. G/100 yields a velocity increment of 800 miles per hour every hour, 18,000 miles per hour each day, or five miles per second each day. At this rate interplanetary distances are readily negotiable—with proper manipulation of the sail, I need hardly say.

"The virtues of the sail, I've mentioned. It is cheap to build and cheap to operate. It requires neither fuel nor ejectant. As it travels through space, the great area captures various ions, which may be expelled in the plasma jet powered by the parabolic reflector, which adds another increment to the acceleration.

"The disadvantages of the sail are those of the glider or sailing ship, in that we must use natural forces with great precision and delicacy.

"There is no particular limit to the size of the sail. On 25 we use about four square miles of sail. For the present voyage we will install a new sail, as the old is well-worn and eroded.

"That will be all for today." Once more Henry Belt limped down from the dais and out the passage. On this occasion there were no comments.

II

The eight cadets shared a dormitory, attended classes together, ate at the same table in the mess hall. In various shops and laboratories they assembled, disassembled—and reassembled computers, pumps, generators, gyro-platforms, star-trackers, communication gear. "It's not enough to be clever with your hands," said Henry Belt. "Dexterity is not enough. Resourcefulness, creativity, the ability to make successful improvisations—these are more important. We'll test you out." And presently each of the cadets was introduced into a room on the floor of which lay a great heap of mingled housings, wires, flexes, gears, components of a dozen varieties of mechanism. "This is a twenty-six hour test," said Henry Belt. "Each of you has an identical set of components and supplies. There shall be no exchange of parts or information between you. Those whom I suspect of this fault will be dropped from the class, without recommendation. What I want you to build is, first, one standard Aminex Mark 9 Computer. Second, a servo-mechanism to orient a mass ten kilograms toward Mu Hercules. Why Mu Hercules?"

"Because, sir, the solar system moves in the direction of Mu Hercules, and we thereby avoid parallax error. Negligible though it may be, sir."

"The final comment smacks of frivolity, Mr. McGrath, which serves only to distract the attention of those who are trying to take careful notes of my instructions. One demerit."

"Sorry, sir. I merely intended to express my awareness that for many practical purposes such a degree of accuracy is unnecessary."

"That idea, cadet, is sufficiently elemental that it need not be labored. I appreciate brevity and precision."

"Yes, sir."

"Thirdly, from these materials, assemble a communication system, operating on one hundred watts, which will permit two-way conversation between Tycho Base and Phobos, at whatever frequency you deem suitable."

The cadets started in identical fashion by sorting the material into various piles, then calibrating and checking the test instruments. Achievement thereafter was disparate. Culpepper and von Gluck, diagnosing the test as partly one of mechanical ingenuity and partly ordeal by frustration, failed to become excited when several indispensable components proved either to be missing or inoperative, and carried each project as far as immediately feasible. McGrath and Weske, beginning with the computer, were reduced to rage and random action. Lynch and Sutton worked doggedly at the computer, Verona at the communication system.

Culpepper alone managed to complete one of the instruments, by the process of sawing, polishing and cementing together sections of two broken crystals into a crude, inefficient but operative maser unit.

The day after this test McGrath and Weske disappeared from the dormitory, whether by their own volition or notification from Henry Belt no one ever knew.

The test was followed by weekend leave. Cadet Lynch, attending a cocktail party, found himself in conversation with a Lieutenant-Colonel Trenchard, who shook his head pityingly to hear that Lynch was training with Henry Belt.

"I was up with Old Horrors myself. I tell you it's a miracle we ever got back. Belt was drunk two-thirds of the voyage."

"How does he escape court-martial?" asked Lynch.

"Very simple. All the top men seem to have trained under Henry Belt. Naturally they hate his guts but they all take a perverse pride in the fact. And maybe they hope that someday a cadet will take him apart."

"Has any ever tried?"

"Oh yes. I took a swing at Henry once. I was lucky to escape with a broken collarbone and two sprained ankles. If you come back alive, you'll stand a good chance of reaching the top."

The next evening Henry Belt passed the word. "Next Tuesday morning we go up. We'll be gone several months."

On Tuesday morning the cadets took their places in the angel-wagon. Henry Belt presently appeared. The pilot readied for takeoff.

"Hold your hats. On the count...." The projectile thrust against the earth, strained, rose, went streaking up into the sky. An hour later the pilot pointed. "There's your boat. Old 25. And 39 right beside it, just in from space."

Henry Belt stared aghast from the port. "What's been done to the ship? The decoration? The red? The white? The yellow? The checkerboard."

"Thank some idiot of a landlubber," said the pilot. "The word came to pretty the old boats for a junket of congressmen."

Henry Belt turned to the cadets. "Observe this foolishness. It is the result of vanity and ignorance. We will be occupied several days removing the paint."

They drifted close below the two sails: No. 39 just down from space, spare and polished beside the bedizened structure of No. 25. In 39's exit port a group of men waited, their gear floating at the end of cords.

"Observe those men," said Henry Belt. "They are jaunty. They have been on a pleasant outing around the planet Mars. They are poorly trained. When you gentlemen return you will be haggard and desperate and well trained. Now, gentlemen, clamp your helmets, and we will proceed."

The helmets were secured. Henry Belt's voice came by radio. "Lynch, Ostrander will remain here to discharge cargo. Verona, Culpepper, von Gluck, Sutton, leap with cords to the ship; ferry across the cargo, stow it in the proper hatches."

Henry Belt took charge of his personal cargo, which consisted of several large cases. He eased them out into space, clipped on lines, thrust them toward 25, leapt after. Pulling himself and the cases to the entrance port, he disappeared within.

Discharge of cargo was effected. The crew from 39 transferred to the carrier, which thereupon swung down and away, thrust itself dwindling back toward earth.

When the cargo had been stowed, the cadets gathered in the wardroom. Henry Belt appeared from the master's cubicle. "Gentlemen, how do you like the surroundings? Eh, Mr. Culpepper?"

"The hull is commodious, sir. The view is superb."

Henry Belt nodded. "Mr. Lynch? Your impressions?"

"I'm afraid I haven't sorted them out yet, sir."

"I see. You, Mr. Sutton?"

"Space is larger than I imagined it, sir."

"True. Space is unimaginable. A good spaceman must either be larger than space or he must ignore it. Both difficult. Well, gentlemen, I will make a few comments, then I will retire and enjoy the voyage. Since this is my last time out, I intend to do nothing whatever. The operation of the ship will be completely in your hands. I will merely appear from time to time to beam benevolently about or alas! to make remarks in my red book. Nominally I shall be in command, but you six will enjoy complete control over the ship. If you return as safely to Earth I will make an approving entry in my red book. If you wreck us or fling us into the sun, you will be more unhappy than I, since it is my destiny to die in space. Mr. von Gluck, do I perceive a smirk on your face?"

"No, sire, it is a thoughtful half-smile."

"What is humorous in the concept of my demise, may I ask?"

"It will be a great tragedy, sir. I merely was reflecting upon the contemporary persistence of, well, not exactly superstition, but, let us say, the conviction of a subjective cosmos."

Henry Belt made a notation in the red book. "Whatever is meant by this barbaric jargon I'm sure I don't know, Mr. von Gluck. It is clear that you fancy yourself a philosopher and dialectician. I will not fault this, so long as your remarks conceal no overtones of malice and insolence, to which I am extremely sensitive. Now as to the persistence of superstition, only an impoverished mind considers itself the repository of absolute knowledge. Hamlet spoke on the subject to Horatio, as I recall, in the well-known work by William Shakespeare. I myself have seen strange and terrifying sights. Were they hallucinations? Were they the manipulation of the cosmos by my mind or the mind of someone—or something—other than myself? I do not know. I therefore counsel a flexible attitude toward matters where the truth is still unknown. For this reason: the impact of an inexplicable experience may well destroy a mind which is too brittle. Do I make myself clear?"

"Perfectly, sir."

"Very good. To return, then. We shall set a system of watches whereby each man works in turn with each of the other five. I thereby hope to discourage the formation of special friendships, or cliques.

"You have inspected the ship. The hull is a sandwich of lithium-beryllium, insulating foam, fiber, and an interior skin. Very light, held rigid by air pressure rather than by any innate strength of the material. We can therefore afford enough space to stretch our legs and provide all of us with privacy.

"The master's cubicle is to the left; under no circumstances is anyone permitted in my quarters. If you wish to speak to me, knock on my door. If I appear, good. If I do not appear, go away. To the right are six cubicles which you may now distribute among yourselves by lot.

"You schedule will be two hours study, four hours on watch, six hours off. I will require no specific rate of study progress, but I recommend that you make good use of your time.

"Our destination is Mars. We will presently construct a new sail, then while orbital velocity builds up, you will carefully test and check all equipment aboard. Each of you will compute sail cant and course and work out among yourselves any discrepancies which may appear. I shall take no hand in navigation. I prefer that you involve me in no disaster. If any such occurs I shall severely mark down the persons responsible.

"Singing, whistling, humming, are forbidden. I disapprove of fear and hysteria, and mark accordingly. No one dies more than once; we are well aware of the risks of this, our chosen occupation. There will be no practical jokes. You may fight, so long as you do not disturb me or break any instruments; however, I counsel against it, as it leads to resentment, and I have known cadets to kill each other. I suggest coolness and detachment in your personal relations. Use of the microfilm projector is of course at your own option. You may not use the radio either to dispatch or receive messages. In fact, I have put the radio out of commission, as is my practice. I do this to emphasize the fact that, sink or swim, we must make do with our own resources. Are there any questions?...Very good. You will find that if you all behave with scrupulous correctness and accuracy, we shall in due course return safe and sound, with a minimum of demerits and no casualties. I am bound to say, however, that in twelve previous voyages this has failed to occur. Now you select your cubicles, stow your gear. The carrier will bring up the new sail tomorrow, and you will go to work."

III

The carrier discharged a great bundle of three-inch tubing: paper-thin lithium hardened with beryllium, reinforced with filaments of mono-crystalline iron—a total length of eight miles. The cadets fitted the tubes end to end, cementing the joints. When the tube extended a quarter-mile it was bent bow-shaped by a cord stretched between two ends, and further sections added. As the process continued, the free end curved far out and around, and began to veer back in toward the hull. When the last tube was in place the loose end was hauled down, socketed home, to form a great hoop two and a half miles in diameter.

Henry Belt came out occasionally in his space suit to look on, and occasionally spoke a few words of sardonic comment, to which the cadets paid little heed. Their mood had changed; this was exhilaration, to be weightlessly afloat above the bright cloud-marked globe, with continent and ocean wheeling massively below. Anything seemed possible, even the training voyage with Henry Belt! When he came out to inspect their work, they grinned at each other with indulgent amusement. Henry Belt suddenly seemed a rather pitiful creature, a poor vagabond suited only for drunken bluster. Fortunate indeed that they were less naive than Henry Belt's previous classes! They had taken Belt seriously; he had cowed them, reduced them to nervous pulp. Not this crew, not by a long shot! They saw through Henry Belt! Just keep your nose clean, do your work, keep cheerful. The training voyage won't last but a few months, and then real life begins. Gut it out, ignore Henry Belt as much as possible. This is the sensible attitude; the best way to keep on top of the situation.

Already the group had made a composite assessment of its members, arriving at a set of convenient labels. Culpepper: smooth, suave, easy-going. Lynch: excitable, argumentative, hot-tempered. Von Gluck: the artistic temperament, delicate with hands and sensibilities. Ostrander: prissy, finicky, over-tidy. Sutton: moody, suspicious, competitive. Verona: the plugger, rough at the edges, but persistent and reliable.

Around the hull swung the gleaming hoop, and now the carrier brought up the sail, a great roll of darkly shining stuff. When unfolded and unrolled, and unfolded many times more it became a tough, gleaming film, flimsy as gold leaf. Unfolded to its fullest extent it was a shimmering disk, already rippling and bulging to the light of the sun. The cadets fitted the film to the hoop, stretched it taut as a drumhead, cemented it in place. Now the sail must carefully be held edge on to the sun or it would quickly move away, under a thrust of about a hundred pounds.

From the rim braided-iron threads were led through a ring at the back of the parabolic reflector, dwarfing this as the reflector dwarfed the hull, and now the sail was ready to move.

The carrier brought up a final cargo: water, food, spare parts, a new magazine for the microfilm viewer, mail. Then Henry Belt said, "Make sail."

This was the process of turning the sail to catch the sunlight while the hull moved around Earth away from the sun, canting it parallel to the sun rays when the ship moved on the sunward leg of its orbit; in short, building up an orbital velocity which in due course would stretch loose the bonds of terrestrial gravity and send Sail 25 kiting out toward Mars.

During this period the cadets checked every item of equipment aboard the vessel. They grimaced with disgust and dismay at some of the instruments: 25 was an old ship, with antiquated gear. Henry Belt seemed to enjoy their grumbling. "This is a training voyage, not a pleasure cruise. If you wanted your noses wiped, you should have taken a post on the ground. And, I have no sympathy for fault-finders. If you wish a model by which to form your own conduct, observe me."

The moody, introspective Sutton, usually the most diffident and laconic of individuals, ventured an ill-advised witticism. "If we modeled ourselves after you, sir, there'd be no room to move for the whisky."

Out came the red book. "Extraordinary impudence, Mr. Sutton. How can you yield so easily to malice?"

Sutton flushed pink; his eyes glistened, he opened his mouth to speak, then closed it firmly. Henry Belt, waiting, politely expectant, turned away. "You gentlemen will perceive that I rigorously obey my own rules of conduct. I am regular as a clock. There is no better, more genial shipmate than Henry Belt. There is no fairer man alive. Mr. Culpepper, you have a remark to make?"

"Nothing of consequence, sir."

Henry Belt went to the port, glared out at the sail. He swung around instantly. "Who is on watch?"

"Sutton and Ostrander, sir."

"Gentlemen, have you noticed the sail? It has swung about and is canting to show its back to the sun. In another ten minutes we shall be tangled in a hundred miles of guy wires."

Sutton and Ostrander sprang to repair the situation. Henry Belt shook his head disparagingly. "This is precisely what is meant by the words 'negligence' and 'inattentiveness.' You two have committed a serious error. This is poor spacemanship. The sail must always be in such a position as to hold the wires taut."

"There seems to be something wrong with the sensor, sir," Sutton blurted. "It should notify us when the sail swings behind us."

"If fear I must charge you an additional demerit for making excuses, Mr. Sutton. It is your duty to assure yourself that all the warning devices are functioning properly, at all times. Machinery must never be used as a substitute for vigilance."

Ostrander looked up from the control console. "Someone has turned off the switch, sir. I do not offer this as an excuse, but as an explanation."

"The line of distinction is often hard to define, Mr. Ostrander. Please bear in mind my remarks on the subject of vigilance."

"Yes, sir, but—who turned off the switch?"

"Both you and Mr. Sutton are theoretically hard at work watching for any such accident or occurrence. Did you not observe it?"

"No, sir."

"I almost accuse you of further inattention and neglect, in this case."

Ostrander gave Henry Belt a long dubious side-glance. "The only person I recall going near the console is yourself, sir. I'm sure you wouldn't do such a thing."

Henry Belt shook his head sadly. "In space you must never rely on anyone for rational conduct. A few moments ago Mr. Sutton unfairly imputed to me an unusual thirst for whiskey. Suppose this were the case? Suppose, as an example of pure irony, that I had indeed been drinking whisky, that I was in fact drunk?"

"I will agree, sir, that anything is possible."

Henry Belt shook his head again. "This is the type of remark, Mr.

Ostrander, that I have come to associate with Mr. Culpepper. A better response would have been, 'In the future, I will try to be ready for any conceivable contingency.' Mr. Sutton, did you make a hissing sound between your teeth?"

"I was breathing, sir."

"Please breathe with less vehemence."

Henry Belt turned away and wandered back and forth about the wardroom, scrutinizing cases, frowning at smudges on polished metal. Ostrander muttered something to Sutton, and both watched Henry Belt closely as he moved here and there. Presently Henry Belt lurched toward them. "You show great interest in my movements, gentlemen."

"We were on the watch for another unlikely contingency, sir."

"Very good, Mr. Ostrander. Stick with it. In space nothing is impossible. I'll vouch for this personally."

IV

Henry Belt sent all hands out to remove the paint from the surface of the parabolic reflector. When this had been accomplished, incident sunlight was focused upon an expanse of photoelectric cells. The power so generated was used to operate plasma jets, expelling ions collected by the vast expanse of sail, further accelerating the ship, thrusting it ever out into an orbit of escape. And finally one day, at an exact instant dictated by the computer, the ship departed from Earth and floated tangentially out into space, off at an angle for the orbit of Mars. At an acceleration of g/100 velocity built up rapidly. Earth dwindled behind; the ship was isolated in space. The cadets' exhilaration vanished, to be replaced by an almost funereal solemnity. The vision of Earth dwindling and retreating is an awesome symbol, equivalent to eternal loss, to the act of dying itself. The more impressionable cadets—Sutton, von Gluck, Ostrander—could not look astern without finding their eyes swimming with tears. Even the suave Culpepper was awed by the magnificence of the spectacle, the sun an aching pit not to be tolerated, Earth a plump pearl rolling on black velvet among a myriad glittering diamonds. And away from Earth, away from the sun, opened an exalted magnificence of another order entirely. For the first time the cadets became dimly aware that Henry Belt had spoken truly of strange visions. Here was death, here was peace, solitude, star-blazing beauty which promised not oblivion in death, but eternity....Streams and spatters of stars....The familiar constellations, the stars with their prideful names presenting themselves like heroes: Achernar, Fomalhaut, Sadal, Suud, Canopus....

Sutton could not bear to look into the sky. "It's not that I feel fear," he told von Gluck, "or yes, perhaps it is fear. It sucks at me, draws me out there....I suppose in due course I'll become accustomed to it."

"I'm not so sure," said von Gluck. "I wouldn't be surprised if space could become a psychological addiction, a need—so that whenever you walked on Earth you felt hot and breathless."

Life settled into a routine. Henry Belt no longer seemed a man, but a capricious aspect of nature, like storm or lightning; and like some natural cataclysm. Henry Belt showed no favoritism, nor forgave one jot or tittle of offense. Apart from the private cubicles, no place on the ship escaped his attention. Always he reeked of whisky, and it became a matter of covert speculation as to exactly how much whiskey he had brought aboard. But no matter how he reeked or how he swayed on his feet, his eyes remained clever and steady, and he spoke without slurring in his paradoxically clear, sweet voice.

One day he seemed slightly drunker than usual, and ordered all hands into space suits and out to inspect the sail for meteoric puncture. The order seemed sufficiently odd that the cadets stared at him in disbelief. "Gentlemen, you hesitate, you fail to exert yourselves, you luxuriate in sloth. Do you fancy yourselves at the Riviera? Into the space suits, on the double, and everybody into space. Check hoop, sail, reflector, struts, and sensor. You will be adrift for two hours. When you return I want a comprehensive report. Mr. Lynch, I believe you are in charge on this watch. You will present the report."

"Yes, sir."

"One more matter. You will notice that the sail is slightly bellied by the continual radiation pressure. It therefore acts as a focusing device, the focal point presumably occurring behind the cab. But this is not a matter to be taken for granted. I have seen a man burnt to death in such a freak accident. Bear this in mind."

For two hours the cadets drifted through space, propelled by tanks of gas and thrust tubes. All enjoyed the experience except Sutton, who found himself appalled by the immensity of emotions. Probably least affected was the practical Verona, who inspected the sail with a care exacting enough even to satisfy Henry Belt.

The next day the computer went wrong. Ostrander was in charge of the watch and knocked on Henry Belt's door to make the report.

Henry Belt appeared in the doorway. He apparently had been asleep. "What is the difficulty, Mr. Ostrander?"

"We're in trouble, sir. The computer has gone out."

Henry Belt rubbed his grizzled pate. "This is not an unusual cicumstance. We prepare for this contingency by schooling all cadets thoroughly in computer design and repair. Have you identified the difficulty?"

"The bearings which suspend the data separation disks have broken.

The shaft has several millimeters' play and as a result there is total confusion in the data presented to the analyzer."

"An interesting problem. Why do you present it to me?"

"I thought you should be notified, sir. I don't believe we carry spares for this particular bearing."

Henry Belt shook his head sadly. "Mr. Ostrander, do you recall my statement at the beginning of this voyage, that you six gentlemen are totally responsible for the navigation of the ship?"

"Yes, sir. But—"

"This is an applicable situation. You must either repair the computer or perform the calculations yourself."

"Very well, sir. I will do my best."

V

Lynch, Verona, Ostrander, and Sutton disassembled the mechanism, removed the worn bearing. "Confounded antique!" said Lynch. "Why can't they give us decent equipment? Or if they want to kill us, why not shoot us and save us all trouble."

"We're not dead yet," said Verona. "You've looked for a spare?"

"Naturally. There's nothing remotely like this."

Verona looked at the bearing dubiously. "I suppose we could cast a babbitt sleeve and machine it to fit. That's what we'll have to do—unless you fellows are awfully fast with your math."

Sutton glanced out the port, quickly turned away his eyes. "I wonder if we should cut sail."

"Why?" asked Ostrander.

"We don't want to build up too much velocity. We're already going 30 miles a second."

"Mars is a long way off."

"And if we miss, we go shooting past. Then where are we?"

"Sutton, you're a pessimist. A shame to find morbid tendencies in one so young." This from von Gluck.

"I'd rather be a live pessimist than a dead comedian."

The new sleeve was duly cast, machined and fitted. Anxiously the alignment of the data disks was checked. "Well," said Verona dubiously, "There's wobble. How much that affects the functioning remains to be seen. We can take some of it out by shimming the mount...."

Shims of tissue paper were inserted and the wobble seemed to be reduced. "Now—feed in the data," said Sutton. "Let's see how we stand."

Coordinates were fed into the system; the indicator swung. "Enlarge sail cant four degrees," said von Gluck, "we're making too much left concentric. Projected course..." he tapped buttons, watched the bright line extend across the screen, swing around a dot representing the center of gravity of Mars. "I make it an elliptical pass, about twenty thousand miles out. That's at present acceleration, and it should toss us right back at Earth."

"Great. Simply great. Let's go, 25!" This was Lynch. "I've heard of guys dropping flat on their faces and kissing Earth when they put down. Me, I'm going to live in a cave the rest of my life."

Sutton went to look at the data disks. The wobble was slight but perceptible. "Good Lord," he said huskily. "The other end of the shaft is loose too."

Lynch started to spit curses; Verona's shoulders slumped. "Let's get to work and fix it."

Another bearing was cast, machined, polished, mounted. The disks wobbled, scraped. Mars, an ocher disk, shouldered ever closer in from the side. With the computer unreliable, the cadets calculated and plotted the course manually. The results were at slight but significant variance with those of the computer. The cadets looked dourly at each other. "Well," growled Ostrander, "There's error. Is it the instruments? The calculation? The plotting? Or the computer?"

Culpepper said in a subdued voice, "Well, we're not about to crash head-on at any rate."

Verona went back to study the computer. "I can't imagine why the bearings don't work better.... The mounting brackets—could they have shifted?" He removed the side housing, studied the frame, then went to the case for tools.

"What are you going to do?" demanded Sutton.

"Try to ease the mounting brackets around. I think that's our trouble."

"Leave me alone! You'll bugger the machine so it'll never work."

Verona paused, looked questioningly around the group. "Well? What's the verdict?"

"Maybe we'd better check with the old man," said Ostrander nervously.

"All well and good—but you know what he'll say."

"Let's deal cards. Ace of spades goes to ask him."

Culpepper received the ace. He knocked on Henry Belt's door. There was no response. He started to knock again, but restrained himself.

He returned to the group. "Wait till he shows himself. I'd rather crash into Mars than bring forth Henry Belt and his red book."

The ship crossed the orbit of Mars well ahead of the looming red planet. It came toppling at them with a peculiar clumsy grandeur, a mass obviously bulking and globular, but so fine and clear was the detail, so absent the perspective, that the distance and size might have been anything. Instead of swinging in a sharp elliptical curve back toward Earth, the ship swerved aside in a blunt hyperbola and proceeded outward, now at a velocity of close to fifty miles a second. Mars receded astern and to the side. A new part of space lay ahead. The sun was noticeably smaller. Earth could no longer be differentiated from the stars. Mars departed quickly and politely, and space seemed lonely and forlorn.

Henry Belt had not appeared for two days. At last Culpepper went to knock on the door—once, twice, three times: a strange face looked out. It was Henry Belt, face haggard, skin like pulled taffy. His eyes were red and glared, his hair seemed matted and more unkempt than hair a quarter-inch long should be.

But he spoke in his quiet, clear voice. "Mr. Culpepper, your merciless din has disturbed me. I am quite put out with you."

"Sorry, sir. We feared that you were ill."

Henry Belt made no response. He looked past Culpepper, around the circle of faces. "You gentlemen are unwontedly serious. Has this presumptive illness of mine caused you all distress?"

Sutton spoke in a rush, "The computer is out of order."

"Why then, you must repair it."

"It's a matter of altering the housing. If we do it incorrectly—"

"Mr. Sutton, please do not harass me with the hour-by-hour minutiae of running the ship."

"But, sir, the matter has become serious; we need your advice. We missed the Mars turnaround—"

"Well, I suppose there's always Jupiter. Must I explain the basic elements of astrogation to you?"

"But the computer's out of order—definitely."

"Then, if you wish to return to Earth, you must perform the calculations with pencil and paper. Why is it necessary to explain the obvious?"

"Jupiter is a long way out," said Sutton in a shrill voice. "Why can't we just turn around and go home?" This last was almost a whisper.

"I see I've been too easy on you cads," said Henry Belt. "You stand around idly; you chatter nonsense while the machinery goes to pieces and the ship flies at random. Everybody into space suits for sail inspection. Come now. Let's have some snap. What are you all? Walking corpses? You, Mr. Culpepper, why the delay?"

"It occurred to me, sir, that we are approaching the asteroid belt. As I am chief of the watch I consider it my duty to cant sail to swing us around the area."

"You may do this; then join the rest in hull-and-sail inspection."

"Yes, sir."

The cadets donned space suits, Sutton with the utmost reluctance. Out into the dark void they went, and now here was loneliness indeed.

When they returned, Henry Belt had returned to his compartment.

"As Mr. Belt points out, we have no great choice," said Ostrander. "We missed Mars, so let's hit Jupiter. Luckily it's in good position—otherwise we'd have to swing out to Saturn or Uranus—"

"They're off behind the sun," said Lynch. "Jupiter's our last chance."

"Let's do it right then. I say, let's make one last attempt to set those confounded bearings...."

But now it seemed as if the wobble and twist had been eliminated. The disks tracked perfectly, the accuracy monitor glowed green.

"Great!" yelled Lynch. "Feed it the dope. Let's get going! All sail for Jupiter. Good Lord, but we're having a trip!"

"Wait till it's over," said Sutton. Since his return from sail inspection, he had stood to one side, cheeks pinched, eyes staring, "It's not over yet. And maybe it's not meant to be."

The other five pretended not to have heard him. The computer spat out figures and angles. There were a billion miles to travel. Acceleration was less, due to the diminution in the intensity of sunlight. At least a month must pass before Jupiter came close.

VI

The ship, great sail spread to the fading sunlight, fled like a ghost—out, always out. Each of the cadets had quietly performed the same calculation, and arrived at the same result. If the swing around Jupiter was not performed with exactitude, if the ship was not slung back like a stone on a string, there was nothing beyond. Saturn, Uranus, Neptune, Pluto were far around the sun; the ship, speeding at a hundred miles a second, could not be halted by the waning gravity of the sun, nor yet sufficiently accelerated in a concentric direction by sail and jet into a true orbit. The very nature of the sail made it useless as a brake, always the thrust was outward.

Within the hull seven men lived and thought, and the interrelationships worked and stirred like yeast in a vat of decaying fruit. The fundamental similarity, the human identity of the seven men, was utterly canceled; apparent only were the disparities. Each cadet appeared to others only as a walking characteristic, and Henry Belt was an incomprehensible Thing, who appeared from his compartment at unpredictable times, to move quietly here and there with the blind, blank grin of an archaic Attic hero.

Jupiter loomed and bulked. The ship, at last within reach of the Jovian gravity, sidled over to meet it. The cadets gave ever more careful attention to the computer, checking and counter-checking the instructions. Verona was the most assiduous at this, Sutton the most harassed and ineffectual. Lynch growled and cursed and sweat; Ostrander complained in a thin, peevish voice. Von Gluck worked with the calm of pessimistic fatalism; Culpepper seemed unconcerned, almost debonair; his blandness bewildered Ostrander, infuriated Lynch, awoke a malignant hate in Sutton. Verona and von Gluck, on the other hand seemed to derive strength and refreshment from Culpepper's placid acceptance of the situation. Henry Belt said nothing. Occasionally he emerged from his compartment to survey the wardroom and the cadets with the detached interest of a visitor to an asylum.

It was Lynch who made the discovery. He signaled it with an odd growl of sheer dismay, which brought a resonant questioning sound from Sutton. "My God, my God," muttered Lynch.

Verona was at his side. "What's the trouble?"

"Look. This gear. When we replaced the disks we dephased the whole apparatus one notch. This white dot and this other white dot should synchronize. They're one sprocket apart. All the results would check and be consistent because they'd all be off by the same factor."

Verona sprang into action. Off came the housing, off came various components. Gently he lifted the gear, set it back into correct alignment. The other cadets leaned over him as he worked, except Culpepper who was chief of the watch.

Henry Belt appeared. "You gentlemen are certainly diligent in your navigation," he said. "Perfectionists almost."

"We do our best," greeted Lynch between set teeth. "It's a damn shame sending us out with a machine like this."

The red book appeared. "Mr. Lynch, I mark you down not for your private sentiments, which are of course yours to entertain, but for voicing them and thereby contributing to an unhealthy atmosphere of despairing and hysterical pessimism."

A tide of red crept up from Lynch's neck. He bent over the computer, made no comment. But Sutton suddenly cried out, "What else do you expect from us? We came out here to learn, not to suffer, or to fly on forever!" He gave a ghastly laugh. Henry Belt listened patiently. "Think of it!" cried Sutton. "The seven of us. In this capsule, forever!"

"I am afraid that I must charge you two demerits for your outburst, Mr. Sutton. A good spaceman maintains his dignity at all costs."

Lynch looked up from the computer. "Well, now we've got a corrected reading. Do you know what it says?"

Henry Belt turned him a look of polite inquiry.

"We're going to miss," said Lynch. "We're going to pass by just as we passed Mars. Jupiter is pulling us around and sending us out toward Gemini."

The silence was thick in the room. Henry Belt turned to look at

Culpepper, who was standing by the porthole, photographing Jupiter with his personal camera.

"Mr. Culpepper?"

"Yes, sir."

"You seemed unconcerned by the prospect which Mr. Sutton has set forth."

"I hope it's not imminent."

"How do you propose to avoid it?"

"I imagine that we will radio for help, sir."

"You forget that I have destroyed the radio."

"I remember noting a crate marked 'Radio Parts' stored in the starboard jet-pod."

"I am sorry to disillusion you, Mr. Culpepper. That case is mislabeled."

Ostrander jumped to his feet, left the wardroom. There was the sound of moving crates. A moment of silence. Then he returned. He glared at Henry Belt. "Whisky. Bottles of whisky."

Henry Belt nodded. "I told you as much."

"But now we have no radio," said Lynch in an ugly voice.

"We never have had a radio, Mr. Lynch. You were warned that you would have to depend on your own resources to bring us home. You have failed, and in the process doomed me as well as yourself. Incidentally, I must mark you all down ten demerits for a faulty cargo check."

"Demerits," said Ostrander in a bleak voice.

"Now, Mr. Culpepper," said Henry Belt. "What is your next proposal?"

"I don't know, sir."

Verona spoke in a placatory voice. "What would you do, sir, if you were in our position?"

Henry Belt shook his head. "I am an imaginative man, Mr. Verona, but there are certain leaps of the mind which are beyond my powers." He returned to his compartment.

Von Gluck looked curiously at Culpepper. "It is a fact. You're not at all concerned."

"Oh, I'm concerned. But I believe that Mr. Belt wants to get home too. He's too good a spaceman not to know exactly what he's doing."

The door from Henry Belt's compartment slid back. Henry Belt stood in the opening. "Mr. Culpepper, I chanced to overhear your remark, and I now note down ten demerits against you. This attitude expresses a complacence as dangerous as Mr. Sutton's utter funk." He looked about the room. "Pay no heed to Mr. Culpepper. He is wrong. Even if I could repair this disaster, I would not raise a hand. For I expect to die in space."

VII

The sail was canted vectorless, edgewise to the sun. Jupiter was a smudge astern. There were five cadets in the wardroom. Culpepper, Verona, and von Gluck sat talking in low voices. Ostrander and Lynch lay crouched, arms to knees, faces to the wall. Sutton had gone two days before. Quietly donning his space suit, he had stepped into the exit chamber and thrust himself headlong into space. A propulsion unit gave him added speed, and before any of the cadets could intervene he was gone.

Shortly thereafter Lynch and Ostrander succumbed to inanition, a kind of despondent helplessness: manic-depression in its most stupefying phase. Culpepper the suave, Verona the pragmatic, and von Gluck the sensitive remained.

They spoke quietly to themselves, out of earshot of Henry Belt's room. "I still believe," said Culpepper, "that somehow there is a means to get ourselves out of this mess, and that Henry Belt knows it."

Verona said, "I wish I could think so.... We've been over it a hundred times. If we set sail for Saturn or Neptune or Uranus, the outward vector of thrust plus the outward vector of our momentum will take us far beyond Pluto before we're anywhere near. The plasma jets could stop us if we had enough energy, but the shield can't supply it, and we don't have another power source...."

Von Gluck hit his fist into his hand. "Gentlemen," he said in a soft delighted voice, "I believe we have sufficient energy at hand. We will use the sail. Remember? It is bellied. It can function as a mirror. It spreads five square miles of surface. Sunlight out here is thin—but so long as we collect enough of it—"

"I understand!" said Culpepper. "We back off the hull till the reactor is at the focus of the sail and turn on the jets!"

Verona said dubiously, "We'll still be receiving radiation pressure. And what's worse, the jets will impinge back on the sail. Effect—cancellation. We'll be nowhere."

"If we cut the center out of the sail—just enough to allow the plasma through—we'd beat that objection. And as for the radiation pressure—we'll surely do better with the plasma drive."

"What do we use to make plasma? We don't have the stock."

"Anything that can be ionized. The radio, the computer, your shoes, my shirt, Culpepper's camera, Henry Belt's whisky...."

VIII

The angel-wagon came up to meet sail 25, in orbit beside Sail 40, which was just making ready to take out a new crew.

The cargo carrier drifted near, eased into position. Three men sprang across to Sail 40, a few hundred yards behind 25, tossed lines back to the carrier, pulled bales of cargo and equipment across the gap.

The five cadets and Henry Belt, clad in space suits, stepped out into the sunlight. Earth spread below, green and blue, white and brown, the contours so precious and dear as to bring tears to the eyes. The cadets transferring cargo to Sail 40 gazed at them curiously as they worked. At last they were finished, and the six men of Sail 25 boarded the carrier.

"Back safe and sound, eh Henry?" said the pilot. "Well, I'm always surprised."

Henry Belt made no answer. The cadets stowed their cargo, and standing by the port, took a final look at Sail 25. The carrier retro-jetted; the two sails seemed to rise above them.

The lighter nosed in and out of the atmosphere; then braking, it extended its wings and glided to an easy landing on the Mojave Desert.

The cadets, their legs suddenly loose and weak to the unaccustomed gravity, limped after Henry Belt to the carry-all, seated themselves, and were conveyed to the administration complex. They alighted from the carry-all, and now Henry Belt motioned the five to the side.

"Here, gentlemen, is where I leave you. Tonight I will check my red book and prepare my official report. But I believe I can present you an unofficial resume of my impressions. Mr. Lynch and Mr. Ostrander, I feel that you are ill-suited either for command or for any situation which might inflict prolonged emotional pressure upon you. I cannot recommend you for space duty.

"Mr. von Gluck, Mr. Culpepper, and Mr. Verona, all of you meet my minimum requirements for a recommendation, although I shall write the words 'Especially Recommended' only beside the names 'Clyde von Gluck' and 'Marcus Verona.' You brought the sail back to Earth by essentially faultless navigation.

"So now our association ends. I trust you have profited by it." Henry Belt nodded briefly to each of the five and limped off around the building.

The cadets looked after him. Culpepper reached in his pocket and brought forth a pair of small metal objects which he displayed in his palm. "Recognize these?"

"Hmf," said Lynch in a flat voice. "Bearings for the computer disks. The original ones."

"I found them in the little spare-parts tray. They weren't there before."

Von Gluck nodded. "The machinery always seemed to fail immediately after sail check, as I recall."

Lynch drew in his breath with a sharp hiss. He turned, strode away. Ostrander followed him. Culpepper shrugged. To Verona he gave one of the bearings, to von Gluck the other. "For souvenirs—or medals. You fellows deserve them."

"Thanks, Ed," said von Gluck.

"Thanks," muttered Verona. "I'll make a stickpin of this thing."

The three, not able to look at each other, glanced up into the sky where the stars of twilight were appearing, then continued on into the building where family and friends and sweethearts awaited them.

WHEN THE FIVE MOONS RISE

Seguilo could not have gone far; there was no place for him to go. Once Perrin had searched the lighthouse and the lonesome acre of rock, there were no other possibilities—only the sky and the ocean.

Seguilo was neither inside the lighthouse nor was he outside.

Perrin went out into the night, squinted up against the five moons. Seguilo was not to be seen on top of the lighthouse.

Seguilo had disappeared.

Perrin looked indecisively over the flowing brine of Maurnilam Var. Had Seguilo slipped on the damp rock and fallen into the sea, he certainly would have called out....The five moons blinked, dazzled, glinted along the surface; Seguilo might even now be floating unseen a hundred yards distant.

Perrin shouted across the dark water: "Seguilo!"

He turned, once more looked up the face of the lighthouse. Around the horizon whirled the twin shafts of red and white light, guiding the barges crossing from South Continent to Spacetown, warning them off Isel Rock.

Perrin walked quickly toward the lighthouse; Seguilo was no doubt asleep in his bunk, or in the bathroom.

Perrin went to the top chamber, circled the lumenifer, climbed down the stairs. "Seguilo!"

No answer. The lighthouse returned a metallic vibrating echo.

Seguilo was not in his room, in the bathroom, in the commissary, or in the storeroom. Where else could a man go?

Perrin looked out the door. The five moons cast confusing shadows. He saw a gray blot—"Seguilo!" He ran outside. "Where have you been?"

Seguilo straightened to his full height, a thin man with a wise, doleful face. He turned his head; the wind blew his words past Perrin's ears.

Sudden enlightenment came to Perrin. "You must have been under the generator!" The only place he could have been.

Seguilo had come closer. "Yes…I was under the generator." He paused uncertainly by the door, stood looking up at the moons, which this evening had risen all bunched together. Puzzlement creased Perrin's forehead. Why should Seguilo crawl under the generator? "Are you…well?"

"Yes. Perfectly well."

Perrin stepped closer and in the light of the five moons, Ista, Bista, Liad, Miad, and Poidel, scrutinized Seguilo sharply. His eyes were dull and noncommittal; he seemed to carry himself stiffly. "Have you hurt yourself? Come over to the steps and sit down."

"Very well." Seguilo ambled across the rock, sat down on the steps.

"You're certain you're all right?"

"Certain."

After a moment, Perrin said, "Just before you…went under the generator, you were about to tell me something you said was important."

Seguilo nodded slowly. "That's true."

"What was it?"

Seguilo stared dumbly up into the sky. There was nothing to be heard but the wash of the sea, hissing and rushing where the rock shelved under.

"Well?" asked Perrin finally. Seguilo hesitated. "You said that when five moons rose together in the sky, it was not wise to believe anything."

"Ah," nodded Seguilo, "so I did."

"What did you mean?"

"I'm not sure."

"Why is not believing anything important?"

"I don't know."

Perrin rose abruptly to his feet. Seguilo normally was crisp, dryly emphatic. "Are you sure you're all right?"

"Right as rain."

That was more like Seguilo. "Maybe a drink of whisky would fix you up."

"Sounds like a good idea."

Perrin knew where Seguilo kept his private store. "You sit here, I'll get you a shot."

"Yes, I'll sit here."

Perrin hurried inside the lighthouse, clambered the two flights of stairs to the commissary. Seguilo might remain seated or he might not; something in his posture, in the rapt gaze out to sea, suggested that he might not. Perrin found the bottle and a glass, ran back down the steps. Somehow he knew that Seguilo would be gone.

Seguilo was gone. He was not on the steps, nowhere on the windy acre of Isel Rock. It was impossible that he had passed Perrin on the stairs. He might have slipped into the engine room and crawled under the generator once more.

Perrin flung open the door, switched on the lights, stooped, peered under the housing. Nothing.

A greasy film of dust, uniform, unmarred, indicated that no one had ever been there.

Where was Seguilo?

Perrin went up to the top-most part of the lighthouse, carefully searched every nook and cranny down to the outside entrance. No Seguilo.

Perrin walked out on the rock. Bare and empty; no Seguilo.

Seguilo was gone. The dark water of Maurnilam Var sighed and flowed across the shelf.

Perrin opened his mouth to shout across the moon-dazzled swells, but somehow it did not seem right to shout. He went back to the lighthouse, seated himself before the radio transceiver.

Uncertainly he touched the dials; the instrument had been Seguilo's responsibility. Seguilo had built it himself, from parts salvaged from a pair of old instruments.

Perrin tentatively flipped a switch. The screen sputtered into light, the speaker hummed and buzzed. Perrin made hasty adjustments. The screen streaked with darts of blue light, a spatter of quick, red blots. Fuzzy, dim, a face looked forth from the screen. Perrin recognized a junior clerk in the Commission office at Spacetown. He spoke urgently, "This is Harold Perrin, at Isel Rock Lighthouse; send out a relief ship."

The face in the screen looked at him as through thick pebbleglass. A faint voice, overlaid by sputtering and crackling, said, "Adjust your tuning...I can't hear you...."

Perrin raised his voice. "Can you hear me now?"

The face in the screen wavered and faded.

Perrin yelled, "This is Isel Rock Lighthouse! Send out a relief ship! Do you hear? There's been an accident!"

"...signals not coming in. Make out a report, send..." the voice sputtered away.

Cursing furiously under his breath, Perrin twisted knobs, flipped switches. He pounded the set with his fist. The screen flashed bright orange, went dead.

Perrin ran behind, worked an anguished five minutes, to no avail. No light, no sound.

Perrin slowly rose to his feet. Through the window he glimpsed the five moons racing for the west. "When the five moons rise together," Seguilo had said, "it's not wise to believe anything." Seguilo was gone. He had been gone once before and come back; maybe he would come back again. Perrin grimaced, shuddered. It would be best now if Seguilo stayed away. He ran down to the outer door, barred and bolted it. Hard on Seguilo, if he came wandering back...Perrin leaned a moment with his back to the door, listening. Then he went to the generator room, looked under the generator. Nothing. He shut the door, climbed the steps.

Nothing in the commissary, the storeroom, the bathroom, the bedrooms. No one in the lightroom. No one on the roof.

No one in the lighthouse but Perrin.

He returned to the commissary, brewed a pot of coffee, sat half an hour listening to the sigh of water across the shelf, then went to his bunk.

Passing Seguilo's room he looked in. The bunk was empty.

When at last he rose in the morning, his mouth was dry, his muscles like bundles of withes, his eyes hot from long staring up at the ceiling. He rinsed his face with cold water and, going to the window, searched the horizon. A curtain of dingy overcast hung halfway up the east; blue-green Magda shone through like an ancient coin covered with verdigris. Over the water oily skeins of blue-green light formed and joined and broke and melted....Out along the south horizon Perrin spied a pair of black hyphens—barges riding the Trade Current to Spacetown. After a few moments they disappeared into the overcast.

Perrin threw the master switch; above him came the fluttering hum of the lumenifer slowing and dimming.

He descended the stairs, with stiff fingers unbolted the door, flung it wide. The wind blew past his ears, smelling of Maurnilam Var. The tide was low; Isel Rock rose out of the water like a saddle. He walked gingerly to the water's edge. Blue-green Magda broke clear of the overcast; the light struck under the water. Leaning precariously over the shelf, Perrin looked down, past shadows and ledges and grottos, down into the gloom....Movement of some kind; Perrin strained to see. His foot slipped, he almost fell.

Perrin returned to the lighthouse, worked a disconsolate three hours at the transceiver, finally deciding that some vital component had been destroyed.

He opened a lunch unit, pulled a chair to the window, sat gazing across the ocean. Eleven weeks to the relief ship. Isel Rock had been lonely enough with Seguilo.

Blue-green Magda sank in the west. A sulfur overcast drifted up to meet it. Sunset brought a few minutes of sad glory to the sky: jade-colored stain with violet streakings. Perrin started the twin shafts of red and white on their nocturnal sweep, went to stand by the window.

The tide was rising, the water surged over the shelf with a heavy sound. Up from the west floated a moon; Ista, Bista, Liad, Miad, or Poidel? A native would know at a glance. Up they came, one after the other, five balls blue as old ice.

"It's not wise to believe..." What had Seguilo meant? Perrin tried to think back. Seguilo had said, "It's not often, very rare, in fact, that the five moons bunch up—but when they do, then there're high tides." He had hesitated, glancing out at the shelf. "When the five moons rise together," said Seguilo, "it's not wise to believe anything."

Perrin had gazed at him with forehead creased in puzzlement. Seguilo was an old hand, who knew the fables and lore, which he brought forth from time to time. Perrin had never known quite what to expect from Seguilo; he had the trait indispensable to a lighthouse-tender—taciturnity. The transceiver had been his hobby; in Perrin's ignorant hands, the instrument had destroyed itself. What the lighthouse needs, thought Perrin, was one of the new transceivers with self-contained power unit, master control, the new organic screen, soft and elastic, like a great eye....A sudden rain squall blanketed half the sky; the five moons hurtled toward the cloud bank. The tide surged high over the shelf, almost over a gray mass. Perrin eyed it with interest; what could it be?....About the size of a transceiver, about the same shape. Of course, it could not possibly *be* a transceiver; yet, what a wonderful thing if it were....He squinted, strained his eyes. There, surely, that was the milk-colored screen; those black spots were dials. He sprang to his feet, ran down the stairs, out the door, across the rock....It was irrational; why should a transceiver appear just when he wanted it, as if in answer to his prayer? Of course it might be part of a cargo lost overboard....

Sure enough, the mechanism was bolted to a raft of Manasco logs, and evidently had floated up on the shelf on the high tide.

Perrin, unable to credit his good fortune, crouched beside the gray case. Brand new, with red seals across the master switch.

It was too heavy to carry. Perrin tore off the seals, threw on the power: here was a set he understood. The screen glowed bright.

Perrin dialed to the Commission band. The interior of an office appeared and facing out was, not the officious subordinate, but Superintendent Raymond Flint himself. Nothing could be better.

"Superintendent," cried out Perrin, "this is Isel Rock Lighthouse, Harold Perrin speaking."

"Oh, yes," said Superintendent Flint. "How are you, Perrin? What's the trouble?"

"My partner, Andy Seguilo, disappeared—vanished into nowhere; I'm alone out here."

Superintendent Flint looked shocked. "Disappeared? What happened? Did he fall into the ocean?"

"I don't know. He just disappeared. It happened last night—"

"You should have called in before," said Flint reprovingly. "I would have sent out a rescue copter to search for him."

"I tried to call," Perrin explained, "but I couldn't get the regular transceiver to work. It burnt up on me....I thought I was marooned here."

Superintendent Flint raised his eyebrows in mild curiosity. "Just what are you using now?"

Perrin stammered, "It's a brand-new instrument...floated up out of the sea. Probably was lost from a barge."

Flint nodded. "Those bargemen are a careless lot—don't seem to understand what good equipment costs....Well, you sit tight. I'll order a plane out in the morning with a relief crew. You'll be assigned to duty along the Floral Coast. How does that suit you?"

"Very well, sir," said Perrin. "Very well indeed. I can't think of anything I'd like better...Isel Rock is beginning to get on my nerves."

"When the five moons rise, it's not wise to believe anything," said Superintendent Flint in a sepulchral voice.

The screen went dead.

Perrin lifted his hand, slowly turned off the power. A drop of rain fell on his face. He glanced skyward. The squall was almost on him. He tugged at the transceiver, although well aware that it was too heavy to move. In the storeroom was a tarpaulin that would protect the transceiver until morning. The relief crew could help him move it inside.

He ran back to the lighthouse, found the tarpaulin, hurried back outside. Where was the transceiver?... Ah—there. He ran through the pelting drops, wrapped the tarpaulin around the box, lashed it into place, ran back to the lighthouse. He barred the box, and whistling, opened a canned dinner unit.

The rain spun and slashed at the lighthouse. The twin shafts of white and red swept wildly around the sky. Perrin climbed into his bunk, lay warm and drowsy....Seguilo's disappearance was a terrible thing; it would leave a scar on his mind. But it was over and done with. Put it behind him; look to the future. The Floral Coast....

In the morning the sky was bare and clean. Maurnilam Var spread mirror-quiet as far as the eye could reach. Isel Rock lay naked to the sunlight. Looking out the window, Perrin saw a rumpled heap—the tarpaulin, the lashings. The transceiver, the Manasco raft had disappeared utterly.

Perrin sat in the doorway. The sun climbed the sky. A dozen times he jumped to his feet, listening for the sound of engines. But no relief plane appeared.

The sun reached the zenith, verged westward. A barge drifted by, a mile from the rock. Perrin ran out on the shelf, shouting, waving his arms.

The lank, red bargemen sprawled on the cargo stared curiously, made no move. The barge dwindled into the east.

Perrin returned to the doorstep, sat with his head in his hands. Chills and fever ran along his skin. There would be no relief plane. On Isel Rock he would remain, day in, day out, for eleven weeks.

Listlessly, he climbed the steps to the commissary. There was no lack of food, he would never starve. But could he bear the solitude, the uncertainty? Seguilo going, coming, going....The unsubstantial transceiver....Who was responsible for these cruel jokes? The five moons rising together—was there some connection?

He found an almanac, carried it to the table. At the top of each page five white circles on a black strip represented the moons. A week ago they strung out at random. Four days ago Liad, the slowest, and Poidel, the fastest, were thirty degrees apart, with Ista, Bista, and Miad between. Two nights ago the peripheries almost touched; last night they were even closer. Tonight Poidel would bulge slightly out in front of Ista, tomorrow night Liad would lag behind Bista....But between the five moons and Seguilo's disappearance—where was the connection?

Gloomily, Perrin ate his dinner. Magda settled into Maurnilam Var without display, a dull dusk settled over Isel Rock, water rose and sighed across the shelf.

Perrin turned on the light, barred the door. There would be no more hoping, no more wishing—no more believing. In eleven weeks the relief ship would convey him back to Spacetown; in the meantime he must make the best of the situation.

Through the window he saw the blue glow in the east, watched Poidel, Ista, Bista, Liad, and Miad climb the sky. The tide came with the moons. Maurnilam Var was still calm, and each moon laid a separate path of reflection along the water.

Perrin looked up into the sky, around the horizon. A beautiful, lonesome sight. With Seguilo he sometimes had felt lonely, but never isolation such as this. Eleven weeks of solitude....If he could select a companion...Perrin let his mind wander.

Into the moonlight a slim figure came walking, wearing tan breeches and a short-sleeved white sports shirt.

Perrin stared, unable to move. The figure walked up to the door, rapped. The muffled sound came up the staircase. "Hello, anybody home?" It was a girl's clear voice.

Perrin swung open the window, called hoarsely, "Go away!"

She moved back, turned up her face, and the moonlight fell upon her features. Perrin's voice died in his throat. He felt his heart beating wildly.

"Go away?" she said in a soft puzzled voice. "I've no place to go."

"Who are you?" he asked. His voice sounded strange to his own ears—desperate, hopeful. After all, she was possible—even though almost impossibly beautiful....She might have flown out from Spacetown. "How did you get here?"

She gestured at Maurnilam Var. "My plane went down about three miles out. I came over on the life raft."

Perrin looked along the water's edge. The outline of a life raft was barely visible.

The girl called up, "Are you going to let me in?"

Perrin stumbled downstairs. He halted at the door, one hand on the bolts, and the blood rushed in his ears.

An impatient tapping jarred his hand. "I'm freezing to death out here."

Perrin let the door swing back. She stood facing him, half-smiling. "You're a very cautious lighthouse—tender—or perhaps a woman-hater?"

Perrin searched her face, her eyes, the expression of her mouth. "Are you...real?"

She laughed, not at all offended. "Of course I'm real." She held out her hand. "Touch me." Perrin stared at her—the essence of night-flowers, soft silk, hot blood, sweetness, delightful fire. "Touch me," she replied softly.

Perrin moved back uncertainly, and she came forward, into the lighthouse. "Can you call the shore?"

She turned him a quick firefly look. "When is your next relief boat?"

"Eleven weeks."

"Eleven weeks!" she sighed a soft shallow sigh.

Perrin moved back another half-step. "How did you know I was alone?"

She seemed confused. "I didn't know....Aren't light housekeepers always alone?"

"No."

She came a step closer. "You don't seem pleased to see me. Are you...a hermit?"

"No," said Perrin in a husky voice. "Quite the reverse. ...But I can't quite get used to you. You're a miracle. Too good to be true. Just now I was wishing for someone...exactly like you. Exactly."

"And here I am."

Perrin moved uneasily. "What's your name?"

He knew what she would say before she spoke. "Sue."

"Sue what?" He tried to hold his mind vacant.

"Oh...just Sue. Isn't that enough?"

Perrin felt the skin of his face tighten. "Where is your home?"

She looked vaguely over her shoulder. Perrin held his mind blank, but the word came through.

"Hell."

Perrin's breath came hard and sharp.

"And what is Hell like?"

"It is...cold and dark."

Perrin stepped back. "Go away. Go away." His vision blurred; her face melted as if tears had come across his eyes.

"Where will I go?"

"Back where you came from."

"But"—forlornly—"there is nowhere but Maurnilam Var. And up here—" She stopped short, took a swift step forward, stood looking up into his face. He could feel the warmth of her body. "Are you afraid of me?"

Perrin wrenched his eyes from her face. "You're not real. You're something which takes the shape of my thoughts. Perhaps you killed Seguilo...I don't know what you are. But you're not real."

"Not real? Of course I'm real. Touch me. Feel my arm." Perrin backed away. She said passionately, "Here, a knife. If you are of a mind, cut me; you will see blood. Cut deeper...you will find bone."

"What would happen," said Perrin, "if I drove the knife into your heart?"

She said nothing, staring at him with big eyes.

"Why do you come here?" cried Perrin. She looked away, back toward the water.

"It's magic...darkness...." The words were a mumbled confusion; Perrin suddenly realized that the same words were in his own mind. Had she merely parroted his thoughts during the entire conversation? "Then comes a slow pull," she said. "I drift, I crave the air, the moons bring me up...I do anything to hold my place in the air...."

"Speak your own words," said Perrin harshly. "I know you're not real—but where is Seguilo?"

"Seguilo?" She reached a hand behind her head, touched her hair, smiled sleepily at Perrin. Real or not, Perrin's pulse thudded in his ears. Real or not....

"I'm no dream," she said. "I'm real...." She came slowly toward Perrin, feeling his thoughts, face arch, ready.

Perrin said in a strangled gasp, "No, no. Go away. *Go away!*"

She stopped short, looked at him through eyes suddenly opaque. "Very well. I will go now—"

"Now! Forever!"

"—but perhaps you will call me back...."

She walked slowly through the door. Perrin ran to the window, watched the slim shape blur into the moonlight. She went to the edge of the shelf; here she paused. Perrin felt a sudden intolerable pang; what was he casting away? Real or not, she was what he wanted her to be; she was identical to reality....He leaned forward to call, "Come back...whatever you are...." He restrained himself. When he looked again she was gone....Why was she gone? Perrin pondered, looking across the moonlit sea. He had wanted her, but he no longer believed in her. He had believed in the shape called Seguilo; he had believed in the transceiver—and both had slavishly obeyed his expectations. So had the girl, and he had sent her away....Rightly, too, he told himself regretfully. Who knows what she might become when his back was turned....

When dawn finally came, it brought a new curtain of overcast. Blue-green Magda glimmered dull and sultry as a moldy orange. The water shone like oil....Movement in the west—a Panapa chieftain's private barge, walking across the horizon like a water-spider. Perrin vaulted the stairs to the lightroom, swung the lumenifer full at the barge, dispatched an erratic series of flashes.

The barge moved on, jointed oars swinging rhythmically in and out of the water. A torn banner of fog drifted across the water. The barge became a dark, jerking shape, disappeared.

Perrin went to Seguilo's old transceiver, sat looking at it. He jumped to his feet, pulled the chassis out of the case, disassembled the entire circuit.

He saw scorched metal, wires fused into droplets, cracked ceramic. He pushed the tangle into a corner, went to stand by the window.

The sun was at the zenith, the sky was the color of green grapes. The sea heaved sluggishly, great amorphous sweeps rising and falling without apparent direction. Now as low tide; the shelf shouldered high up, the black rock showing naked and strange. The sea palpitated, up, down, up, down, sucking noisily at bits of sea-wrack.

Perrin descended the stairs. On his way down he looked in at the bathroom mirror, and his face stared back at him, pale, wide-eyed, cheeks hollow and lusterless. Perrin continued down the stairs, stepped out into the sunlight.

Carefully he walked out on the shelf, looked in a kind of fascination down over the edge. The heave of the swells distorted his vision; he could see little more than shadows and shifting fingers of light.

Step by step he wandered along the shelf. The sun leaned to the west. Perrin retreated up the rock.

At the lighthouse he seated himself in the doorway. Tonight the door remained barred. No inducement could persuade him to open up; the most entrancing visions would beseech him in vain. His thoughts went to Seguilo. What had Seguilo believed; what being had he fabricated out of his morbid fancy with the power and malice to drag him away?... It seemed that every man was victim to his own imaginings, Isel Rock was not the place for a fanciful man when the five moons rose together.

Tonight he would bar the door, he would bed himself down and sleep, secure both in the barrier of welded metal and his own unconsciousness.

The sun sank in a bank of heavy vapor. North, east, south flushed with violet; the west glowed lime and dark green, dulling quickly through tones of brown. Perrin entered the lighthouse, bolted the door, set the twin shafts of red and white circling the horizon.

He opened a dinner unit, ate listlessly. Outside was dark night, emptiness to all the horizons. As the tide rose, the water hissed and moaned across the shelf.

Perrin lay in his bed, but sleep was far away. Through the window came an electric glow, then up rose the five moons, shining through a high overcast as if wrapped in blue gauze.

Perrin heaved fitfully. There was nothing to fear, he was safe in the lighthouse. No human hands could force the door; it would take the strength of a mastodon, the talons of a rock choundril, the ferocity of a Maldene land-shark....

He elbowed himself up on his bunk....A sound from outside? He peered through the window, heart in his mouth. A tall shape, indistinct. As he watched it, it slouched toward the lighthouse—as he knew it would.

"No, no," cried Perrin softly. He flung himself into his bunk, covered his head in the blankets. "It's only what I think up myself, it's not real....Go away," he whispered fiercely. "Go away." He listened. It must be near the door now. I would be lifting a heavy arm, the talons would glint in the moonlight.

"No, no," cried Perrin. "There's nothing there...." He held up his head and listened.

A rattle, a rasp at the door. A thud as a great mass tested the lock.

"Go away!" screamed Perrin. "You're not real!"

The door groaned, the bolts sagged.

Perrin stood at the head of the stairs, breathing heavily through his mouth. The door would slam back in another instant. He knew what he would see: a black shape tall and round as a pole, with eyes like coach-lamps. Perrin even knew the last sound his ears would hear—a terrible grinding discord....

The top bolt snapped, the door reeled. A huge black arm shoved inside. Perrin saw the talons gleam as the fingers reached for the bolt.

His eyes flickered around the lighthouse for a weapon....Only a wrench, a table knife.

The bottom bolt shattered, the door twisted. Perrin stood staring, his mind congealed. A thought rose up from some hidden survival-node. Here, Perrin thought, was the single chance.

He ran back into his room. Behind him the door clattered, he heard heavy steps. He looked around the room. His shoe.

Thud! Up the stairs, and the lighthouse vibrated. Perrin's fancy explored the horrible, he knew what he would hear. And so came a voice—harsh, empty, but like another voice which had been sweet. "I told you I'd be back."

Thud—thud—up the stairs. Perrin took the shoe by the toe, swung, struck the side of his head.

Perrin recovered consciousness. He stumbled to the wall, supported himself. Presently he groped to his bunk, sat down.

Outside there was still dark night. Grunting, he looked out the window into the sky. The five moons hung far down in the west. Already Poidel ranged ahead, while Liad trailed behind.

Tomorrow night the five moons would rise apart.

Tomorrow night there would be no high tides, sucking and tremulous along the shelf.

Tomorrow night the moons would call up no yearning shapes from the streaming dark.

Eleven weeks to relief. Perrin gingerly felt the side of his head....Quite a respectable lump.

THE NEW PRIME

Music, carnival lights, the slide of feet on waxed oak, perfume, muffled talk and laugher.

Arthur Caversham of twentieth-century Boston felt air along his skin, and discovered himself to be stark naked.

It was at Janice Paget's coming-out party: three hundred guests in formal evening-wear surrounded him.

For a moment he felt no emotion beyond vague bewilderment. His presence seemed the outcome of logical events, but his memory was fogged and he could find no definite anchor of certainty.

He stood a little apart from the rest of the stag line, facing the red and gold calliope where the orchestra sat. The buffet, the punch bowl, the champagne wagons, tended by clowns, were to his right; to the left, through the open flap of the circus tent, lay the garden, now lit by strings of colored lights, red, green, yellow, blue, and he caught a glimpse of a merry-go-round across the lawn.

Why was he here? He had no recollection, no sense of purpose....The night was warm; the other young men in the full-dress suits must feel rather sticky, he thought....An idea tugged at a corner of his mind. There was a significant aspect of the affair that he was overlooking.

He noticed that the young men nearby had moved away from him. He heard chortles of amusement, astonished exclamations. A girl dancing past saw him over the arm of her escort; she gave a startled squeak, jerked her eyes away, giggling and blushing.

Something was wrong. These young men and women were startled and amazed by his naked skin to the point of embarrassment. The gnaw of urgency came closer to the surface. He must do something. Taboos felt with such intensity might not be violated without unpleasant consequences; such was his understanding. He was lacking garments; these he must obtain.

He looked about him, inspecting the young men who watched him with ribald delight, disgust, or curiosity. To one of these latter he addressed himself.

"Where can I get some clothing?"

The young man shrugged. "Where did you leave yours?"

Two heavyset men in dark blue uniforms entered the tent; Arthur Caversham saw them from the corner of his eye, and his mind worked with desperate intensity.

This young man seemed typical of those around him. What sort of appeal would have meaning for him? Like any other human being, he could be moved to action if the right chord were struck. By what method could he be moved?

Sympathy?

Threats?

The prospect of advantage or profit?

Caversham rejected all of these. By violating the taboo he had forfeited his claim to sympathy. A threat would excite derision, and he had no profit or advantage to offer. The stimulus must be more devious....He reflected that young men customarily banded together in secret societies. In the thousand cultures he had studied this was almost infallibly true. Long-houses, drug-cults, tongs, instruments of sexual initiation—whatever the name, the external aspects were near-identical: painful initiation, secret signs and passwords, uniformly of group conduct, obligation to service. If this young man were a member of such an association, he might react to an appeal to this group-spirit.

Arthur Caversham said, "I've been put in this taboo situation by the brotherhood; in the name of the brotherhood, find me some suitable garments."

The young man stared, taken aback. "Brotherhood?... You mean fraternity?" Enlightenment spread over his face. "Is this some kind of hell-week stunt?" He laughed. "If it is, they sure go all the way."

"Yes," said Arthur Caversham. "My fraternity."

The young man said, "This way, then—and hurry, here comes the law. We'll take off under the tent. I'll lend you my topcoat till you make it back to your house."

The two uniformed men, pushing quietly through the dancers, were almost upon them. The young man lifted the flap of the tent, Arthur Caversham ducked under, his friend followed. Together they ran through the man-colored shadows to a little booth painted with gay red and white stripes that was near the entrance to the test.

"You stay back, out of sight," said the young man. "I'll check out my coat."

"Fine," said Arthur Caversham.

The young man hesitated. "What's your house? Where do you go to school."

Arthur Caversham desperately searched his mind for an answer. A single fact reached the surface.

"I'm from Boston."

"Boston U? Or MIT? Or Harvard?"

"Harvard."

"Ah." The young man nodded. "I'm Washington and Lee myself. What's your house?"

"I'm not supposed to say."

"Oh," said the young man, puzzled but satisfied. "Well—just a minute...."

Bearwald the Halforn halted, numb with despair and exhaustion. The remnants of his platoon sank to the ground around him, and they stared back to where the rim of the night flickered and glowed with fire. Man villages, many wood-gabled farmhouses had been given the torch, and the Brands from Mount Medallion reveled in human blood.

The pulse of a distant drum touched Bearwald's skin, a deep *thrumm-thrumm-thrumm*, almost inaudible. Much closer he heard a hoarse human cry of fright, then exultant killing-calls, not human. The Brands were tall, black, man-shaped but not men. They had eyes like lamps of red glass, bright white teeth, and tonight they seemed bent on slaughtering all the men of the world.

"Down," hissed Kanaw, his right arm-guard, and Bearwald crouched. Across the flaring sky marched a column of tall Brand warriors, rocking jauntily, without fear.

Bearwald said suddenly. "Men—we are thirteen. Fighting arm to arm with these monsters we are helpless. Tonight their total force is down from the mountain; the hive must be near deserted. What can we lose if we undertake to burn the home-hive of the Brands? Only our lives, and what are these now?"

Kanaw said. "Our lives are nothing; let us be off at once."

"May our vengeance be great," said Broctan the left armguard. "May the home-hive of the Brands be white ashes this coming morn...."

Mount Medallion loomed overhead; the oval hive lay in Pangborn Valley. At the mouth of the valley, Bearwald divided the platoon into two halves, and placed Kanaw in the van of the second. "We move silently twenty yards apart; thus if either party rouses a Brand, the other may attack from the rear and so kill the monster before the vale is roused. Do all understand?"

"We understand."

"Forward then, to the hive."

The valley reeked with an odor like sour leather. From the direction of the hive came a muffled clanging. The ground was soft, covered with runner moss; careful feet made no sound. Crouching low, Bearwald could see the shapes of his men against the sky—here indigo with a violet rim. The angry glare of burning Echevasa lay down the slope to the south.

A sound. Bearwald hissed, and the columns froze. They waited. *Thud-thud-thud-thud* came the steps—then a hoarse cry of rage and alarm.

"Kill, kill the beast!" yelled Bearwald.

The Brand swung his club like a scythe, lifting one man, carrying the body around with the after-swing. Bearwald leapt close, struck with his blade, slicing as he hewed; he felt the tendons part, smelled the hot gush of Brand blood.

The clanging had stopped now, and Brand cries carried across the night.

"Forward," panted Bearwald. "Out with your tinder, strike fire to the hive. Burn, burn, burn...."

Abandoning stealth he ran forward; ahead loomed the dark dome. Immature Brands came surging forth, squeaking and squalling, and with them came the genetrices—twenty-foot monsters crawling on hands and feet, grunting and snapping as they moved.

"Kill!" yelled Bearwald the Halform. "Kill! Fire, fire, fire!"

He dashed to the hive, crouched, struck spark to tinder, puffed. The rag, soaked with saltpeter, flared; Bearwald fed it straw, thrust it against the hive. The reed-pulp and withe crackled.

He leapt up as a horde of young Brands darted at him. His blade rose and fell; they were cleft, no match for his frenzy. Creeping close came the great Brand genetrices, three of them, swollen of abdomen, exuding an odor vile to his nostrils.

"Out with the fire!" yelled the first. "Fire, out. The Great Mother is tombed within; she lies too fecund to move....Fire, woe, destruction!" And they wailed, "Where are the mighty? Where are our warriors?"

Thrumm—thrumm-thrumm came the sound of skindrums. Up the valley rolled the echo of hoarse Brand voices.

Bearwald stood with his back to the blaze. He darted forward, severed the head of a creeping genetrix, jumped back....Where were his men? "Kanaw!" he called. "Laida! Theyat! Gyorg! Broctan!"

He craned his neck, saw the flicker of fires. "Men! Kill the creeping mothers!" And leaping forward once more, he hacked and hewed, and another genetrix sighed and groaned and rolled flat.

The Brand voices changed to alarm; the triumphant drumming halted; the thud of footsteps came loud.

At Bearwald's back the hive burnt with a pleasant heat. Within came a shrill keening, a cry of vast pain.

In the leaping blaze he saw the charging Brand warriors. Their eyes glared like embers, their teeth shone like white sparks. They came forward, swinging their clubs, and Bearwald gripped his sword, too proud to flee.

After grounding his air sled Ceistan sat a few minutes inspecting the dead city Therlatch: a wall of earthen brick a hundred feet high, a dusty portal, and a few crumbled roofs lifting above the battlements. Behind the city the desert spread across the near, middle, and far distance to the hazy shapes of the Allune Mountains at the horizon, pink in the light of the twin suns Mig and Pag.

Scouting from above he had seen no sign of life, nor had he expected any, after a thousand years of abandonment. Perhaps a few sand-crawlers wallowed in the heat of the ancient bazaar. Otherwise the streets would feel his presence with great surprise.

Jumping from the air sled, Ceistan advanced toward the portal. He passed under, stood looking right and left with interest. In the parched air the brick buildings stood almost eternal. The wind smoothed and rounded all harsh angles; the glass had been cracked by the heat of day and chill of night; heaps of sand clogged the passageways.

Three streets led away from the portal and Ceistan could find nothing to choose between them. Each was dusty, narrow, and each twisted out of his line of vision after a hundred yards.

Ceistan rubbed his chin thoughtfully. Somewhere in the city lay a brassbound coffer, containing the Crown and Shield Parchment. This, according to tradition set a precedent for the fiefholder's immunity from energy-tax. Glay, who was Ceistan's liege-lord, having cited the parchment as justification for his delinquency, had been challenged to show validity. Now he lay in prison on charge of rebellion, and in the morning he would be nailed to the bottom of an air sled and send drifting into the west, unless Ceistan returned with the parchment.

After a thousand years, there was small cause for optimism, thought Ceistan. However, the lord Glay was a fair man and he would leave no stone unturned....If it existed, the chest presumably would lie in state, in the town's Legalic, or the Mosque, or the Hall of Relics, or possibly in the Sumptuar. He would search all of these, allowing two hours per building; the eight hours so used would see the end to the pink daylight.

At random he entered the street in the center and shortly came to a plaza at whose far end rose the Legalic, the Hall of Records and Decisions. At the facade Ceistan paused, for the interior was dim and gloomy. No sound came from the dusty void save the sigh and whisper of the dry wind. He entered.

The great hall was empty. The walls were illuminated with frescoes of red and blue, as bright as if painted yesterday. There were six to each wall, the top half displaying a criminal act and the bottom half the penalty.

Ceistan passed through the hall, into the chambers behind. He found but dust and the small of dust. Into the crypts he ventured, and these were lit by embrasures. There was much litter and rubble, but no brass coffer.

Up and out into the clean air he went, and strode across the plaza to the Mosque, where he entered under the massive architrave.

The Nunciator's Confirmatory lay wide and bare and clean, for the tessellated floor was swept by a powerful draft. A thousand apertures opened from the low ceiling, each communicating with a cell overhead; thus arranged so that the devout might seek counsel with the Nunciator as he passed below without disturbing their attitudes of supplication. In the center of the pavilion a disk of glass roofed a recess. Below was a coffer and in the coffer rested a brass-bound chest. Ceistan sprang down the steps in high hopes.

But the chest contained jewels—the tiara of the Old Queen, the chest vellopes of the Gonwand Corps, the great ball, half emerald, half ruby, which in the ancient ages was rolled across the plaza to signify the passage of the old year.

Ceistan tumbled them all back in the coffer. Relics on this planet of dead cities had no value, and synthetic gems were infinitely superior in luminosity and water.

Leaving the Mosque, he studied the height of the suns. The zenith was past, the moving balls of pink fire leaned to the west. He hesitated, frowning and blinking at the hot earthen walls, considering that not impossibly both coffer and parchment were fable, like so many others regarding dead Therlatch.

A gust of wind swirled across the plaza and Ceistan choked on a dry throat. He spat, and an acrid taste bit his tongue. An old fountain opened in the wall nearby; he examined it wistfully, but water was not even a memory along these dead streets.

Once again he cleared his throat, spat, turned across the city toward the Hall of Relics.

He entered the great nave, past square pillars built of earthen brick. Pink shafts of light struck down from the cracks and gaps in the roof, and he was like a midge in the vast space. To all sides were niches cased in glass, and each held an object of ancient reverence: the armor in which Plange the Forewarned led the Blue Flags; the coronet of the First Serpent; an array of antique Padang skulls; Princess Thermosteraliam's bridal gown of woven cobweb palladium, as fresh as the day she wore it; the original Tablets of Legality; the great conch throne of an early dynasty; a dozen other objects. But the coffer was not among them.

Ceistan sought for entrance to a possible crypt, but except where the currents of dusty air had channeled grooves in the porphyry, the floor was smooth.

Out once more into the dead streets, and now the suns had passed behind the crumbled roofs, leaving the streets in magenta shadow.

With leaden feet, burning throat, and a sense of defeat, Ceistan turned to the Sumptuar, on the citadel. Up the wide steps, under the verdigris-fronted portico into a lobby painted with vivid frescoes. These depicted the maidens of ancient Therlatch at work, at play, amid sorrow and joy: slim creatures with short, black hair and glowing ivory skin, as graceful as water vanes, as round and delectable as chermoyan plums. Ceistan passed through the lobby with many side-glances, reflecting that these ancient creatures of delight were now the dust he trod under his feet.

He walked down a corridor which makes a circuit of the building, and from which the chambers and apartments of the Sumptuar might be entered. The wisps of a wonderful rug crunched under his feet, and the walls displayed moldy tatters, once tapestries of the finest weave. At the entrance to each chamber a fresco pictured the Sumptuar maiden and the sign she served; at each of these chambers Ceistan paused, made a quick investigation, and so passed on to the next. The beams slanting in through the cracks served him as a gauge of time, and they flattened ever more toward the horizontal.

Chamber after chamber after chamber. There were chests in some, altars in others, cases of manifestos, triptychs, and fonts in others. But never the chest he sought.

And ahead was the lobby where he had entered the building. Three more chambers were to be searched, then the light would be gone.

He came to the first of these, and this was hung with a new curtain. Pushing it aside, he found himself looking into an outside court, full in the long light of the twin suns. A fountain of water trickled down across steps of apple-green jade into a garden as soft and fresh and green as any in the north. And rising in alarm from a couch was a maiden, as vivid and delightful as any in the frescoes. She had short, dark hair, a face as pure and delicate as the great white frangipani she wore over her ear.

For an instant Ceistan and the maiden stared eye to eye; then her alarm faded and she smiled shyly.

"Who are you?" Ceistan asked in wonder. "Are you a ghost or do you live here in the dust?"

"I am real," she said. "My home is to the south, at the Palram Oasis, and this is the period of solitude to which all maidens of the race submit when aspiring for Upper Instruction....So without fear may you come beside me, and rest, and drink of fruit wine and be my companion through the lonely night, for this is my last week of solitude and I am weary of my aloneness."

Ceistan took a step forward, then hesitated. "I must fulfill my mission. I seek the brass coffer containing the Crown and Shield Parchment. Do you know of this?"

She shook her head. "It is nowhere in the Sumptuar." She rose to her feet, stretching her ivory arms as a kitten stretches. "Abandon your search, and come let me refresh you."

Ceistan looked at her, looked up at the fading light, looked down the corridor to the two doors yet remaining. "First I must complete my search; I owe duty to my lord Glay, who will be nailed under an air sled and sped west unless I bring him aid."

The maiden said with a pout, "Go then to your dusty chamber; and go with a dry throat. You will find nothing, and if you persist so stubbornly, I will be gone when you return."

"So let it be," said Ceistan.

He turned away, marched down the corridor. The first chamber was bare and dry as a bone. In the second and last, a man's skeleton lay tumbled in a corner; this Ceistan saw in the last rosy light of the twin suns.

There was no brass coffer, no parchments. So Glay must die, and Ceistan's heart hung heavy.

He returned to the chamber where he had found the maiden, but she had departed. The fountain had been stopped, and moisture only filmed the stones.

Ceistan called, "Maiden, where are you? Return; my obligation is at an end...."

There was no response.

Ceistan shrugged, turned to the lobby and so outdoors, to grope his way through the deserted twilight street to the portal and his air sled.

Dobnor Daksat became aware that the big man in the embroidered black cloak was speaking to him.

Orienting himself to his surroundings, which were at once familiar and strange, he also became aware that the man's voice was condescending, supercilious.

"You are competing in a highly advanced classification," he said. "I marvel at your...ah, confidence." And he eyed Daksat with a gleaming and speculative eye.

Daksat looked down at the floor, frowned at the sight of his clothes. He wore a long cloak of black-purple velvet, swinging like a bell around his ankles. His trousers were of scarlet corduroy, tight at the waist, thigh, and calf, with a loose puff of green cloth between calf and ankle. The clothes were his own, obviously: they looked wrong and right at once, as did the carved gold knuckle-guards he wore on his hands.

The big man in the dark cloak continued speaking, looking at a point over Daksat's head, as if Daksat were nonexistent.

"Clauktaba has won Imagist honors over the years. Bel-Washab was the Korsi Victor last month; Tol Morabait is an acknowledged master of the technique. And then there is Ghisel Ghang of West Ind, who knows no peer in the creation of fire-stars, and Pulakt Havjorska, the Champion of the Island Realm. So it becomes a matter of skepticism whether you, new, inexperienced, without a fund of images, can do more than embarrass us with all your mental poverty."

Daksat's brain was yet wrestling with his bewilderment, and he could feel no strong resentment at the big man's evident contempt. He said, "Just what is all this? I'm not sure that I understand my position."

The man in the black cloak inspected him quizzically. "So, now you commence to experience trepidation? Justly, I assure you." He sighed, waved his hands. "Well, well—young men will be impetuous, and perhaps you have formed images you considered not discreditable. In any event, the public eye will ignore you for the glories of Clauktaba's geometrics and Ghisel Ghang's star-bursts. Indeed, I counsel you, keep your images small, drab, and confined; you will so avoid the faults of bombast and discord....Now, it is time to go to your Imagicon. This way, then. Remember, grays, browns, lavenders, perhaps a few tones of ocher and rust; then the spectators will understand that you compete for the schooling alone, and do not actively challenge the masters. This way then...."

He opened a door and led Dobnor Daksat up a stair and so out into the night.

They stood in a great stadium, facing six great screens forty feet high. Behind them in the dark sat tier upon tier of spectators—thousands and thousands, and their sounds came as a soft crush. Daksat turned to see them, but all their faces and their individualities had melted into the entity as a whole.

"Here," said the big man, "this is your apparatus. Seat yourself and I will adjust the ceretemps."

Daksat suffered himself to be placed in a heavy chair, so soft and deep that he felt himself to be floating. Adjustments were made at his head and neck and the bridge of his nose. He felt a sharp prick, a pressure, a throb, and then a soothing warmth. From the distance, a voice called out over the crowd:

"Two minutes to gray mist! Two minutes to gray mist! Attend, Imagists, two minutes to gray mist!"

The big man stooped over him. "Can you see well?"

Daksat raised himself a trifle. "Yes...all is clear."

"Very well. At 'gray mist' this little filament will glow. When it dies, then it is your screen, and you must imagine your best."

The far voice said, "One minute to gray mist! The order is Pulakt Havjorska, Tol Marabait, Ghisel Ghang, Dobnor Daksat, Clauktaba, and Bel-Washab. There are no handicaps; all color and shapes are permitted. Relax then, ready your lobes, and now—gray mist!"

The light glowed on the panel of Daksat's chair, and he saw five of the six screens light to a pleasant pear-gray, swirling a trifle as if agitated, excited. Only the screen before him remained dull. The big man, who stood behind him, reached down, prodded. "Gray mist, Daksat; are you deaf and blind?"

Daksat thought gray mist, and instantly his screen sprang to life, displaying a cloud of silver-gray, clean and clear.

"Humph," he heard the big man shout. "Somewhat dull and without interest—but I suppose good enough....See how Cluktaba's rings with hints of passion already, quivers with emotion."

And Daksat, noting the screen to his right, saw this to be true. The gray, without actually displaying color, flowed and filmed as if suppressing a vast flood of light.

Now, to the far left, on Pulakt Havjorska's screen, color glowed. It was a gambit image, modest and restrained—a green jewel dripping a rain of blue and silver drops which struck a black ground and disappeared in little orange explosions.

Then Tol Morabait's screen glowed: a black and white checkerboard with certain of the squares flashing suddenly green, red, blue, and yellow—warm, searching colors, pure as shafts from a rainbow. The image disappeared in a flush mingled of rose and blue.

Ghisel Ghang wrought a circle of yellow which quivered, brought forth a green halo, which in turn bulged giving rise to larger band of brilliant black and white. In the center formed a complex kaleidoscopic pattern. The pattern suddenly vanished in a brilliant flash of light; on the screen for an instant or two appeared the identical pattern in a complete new suit of colors. A ripple of sound from the spectators greeted this *tour de force*.

The light on Daksat's panel died. Behind him he felt a prod. "Now."

Daksat eyed the screen and his mind was blank of ideas. He ground his teeth. Anything. Anything. A picture...he imagined a view across the meadowlands beside the River Melramy.

"Hm," said the big man behind him. "Pleasant. A pleasant fantasy and rather original."

Puzzled, Daksat examined the picture on the screen. So far as he could distinguish, it was an uninspired reproduction of a scene he knew well. Fantasy? Was that what was expected? Very well, he'd produce fantasy. He imagined the meadows glowing, molten, white-hot. The vegetation, the old cairns slumped into a viscous seethe. The surface smoothed, became a mirror which reflected the Copper Crags.

Behind him the big man grunted. "A little heavy-handed, that last, and thereby you destroyed the charming effect of those unearthly colors and shapes...."

Daksat slumped back in his chair, frowning, eager for his turn to come again.

Meanwhile Clauktaba created a dainty white blossom with purple stamens on a green stalk. The petals wilted, the stamens discharged a cloud of swirling yellow pollen.

Then Bel-Washab, at the end of the line, painted his screen a luminous underwater green. It rippled, bulged, and a black irregular blot marred the surface. From the center of the blot seeped a trickle of hot gold that quickly meshed and veined the black blot.

Such was the first passage.

There was a pause of several seconds. "Now," breathed the voice behind Daksat, "now the competition begins."

On Pulakt Havjorska's screen appeared an angry sea of color: waves of red, green, blue, an ugly mottling. Dramatically, a yellow shape appeared at the lower right, vanquished the chaos. It spread over the screen, the center went lime-green. A black shape appeared, split, bowed softly and easily to both sides. Then turning, the two shapes wandered into the background, twisting, bending with supple grace. Far down a perspective they merged, darted forward like a lance, spread out into a series of lances, formed a slanting pattern of slim black bars.

"Superb!" hissed the big man. "The timing, so just, so exact!"

Tol Morabait replied with a fuscous brown field threaded with crimson lines and blots. Vertical green hatching formed at the left, strode across the screen to the right. The brown field pressed forward, bulged through the green bars, pressed hard, broke, and segments flitted forward to leave the screen. On the black background behind the green hatching, which now faded, lay a human brain, pink, pulsing. The brain sprouted six insectlike legs, scuttled crabwise back into the distance.

Ghisel Ghang brought forth one of his fire-bursts—a small pellet of bright blue exploding in all directions, the tips working and writhing through wonderful patterns in the five colors, blue, violet, white, purple, and light green.

Dobnor Daksat, rigid as a bar, sat with hands clenched and teeth grinding into teeth. Now! Was not his brain as excellent as those of the far lands? Now!

On the screen appeared a tree, conventionalized in greens and blues, and each leaf was a tongue of fire. From these fire wisps of smoke arose on high to form a cloud which worked and swirled, then emptied a cone of rain about the tree. The flames vanished and in their places appeared star-shaped white flowers. From the cloud came a bolt of lightning, shattering the tree to agonized fragments of glass. Another bolt into the brittle heap and the screen exploded in a great gout of white, orange, and black.

The voice of the big man said doubtfully, "On the whole, well done, but mind my warning, and create more modest images, since—"

"Silence!" said Dobnor Daksat in a harsh voice.

So the competition went, round and round of spectacles, some sweet as canmel honey, others as violent as the storms that circle the poles. Color strove with color, patterns evolved and changed, sometimes in glorious cadence, sometimes in the bitter discord necessary to the strength of the image.

And Daksat built dream after dream, while his tension vanished, and he forgot all save the racing pictures in his mind and on the screen, and his images became as complex and subtle as those of the masters.

"One more passage," said the big man behind Daksat, and now the imagists brought forth the master-dreams: Pulakt Havjorska, the growth and decay of a beautiful city. Tol Morabait, a quiet composition of green and white interrupted by a marching army of insects who left a dirty wake, and who were joined in battle by men in painted leather armor and tall hats, armed with short swords and flails. The insects were destroyed and chased off the screen; the dead warriors became bones and faded to twinkling blue dust. Ghisel Ghang created three fire-bursts simultaneously, each different, a gorgeous display.

Daksat imagined a smooth pebble, magnified it to a block of marble, chipped it away to create the head of a beautiful maiden. For a moment she stared forth and varying emotions crossed her face—joy at her sudden existence, pensive thought, and at last fright. Her eyes turned milky opaque blue, the face changed to a laughing sardonic mask, black-cheeked with a fleering mouth. The head tilted, the mouth spat into the air. The head flattened into a black background, the drops of spittle shone like fire, became stars, constellations, and one of these expanded, became a planet with configurations dear to Daksat's heart. The planet hurtled off into darkness, the constellations faded. Dobnor Daksat relaxed. His last image. He sighed, exhausted.

The big man in the black cloak removed the harness in brittle silence. At last he asked, "The planet you imagined in that last screening, was that a creation or a remembrance of actuality? It was none of our system here, and it rang with the clarity of truth."

Dobnor Daksat stared at him, puzzled, and the words faltered in his throat. "But it is—home! This world! Was it not this world?"

The big man looked at him strangely, shrugged, turned away. "In a moment now the winner of the contest will be made known and the jeweled brevet awarded."

. . .

The day was gusty and overcast, the galley was low and black, manned by the oarsmen of Belaclaw. Ergan stood on the poop, staring across the two miles of bitter sea to the coast of Racland, where he knew the sharp-faced Racs stood watching from the headlands.

A gout of water erupted a few hundred yards astern.

Ergan spoke to the helmsman. "Their guns have better range than we bargained for. Better stand offshore another mile and we'll take our chances with the current."

Even as he spoke, there came a great whistle and he glimpsed a black pointed projectile slanting down at him. It struck the waist of the galley, exploded. Timber, bodies, metal flew everywhere, and the galley laid its broken back into the water, doubled up and sank.

Ergan, jumping clear, discarded his sword, casque, and greaves almost as he hit the chill gray water. Gasping from the shock, he swam in circles, bobbing up and down in the chop; then, finding a length of timber, he clung to it for support.

From the shores of Racland a longboat put forth and approached, bow churning white foam as it rose and fell across the waves. Ergan turned loose the timber and swam as rapidly as possible from the wreck. Better drowning than capture; there would be more mercy from the famine-fish that swarmed the waters than from the pitiless Racs.

So he swam, but the current took him to the shore, and at last, struggling feebly, he was cast upon a pebbly beach.

Here he was discovered by a gang of Rac youths and marched to a nearby command post. He was tied and flung into a cart and so conveyed to the city Korsapan.

In a gray room he was seated facing an intelligence officer of the Rac secret police, a man with the gray skin of a toad, a moist gray mouth, eager, searching eyes.

"You are Ergan," said the officer. "Emissary to the Bargee of Salomdek. What was your mission?"

Ergan stared back eye to eye, hoping that a happy and convincing response would find his lips. None came, and the truth would incite an immediate invasion of both Belaclaw and Salomdek by the tall, thin-headed Rac soldiers, who wore black uniforms and black boots.

Ergan said nothing. The officer leaned forward. "I ask you once more; then you will be taken to the room below." He said "Room Below" as if the words were capitalized, and he said it with soft relish.

Ergan, in a cold sweat, for he knew of the Rac torturers, said, "I am not Ergan, my name is Ervard; I am an honest trader in pearls."

"This is untrue," said the Rac. "Your aide was captured, and under the compression pump he blurted up your name with his lungs."

"I am Ervard," said Ergan, his bowels quaking.

The Rac signaled. "Take him to the Room Below."

A man's body, which has developed nerves as outposts against danger, seems especially intended for pain, and cooperates wonderfully with the craft of the torturer. These characteristics of the body had been studied by the Rac specialists, and other capabilities of the human nervous system had been blundered upon by accident. It had been found that certain programs of pressure, heat, strain, friction, torque, surge, jerk, sonic and visual shock, vermin, stench, and vileness created cumulative effects, whereas a single method, used to excess, lost its stimulation thereby.

All this lore and cleverness was lavished upon Ergan's citadel of nerves, and they inflicted upon him the entire gamut of pain: the sharp twinges, the dull, lasting joint-aches which groaned by night, the fiery flashes, the assaults of filth and lechery, together with shocks of occasional tenderness when he would be allowed to glimpse the world he had left.

Then back to the Room Below.

But always: "I am Ervard the trader." And always he tried to goad his mind over the tissue barrier to death, but always the mind hesitated at the last toppling step, and Ergan lived.

The Racs tortured by routine, so that the expectation, the approach of the hour, brought as much torment as the act itself. And then the heavy, unhurried steps outside the cell, the feeble thrashing around to evade, the harsh laughs when they cornered him and carried him forth, and the harsh laughs when three hours later they threw him sobbing and whimpering back to the pile of straw that was his bed.

"I am Ervard," he said, and trained his mind to believe that this was the truth, so that never would they catch him unaware. "I am Ervard! I am Ervard, I trade in pearls!"

He tried to strangle himself on straw, but a slave watched always, and this was not permitted.

He attempted to die by self-suffocation, and would have been glad to succeed, but always as he sank into blessed numbness, so did his mind relax and his motor nerves take up the mindless business of breathing once more.

He ate nothing, but this meant little to the Racs, as they injected him full of tonics, sustaining drugs, and stimulants, so that he might always be keyed to the height of his awareness.

"I am Ervard," said Ergan, and the Racs gritted their teeth angrily. The case was now a challenge; he defied their ingenuity, and they puzzled long and carefully upon refinements and delicacies, new shapes to the iron tools, new types of jerk ropes, new direction for the strains and pressures. Even when it was no longer important whether he was Ergan or Ervard, since war now raged, he was kept and maintained as a problem, an ideal case; so he was guarded and cosseted with even more than usual care, and the Rac torturers mulled over their techniques, making changes here, improvements there.

Then one day the Belaclaw galleys landed and the feather-crested soldiers fought past the wall of Korsapan.

The Racs surveyed Ergan with regret. "Now we must go, and still you will not submit to us."

"I am Ervard," croaked that which lay on the table. "Ervard the trader."

A splintering crash sounded overhead.

"We must go," said the Racs. "Your people have stormed the city. If you tell the truth, you may live. If you lie, we kill you. So there is your choice. Your life for the truth."

"The truth?" muttered Ergan. "It is a trick—" and then he caught the victory chant of the Belaclaw soldiery. "The truth? Why not?... Very well." And he said, "I am Ervard," for now he believed this to be the truth.

Galactic Prime was a lean man with reddish-brown hair, sparse across a fine arch of skull. His face, undistinguished otherwise, was given power by great dark eyes, flickering with a light like fire behind smoke. Physically, he had passed the peak of his youth; his arms and legs were thin and loose-jointed; his head inclined forward as if weighted by the intricate machinery of his brain.

Arising from the couch, smiling faintly, he looked across the arcade to the eleven Elders. They sat at a table of polished wood, backs to a wall festooned with vines. They were grave men, slow in their motions, and their faces were lined with wisdom and insight. By the ordained system, Prime was the executive of the universe, the Elders the deliberative body, invested with certain restrictive powers.

"Well?"

The Chief Elder without haste raised his eyes from the computer. "You are the first to arise from the couch."

Prime turned a glance up the arcade, still smiling faintly. The others lay variously: some with arms clenched, rigid as bars; others huddled in fetal postures. One had slumped from the couch half to the floor; his eyes were open, staring at remoteness.

Prime returned his gaze to the Chief Elder, who watched him with detached curiosity. "Has the optimum been established?"

The Chief Elder consulted the computer. "Twenty-six thirty-seven is the optimum score."

Prime waited, but the Chief Elder said no more. Prime stepped to the alabaster balustrade beyond the couches. He leaned forward, looked out across the vista—miles and miles of sunny haze, with a twinkling sea in the distance. A breeze blew past his face, ruffling the scant russet strands of his hair. He took a deep breath, flexed his fingers and hands, for the memory of the Rac torturers was still heavy on his mind. After a moment he swung around, leaned back, resting his elbows upon the balustrade. He glanced once more down the line of couches; there were still no signs of vitality from the candidates.

"Twenty-six thirty-seven," he muttered. "I venture to estimate my own score at twenty-five ninety. In the last episode I recall an incomplete retention of personality."

"Twenty-five seventy-four," said the Chief Elder. "The computer judge Bearwald the Halforn's final defiance of the Brand warriors unprofitable."

Prime considered. "The point is well made. Obstinacy serves no purpose unless it advances a predetermined end. It is a flaw I must seek to temper." He looked along the line of Elders, from face to face. "You make no enunciations, you are curiously mute."

He waited; the Chief Elder made no response.

"May I inquire the high score?"

"Twenty-five seventy-four."

Prime nodded. "Mine."

"Yours is the high score," said the Chief Elder.

Prime's smile disappeared: a puzzled line appeared across his brow. "In spite of this, you are still reluctant to confirm my second span of authority; there are still doubts among you."

"Doubts and misgivings," replied the Chief Elder.

Prime's mouth pulled in at the corners, although his brows were still raised in polite inquiry. "Your attitude puzzles me. My record is one of selfless service. My intelligence is phenomenal, and in this final test, which I designed to dispel your last doubts, I attained the highest score. I have proved my social intuition and flexibility, my leadership, devotion to duty, imagination, and resolution. In every commensurable aspect, I fulfill best the qualifications for the office I hold."

The Chief Elder looked up and down the line of his fellows. There were none who wished to speak. The Chief Elder squared himself in his chair, sat back.

"Our attitude is difficult to represent. Everything is as you say. Your intelligence is beyond dispute, your character is exemplary, you have served your term with honor and devotion. You have earned our respect, admiration, and gratitude. We realize also that you seek this second term from praiseworthy motives: you regard yourself as the man best able to coordinate the complex business of the galaxy."

Prime nodded grimly. "But you think otherwise."

"Our position is perhaps not quite so blunt."

"Precisely what is your position?" Prime gestured along the couches. "Look at these men. They are the finest of the galaxy. One man is dead. That one stirring on the third couch has lost his mind; he is a lunatic. The others are sorely shaken. And never forget that this test has been expressly designed to measure the qualities essential to the Galactic Prime."

"This test has been of great interest to us," said the Chief Elder mildly. "It has considerably affected our thinking."

Prime hesitated, plumbing the unspoken overtones of the words. He came forward, seated himself across from the line of Elders. With a narrow glance he searched the faces of the eleven men, tapped once, twice, three times with his fingertips on the polished wood, leaned back in the chair.

"As I have pointed out, the test has gauged each candidate for the exact qualities essential to the optimum conduct of office, in this fashion: Earth of the twentieth century is a planet of intricate conventions; on Earth the candidate, as Arthur Caversham, is required to use his social intuition—a quality highly important in this galaxy of two billion suns. On Belotsi, Bearwald the Halforn is tested for courage and the ability to conduct positive action. At the dead city Therlatch on Praesepe Three, the candidate, as Ceistan, is rated for devotion to duty, and as Dobnor Daksat at the Imagicon on Staff, his creative conceptions are rated against the most fertile imaginations alive. Finally as Ergan, on Chankozar, his will, persistence, and ultimate fiber are explored to their extreme limits.

"Each candidate is placed in the identical set of circumstances by a trick of temporal, dimensional, and cerebroneural meshing, which is rather complicated for the present discussion. Sufficient that each candidate is objectively rated by his achievements, and that the results are commensurable."

He paused, looking shrewdly along the line of grave faces. "I must emphasize that although I myself designed and arranged the test, I thereby gained no advantage. The mnemonic synapses are entirely disengaged from incident to incident, and only the candidate's basic personality acts. All were tested under precisely the same conditions. In my opinion the scores registered by the computer indicate an objective and reliable index of the candidate's ability for the highly responsible office of Galactic Executive."

The Chief Elder said, "The scores are indeed significant."

"Then—you approve my candidacy?"

The Chief Elder smiled. "Not so fast. Admittedly you are intelligent, admittedly you have accomplished much during your term as Prime. But much remains to be done."

"Do you suggest that another man would have achieved more?"

The Chief Elder shrugged. "I have no conceivable way of knowing. I point out your achievements, such as the Glenart civilization, the Dawn Time on Masilis, the reign of King Karal on Aevir, the suppression of the Arkid Revolt. There are many such examples. But there are also short-comings: the totalitarian governments on Earth, the savagery on Belotsi and Chankozar, so pointedly emphasized in your test. Then there is the decadence of the planets in the Eleven Hundred Ninth Cluster, the rise of the priest-kinds on Fiir, and much else."

Prime clenched his mouth and the fires behind his eyes burnt more brightly.

The Chief Elder continued. "One of the most remarkable phenomena of the galaxy is the tendency of humanity to absorb and manifest the personality of the Prime. There seems to be a tremendous resonance which vibrates from the brain of the Prime through the minds of man from Center to the outer fringes. It is a matter which should be studied, analyzed, and subjected to control. The effect is as if every thought of the Prime is magnified a billion-fold, as if every mood sets the tone for a thousand civilizations, every facet of his personality reflects in the ethics of a thousand cultures."

Prime said tonelessly, "I have remarked this phenomenon and have thought much on it. Prime's commands are promulgated in such a way as to exert subtle rather than overt influence; perhaps here is the background of the matter. In any event, the fact of this influence is even more reason to select for the office a man of demonstrated virtue."

"Well put," said the Chief Elder. "Your character is indeed beyond reproach. However, we of the Elders are concerned by the rising tide of authoritarianism among the planets of the galaxy. We suspect that this principle of resonance is at work. You are a man of intense and indomitable will, and we feel that your influence has unwittingly prompted an irruption of autarchies."

Prime was silent a moment. He looked down the line of couches where the other candidates were recovering awareness. They were men of various races: a pale Northkin of Palast, a stocky red Hawolo, a gray-haired gray-eyed Islander from the Sea Planet—each the outstanding man of the planet of his birth. Those who had returned to consciousness sat quietly, collecting their wits, or lay back on the couch, trying to expunge the test from their minds. There had been a toll taken: one lay dead, another bereft of his wits crouched whimpering beside his couch.

The Chief Elder said, "The objectionable aspects of your character are perhaps best exemplified by the test itself."

Prime opened his mouth; the Chief Elder held up his hand. "Let me speak; I will try to deal fairly with you. When I am done, you may say your say.

"I repeat that your basic direction is displayed by the details of the test that you devised. The qualities you measured were those which you considered the most important: that is, those ideals by which you guide your own life. This arrangement I am sure was completely unconscious, and hence completely revealing. You conceive the essential characteristics of the Prime to be social intuition, aggressiveness, loyalty, imgination, and dogged persistence. As a man of strong character you seek to exemplify these ideals in your own conduct; therefore it is not at all surprising that in this test, designed by you, with a scoring system calibrated by you, your score should be highest.

"Let me clarify the idea by an analogy. If the Eagle were conducting a test to determine the King of Beasts, he would rate all the candidates on their ability to fly; necessarily he would win. In this fashion the Mole would consider ability to dig important; by his system of testing *he* would inevitably emerge King of Beasts."

Prime laughed sharply, ran a hand through his sparse red-brown locks. "I am neither Eagle nor Mole."

The Chief Elder shook his head. "No. You are zealous, dutiful, imaginative, indefatigable—so you have demonstrated, as much by specifying tests for these characteristics as by scoring high in these same tests. But conversely, by the very absence of other tests you demonstrate deficiencies in your character."

"And these are?"

"Sympathy. Compassion. Kindness." The Chief Elder settled back in his chair. "Strange. Your predecessor two times removed was rich in these qualities. During his term, the great humanitarian systems based on the idea of human brotherhood sprang up across the universe. Another example of resonance—but I digress."

Prime said with a sardonic twitch of his mouth, "May I ask this: have you selected the next Galactic Prime?"

The Chief Elder nodded. "A definite choice has been made."

"What was his score in the test?"

"By your scoring system—seventeen eighty. He did poorly as Arthur Caversham; he tried to explain the advantages of nudity to the policeman. He lacked the ability to concoct an instant subterfuge; he has little of your quick craft. As Arthur Caversham he found himself naked. He is sincere and straightforward, hence tried to expound the positive motivations for his state, rather than discover the means to evade the penalties."

"Tell me more about this man," said Prime shortly.

"As Bearwald the Halforn, he led his band to the hive of the Brands on Mount Medallion, but instead of burning the hive, he called forth the queen, begging her to end the useless slaughter. She reached out from the doorway, drew him within and killed him. He failed—but the computer still rated him highly on his forthright approach.

"At Therlatch, his conduct was as irreproachable as yours, and at the Imagicon his performance was adequate. Yours approached the brilliance of the Master Imagists, which is high achievement indeed.

"The Rac tortures are the most trying element of the test. You knew well you could resist limitless pain; therefore you ordained that all other candidates must likewise possess this attribute. The new Prime is sadly deficient here. He is sensitive, and the idea of one man intentionally inflicting pain upon another sickens him. I may add that none of the candidates achieved a perfect count in the last episode. Two others equaled your score—"

Prime evinced interest. "Which are they?"

The Chief Elder pointed them out—a tall hard-muscled man with rock-hewn face standing by the alabaster balustrade gazing moodily out across the sunny distance, and a man of middle age who sat with his legs folded under him, watching a point three feet before him with an expression of imperturbable placidity.

"One is utterly obstinate and hard," said the Chief Elder. "He refused to say a single word. The other assumes an outer objectivity when unpleasantness overtakes him. Others among the candidates fared not so well; therapy will be necessary in almost all cases."

Their eyes went to the witless creature with vacant eyes who padded up and down the aisle, humming and muttering quietly to himself.

"The tests were by no means valueless," said the Chief Elder. "We learned a great deal. By your system of scoring, the competition rated you most high. By other standards which we Elders postulated, your place was lower."

With a tight mouth, Prime inquired, "Who is this paragon of altruism, kindliness, sympathy and generosity?"

The lunatic wandered close, fell on his hands and knees, crawled whimpering to the wall. He pressed his face to the cool stone, stared blankly up at Prime. His mouth hung loose, his chin was wet, his eyes rolled apparently free of each other.

The Chief Elder smiled in great compassion; he stroked the mad creature's head. "This is he. Here is the man we select."

The old Galactic Prime sat silent, mouth compressed, eyes burning like far volcanoes.

At his feet the new Prime, Lord of Two Billion Suns, found a dead leaf, put it into his mouth and began to chew.

MEN OF THE TEN BOOKS

They were as alone as it is possible for living man to be in the black gulf between stars. Far astern shone the suns of the home worlds—ahead the outer stars and galaxies in a fainter ghostly glimmer.

The cabin was quiet. Betty Welstead sat watching her husband at the assay table, her emotions tuned to his. When the centrifuge scale indicated heavy metal and Welstead leaned forward she leaned forward too, in unconscious sympathy. When he burnt scrapings in the spectroscope and read *Lead* from the brightest pattern and chewed at his lips Betty released her pent-up breath, fell back in her seat.

Ralph Welstead stood up, a man of medium height—rugged, tough-looking—with hair and skin and eyes the same tawny color. He brushed the clutter of rock and ore into the waste chute and Betty followed him with her eyes.

Welstead said sourly, "We'd be millionaires if that asteroid had been inside the solar system. Out here, unless it's pure platinum or uranium, it's not worth mining."

Betty broached a subject which for two months had been on the top of her mind. "Perhaps we should start to swing back in."

Welstead frowned, stepped up into the observation dome. Betty watched after him anxiously. She understood very well that the instinct of the explorer as much as the quest for minerals had brought them out so far.

Welstead stepped back down into the cabin. "There's a star ahead"—he put a finger into the three-dimensional chart—"this one right here, Eridanus two thousand nine hundred and thirty-two. Let's make a quick check—and then we'll head back in."

Betty nodded, suddenly happy. "Suits me." She jumped up, and together they went to the screen. He aimed the catch-all vortex, dialed the hurrying blur to stability and the star pulsed out like a white-hot coin. A single planet made up the entourage.

"Looks about Earth-size," said Welstead, interest in his voice, and Betty's heart sank a trifle. He tuned the circuit finer, turned up the magnification and the planet leapt at them.

"Look at that atmosphere! *Thick!*"

He swiveled across the jointed arm holding the thermocouple and together they bent over the dial.

"Nineteen degrees Centigrade. About Earth-norm. Let's look at that atmosphere. You know, dear, we might have something tremendous here! Earth size, Earth temperature...." His voice fell off in a mutter as he peered through the spectroscope, flipping screen after screen past the pattern from the planet. He stood up, cast Betty a swift exultant glance, then squinted in sudden reflection. "Better make sure before we get too excited."

Betty felt no excitement. She watched without words as Welstead thumbed through the catalogue.

"*Whee!*" yelled Welstead, suddenly a small boy. "No listing! It's ours!" And Betty's heart melted at the news. Delay, months of delay, while Welstead explored the planet, charted its oceans and continents, classified its life. At the same time, a spark of her husband's enthusiasm caught fire in her mind and interest began to edge aside her gloom.

"We'll name it 'Welstead,'" he said. "Or, no—'Elizabeth' for you. A planet of your own! Some day there'll be cities and millions of people. And every time they write a letter or throw a shovelful of dirt or a ship lands—they'll use your name."

"No, dear," she said. "Don't be ridiculous. We'll call it 'Welstead'—for us both."

They felt an involuntary pang of disappointment later, when they found the planet already inhabited, and by men.

Yet their reception astonished them as much as the discovery of the planet and its people. Curiosity, hostility might have been expected....

They had been in no hurry to land, preferring to fall into an orbit just above the atmosphere, the better to study the planet and its inhabitants.

It looked to be a cheerful world. There were a thousand kinds of forest, jungle, savannah. Sunny rivers coursed green fields. A thousand lakes and three oceans glowed blue. To the far north and far south snowfields glittered, dazzled. Such cities as they found—the world seemed sparsely settled—merged indistinguishably with the countryside.

They were wide low cities, very different from the clanging hives of Earth, and lay under the greenery like carvings in alabaster or miraculous snowflakes. Betty, in whose nature ran a strong streak of the romantic, was entranced.

"They look like cities of Paradise—cities in a dream!"

Welstead said reflectively, "They're evidently not backward. See that cluster of long gray buildings off to the side? Those are factories."

Betty voiced a doubt which had been gradually forming into words. "Do you think that they might—resent our landing? If they've gone to the trouble of creating a secret—well, call it Utopia—they might not want to be discovered."

Welstead turned his head, gazed at her eye to eye. "Do you want to land?" he asked soberly.

"Yes—if you do. If you don't think it's dangerous."

"I don't know whether it's dangerous or not. A people as enlightened as those settlements would seem to indicate would hardly maltreat strangers."

Betty searched the face of the planet. "I think it might be safe."

Welstead laughed. "I'm game. We've got to die sometime. Why not out here?"

He jumped up to the controls, nosed the ship down.

"We'll land right in their laps, right in the middle of that big city there."

Betty looked at him questioningly.

"No sense sneaking down out in the wilds," said Welstead. "If we're landing we'll land with a flourish."

"And if they shoot us for our insolence?"

"Call it Fate."

They bellied down into a park in the very center of the city. From the observation dome Welstead glimpsed hurrying knots of people coming toward them.

"Go to the port, Betty. Open it just a crack and show yourself. I'll stay at the controls. One false move, one dead cat heaved at us, and we'll be away so fast they won't remember we arrived."

Thousands of men and women of all ages had surrounded the ship, all shouting, all agitated by strong emotion.

"They're throwing flowers!" Betty gasped. She opened the port and stood in the doorway and the people below shouted, chanted, wept. Feeling rather ridiculous, Betty waved, smiled.

She turned to look back up at Welstead. "I don't know what we've done to deserve all this but we're heroes. Maybe they think we're somebody else."

Welstead craned his neck through the observation dome. "They look healthy—normal."

"They're beautiful," said Betty. "All of them."

The throng opened; a small group of elderly men and women approached. The leader, a white-haired man, tall, lean, with much the same face as Michelangelo's Jehovah, stood forth.

"Welcome!" he called resonantly. "Welcome from the people of Haven!"

Betty stared, and Welstead clambered down from the controls. The words were strangely pronounced, the grammar was archaic—but it was the language of Earth.

The white-haired man spoke on, without calculation, as if delivering a speech of great familiarity. "We have waited two hundred and seventy-one years for your coming, for the deliverance you will bring us."

Deliverance? Welstead considered the word. "Don't see much to deliver 'em from," he muttered aside to Betty. "The sun's shining, there's flowers on all the trees, they look well fed—a lot more enthusiastic than I do. Deliver 'em from what?"

Betty was climbing down to the ground and Welstead followed.

"Thanks for the welcome," said Welstead, trying not to sound like a visiting politician. "We're glad to be here. It's a wonderful experience, coming unexpectedly on a world like this."

The white-haired man bowed gravely. "Naturally you must be curious—as curious as we are about the civilized universe. But for the present, just one question for the ears of our world. How goes it with Earth?"

Welstead rubbed his chin, acutely conscious of the thousands of eyes, the utter silence.

"Earth," he said, "goes about as usual. There's the same seasons, the same rain, sunshine, frost and wind." And the people of Haven breathed in his words as devoutly as if they were the purest poetry. "Earth is still the center of the Cluster and there's more people living on Earth than ever before. More noise, more nuisance...."

"Wars? New governments? How far does science reach?"

Welstead considered. "Wars? None to speak of—not since the Hieratic League broke up. The central government still governs. There's still graft, robbery, inefficiency, if that's what you mean.

"Science—that's a big subject. We know a lot but there's much we don't know, the way it's always been. Everything considered, it's the same Earth it's always been—some good, a lot of bad."

He paused, and the pent breath of the listeners went in a great sigh. The white-haired man nodded again, serious, sober—though evidently infected with the excitement that fired his fellows.

"No more for the present! You'll be tired and there's much time for talk. May I offer you the hospitality of my house?"

Welstead looked uncertainly at Betty. Instinct urged him not to leave his ship.

"Or if you'd prefer to remain aboard...." suggested the man of Haven.

"No," said Welstead. "We'll be delighted." If harm were intended—as emphatically did not seem likely—their presence aboard the ship would not prevent it. He craned his neck, looked here and there for the officialdom that would be bumptiously present on Earth.

"Is there anyone we should report to? Any law we'll be breaking by parking our ship here?"

The white-haired man laughed. "What a question! I am Alexander Clay, Mayor of this city Mytilene and Guide of Haven. By my authority and by common will you are free of anything the planet can offer you. Your ship will not be molested."

He led them to a wide low car and Betty was uncomfortably conscious of her blue shorts, rumpled and untidy by comparison with the many-colored tunics of the women in the crowd.

Welstead was interested in the car as providing a gauge of Haven's technics. Built of shiny gray metal it hung a foot above the ground, without the intervention of wheels. He gave Clay a startled look. "Antigravity? Your fortune's made."

Clay shook his head indulgently. "Magnetic fields, antipathetic to the metal in the road. Is it not a commonplace on Earth?"

"No," said Welstead. "The theory, of course, is well known but there is too much opposition, too many roads to dig up. We still use wheels."

Clay said reflectively, "The force of tradition. The continuity which generates the culture of races. The steam from which we have been so long lost...."

Welstead shot him a sidelong glance. Clay was entirely serious.

The car had been sliding down the road at rather high speed through vistas of wonderful quiet and beauty. Every direction showed a new and separate enchantment—a glade surrounded by great trees, a small home of natural wood, a cluster of public buildings around a plaza, a terrace checkered with trees and lined with many-colored shops.

Occasionally there were touches of drama, such as the pylon at the end of a wide avenue. It rose two hundred feet into the air, a structure of concrete, bronze and black metal, and it bore the heroic figure of a man grasping vainly for a star.

Welstead craned his neck like a tourist. "Magnificent!"

Clay assented without enthusiasm. "I suppose it's not discreditable. Of course, to you, fresh from the worlds of civilization—" He left the sentence unfinished. "Excuse me, while I call my home." He bent his head to a telephone.

Betty said in Welstead's ear, "This is a city every planner on Earth would sell his soul to build."

Welstead grunted. "Remember Halleck?" he muttered. "He was a city planner. He wanted to tear down a square mile of slums in Lanchester, eighteen stories high on the average, nothing but airless three-room apartments.

"First the real estate lobby tore into him, called him a Chaoticist. The poor devils that lived there tried to lynch him because they'd be evicted. The Old Faithfuls read him out of the party because they controlled the votes of the district. The slums are still there and Halleck's selling farm implements on Arcturus Five."

Betty looked off through the trees. "Maybe Haven will turn out to be an object lesson for the rest of the cluster."

Welstead shrugged. "Maybe, maybe not. Peace and seclusion are not something you can show to a million people because then it isn't peace and seclusion any more."

Betty sat up straighter in her seat. "The only way to convince the unbelievers is by showing them, setting them an example. Do you think that if the Lanchester slum-dwellers saw this city they'd go back to their three-room apartments without wanting to do something about them?"

"If they saw this city," said Welstead, "they'd never leave Haven. By hook or crook, stowaway or workaway, they'd emigrate."

"Include me in the first wave!" said Betty indignantly.

The car turned into a leafy tunnel, crossed a carpet of bright green turf, stopped by a house built of dark massive wood. Four high gables in a row overlooked a terrace, where a stream followed its natural bed. The house looked spacious, comfortable—rather like the best country villas of Earth and the garden planets without the sense of contrived effect, the strain, the staging.

"My home," said Clay. He slid back a door of waxed blond wood, ushered them into an entry carpeted with golden rattan, walled with a fabric the color of the forest outside. A bench of glowing dark wood crossed a wall under a framed painting. From no apparent source light flooded the room, like water in a tank.

"One moment," said Clay with a trace of embarrassment. "My home is poor and makeshift enough without exposing it to your eyes at its worst." He was clearly sincere; this was no conventional deprecation.

He started away, paused and said to his half-comprehending guests, "I must apologize for our backwardness but we have no facilities for housing notable guests, no great inns or embassies or state-houses such as must add to the dignity of life on Earth. I can only offer you the hospitality of my home."

Welstead and Betty both protested. "We don't deserve as much. After all we're only a pair of fly-by-night prospectors."

Clay smiled and they could see that he had been put more at his ease.

"You're the link between Haven and civilization—the most important visitors we've ever had. Excuse me." He departed.

Betty went to the picture on the wall, a simple landscape—the slope of a hill, a few trees, a distant range of mountains. Welstead, with small artistic sensibility, looked around for the source of the light—without success. He joined Betty beside the picture. She said half-breathlessly. "This is a—I'm afraid to say it—a masterpiece."

Welstead squinted, trying to understand the basis of his wife's awe and wonderment. Indeed the picture focused his eyes, drew them in and around the frame, infused him with a pleasant exhilaration, a warmth and serenity.

Clay, returning, noticed their interest. "What do you think of it?" he asked.

"I think it's—exceedingly well done," said Betty, at a loss for words which would convey her admiration without sounding fulsome.

Clay shook his head ruefully, turned away. "You need not praise an inconsequentiality out of courtesy, Mrs. Welstead. We know our deficiencies. Your eyes have seen the Giottos, the Rembrandts, the Cezannes. This must seem a poor thing."

Betty began to remonstrate but halted. Words evidently would not convince Clay—or perhaps a convention of his society prompted him to belittle the works of his people and it might be discourteous to argue too vehemently.

"Your quarters are being prepared," Clay told them. "I've also ordered fresh clothing for you both as I see yours are stained with travel."

Betty blushed, smoothed the legs of her blue shorts. Welstead sheepishly brushed at his faded blouse. He reached in his pocket, pulled out a bit of gravel. "From an asteroid I prospected a few weeks ago." He twisted it around in his fingers. "Nothing but granite, with garnet inclusions."

Clay took the bit of rock, inspected it with a peculiar reverence. "May I keep this?"

"Why, of course."

Clay laid the bit of stone on a silver plate. "You will not understand what this small stone symbolizes to us of Haven. Interstellar travel—our goal, our dream for two hundred and seventy-one years."

The recurrence of the period two hundred and seventy-one years! Welstead calculated. That put them back into the Era of the Great Excursives, when the over-under drive had first come into use, when men drove pell-mell through the galaxy, like bees through a field of flowers and human culture flared through space like a super-nova.

Clay led them through a large room, simple in effect, rich in detail. Welstead's vision was not analytical enough to catch every particular at first. He sensed overall tones of tan, brown, mellow blue, watery green, in the wood, fabric glass, pottery—the colors combined to marvelous effect with the waxy umber gleam of natural wood. At the end of the room a case held ten large books bound in black leather and these, by some indefinable emphasis, seemed to bear the significance of an icon.

They passed through a passage open along one side into a garden filled with flowers, low trees, tame birds. Clay showed them into a long apartment streaming with sunlight.

"Your bath is through the door," said Clay. "Fresh clothes are laid out on the bed. When you are rested I shall be in the main hall. Please be at leisure—the house is yours."

They were alone. Betty sighed happily, sank down on the bed. "Isn't it wonderful, dear?"

"It's queer," said Welstead, standing in the middle of the room.

"What's queer?"

"Mainly why these people, apparently gifted and efficient, act so humble, so self-deprecating."

"They look confident."

"They *are* confident. Yet as soon as the word Earth is mentioned it's like saying Alakland to an exiled Lak. There's nothing like it."

Betty shrugged, began to remove her clothes. "There's probably some very simple explanation. Right now I'm tired of speculating. I'm for that bath. Water, water, water! *Tons* of it!"

They found Clay in the long hall with his pleasant-faced wife, his four youngest children, whom he gravely introduced.

Welstead and Betty seated themselves on a divan and Clay poured them small china cups of pale yellow-green wine, then settled back in his own seat.

"First I'll explain our world of Haven to you—or have you surmised our plight?"

Welstead said, "I guess a colony was planted here and forgotten—lost."

Clay smiled sadly. "Our beginnings were rather more dramatic. Two hundred and seventy-one years ago the passenger packet *Etruria*, en route to Rigel, lost control. According to the story handed down to us the bars fused inside the drive. If the case were opened the fields would collapse. If it were not, the ship would fly until there was no more energy."

Welstead said, "That was a common accident in the old days. Usually the engineer cut away the thrust-blocks on one side of the hull. Then the ship flew in circles until help arrived."

Clay made a wry sad grimace. "No one on the *Etruria* thought of that. The ship left the known universe and finally passed close to a planet that seemed capable of sustaining life. The sixty-three aboard took to the life-boats and so landed on Haven.

"Thirty-four men, twenty-five women, four children—ranging in age from Dorothy Pell, eight, to Vladimir Hocha, seventy-four, with representatives of every human race. We're the descendants of the sixty-three—three hundred million of us."

Fast work," said Betty, with admiration.

"Large families," returned Clay. "I have nine children, sixteen grandchildren. From the start our guiding principle has been to keep the culture of Earth intact for our descendants, to teach them what we knew of human tradition.

"So that when rescue came—as it must finally—then our children or our children's children could return to Earth, not as savages but as citizens. And our invaluable source has been the Ten Books, the only books brought down from the *Etruria*. We could not have been favored with books more inspiring...."

Clay's gaze went to the black bound books at the end of the room, and his voice lowered a trifle.

"The *Encyclopedia of Human Achievement*. The original edition was in ten little plastrol volumes, none of them larger than your hand—but in them was such a treasury of human glory that never could we forget our ancestry, or rest in our efforts to achieve somewhere near the level of the great masters. All the works of the human race we set as our standards—music, art, literature—all were described in the *Encyclopedia*."

"Described, you say," mused Welstead.

"There were no illustrations?" asked Betty.

"No," said Clay, "there was a small compass for pictures in the original edition. However" he went to the case, selected a volume at random—"the words left little to the imagination. For example, on the music of Bach—'When Bach arrived on the scene the toccata was tentative, indecisive—a recreation, a *tour de force*, where the musician might display his virtuosity.

"'In Bach the toccata becomes a medium of the noblest plasticity. The theme he suggests by casual fingering of the keyboard, unrelated runs. Then comes a glorious burst into harmony—the original runs glow like prisms, assume stature, gradually topple together into a miraculous pyramid of sound.'

"And on Beethoven—'A God among men. His music is the voice of the world, the pageant of all imagined splendor. The sounds he invokes are natural forces of the same order as sunsets, storms at sea, the view from mountain crags.'

"And on Leon Bismarck Beiderbecke—'His trumpet pours out such a torrent of ecstasy, such triumph, such overriding joys that the heart of man freezes in anguish at not being wholly part of it.'" Clay closed the book, replaced it. "Such is our heritage. We have tried to keep alive, however poorly, the stream of our original culture."

"I would say that you have succeeded," Welstead remarked dryly.

Betty sighed, a long slow suspiration.

Clay shook his head. "You can't judge until you've seen more of Haven. We're comfortable enough, though our manner of living must seem unimpressive in comparison with the great cities, the magnificent palaces of Earth."

"No, not at all," said Betty, but Clay made a polite gesture.

"Don't feel obliged to flatter us. As I've said, we're aware of our deficiencies. Our music for instance—it is pleasant, sometimes exciting, sometimes profound, but never does it reach the heights of poignancy that the Encyclopedia describes.

"Our art is technically good but we despair of emulating Seurat, who 'out-lumens light,' or Braque, 'the patterns of the mind in patterns of color on the patterns of life,' or Cezanne—'the planes which under the guise of natural objects march, merge, meet in accord with remorseless logic, which wheel around and impel the mind to admit the absolute justice of the composition.'"

Betty glanced at her husband, apprehensive lest he speak what she knew must be on his mind. To her relief he kept silent, squinting thoughtfully. Betty resolved to maintain a noncommittal attitude.

"No," Clay said heavily, "we do the best we can, and in some fields we've naturally achieved more than in others. To begin with we had the benefit of all human experience in our memories. The paths were charted out for us—we knew the mistakes to avoid. We've never had wars or compulsion. We've never permitted unreined authority. Still we've tried to reward those who are willing to accept responsibility.

"Our criminals—very few now—are treated for mental disorder on the first and second offense, sterilized on the third, executed on the fourth—our basic law being cooperation and contribution to the society, though there is infinite latitude in how this contribution shall be made. We do not make society a juggernaut; a man may live as integrally or as singularly as he wishes so long as he complies with the basic law."

Clay paused, looking from Welstead to Betty. "Now do you understand our way of living?"

"More or less," said Welstead. "In the outline at least. You seem to have made a great deal of progress technically."

Clay considered. "From one aspect, yes. From another no. We had the lifeboat tools, we had the technical skills and most important we knew what we were trying to do. Our main goal naturally has been the conquest of space. We've gone up in rockets but they can take us nowhere save around the sun and back. Our scientists are close on the secret of the space-drive but certain practical difficulties are holding them up."

Welstead laughed. "Space-drive can never be discovered by rational effort. That's a philosophical question which has been threshed back and forth for hundreds of years. Reason—the abstract idea—is a function of ordinary time and space. The space-drive has no qualities in common with these ideas and for this reason human thought can never consciously solve the problem of the over-drive. Experiment, trial and error can do it. Thinking about it is useless."

"Hm," said Clay. "That's a new concept. But now your presence makes it beside the point, for you will be the link back to our homeland."

Betty could see words trembling on her husband's tongue. She clenched her hands, willed—willed—*willed*. Perhaps the effort had some effect because Welstead merely said, "We'll do anything we can to help."

All of Mytilene they visited and nearby Tiryns, Dicte and Ilium. They saw industrial centers, atomic power generators, farms, schools. They attended a session of the Council of Guides, both making brief speeches, and they spoke to the people of Haven by television. Every news organ on the planet carried their words.

They heard music from a green hillside, the orchestra playing from under tremendous smoke black trees. They saw the art of Haven in public galleries; in homes and in common use. They read some of the literature, studied the range of the planet's science, which was roughly equivalent to that of Earth. And they marveled continually how so few people in so little time could accomplish so much.

They visited the laboratories, where three hundred scientists and engineers strove to force magnetic, gravitic and vortigial fields into the fusion that made star-to-star flight possible. And the scientists watched in breathless tension as Welstead inspected their apparatus.

He saw at a single glance the source of their difficulty. He had read of the same experiments on Earth three hundred years ago and of the fantastic accident that had led Roman-Forteski and Gladheim to enclose the generatrix in a dodecahedron of quartz. Only by such a freak—or by his information—would these scientists of Haven solve the mystery of space-drive.

And Welstead walked thoughtfully from the laboratory, with the disappointed glances of the technicians following him out. And Betty had glanced after him in wonder, and the rest of the day there had been a strain between them.

That night as they lay in the darkness, rigid, wakeful, each could feel the pressure of the other's thoughts. Betty finally broke the silence, in a voice so blunt that there was no mistaking her feeling.

"Ralph!"

"What?"

"Why did you act as you did in the laboratory?"

"Careful," muttered Welstead. "Maybe the room is wired for sound."

Betty laughed scornfully. "This isn't Earth. These people are trusting, honest...."

It was Welstead's turn to laugh—a short cheerless laugh. "And that's the reason I'm ignorant when it comes to space-drive."

Betty stiffened. "What do you mean?"

"I mean that these people are too damn good to ruin."

Betty relaxed, sighed, spoke slowly, as if she knew she was in for a long pull. "How—'ruin?'"

Welstead snorted. "It's perfectly plain. You've been to their homes, you've read their poetry, listened to their music...."

"Of course. These people live every second of their lives with—well, call it exaltation. A devotion to creation like nothing I've ever seen before!"

Welstead said somberly, "They're living in the grandest illusion ever imagined and they're riding for an awful fall. They're like a man on a glorious drunk."

Betty stared through the dark. "Are you crazy?"

"They're living in exaltation now," said Welstead, "but what a bump when the bubble breaks!"

"But why should it break?" cried Betty. "Why can't—"

"Betty," said Welstead with a cold sardonic voice, "have you ever seen a public park on Earth after a holiday?"

Betty said hotly. "Yes—it's dreadful. Because most people of Earth have no feeling of community."

"Right," said Welstead. "And these people have. They're knit very tightly by a compulsion that made them achieve in two hundred-odd years what took seven thousand on Earth. They're all facing the same direction, geared to the same drive. Once that drive is gone how do you expect they'll hold on to their standards?"

Betty was silent.

"Human beings," said Welstead dreamily, "are at their best when the going's toughest. They're either at their best or else they're nothing. The going's been tough here—these people have come through. Give them a cheap living, tourist money—then what?

"But that's not all. In fact it's only half the story. These people here," he stated with emphasis, "are living in a dream. They're the victims of the Ten Books. They take every word literally and they've worked their hearts out trying to come somewhere near what they expect the standards to be.

"Their own stuff doesn't do half the things to them that the Ten Books says good art ought to do. Whoever wrote those Ten Books must have been a copywriter for an advertising agency," Welstead laughed. "Shakespeare wrote good plays—sure, I concede it. But I've never seen 'fires flickering along the words, gusty winds rushing through the pages.'

"Sibelius I suppose was a great composer—I'm no expert on these things—but whoever listened and became 'part of Finland's ice, moss-smelling earth, hoarse-breathing forest,' the way the Ten Books said everyone did?"

Betty said, "He was merely trying to express vividly the essence of the artists and musicians."

"Nothing wrong in that," said Welstead. "On Earth we're conditioned to call everything in print a lie. At least we allow for several hundred percent over-statement. These people out here aren't immunized. They've taken every word at its face value. The Ten Books is their Bible. They're trying to equal accomplishments which never existed."

Betty raised herself up on an elbow, said in a voice of hushed triumph. "And they've *succeeded*! Ralph, they've *succeeded*! They've met the challenge, they've equaled or beaten anything Earth has ever produced! Ralph, I'm proud to belong to the same race."

"Same species," Welstead corrected dryly. "These people are a mixed race. They're all races."

"What's the difference?" Betty snapped. "You're just quibbling. You know what I mean well enough."

"We're on a sidetrack," said Welstead wearily. "The question is not the people of Haven and their accomplishments. Of course they're wonderful—*now*. But how do you think contact with Earth will affect them?

"Do you think they'll continue producing when the challenge is gone? When they find the Earth is a rookery—nagging, quarreling—full of mediocre hacks and cheap mischief? Where the artists draw nothing but nude women and the musicians make their living reeling out sound, sound, sound—of any kind of sound—for television sound-track. Where are all their dreams then?

"Talk about disappointment, staleness! Mark my words, half the population would be suicides and the other half would turn to prostitution and cheating the tourists. It's a tough proposition. I say, leave them with their dreams. Let them think we're the worst sort of villains. I say, get off the planet, get back where we belong."

Betty said in a troubled voice, "Sooner or later somebody else will find them."

"Maybe—maybe not. We'll report the region barren—which it is except for Haven."

Betty said in a small voice, "Ralph I couldn't do it. I couldn't violate their trust."

"Not even to keep them trusting?"

Betty said wildly, "Don't you think there'd be an equal deflation if we sneaked away and left them? We're the climax to their entire two hundred and seventy-one years. Think of the listlessness after we left!"

"They're working on their space-drive," said Welstead. "Chances are a million to one against their stumbling on it. They don't know that.

They've got a flicker of a field and they think all they have to do is adjust the power feed, get better insulation. They don't have the Mardi Gras lamp that Gladheim snatched up when the lead tank melted."

"Ralph," said Betty, "your words are all very logical. Your arguments stay together—but they're not satisfying emotionally. I don't have the feeling of rightness."

"Come on!" said Welstead. "let's not get spiritual."

"And," said Betty softly, "let's not try to play God either."

There was a long silence.

"Ralph?" said Betty.

"What?"

"Isn't there *some* way...."

"Some way to do what?"

"Why should it be *our* responsibility?"

"I don't know whose else it is. We're the instruments—"

"But it's *their* lives."

"Betty," said Welstead wearily, "here's one time we can't pass the buck. We're the people who in the last resort say yes or no. We're the only people that see on both sides of the fence. It's an awful decision to make—but I say no."

There was no more talking and after an unmeasured period they fell asleep.

Three nights later Welstead stopped Betty as she began to undress for bed. She gave him a dark wide-eyed stare.

"Throw whatever you're taking into a bag. We're leaving."

Betty's body was rigid and tense, slowly relaxing as she took a step toward him. "Ralph...."

"What?" And she could find no softness, no indecision in his topaz eyes.

"Ralph—it's *dangerous* for us to go. If they caught us, they'd execute us—for utter depravity." And she said in a murmur, looking away, "I suppose they'd be justified too."

"It's a chance we'll have to take. Just what we said the day we decided to land. We've got to die sometime. Get your gear and let's take off."

"We should leave a note, Ralph. Something...."

He pointed to an envelope. "There it is. Thanking them for their hospitality. I told them we were criminals and couldn't risk returning to Earth. It's thin but it's the best I could do."

A hint of fire returned to Betty's voice. "Don't worry, they'll believe it."

Sullenly she tucked a few trinkets into a pouch. "It's a long way to the ship you know," she warned him.

"We'll take Clay's car. I've watched him and I know how to drive it."

She jerked in a small bitter spasm of laughter. "We're even car thieves."

"Got to be," said Welstead stonily. He went to the door, listened. The utter silence of honest sleep held the rest of the house. He returned to where Betty stood waiting, watching him coldly with an air of dissociation.

"This way," said Welstead. "Out through the terrace."

They passed out into the moonless night of Haven and the only sound was the glassy tinkle of the little stream that ran in its natural bed through the terrace.

Welstead took Betty's hand. "Easy now, don't walk into that bamboo." He clutched and they froze to a halt. Through a window had come a sound—a gasp—and then the relieved mutter a person makes on waking from a bad dream.

Slowly, like glass melting under heat, the two came to life, stole across the terrace, out upon the turf beside the house. They circled the vegetable garden and the loom of the car bulked before them.

"Get in," whispered Welstead. "I'll push till we're down around the bend."

Betty climbed into the seat and her foot scraped against the metal. Welstead stiffened, listened, pierced the darkness like an eagle. Quiet from the house, the quiet of relaxation, of trust....He pushed at the car and it floated easily across the ground, resisting his hand only through inertia.

It jerked to a sudden halt. And Welstead froze in his tracks again. A burglar alarm of some sort. No, there were no thieves on Haven—except two recently landed people from Earth. A trap?

"The anchor," whispered Betty.

Of course—Welstead almost groaned with relief. He found, hooked it into place on the car's frame and now the car floated without hindrance down the leafy tunnel that was Clay's driveway. Around a bend he ran to the door, jumped in, pressed his foot on the power pedal, and the car slid away with the easy grace of a canoe. Out on the main road he switched on the lights and they rushed off through the night.

"And we still use wheels on Earth," said Welstead. "If we only had a tenth of the guts these people have—"

Cars passed them from the other direction. The lights glowed briefly into their faces and they cringed low behind the windscreen.

They came to the park where the ship lay. "If anyone stops us," Welstead said in Betty's ear, "we've just driven down to get some personal effects. After all we're not prisoners."

But he circled the ship warily before stopping beside it and then he waited a few seconds, straining his eyes through the darkness. But there was no sound, no light, no sign of any guard or human presence.

Welstead jumped from the car. "Fast now. Run over, climb inside. I'll be right behind you."

They dashed through the dark, up the rungs welded to the hull, and the cold steel felt like a caress to Welstead's hot hands. Into the cabin he thudded the port shut, slammed home the dogs.

Welstead vaulted to the controls, powered the reactors. Dangerous business—but once clear of the atmosphere they could take time to let them warm properly. The ship rose, the darkness and lights of Mytilene fell below. Welstead sighed, suddenly tired, but warm and relaxed.

Up, up—and the planet became a ball, and Eridanus two thousand nine hundred and thirty-two peered around the edge and suddenly, without any noticeable sense of boundary passed, they were out in space.

Welstead sighed. "Lord, what a relief! I never knew how good empty space could look."

"It looks beautiful to me also," said Alexander Clay. "I've never seen it before."

Welstead whirled, jumped to his feet.

Clay came forward from the reaction chamber, watching with a peculiar expression Welstead took to be deadly fury. Betty stood by the bulkhead, looking from one to the other, her face blank as a mirror.

Welstead came slowly down from the controls. "Well—you've caught us in the act. I suppose you think we're treating you pretty rough. Maybe we are. But my conscience is clear. And we're not going back. Looks like you asked for a ride, and you're going to get one. If necessary—" He paused meaningfully.

Then, "How'd you get aboard?" and after an instant of narrow-eyed speculation, "And why? Why tonight?"

Clay shook his head slowly. "Ralph—you don't give us any credit for ordinary intelligence, let alone ordinary courage."

"What do you mean?"

"I mean that I understand your motives—and I admire you for them. Although I think you've been bull-headed putting them into action without discussing it with the people most directly concerned."

Welstead lowered his head, stared with hard eyes. "It's basically my responsibility. I don't like it but I'm not afraid of it."

"It does you credit," said Clay mildly. "On Haven we're used to sharing responsibility. Not diluting it, you understand, but putting a dozen—a hundred—a thousand minds on a problem that might be too much for one. You don't appreciate us, Ralph. You think we're soft, spiritless."

"No," said Welstead. "Not exactly—"

"Our civilization is built on adaptability, on growth, on flexibility," continued Clay. "We—"

"You don't understand just what you'd have to adapt to," said

Welstead harshly. "It's nothing nice. It's graft, scheming sharp-shooters, tourists by the million, who'll leave your planet the way a platoon of invading soldiers leaves the first pretty girl they find."

"There'll be problems," said Clay. His voice took on power. "But that's what we want, Ralph—problems. We're hungry for them, for the problems of ordinary human existence. We want to get back into the stream of life. And if it means grunting and sweating we want it. We're flesh and blood, just like you are.

"We don't want Nirvana—we want to test our strength. We want to fight along with the rest of decent humanity. Don't you fight what you think is unjust?"

Welstead slowly shook his head. "Not any more. It's too big for me. I tried when I was young, then I gave up. Maybe that's why Betty and I roam around the outer edges."

"No," said Betty. "That's not it at all, Ralph, and you know it. You explore because you like exploring. You like the rough and tumble of human contact just as much as anyone else."

"Rough and tumble," said Clay, savoring the words. "That's what we need on Haven. They had it in the old days. They gave themselves to it, beating the new world into submission. It's ours now. Another hundred years of nowhere to go and we'd be drugged, lethargic, decadent."

Welstead was silent.

"The thing to remember, Ralph," said Clay, "is that we're part of humanity. If there are problems we want to help solve them. You said you'd given up because it was too big for you. Do you think it would be too big for a whole planet? Three hundred million hard honest brains?"

Welstead stared, his imagination kindled. "I don't see how—"

Clay smiled. "I don't either. It's a problem for three hundred million minds. Thinking about it that way it doesn't seem so big. If it takes three hundred brains three days to figure out a dodecahedron of quartz—"

Welstead jerked, looked accusingly at his wife. "Betty!"

She shook her head. "Ralph, I told Clay about our conversation, our argument. We discussed it all around, Ralph, and I told him everything—and I told him I'd give a signal whenever we started to leave. But I never mentioned space-drive. If they discovered it they did it by themselves."

Welstead turned slowly back to Clay. "*Discovered* it? But—that's impossible."

Said Clay, "Nothing's impossible. You yourself gave me the hint when you told me human reason was useless because the space-drive worked out of a different environment. So we concentrated not on the drive itself but on the environment. The first results came at us in terms of twelve directions—hence the dodecahedron. Just a hunch, an experiment and it worked."

Welstead sighed. "I'm licked. I give in. Clay, the headache is yours. You've *made* it yours. What do you want to do? Go back to Haven?"

Clay smiled, almost with affection. "We're this far. I'd like to see Earth. For a month, incognito. Then we'll come back to Haven and make a report to the world. There's three hundred million of us, waiting for the signal to start."

THE MASQUERADE ON DICANTROPUS

Two puzzles dominated the life of Jim Root. The first, the pyramid out in the desert, tickled and prodded his curiosity, while the second, the problem of getting along with his wife, kept him keyed to a high pitch of anxiety and apprehension. At the moment the problem had crowded the mystery of the pyramid into a lost alley of his brain.

Eyeing his wife uneasily, Root decided that she was in for another of her fits. The symptoms were familiar—a jerking over of the pages of an old magazine, her tense back and bolt-upright posture, her pointed silence, the compression at the corners of her mouth.

With no preliminary motion she threw the magazine across the room, jumped to her feet. She walked to the doorway, stood looking out across the plain, fingers tapping on the sill. Root heard her voice, low, as if not meant for him to hear.

"Another day of this and I'll lose what little's left of my mind."

Root approached warily. If he could be compared to a Labrador retriever, then his wife was a black panther—a woman tall and well-covered with sumptuous flesh. She had black flowing hair and black flashing eyes. She lacquered her fingernails and wore black lounge pajamas even on desiccated deserted inhospitable Dicantropus.

"Now, dear," said Root, "take it easy. Certainly it's not as bad as all that."

She whirled and Root was surprised by the intensity in her eyes. "It's not bad, you say? Very well for you to talk—*you* don't care for anything human to begin with. I'm sick of it. Do you hear? I want to go back to Earth! I never want to see another planet in my whole life. I never want to hear the word archaeology, I never want to see a rock or a bone or a microscope—"

She flung a wild gesture around the room that included a number of rocks, bones, microscopes, as well as books, specimens in bottles, photographic equipment, a number of native artifacts.

Root tried to soothe her with logic. "Very few people are privileged to live on an outside planet, dear."

"They're in their right minds. If I'd known what it was like, I'd never have come out here." Her voice dropped once more. "Same old dirt every day, same stinking natives, same vile canned food, nobody to talk to—"

Root uncertainly picked up and laid down his pipe. "Lie down, dear," he said with unconvincing confidence. "Take a nap! Things will look different when you wake up."

Stabbing him with a look, she turned and strode out into the blue-white glare of the sun. Root followed more slowly, bringing Barbara's sun-helmet and adjusting his own. Automatically he cocked an eye up the antenna, the reason for the station and his own presence, Dicantropus being a relay point for ULR messages between Clave II and Polaris. The antenna stood as usual, polished metal tubing four hundred feet high.

Barbara halted by the shore of the lake, a brackish pond in the neck of an old volcano, one of the few natural bodies of water on the planet. Root silently joined her, handed her her sun-helmet. She jammed it on her head, walked away.

Root shrugged, watched her as she circled the pond to a clump of feather-fronded cycads. She flung herself down, relaxed into a sulky lassitude, her back to a big gray-green trunk, and seemed intent on the antics of the natives—owlish leather-gray little creatures popping back and forth into holes in their mound.

This was a hillock a quarter-mile long, covered with spinescrub and a rusty black creeper. With one exception it was the only eminence as far as the eye could reach, horizon to horizon, across the baked helpless expanse of the desert.

The exception was the stepped pyramid, the mystery of which irked Root. It was built of massive granite blocks, set without mortar but cut so carefully that hardly a crack could be seen. Early on his arrival Root had climbed all over the pyramid, unsuccessfully seeking entrance.

When finally he brought out his atomite torch to melt a hole in the granite a sudden swarm of natives pushed him back and in the pidgin of Dicantropus gave him to understand that entrance was forbidden. Root desisted with reluctance, and had been consumed by curiosity ever since....

Who had built the pyramid? In style it resembled the *ziggurats* of ancient Assyria. The granite had been set with a skill unknown, so far as Root could see, to the natives. But if not the natives—who? A thousand times Root had chased the question through his brain. Were the natives debased relics of a once-civilized race? If so, why were there no other ruins? And what was the purpose of the pyramid? A temple? A mausoleum? A treasure-hunt? Perhaps it was entered from below by a tunnel.

As Root stood on the shore of the lake, looking across the desert, the questions flicked automatically through his mind though without their usual pungency. At the moment the problem of soothing his wife lay heavy on his mind. He debated a few moments whether or not to join her; perhaps she had cooled off and might like some company. He circled the pond and stood looking down at her glossy black hair.

"I came over here to be alone," she said without accent and the indifference chilled him more than an insult.

"I thought—that maybe you might like to talk," said Root. "I'm very sorry, Barbara, that you're unhappy."

Still she said nothing, sitting with her head pressed back against the tree trunk.

"We'll go home on the next supply ship," Root said. "Let's see, there should be one—"

"Three months and three days," said Barbara flatly.

Root shifted his weight, watched her from the corner of his eye. This was a new manifestation. Tears, recriminations, anger—there had been plenty of these before.

"We'll try to keep amused till then," he said desperately. "Let's think up some games to play. Maybe badminton—or we could do more swimming."

Barbara snorted in sharp sarcastic laughter. "With things like that popping up around you?" She gestured to one of the Dicantrops who had lazily paddled close. She narrowed her eyes, leaned forward. "What's that he's got around his neck?"

Root peered. "Looks like a diamond necklace more than anything else."

"My Lord!" whispered Barbara.

Root walked down to the water's edge. "Hey, boy!" The Dicantrop turned his great velvety eyes in their sockets. "Come here!"

Barbara joined him as the native paddled close.

"Let's see what you've got there," said Root, leaning close to the necklace.

"Why, those are *beautiful*!" breathed his wife.

Root chewed his lip thoughtfully. "They certainly look like diamonds. The setting might be platinum or iridium. Hey, boy where did you get these?"

The Dicantrop paddled backward. "We find."

"Where?"

The Dicantrop blew froth from his breath-holes but it seemed to Root as if his eyes had glanced momentarily toward the pyramid.

"You find in big pile of rock?"

"No," said the native and sank below the surface.

Barbara returned to her seat by the tree, frowned at the water. Root joined her. For a moment there was silence. Then Barbara said, "That pyramid must be full of things like that!"

Root made a deprecatory noise in his throat. "Oh—I suppose it's possible."

"Why don't you go out and see?"

"I'd like to—but you know it would make trouble."

"You could go out at night."

"No," said Root uncomfortably. "It's really not right. If they want to keep the thing closed up and secret it's their business. After all it belongs to them."

"How do you know it does?" his wife insisted, with a hard and sharp directness. "They didn't build it and probably never put those diamonds there." Scorn crept into her voice. "Are you afraid?"

"Yes," said Root. "I'm afraid. There's an awful lot of them and only two of us. That's one objection. But the other, most important—"

Barbara let herself slump back against the trunk. "I don't want to hear it."

Root, now angry himself, said nothing for a minute. Then, thinking of the three months and three days till the arrival of the supply ship, he said, "It's no use our being disagreeable. It just makes it harder on both of us. I made a mistake bringing you out here and I'm sorry. I thought you'd enjoy the experience, just the two of us alone on a strange planet—"

Barbara was not listening to him. Her mind was elsewhere.

"*Barbara!*"

"*Shh!*" she snapped. "Be still! Listen!"

He jerked his head up. The air vibrated with a far *thrum-m-m-m.* Root sprang out into the sunlight, scanned the sky. The sound grew louder. There was no question about it, a ship was dropping down from space.

Root ran into the station, flipped open the communicator—but there were no signals coming in. He returned to the door and watched as the ship sank down to a bumpy rough landing two hundred yards from the station.

It was a small ship, the type rich men sometimes used as private yachts, but old and battered. It sat in a quiver of hot air, its tubes creaking and hissing as they cooled. Root approached.

The dogs on the port began to turn, the port swung open. A man stood in the opening. For a moment he teetered on loose legs, then fell headlong.

Root, springing forward, caught him before he struck ground. "Barbara!" Root called. His wife approached. "Take his feet. We'll carry him inside. He's sick."

They laid him on the couch and his eyes opened halfway.

"What's the trouble?" asked Root. "Where do you feel sick?"

"My legs are like ice," husked the man. "My shoulders ache. I can't breathe."

"Wait till I look in the book," muttered Root. He pulled out the Official Spaceman's Self-Help Guide, traced down the symptoms. He looked across to the sick man. "You been anywhere near Alphard?"

"Just came from there," panted the man.

"Looks like you got a dose of Lyma's Virus. A shot of mycosetin should fix you up, according to the book."

He inserted an ampule into the hypo-spray, pressed the tip to his patient's arm, pushed the plunger home. "That should do it—according to the *Guide*."

"Thanks," said his patient. "I feel better already." He closed his eyes. Root stood up, glanced at Barbara She was scrutinizing the man with a peculiar calculation. Root looked down again, seeing the man for the first time. He was young, perhaps thirty, thin but strong with a tight nervous muscularity. His face was lean, almost gaunt, his skin very bronzed. He had short black hair, heavy black eyebrows, a long jaw, a thin high nose.

Root turned away. Glancing at his wife he foresaw the future with a sick certainty.

He washed out the hypospray, returned the Guide to the rack, with sudden self-conscious awkwardness. When he turned around, Barbara was staring at him with wide thoughtful eyes. Root slowly left the room.

A day later Marville Landry was on his feet and when he had shaved and changed his clothes there was no sign of the illness. He was by profession a mining engineer, so he revealed to Root, en route to a contract on Thuban XIV.

The virus had struck swiftly and only by luck had he noticed the proximity of Dicantropus on his charts. Rapidly weakening, he had been forced to decelerate so swiftly and land so uncertainly that he feared his fuel was low. And indeed, when they went out to check, they found only enough fuel to throw the ship a hundred feet into the air.

Landry shook his head ruefully. "And there's a ten-million-munit contract waiting for me on Thuban Fourteen."

Said Root dismally, "The supply packet's due in three months."

Landry winced. "Three months—in this hell-hole? That's murder." They returned to the station. "How do you stand it here?"

Barbara heard him. "We don't. I've been on the verge of hysterics every minute the last six months. Jim"—she made a wry grimace toward her husband—"he's got his bones and rocks and the antenna. He's not too much company."

"Maybe I can help out," Landry offered airily.

"Maybe," she said with a cool blank glance at Root. Presently she left the room, walking more gracefully now, with an air of mysterious gaiety.

Dinner that evening was a gala event. As soon as the sun took its blue glare past the horizon Barbara and Landry carried a table down to the lake and there they set it with all the splendor the station could afford. With no word to Root she pulled the cork on the gallon of brandy he had been nursing for a year and served generous highballs with canned lime juice, Maraschino cherries and ice.

For a space, with the candles glowing and evoking lambent ghosts in the highballs, even Root was gay. The air was wonderfully cool and the sands of the desert spread white and clean as damask out into the dimness. So they feasted on canned fowl and mushrooms and frozen fruit and drank deep of Root's brandy, and across the pond the natives watched from the dark.

And presently, while Root grew sleepy and dull, Landry became gay, and Barbara sparkled—the complete hostess, charming, witty and the Dicantropus night tinkled and throbbed with her laughter. She and Landry toasted each other and exchanged laughing comments at Root's expense—who now sat slumping, stupid, half-asleep. Finally he lurched to his feet and stumbled off to the station.

On the table by the lake the candles burnt low. Barbara poured more brandy. Their voices became murmurs and at last the candles guttered.

In spite of any human will to hold time in blessed darkness, morning came and brought a day of silence and averted eyes. Then other days and nights succeeded each other and time proceeded as usual. And there was now little pretense at the station.

Barbara frankly avoided Root and when she had occasion to speak her voice was one of covert amusement. Landry, secure, confident, aquiline, had a trick of sitting back and looking from one to the other as if inwardly chuckling over the whole episode. Root preserved a studied calm and spoke in a subdued tone which conveyed no meaning other than the sense of his words.

There were a few minor clashes. Entering the bathroom one morning Root found Landry shaving with his razor. Without heat Root took the shaver out of Landry's hand.

For an instant Landry stared blankly, then wrenched his mouth into the beginnings of a snarl.

Root smiled almost sadly. "Don't get me wrong, Landry. There's a difference between a razor and a woman. The razor is mine. A human being can't be owned. Leave my personal property alone."

Landry's eyebrows rose. "Man, you're crazy." He turned away. "Heat's got you."

The days went past and now they were unchanging as before but unchanging with a new leaden tension. Words became even fewer and dislike hung like tattered tinsel. Every motion, every line of the body, became a detestable sight, an evil which the other flaunted deliberately.

Root burrowed almost desperately into his rocks and bones, peered through his microscope, made a thousand measurements, a thousand notes. Landry and Barbara fell into the habit of taking long walks in the evening, usually out to the pyramid, then slowly back across the quiet cool sand.

The mystery of the pyramid suddenly fascinated Landry and he even questioned Root.

"I've no idea," said Root. "Your guess is as good as mine. All I know is that the natives don't want anyone trying to get into it."

"Mph," said Landry, gazing across the desert. "No telling what's inside. Barbara said one of the natives was wearing a diamond necklace worth thousands."

"I suppose anything's possible," said Root. He had noticed the acquisitive twitch to Landry's mouth, the hook of the fingers. "You'd better not get any ideas. I don't want any trouble with the natives. Remember that, Landry."

Landry asked with seeming mildness, "Do you have any authority over that pyramid?"

"No," said Root shortly. "None whatever."

"It's not—yours?" Landry sardonically accented the word and Root remembered the incident of the shaver.

"No."

"Then," said Landry, rising, "mind your own business."

He left the room.

During the day Root noticed Landry and Barbara deep in conversation and he saw Landry rummaging through his ship. At dinner no single word was spoken.

As usual, when the afterglow had died to a cool blue glimmer, Barbara and Landry strolled into the desert. But tonight Root watched after them and he noticed a pack on Landry's shoulders and Barbara seemed to be carrying a handbag.

He paced back and forth, puffing furiously at his pipe. Landry was right—it was none of his business. If there were profit, he wanted none of it. And if there were danger, it would strike only those who provoked it. Or would it? Would he, Root, be automatically involved because of his association with Landry and Barbara? To the Dicantrops, a man was a man, and if one man needed punishment, all men did likewise.

Would there be—killing? Root puffed at his pipe, chewed the stem, blew smoke out in gusts between his teeth. In a way he was responsible for Barbara's safety. He had taken her from a sheltered life on Earth. He shook his head, put down his pipe, went to the drawer where he kept his gun. It was gone.

Root looked vacantly across the room. Landry had it. No telling how long since he'd taken it. Root went to the kitchen, found a meat-axe, tucked it inside his jumper, set out across the desert.

He made a wide circle in order to approach the pyramid from behind. The air was quiet and dark and cool as water in an old well. The crisp sand sounded faintly under his feet. Above him spread the sky and the sprinkle of the thousand stars. Somewhere up there was the Sun and old Earth.

The pyramid loomed suddenly large and now he saw a glow, heard the muffled clinking of tools. He approached quietly, halted several hundred feet out in the darkness, stood watching, alert to all sounds.

Landry's atomite torch ate at the granite. As he cut, Barbara hooked the detached chunks out into the sand. From time to time Landry stood back, sweating and gasping from radiated heat.

A foot he cut into the granite, two feet, three feet, and Root heard the excited murmur of voices. They were through, into empty space. Careless of watching behind them they sidled through the hole they had cut. Root, more wary, listened, strove to pierce the darkness...Nothing.

He sprang forward, hastened to the hole, peered within. The yellow gleam of Landry's torch swept past his eyes. He crept into the hole, pushed his head out into emptiness. The air was cold, smelled of dust and damp rock.

Landry and Barbara stood fifty feet away. In the desultory flash of the lamp Root saw stone walls and a stone floor. The pyramid appeared to be an empty shell. Whey then were the natives so particular? He heard Landry's voice, edged with bitterness.

"Not a damn thing, not even a mummy for your husband to gloat over."

Root could sense Barbara shuddering. "Let's go. It gives me the shivers. It's like a dungeon."

"Just a minute, we might as well make sure...Hm." He was playing the light on the walls. "That's peculiar."

"What's peculiar?"

"It looks like the stone was sliced with a torch. Notice how it's fused here on the inside...."

Root squinted, trying to see. "Strange," he heard Landry mutter. "Outside it's chipped, inside it's cut by a torch. It doesn't look so very old here inside, either."

"The air would preserve it," suggested Barbara dubiously.

"I suppose so—still, old places look old. There's dust and a kind of dullness. This looks raw."

"I don't understand how that could be."

"I don't either. There's something funny somewhere."

Root stiffened. Sound from without? Shuffle of splay feet in the sand—he started to back out. Something pushed him, he sprawled forward, fell. The bright eye of Landry's torch stared in his direction. "What's that?" came a hard voice. "Who's there?"

Root looked over his shoulder. The light passed over him, struck a dozen gray bony forms. They stood quietly just inside the hole, their eyes like balls of black plush.

Root gained his feet. "Hah!" cried Landry. "So *you're* here too."

"Not because I want to be," returned Root grimly.

Landry edged slowly forward, keeping his light on the Dicantrops. He asked Root sharply, "Are these lads dangerous?"

Root appraised the natives. "I don't know."

"Stay still," said one of these in the front rank. "Stay still." His voice was a deep croak.

"Stay still, *hell!*" exclaimed Landry. "We're leaving. There's nothing here I want. Get out of the way." He stepped forward.

"Stay still...We kill..."

Landry paused.

"What's the trouble now?" interposed Root anxiously. "Surely there's no harm in looking. There's nothing here."

"That is why we kill. Nothing here, now you know. Now you look other place. When you think the place important, then you not look other place. We kill, new man come, he think this place important."

Landry muttered. "Do you get what he's driving at?"

Root said slowly, "I don't know for sure." He addressed the Dicantrop. "We don't care about your secrets. You've no reason to hide things from us."

The native jerked his head. "Then why do you come here? You look for secrets."

Barbara's voice came from behind. "What *is* your secret? Diamonds?"

The native jerked his head again. Amusement? Anger? His emotions, unearthly, could be matched by no earthly words. "Diamonds are nothing—rocks."

"I'd like a carload," Landry muttered under his breath.

"Now look here," said Root persuasively. "You let us out and we won't pry into any of your secrets. It was wrong of us to break in and I'm sorry it happened. We'll repair the damage—"

The Dicantrop made a faint sputtering sound. "You do not understand. You tell other men—pyramid is nothing. Then other men look all around for other thing. They bother, look, look, look. All this no good. You die, go like before."

"There's too much talk," said Landry viciously, "and I don't like the sound of it. Let's go out of here." He pulled out Root's gun. "Come on," he snapped at Root, "let's move."

To the natives, "Get out of the way or I'll do some killing myself!"

A rustle of movement from the natives, a thin excited whimper.

"We've got to rush 'em," shouted Landry. "If they get outside they can knock us over as we leave. Let's go!"

He sprang forward and Root was close behind. Landry used the gun as a club and Root used his fist and the Dicantrops rattled like cornstalks against the walls. Landry erupted through the hole. Root pushed Barbara through and kicking back at the natives behind him, struggled out into the air.

Landry's momentum had carried him away from the pyramid, out into a seething mob of Dicantrops. Root, following more slowly, pressed his back to the granite. He sensed the convulsive movement in the wide darkness. "The whole colony must be down here," he shouted into Barbara's ear. For a minute he was occupied with the swarming natives, keeping Barbara behind him as much as possible. The first ledge of granite was about shoulder height.

"Step on my hands," he panted. "I'll shove you up."

"But—Landry!" came Barbara's choked wail.

"Look at that crowd!" bit Root furiously. "We can't do anything." A sudden rush of small bony forms almost overwhelmed him. "Hurry up!"

Whimpering she stepped into his clasped hands. He thrust her up on the first ledge. Shaking off the clawing natives who had leapt on him, he jumped, scrambled up beside her. "Now run!" he shouted in her ear and she fled down the ledge.

From the darkness came a violent cry. "Root! *Root!* For *God's* sake—they've got me down—" Another hoarse yell, rising to a scream of agony. Then silence.

"Hurry!" said Root. They came to the far corner of the pyramid. "Jump down," panted Root. "Down to the ground."

"Landry!" moaned Barbara, teetering at the edge.

"Get *down!*" snarled Root. He thrust her down to the white sand and, seizing her hand, ran across the desert, back toward the station. A minute or so later, with pursuit left behind, he slowed to a trot.

"We should go back," cried Barbara. "Are you going to leave him to those devils?"

Root was silent a moment. Then, choosing his words, he said, "I told him to stay away from the place. Anything that happens to him is his own fault. And whatever it is, it's already happened. There's nothing we can do now."

A dark hulk shouldered against the sky—Landry's ship.

"Let's get in here," said Root. "We'll be safer than in the station."

He helped her into the ship, clamped tight the port. "*Phew!*" He shook his head. "Never thought it would come to this."

He climbed into the pilot's seat, looked out across the desert. Barbara huddled somewhere behind him, sobbing softly.

An hour passed, during which they said no word. Then, without warning, a fiery orange ball rose from the hill across the pond, drifted toward the station. Root blinked, jerked upright in his seat. He scrambled for the ship's machine-gun, yanked at the trigger—without result.

When at last he found and threw off the safety the orange ball hung over the station and Root held his fire. The ball brushed against the antenna—a tremendous explosion spattered to every corner of vision. It seared Root's eyes, threw him to the deck, rocked the ship, left him dazed and half-conscious.

Barbara lay moaning. Root hauled himself to his feet. A seared pit, a tangle of metal, showed where the station had stood. Root dazedly slumped into the seat, started the fuel pump, plunged home the catalyzers. The boat quivered, bumped a few feet along the ground. The tubes sputtered, wheezed.

Root looked at the fuel gauge, looked again. The needle pointed to zero, a fact which Root had known but forgotten. He cursed his own stupidity. Their presence in the ship might have gone ignored if he had not called attention to it.

Up from the hill floated another orange ball. Root jumped for the machine gun, sent out a burst of explosive pellets. Again the roar and the blast and the whole top of the hill was blown off, revealing what appeared to be a smooth strata of black rock.

Root looked over his shoulder to Barbara. "This is it."

"Wha—what do you mean?"

"We can't get away. Sooner or later—" His voice trailed off. He reached up, twisted a dial labeled EMERGENCY. The ship's ULR unit hummed. Root said into the mesh, "Dicantropus station—we're being attacked by natives. Send help at once."

Root sank back into the seat. A tape would repeat his message endlessly until cut off.

Barbara staggered to the seat beside Root. "What were those orange balls?"

"That's what *I've* been wondering—some sort of bomb."

But there were no more of them. And presently the horizon began to glare, the hill became a silhouette on the electric sky. And over their heads the transmitter pulsed an endless message into space.

"How long before we get help?" whispered Barbara.

"Too long," said Root, staring off toward the hill. "They must be afraid of the machine gun—I can't understand what else they're waiting for. Maybe good light."

"They can—" Her voice stopped. She stared. Root stared, held by unbelief—amazement. The hill across the pond was breaking open, crumbling....

Root sat drinking brandy with the captain of the supply ship *Method*, which had come to their assistance, and the captain was shaking his head.

"I've seen lots of strange things around this cluster but this masquerade beats everything."

Root said, "It's strange in one way, in another it's as cold and straightforward as ABC. They played it as well as they could and it was pretty darned good. If it hadn't been for that scoundrel Landry they'd have fooled us forever."

The captain banged his glass on the desk, stared at Root. "But *why*?"

Root said slowly, "They liked Dicantropus. It's a hell-hole, a desert to us, but it was heaven to them. They liked the heat, the dryness. But they didn't want a lot of off-world creatures prying into their business—as we surely would have if we'd seen through the masquerade. It must have been an awful shock when the first Earth ship set down here."

"And that pyramid...."

"Now that's a strange thing. They were good psychologists, these Dicantrops, as good as you could expect an off-world race to be. If you'll read a report of the first landing, you'll find no mention of the pyramid. Why? Because it wasn't here. Landry thought it looked new. He was right. It *was* new. It was a fraud, a decoy—just strange enough to distract our attention.

"As long as that pyramid sat out there, with me focusing all my mental energy on it, they were safe—and how they must have laughed. As soon as Landry broke in and discovered the fraud, then it was all over...."

"That might have been their miscalculation," mused Root. "Assume that they knew nothing of crime, of anti-social action. If everybody did what he was told to do their privacy was safe forever." Root laughed. "Maybe they didn't know human beings so well after all."

The captain refilled the glasses and they drank in silence. "Wonder where they came from," he said at last.

Root shrugged. "I suppose we'll never know. Some other hot dry planet, that's sure. Maybe they were refugees or some peculiar religious sect or maybe they were a colony."

"Hard to say," agreed the captain sagely. "Different race, different psychology. That's what we run into all the time."

"Thank God they weren't vindictive," said Root, half to himself. "No doubt they could have killed us any one of a dozen ways after I'd sent out that emergency call and they had to leave."

"It all ties in," admitted the captain.

Root sipped the brandy, nodded. "Once that ULR signal went out, their isolation was done for. No matter whether we were dead or not, there'd be Earthmen swarming around the station, pushing into their tunnels—and right there went their secret."

And he and the captain silently inspected the hole across the pond where the tremendous space-ship had lain buried under the spine-scrub and rusty black creeper.

"And once that space-ship was laid bare," Root continued, "there'd be a hullabaloo from here to Fomalhaut. A tremendous mass like that? We'd have to know everything—their space-drive, their history, everything about them. If what they wanted was privacy that would be a thing of the past. If they were a colony from another star they had to protect their secrets the same way we protect ours."

Barbara was standing by the ruins of the station, poking at the tangle with a stick. She turned and Root saw that she held his pipe. It was charred and battered but still recognizable.

She slowly handed it to him.

"Well?" said Root.

She answered in a quiet withdrawn voice: "Now that I'm leaving I think I'll miss Dicantropus." She turned to him, "Jim...."

"What?"

"I'd stay on another year if you'd like."

"No," said Root. "I don't like it here myself."

She said, still in the low tone: "Then—you don't forgive me for being foolish...."

Root raised his eyebrows. "Certainly I do. I never blamed you in the first place. You're human. Indisputably human."

"Then—why are you acting—like Moses?"

Root shrugged.

"Whether you believe me or not," she said with an averted gaze, "I never—"

He interrupted with a gesture. "What does it matter? Suppose you did—you had plenty of reason to. I wouldn't hold it against you."

"You would—in your heart."

Root said nothing.

"I wanted to hurt you. I was slowly going crazy—and you didn't seem to care one way or another. Told—him I wasn't—your property."

Root smiled his sad smile. "I'm human too."

He made a casual gesture toward the hole where the Dicantrop spaceship had lain. "If you still want diamonds, go down that hole with a bucket. There're diamonds big as grapefruit. It's an old volcanic neck, it's the grand-daddy of all diamond mines. I've got a claim staked out around it; we'll be using diamonds for billiard balls as soon as we get some machinery out here."

They turned slowly back to the *Method.*

"Three's quite a crowd on Dicantropus," said Root thoughtfully. "On Earth, where there're three billion, we can have a little privacy."

WHERE HESPERUS FALLS

My servants will not allow me to kill myself. I have sought self-extinction by every method, from throat-cutting to the intricate routines of Yoga, but so far they have thwarted my most ingenious efforts.

I grow ever more annoyed. What is more personal, more truly one's own, than a man's own life? It is his basic possession, to retain or relinquish as he sees fit. If they continue to frustrate me, someone other than myself will suffer. I guarantee this.

My name is Henry Revere. My appearance is not remarkable, my intelligence is hardly noteworthy, and my emotions run evenly. I live in a house of synthetic shell, decorated with wood and jade, and surrounded by a pleasant garden. The view to one side is the ocean, the other, a valley sprinkled with houses similar to my own. I am by no means a prisoner, although my servants supervise me with the most minute care. Their first concern is to prevent my suicide, just as mine is to achieve it.

It is a game in which they have all the advantages—a detailed knowledge of my psychology, corridors behind the walls from which they can observe me, and a host of technical devices. They are men of my own race, in fact my own blood. But they are immeasurably more subtle than I.

My latest attempt was clever enough—although I had tried it before without success. I bit deeply into my tongue and thought to infect the cut with a pinch of garden loam. The servants either noticed me placing the soil in my mouth or observed the tension of my jaw.

They acted without warning. I stood on the terrace, hoping the soreness in my mouth might go undetected. Then, without conscious hiatus, I found myself reclining on a pallet, the dirt removed, the wound healed. They had used a thought-damping ray to anaesthetize me, and their sure medical techniques, aided by my almost invulnerable constitution, defeated the scheme.

As usual, I concealed my annoyance and went to my study. This is a room I have designed to my own taste, as far as possible from the complex curvilinear style which expresses the spirit of the age.

Almost immediately the person in charge of the household entered the room. I call him Dr. Jones because I cannot pronounce his name. He is taller than I, slender and fine-boned. His features are small, beautifully shaped, except for his chin which to my mind is too sharp and long, although I understand that such a chin is a contemporary criterion of beauty. His eyes are very large, slightly protuberant; his skin is clean of hair, by reason both of the racial tendency toward hairlessness, and the depilation which every baby undergoes upon birth.

Dr. Jones' clothes are vastly fanciful. He wears a body mantle of green film and a dozen vari-colored disks which spin slowly around his body like an axis. The symbolism of these disks, with their various colors, patterns, and directions of spin, are discussed in a chapter of my *History of Man*—so I will not be discursive here. The disks serve also as gravity deflectors, and are used commonly in personal flight.

Dr. Jones made me a polite salute, and seated himself upon an invisible cushion of anti-gravity. He spoke in the contemporary speech, which I could understand well enough, but whose nasal trills, gutturals, sibilants and indescribable friccatives, I could never articulate.

"Well, Henry Revere, how goes it?" he asked.

In my pidgin-speech I made a noncommittal reply.

"I understand," said Dr. Jones, "that once again you undertook to deprive us of your company."

I nodded. "As usual I failed," I said.

Dr. Jones smiled slightly. The race had evolved away from laughter, which, as I understand, originated in the cave-man's bellow of relief at the successful clubbing of an adversary.

"You are self-centered," Dr. Jones told me. "You consider only your own pleasure."

"My life is my own. If I want to end it, you do great wrong in stopping me."

Dr. Jones shook his head. "But you are not your own property. You are the ward of the race. How much better if you accepted this fact!"

"I can't agree," I told him.

"It is necessary that you so adjust yourself." He studied me ruminatively. "You are something over ninety-six thousand years old. In my tenure at this house you have attempted suicide no less than a hundred times. No method has been either too crude or too painstaking."

He paused to watch me but I said nothing. He spoke no more than the truth, and for this reason I was allowed no object sharp enough to cut, long enough to strangle, noxious enough to poison, heavy enough to crush—even if I could have escaped surveillance long enough to use any deadly weapon.

I was ninety-six thousand, two hundred and thirty-two years old, and life long ago had lost that freshness and anticipation which makes it enjoyable. I found existence not so much unpleasant, as a bore. Events repeated themselves with a deadening familiarity. It was like watching a rather dull drama for the thousandth time: the boredom becomes almost tangible and nothing seems more desirable than oblivion.

Ninety-six thousand, two hundred and two years ago, as a student of bio-chemistry. I had offered myself as a guinea pig for certain tests involving glands and connective tissue. An incalculable error had distorted the experiment, with my immortality as the perverse result. To this day I appear not an hour older than my age at the time of the experiment, when I was so terribly young.

Needless to say, I suffered tragedy as my parents, my friends, my wife, and finally my children grew old and died, while I remained a young man. So it has been. I have seen untold generations come and go; faces flit before me like snowflakes as I sit here. Nations have risen and fallen, empires extended, collapsed, forgotten. Heroes have lived and died; seas drained, deserts irrigated, glaciers melted, mountains levelled. Almost a hundred thousand years I have persisted, for the most part effacing myself, studying humanity. My great work has been the *History of Man*.

Although I have lived unchanging, across the years the race evolved. Men and women grew taller, and more slender. Every century saw features more refined, brains larger, more flexible. As a result, I, Henry Revere, *homo sapiens* of the twentieth century, today am a freakish survival, somewhat more advanced than the Neanderthal, but essentially a precursor to the true Man of today.

I am a living fossil, a curio among curios, a public ward, a creature denied the option of life or death. This was what Dr. Jones had come to explain to me, as if I were a retarded child. He was kindly, but unusually emphatic. Presently he departed and I was left to myself, in whatever privacy the scrutiny of a half a dozen pairs of eyes allows.

It is harder to kill one's self than one might imagine. I have considered the matter carefully, examining every object within my control for lethal potentialities. But my servants are preternaturally careful. Nothing in this house could so much as bruise me. And when I leave the house, as I am privileged to do, gravity deflectors allow me no profit from high places, and in the exquisitely organized civilization there are no dangerous vehicles or heavy machinery in which I could mangle myself.

In the final analysis I am flung upon my own resources. I have an idea. Tonight I shall take a firm grasp on my head and try to break my neck....

Dr. Jones came as always, and inspected me with his usual reproach. "Henry Revere, you trouble us all with your discontent. Why can't you reconcile yourself to life as you have always known it?"

"Because I am bored! I have experienced everything. There is no more possibility of novelty or surprise! I feel so sure of events that I could predict the future!"

He was rather more serious than usual. "You are our guest. You must realize that our only concern is to ensure your safety."

"But I don't want safety! Quite the reverse!"

Dr. Jones ignored me. "You must make up your mind to cooperate. Otherwise—" he paused significantly "—we will be forced into a course of action that will detract from the dignity of us all."

"Nothing could detract any further from my dignity," I replied bitterly. "I am hardly better than an animal in a zoo."

"That is neither your fault nor ours. We all must fulfill our existences to the optimum. Today your function is to serve as vinculum with the past."

He departed. I was left to my thoughts. The threats had been veiled but were all too clear. I was to desist from further attempts upon my life or suffer additional restraint.

I went out on the terrace, and stood looking across the ocean, where the sun was setting into a bed of golden clouds. I was beset by a dejection so vast that I felt stifled. Completely weary of a world to which I had become alien, I was yet denied freedom to take my leave. Everywhere I looked were avenues to death: the deep ocean, the heights of the palisade, the glitter of energy in the city. Death was a privilege, a bounty, a prize, and it was denied to me.

I returned to my study and leafed through some old maps. The house was silent—as if I were alone. I knew differently. Silent feet moved behind the walls, which were transparent to the eyes above these feet, but opaque to mine. Gauzy webs of artificial nerve tissue watched me from various parts of the room. I had only to make a sudden gesture to bring an anaesthetic beam snapping at me.

I sighed, slumped into my chair. I saw with the utmost clarity that never could I kill myself by my own instrumentality. Must I then submit to an intolerable existence? I sat looking bleakly at the nacreous wall behind which eyes noted my every act.

No, I would never submit. I must seek some means outside myself, a force of destruction to strike without warning: a lightning bolt, an avalanche, an earthquake.

Such natural cataclysms, however, were completely beyond my power to ordain or even predict.

I considered radioactivity. If by some pretext I could expose myself to a sufficient number of roentgens....

I sat back in my chair, suddenly excited. In the early days atomic wastes were sometimes buried, sometimes blended with concrete and dropped into the ocean. If only I were able to—but no. Dr. Jones would hardly allow me to dig in the desert or dive in the ocean, even if the radioactivity were not yet vitiated.

Some other disaster must be found in which I could serve the role of a casualty. If, for instance, I had foreknowledge of some great meteor, and where it would strike....

The idea awoke an almost forgotten association. I sat up in my chair. Then, conscious that knowledgeable minds speculated upon my every expression, I once again slumped forlornly.

Behind the passive mask of my face, my mind was racing, recalling ancient events. The time was too far past, the circumstances obscured. But details could be found in my great *History of Man*.

I must by all means avoid suspicion. I yawned, feigned acute ennui. Then with an air of surly petulance, I secured the box of numbered rods which was my index. I dropped one of them into the viewer, focused on the molecule-wide items of information.

Someone might be observing me. I rambled here and there, consulting articles and essays totally unrelated to my idea: *The Origin and Greatest Development of the Dithyramb; The Kalmuk Tyrants; New Camelot, 18119 A.D.; Oestheotics; The Caves of Phrygia; The Exploration of Mars; The Launching of the Satellites.* I undertook no more than a glance at this last; it would not be wise to show any more than a flicker of interest. But what I read corroborated the inkling which had tickled the back of my mind.

The data was during the twentieth century, during what would have been my normal lifetime.

The article read in part:

Today HESPERUS, *last of the unmanned satellites was launched into orbit around Earth. This great machine will swing above the equator at a height of a thousand miles, where atmospheric resistance is so scant as to be negligible. Not quite negligible, of course; it is estimated that in something less than a hundred thousand years* HESPERUS *will lose enough momentum to return to Earth.*

Let us hope that no citizen of that future age suffers injury when HESPERUS *falls.*

I grunted and muttered. A fatuous sentiment! Let us hope that one person, at the very least, suffers injury. Injury enough to erase him from life!

I continued to glance through the monumental work which had occupied so much of my time. I listened to acquaclave music from the old

Poly-Pacific Empire; read a few pages from the Revolt of the Manitobans. Then, yawning and simulating hunger, I called for my evening meal.

Tomorrow I must locate more exact information, and brush up on orbital mathematics.

The *Hesperus* will drop into the Pacific Ocean at Latitude 0° 0' 0.0" + 0.1", Longitude 141° 12" 63.9" + 0.2", at 2 hours 22 minutes 18 seconds after standard noon on January 13 of next year. It will strike with a velocity of approximately one thousand miles an hour, and I hope to be on hand to absorb a certain percentage of its inertia.

I have been occupied seven months establishing these figures. Considering the necessary precautions, the dissimulation, the delicacy of the calculations, seven months is a short time to accomplish as much as I have. I see no reason why my calculations should not be accurate. The basic data were recorded to the necessary refinement and there have been no variables or fluctuations to cause error.

I have considered light pressure, hysteresis, meteoric dust; I have reckoned the calendar reforms which have occurred over the years; I have allowed for any possible Einsteinian, Gambade, or Bolbinski perturbation. What is there left to disturb the *Hesperus*? Its orbit lies in the equatorial plane, south of spaceship channels; to all intents and purposes it has been forgotten.

The last mention of the *Hesperus* occurs about eleven thousand years after it was launched. I find a note to the effect that its orbital position and velocity were in exact accordance with theoretical values. I believe I can be certain that the *Hesperus* will fall on schedule.

The most cheerful aspect to the entire affair is that no one is aware of the impending disaster but myself.

The date is *January 9*. To every side long blue swells are rolling, rippled with cat's-paws. Above are blue skies and dazzling white clouds. The yacht slides quietly southwest in the general direction of the Marquesas Islands.

Dr. Jones had no enthusiasm for this cruise. At first he tried to dissuade me from what he considered a whim but I insisted, reminding him that I was theoretically a free man and he made no further difficulty.

The yacht is graceful, swift, and seems as fragile as a moth. But when we cut through the long swells there is no shudder or vibration—only a gentle elastic heave. If I had hoped to lose myself overboard, I would have suffered disappointment. I am shepherded as carefully as in my own house. But for the first time in many years I am relaxed and happy. Dr. Jones notices and approves.

The weather is beautiful—the water so blue, the sun so bright, the air so fresh that I almost feel a qualm at leaving this life. Still, now is my chance and I must seize it. I regret that Dr. Jones and the crew must die with me. Still—what do they lose? Very little. A few short years. This is the risk they assume when they guard me. If I could allow them survival I would do so—but there is no such possibility.

I have requested and have been granted nominal command of the yacht. That is to say, I plot the course. I set the speed. Dr. Jones looks on with indulgent amusement, pleased that I interest myself in matters outside myself.

January 12. Tomorrow is my last day of life. We passed through a series of rain squalls this morning, but the horizon ahead is clear. I expect good weather tomorrow.

I have throttled down to Dead-Slow, as we are only a few hundred miles from our destination.

January 13. I am tense, active, charged with vitality and awareness. Every part of me tingles. On this day of my death it is good to be alive. And why? Because of anticipation, eagerness, hope.

I am trying to mask my euphoria. Dr. Jones is extremely sensitive; I would not care to start his mind working at this late date.

The time is noon. I keep my appointment with *Hesperus* in two hours and twenty-two minutes. The yacht is coasting easily over the water. Our position, as recorded by a pin-point of light on the chart, is only a few miles from our final position. At this present rate we will arrive in about two hours and fifteen minutes. Then I will halt the yacht and wait....

The yacht is motionless on the ocean. Our position is exactly at Latitude 0° 0' 0.0", Longitude 141° 12" 63.9". The degree of error represents no more than a yard or two. This graceful yacht with the unpronounceable name sits directly on the bull's eye. There is only five minutes to wait.

Dr. Jones comes into the cabin. He inspects me curiously. "You seem very keyed up, Henry Revere."

"Yes, I feel keyed up, stimulated. This cruise is affording me much pleasure."

"Excellent!" He walks to the chart, glances at it. "Why are we halted?"

"I took it into mind to drift quietly. Are you impatient?"

Time passes—minutes, seconds. I watch the chronometer. Dr. Jones follows my glance. He frowns in sudden recollection, goes to the telescreen. "Excuse me; something I would like to watch. You might be interested."

The screen depicts an arid waste. "The Kalahari Desert," Dr. Jones tells me. "Watch."

I glance at the chronometer. Ten seconds—they tick off. Five—four—three—two—one. A great whistling sound, a roar, a crash, an explosion! It comes from the telescreen. The yacht rides on a calm sea.

"There went *Hesperus*," said Dr. Jones. "Right on schedule!"

He looks at me, where I have sagged against a bulkhead. His eyes narrow, he looks at the chronometer, at the chart, at the telescreen, back to me. "Ah, I understand you now! All of us you would have killed!"

"Yes," I mutter, "all of us."

"Aha! You savage!"

I pay him no heed. "Where could I have miscalculated? I considered everything. Loss of entropic mass, lunar attractions—I know the orbit of *Hesperus* as I know my hand. How did it shift, and so far?"

Dr. Jones eyes shine with a baleful light. "You know the orbit of *Hesperus* then?"

"Yes. I considered every aspect."

"And you believe it shifted?"

"It must have. It was launched into an equatorial orbit; it falls into the Kalahari."

"There are two bodies to be considered."

"Two?"

"*Hesperus* and Earth."

"Earth is constant...Unchangeable." I say this last word slowly, as the terrible knowledge comes.

And Dr. Jones, for the first time in my memory, laughs, an unpleasant harsh sound. "Constant—unchangeable. Except for libration of the poles. *Hesperus* is the constant. Earth shifts below."

"Yes! What a fool I am!"

"An insensate murdering fool! I see you cannot be trusted!"

I charge him. I strike him once in the face before the anaesthetic beam hits me.

TELEK

Geskamp and Shorn stood in the sad light of sundown, high on the rim of the new Telek-ordained arena, which seemed to them so eccentric and arbitrary. They were alone: no sound was to be heard but the murmur of their voices. Wooded hills rose to right and left; far to the west, the skyline of Tran crossed the sunset.

Geskamp pointed east, up Swanscomb Valley. "There, by that row of poplars, is where I was born. I knew the valley well in the old days." He spent a moment in reflection. "I hate to see the changes, the old things wiped out." He pointed. "By the stream yonder was Pim's Croft and the old stone barn. Where you see the grove of oaks, that was the village Cobent. Can you believe it? And there, by Poll Point, the old aqueduct crossed the river. Only six months ago! Already it seems a hundred years."

Shorn, intending to make a delicate request, considered how best to take advantage of Geskamp's nostalgia for the irretrievable past; he was faintly surprised to find Geskamp, a big jut-faced man with gray-blond hair, indulging in sentiment of any kind. "There certainly is no recognizing it now."

"No. It's all tidy and clean. Like a park. I liked it better in the old days. Now it's waste, nothing else." Geskamp cocked his bristling eyebrows at Shorn. "Do you know, they hold me responsible, the farms and villagers? Because I'm in charge, I gave the orders?"

"They strike out at what's closest."

"I merely earn my salary. I did what I could for them. Completely

107

useless, of course; there never were people so obdurate as the Teleks. Level the valley, build a stadium. Hurry, in time for their midsummer get-together. I said, why not build in Mismarch Valley, around the mountain, where only sheepherders would be disturbed, no crofts and farms to be broken up, no village to be razed."

"What did they say to that?"

"It was Forence Nollinrude I spoke to; you know him?"

"I've seen him; one of their liaison committee. A young man, rather more lofty than the average."

Geskamp spat on the concrete under his feet. "The young ones are the worst." He asked, "Do we not give you enough money? Pay them well, clear them out. Swanscomb Valley is where we will have our arena. So"—Geskamp held out his hands in a quick gesticulation—"I bring out my machines, my men. We fly in material. For those who have lived here all their lives there is no choice; they take their money and go. Otherwise some morning perhaps they look out their door and find polar ice or mountains of the moon. I'd not put such refinement past the Teleks."

"Strange tales are told," Shorn agreed.

Geskamp pointed to the grove of oaks. His shadow, cast against the far side of the stadium by the level rays of the sun, followed the motion. "The oaks they brought, so much did they condescend. I explained that transplanting a forest was a job of great delicacy and expense. They were indifferent. 'Spend as much as you like.' I told them there wasn't enough time, if they wanted the stadium inside the month; finally they were aroused. Nollinrude and the one called Henry Motch stirred themselves, and the next day we had all our forest. But would they dispose of the waste from the aqueduct, cast it in the sea? No. 'You hire four thousand men, let them move the rubble, brick by brick if need be; we have business elsewhere.' And they were gone."

"A peculiar people."

" 'Peculiar?' " Geskamp gathered his busy eyebrows into arches of vast scorn. "Madmen. For a whim—a town erased, men and women sent forth homeless." He waved his hand around the stadium. "Two hundred million crowns spent to gratify irresponsible popinjays whose only—"

A droll voice above them said, "I hear myself bespoken."

The two men jerked around. A man stood in the air ten feet above them. His face was mercurial and lighthearted; a green cap clung waggishly to the side of his head; dark hair hung below, almost to his shoulders. He wore a flaring red cape, tight green trousers, black velvet shoes. "You speak in anger, with little real consideration. We are your benefactors; where would you be without us?"

"Living normal lives," growled Geskamp.

The Telek was disposed to facetiousness. "Who is to say that yours is a normal life? In any event, our whim is your employment; we formulate our idle dreams, you and your men enrich yourselves fulfilling them, and we're both the better for it."

"Somehow the money always ends up back with the Teleks. A mystery."

"No, no mystery whatever. It is the exercise of economic law. In any event, we procure the funds, and we would be fools to hoard. In our spending you find occupation."

"We would not be idle otherwise."

"Perhaps not. Perhaps...well, look." He pointed across the stadium to the shadows on the far wall. "Perhaps there is your bent." And as they watched their shadows became active. Shorn's shadow bent forward, Geskamp's shadow drew back, aimed and delivered a mighty kick, then turned, bent, and Shorn's shadow kicked.

The Telek cast no shadow.

Geskamp snorted, Shorn smiled grimly. They looked back overhead, but the Telek had moved high and was drifting south.

"Offensive creature," said Geskamp. "A law should be passed confiscating their every farthing."

Shorn shook his head. "They'd have it all back by nightfall. That's not the answer." He hesitated, as if about to add something further.

Geskamp, already irked by the Telek, did not take the contradiction kindly. Shorn, an architectural draughtsman, was his subordinate. "I suppose you know the answer?"

"I know several answers. One of them is that they should all be killed."

Geskamp's irritation had never carried him quite so far. Shorn was a strange, unpredictable fellow. "Rather bloodthirsty," he said heavily.

Shorn shrugged. "It might be best in the long run."

Geskamp's eyebrows lowered into a straight bar of gold-gray bristle across his face. "The idea is impractical. The creatures are hard to kill."

Shorn laughed. "It's more than impractical—it's dangerous. If you recall the death of Vernisaw Knerwig...."

Vernisaw Knerwig had been punctured by a pellet from a high-power rifle, fired from a window. The murderer, a wildeyed stripling, was apprehended. But the jail had not been tight enough to keep him. He disappeared. For months misfortune dogged the town. Poison appeared in the water supply. A dozen fires roared up one night. The roof of the town school collapsed. And one afternoon a great meteor struck down from space and obliterated the central square.

"Killing Teleks is dangerous work," said Geskamp. "It's not a realistic thought. After all," he said hurriedly, "they're men and women like ourselves; nothing illegal has ever been proved."

Shorn's eyes glittered. "Illegality? When they damn the whole stream of human development?"

Geskamp frowned. "I'd hardly say—"

"The signs are clear enough when a person pulls his head up out of the sand."

The conversation had got out of hand; Geskamp had been left behind. Waste and excess he admitted, but there were so few Teleks, so many ordinary people. How could they be dangerous? It was strange talk for an architect. He looked sidewise in cautious calculation.

Shorn was faintly smiling. "Well, what do you make of it?"

"You take an extreme position. It's hardly conceivable—"

"The future is unknown. Almost anything is conceivable. We might become Teleks, all of us. Unlikely? I think so myself. The Teleks might die out, disappear. Equally unlikely. They've always been with us, all of history, latent in our midst. What are the probabilities for the future? Something like the present situation, a few Teleks among the great mass of common people?"

Geskamp nodded. "That's my opinion."

"Picture the future, then. What do you see?"

"Nothing extraordinary. I imagine things will move along much as they have been."

"You see no trend, no curve of shifting relationships?"

"The Teleks are an irritation, certainly, but they interfere very little in our lives. In a sense they're an asset. They spend their money like water; they contribute to the general prosperity." He looked anxiously into the sky through the gathering dusk. "Their wealth, it's honestly acquired; no matter where they find those great blocks of metal."

"The metal comes from the Moon, from the asteroids, from the outer planets."

Geskamp nodded. "Yes, that's the speculation."

"The metal represents restraint. The Teleks are giving value in return for what they could take.

"Of course. Why shouldn't they give value in return?"

"No reason at all. They should. But now—consider the trend. At the outset they were ordinary citizens. They lived by ordinary conventions; they were decent people. After the first Congress they made their fortunes by performing dangerous and unpleasant tasks. Idealism, public service was the keynote. They identified themselves with all of humanity, and very praiseworthy, too. Now, sixty years later! Consider the Teleks of today. Is there any pretension to public service? None. They dress differently, speak differently, live differently. They no longer load ships or clear jungles or build roads; they take an easier way, which makes less demands on their time. Humanity benefits; they bring us platinum, palladium, uranium, rhodium, all the precious metals, which they sell at half the old price, and they pour the money back into circulation." He gestured across the stadium. "And meanwhile the old ones are dying and the new Teleks have no roots, no connection with common man. They draw ever farther away, developing a way of living entirely different from ours."

Geskamp said half-truculently, "What do you expect? It's natural, isn't it?"

Shorn put on a patient face. "That's exactly the point I'm trying to make. Consider the trend, the curve. Where does this 'natural' behavior lead? Always away from common humanity, the old traditions, always toward an elite-herd situation."

Geskamp rubbed his heavy chin. "I think that you're—well, making a mountain out of a molehill."

"Do you think so? Consider the stadium, the eviction of the old property-owners. Think of Vernisaw Knerwig and the revenge they took."

"Nothing was proved," said Geskamp uneasily. What was the fellow up to? Now he was grinning, a superior sort of grin.

"In your heart your agree with what I say; but you can't bring yourself to face the facts—because then you'd be forced to take a stand. For or against."

Geskamp stared out across the valley, wholly angry, but unable to dispute Shorn's diagnosis. "I don't see the facts clearly."

"There are only two courses for us. We must either control the Teleks, that is, make them answerable to human law—or we must eliminate them entirely. In blunt words—kill them. If we don't—they become the masters; we the slaves. It's inevitable."

Geskamp's anger broke surface.

"Why do you tell me all these things? What are you driving at? This is strange talk to hear from an architect; you sound like one of the conspirators I've heard rumors of."

"I'm talking for a specific purpose. I want to bring you to our way of thinking."

"Oh. So that's the way of it."

"And with this accomplished, recruit your ability and your authority toward a definite end."

"Who are you? What is this group?"

"A number of men worried by the trend I mentioned."

"A subversive society?" Geskamp's voice held a tinge of scorn.

Shorn laughed. "Don't let the flavor of words upset you. Call us a committee of public-spirited citizens."

"You'd be in trouble if the Teleks caught wind of you," said Geskamp woodenly.

"They're aware of us. But they're not magicians. They don't know who we are."

"I know who you are," said Geskamp. "Suppose I reported this conversation to Nollinrude?"

Shorn grinned. "What would you gain?"

"A great deal of money."

"You'd live the rest of your life in fear of revenge."

"I don't think it," said Geskamp in a brutal voice, "I don't care to be involved in any undercover plots."

"Examine your conscience. Think it over."

II

The attack on Forence Nollinrude came two days later.

The construction office was a long L-shaped building to the west of the stadium. Geskamp stood in the yard angrily refusing to pay a trucker more than the agreed scale for his concrete aggregate.

"I can buy it cheaper in half a dozen places," roared Geskamp. "You only got the contract in the first place because I went to bat for you."

The trucker had been one of the dispossessed farmers. He shook his head mulishly. "You did me no favor. I'm losing money. It's costing me three crowns a meter."

Geskamp waved an arm angrily toward the man's equipment, a small hopper carried by a pair of ramcopters. "How do you expect to make out with that kind of gear? All your profit goes in running back and forth to the quarry. Get yourself a pair of Samson lifts; you'll cut your costs to where you can take a few crowns."

"I'm a farmer, not a trucker. I took this contract because I had what I have. If I go in the hole for heavy equipment, then I'm stuck with it. It'll do me no more good now, the job's three-quarters done. I want more money, Geskamp, not good advice."

"Well, you can't get it from me. Talk to the purchasing agent; maybe he'll break down. I got you the contract, that's as far as I go."

"I already talked to the purchasing agent; he said nothing doing."

"Strike up one of the Teleks then; they've got the money. I can't do anything for you."

The trucker spat on the ground. "The Teleks, they're the devils who started this whole thing. A year ago I had my dairy—right where that patch of water is now. I was doing good. Now I've got nothing; the money they gave me to get out, most of it's gone in this gravel. Now where do I go?"

Geskamp drew his bushy gray-blond eyebrows together. "I'm sorry, Hopson. But there's nothing I can do. There's a Telek now; tell him your troubles."

The Telek was Forence Nollinrude, a tall yellow-haired man, magnificent in a rust cape, saffron trousers, black velvet slippers. The trucker looked across the yard to where Nollinrude floated a fastidious three feet above the ground, then resolved himself and trudged sullenly forward.

Shorn, inside the office, could hear nothing of the interview. The trucker stared up belligerently, legs spread out. Forence Nollinrude turned himself a little to the side, looked down with distaste deepening the lines at the corners of his mouth.

The trucker did most of the talking. The Telek replied in curt monosyllables, and the trucker became progressively more furious.

Geskamp had been watching with a worried frown. He started across the yard with the evident intention of calming the trucker. As he approached, Nollinrude pulled himself a foot or two higher, drew slightly away, turned toward Geskamp, motioned toward the trucker, as if requiring Geskamp to remove the annoyance.

The trucker suddenly seized a bar of reinforcing iron, swung mightily.

Geskamp bawled hoarsely: Forence Nollinrude jerked away, but the iron caught him across the shins. He cried in agony, drew back, looked at the trucker. The trucker rose like a rocket a hundred feet into the air, turned end for end, dived head-first to the ground. He struck with crushing force, pulping his head, his shoulders. But, as if Nollinrude were not yet satisfied, the bar of iron rose and beat the limp body with enormous savage strokes.

Had Nollinrude been less anguished by the pain of his legs he would have been more wary. Almost as the trucker struck the ground, Geskamp seized a laborer's mattock. As Nollinrude plied the bar of iron, Geskamp stalked close behind, swung. The Telek collapsed to the ground.

"Now," said Shorn to himself, "there will be hell to pay." He ran from the office. Geskamp stood panting, looking down at the body huddled in the finery that suddenly seemed not chosen human vestments, but the gaudy natural growth of a butterfly or flash-beetle in pathetic disarray. He became aware of the mattock he still held, flung it away as if it were red-hot and stood wiping his hands nervously together.

Shorn knelt beside the body; searched with practiced swiftness. He found and pocketed a wallet, a small pouch, then rose to his feet.

"We've got to work fast." He looked around the yard. Possibly half a dozen men had witnessed the occurrence—a toolroom attendant, a form foreman, a couple of time-clerks, a laborer or two. "Get them all together, everyone who saw what happened; I'll take care of the body. "Here, you!" He called to a white-faced lift-operator. "Get a hopper down here."

They rolled the gorgeous hulk into the hopper. Shorn jumped up beside the operator, pointed. "Up there where they're pouring that abutment."

They swept diagonally up the great north wall, to where a pour-crew worked beside a receptor designed to receive concrete from loaded hoppers. Shorn jumped four feet from the hopper to the deck, went to the foreman. "There's a hold-up here; take your crew down to B-142 Pilaster and work there for a while."

The foreman grumbled, protested. The receptor was half full of concrete.

Shorn raised his voice impatiently. "Leave it set. I'll send a lift up to move the whole thing."

The foreman turned away, barked ill-naturedly to his men. They moved with exaggerated slowness. Shorn stood tautly while they gathered their equipment and trooped down the ramp.

He turned to the lift operator. "Now."

The bedizened body rolled into the pour.

Shorn guided the dump-hose into position, pulled the trigger. Gray slush pressed down the staring face that had known so much power.

Shorn sighed slightly. "That's good. Now—we'll get the crew back on the job."

At Pilaster B-142 Shorn signaled the foreman, who glowered belligerently. Shorn was a mere draughtsman, therefore a fumbler and impractical. "You can go back to work up above now."

Before the foreman could find words for an adequate retort, Shorn was back in the hopper.

In the yard he found Geskamp standing at the center of an apprehensive group.

"Nollinrude's gone." He looked at the body of the trucker who had caused the original outburst. "Somebody will have to take him home."

He surveyed the group, trying to gauge their strength, and found nothing to reassure him. Eyes shifted sullenly from his. With an empty feeling in his stomach Shorn knew that the fact of the killing could not be disposed of as easily as the body. He looked from face to face. "A lot of people to keep a secret. If one of us talks—even to this brother or his friend or his wife—then there's no more secret. You will remember Vernisaw Knerwig?"

A nervous mutter assured him that they did: that their urgent hope was to disassociate themselves from any part of the episode.

Geskamp's face was working irritably. Shorn remembered that Geskamp was nominally in charge and was possibly sensitive to any usurpations of his authority. "Yes, Mr. Geskamp? Did you have something to add?"

Geskamp drew back his heavy lips, grinning like a big blond dog. With an effort he restrained himself. "You're doing fine."

Shorn turned back to the others. "You men are leaving the job now. You won't be questioned by the Teleks. Naturally they'll know that Nollinrude has disappeared, but I hope they won't know where. Just in case you are asked—Nollinrude came and went. That's all you know. Another thing." He paused weightily. "If any of us becomes wealthy and the Teleks become full of knowledge—this person will regret that he sold his voice." And he added, as if it were an inconsequential matter, "There's a group to cope with situations of this sort." He looked at Geskamp, but Geskamp kept stonily silent. "Now, I'll get your names—for future reference. One at a time...."

Twenty minutes later a carry-all floated off toward Tran.

"Well," said Geskamp bitterly, "I'm up to my neck in it now. Is that what you wanted?"

"I didn't want it this way. You're in a tough spot. So am I. With luck we'll come through. But—just in case—tonight we'll have to do what I was leading up to."

Geskamp squinted angrily. "Now I'm to be your cat's-paw. In what?"

"You can sign a requisition. You can send a pair of lifts to the explosives warehouse—"

Geskamp's bushy eyebrows took on a odd reverse tilt. "Explosives? How much?"

"A ton of mitrox."

Geskamp said in a tone of hushed respect: "That's enough to blow the stadium ten miles high!"

Shorn grinned. "Exactly. You'd better get that requisition off right now. Then you have the key to the generator room. Tomorrow the main pile is going in. Tonight you and I will arrange the mitrox under the piers."

Geskamp's mouth hung open. "But—"

Shorn's dour face became almost charming. "I know. Wholesale murder. Not sporting. I agree with you. A sneak attack. I agree. Stealth and sneak attacks and back-stabbing are our weapons. However, we don't have any others. None at all."

But—why are you so confident of bloodshed?"

Shorn suddenly exploded in anger. "Man, get your head up out of the sand. When will we have another chance of getting every single one without exception?"

Geskamp jumped out of the company airboat assigned to his use, stalked with a set face around the arena toward the construction office. Above him rose two hundred feet of sheer concrete, glowing in the morning sun. In his mind's eye Geskamp saw the dark cartons that he and Shorn had carried below like moles on the night previous; he still moved with reluctance and uncertainty, carried only by Shorn's fire and direction.

Now the trap was set. A single coded radio signal would pulverize the new concrete, fling a molten gout miles into the air, pound a gigantic blow at the earth.

Geskamp's honest face became taut as he wrestled with his conscience. Had he been too malleable? Think what a revenge the Teleks would take for such a disaster! Still, if the Teleks were as terrible a threat to human freedom as Shorn had half made him believe, then the mass killing was a deed to be resolutely carried through, like the killing of dangerous beasts. And certainly the Teleks paid only lip service to human laws. His mind went to the death of Forence Nollinrude. Under ordinary circumstances there would be an inquiry. Nollinrude had killed the trucker; Geskamp, swept by overwhelming rage and pity, had killed the Telek. At the worst, a human court would have found him guilty of manslaughter, and no doubt would have granted probation. But with a Telek—Geskamp's blood chilled in his veins. Maybe there was something to Shorn's extreme methods after all; certainly the Teleks could be controlled by no normal methods of law.

He rounded the corner of the toolroom, noted an unfamiliar face within. Good. Home office had acted without inquisitiveness; the shifting of employees had interested no one with authority to ask questions.

He looked into the expediter's room. "Where's the draughtsman?" he asked Cole, the steel detailer.

"Never showed up this morning, Mr. Geskamp."

Geskamp cursed under his breath. Just like Shorn, getting him into trouble, then ducking out, leaving him to face it. Might be better to come clean with the whole incident; after all, it had been an accident, a fit of blood-rage. The Teleks could understand so much, surely.

He turned his head. Something flickered at the edge of his vision. He looked sharply. Something like a big black bug whisked up behind a shelf of books. Big cockroach, thought Geskamp. A peculiar cockroach.

He attacked his work in a vicious humor, and foremen around the job asked themselves wonderingly what had got into Geskamp. Three times during the morning he looked into the office for Shorn, but Shorn had made no appearance.

And once, as he ducked under a low soffit on one of the upper decks, a black object darted up behind him. He jerked his eyes around, but the thing had disappeared under the beams.

"Funny bug," he said to the new form foreman, whom he was showing around the job.

"I didn't see it, Mr. Geskamp."

Geskamp returned to the office, obtained Shorn's home address—a hotel in the Marmion Tower—and put in a visiphone call.

Shorn was not in.

Geskamp turned away, and almost bumped into the feet of a Telek standing in the air before him: a thin somber man with silver hair and oil-black eyes. He wore two tones of gray, with a sapphire clasp at the collar of his cape, and the usual Telek slippers of black velvet.

Geskamp's heart started thudding; his hand became moist. The moment he had been dreading. Where was Shorn?

"You are Geskamp?"

"Yes," said Geskamp. "I—"

He was picked up, hurled through the air. Far, fleeting below, went the stadium, Swanscomb Valley, the entire countryside. Tran was a gray and black honeycomb, he was in the sunny upper air, hurtling with unthinkable speed. Wind roared past his ears, but he felt no pressure on his skin, no tear at his clothes.

The ocean spread blue below, and something glittered ahead—a complex edifice of shiny metal, glass, and bright color. It floated high in the sunny air, with no support above or below.

Geskamp saw a glitter, a flash; he was standing on a floor of glass threaded and drawn with strands of green and gold. The thin gray man sat behind a table in a yellow chair. The room was flooded with sunlight; Geskamp was too dazed to notice further details.

The Telek said, "Geskamp, tell me what you know of Forence Nollinrude."

It appeared to Geskamp that the Telek was watching him with superior knowledge, as if any lie would be instantly known, dismissed with grim humor. He was a poor liar to begin with. He looked around for a place to rest his big body. A chair appeared.

"Nollinrude?" He seated himself. "I saw him yesterday. What about him?"

"Where is he now?"

Geskamp forced a painful laugh. "How would I know?"

A sliver of glass darted through the air, stung the back of Geskamp's neck. He rose to his feet, startled and angry.

"Sit down," said the Telek, in a voice of unnatural coolness.

Geskamp slowly sat down. A kind of faintness dimmed his vision, his brain seemed to move away, seemed to watch dispassionately.

"Where is Nollinrude?"

Geskamp held his breath. A voice said, "He's dead. Down in the concrete."

"Who killed him?"

Geskamp listened to hear what the voice would say.

III

Shorn sat in a quiet tavern in that section of Tran where the old suddenly changes to the new. South were the towers, the neat intervening plazas and parks; north spread the ugly crust of three and four-story apartment buildings gradually blending into the industrial district.

A young woman with straight brown hair sat across the table from Shorn. She wore a brown cloak without ornament; looking into her face there was little to notice but her eyes—large, brown-black, somber; the rest of her face was without accent.

Shorn was drinking strong tea, his thin dark face in repose.

The young woman seemed to see an indication that the surface calm was false. She put out her hand, rested it on his, a quick exquisite gesture, the first time she had touched him in the three months of their acquaintance. "How could you have done differently?" Her voice became mildly argumentative. "What could you have done?"

"Taken the whole half-dozen underground. Kept Geskamp with me."

"How would that have helped? There'll be a certain number of deaths, a certain amount of destruction—how many and how much is out of our hands. Is Geskamp a valuable man?"

"No. He's a hard-working fellow, hardly devious or many-tracked enough to be of use. And I don't think he would have come with me. He was to the point of open rebellion as it was—the type who resents infringement."

"It's not impossible that your arrangements are still effective."

"Not a chance. The only matter for speculation is how many the Teleks destroy and whom."

The young woman leaned somberly back in her chair, stared straight ahead. "If nothing else, this episode marks a new place in the...in the...I don't know what to call it. Struggle? Campaign? War?"

"Call it war."

"We're almost out in the open. Public opinion may be aroused, swung to our side."

Shorn shook his head gloomily. "The Teleks have bought most of the police, and I suspect that they own the big newspapers, through fronts, of course. No, we can't expect much public support yet. We'll be called Nihilists, Totalitarists...."

The young woman quoted Turgenev. " 'If you want to annoy an opponent thoroughly or even harm him, you reproach him with every defect or vice you are conscious of in yourself.' "

"It's just as well." Shorn laughed bitterly. "If everyone were anti-Telek, the Teleks would have an easy job. Kill everybody."

"Then they'd have to do all their own work."

"That's right, too."

She made a fluttering gesture, her voice was strained. "It's a blood penance on our century, on humanity—"

Shorn snorted. "Mysticism."

She went on as if she had not heard. "If men were to develop from subapes a thousand times—each of those thousand rises would show the same phases, and there would be a Telek phase in all of them. It's as much a part of humanity as hunger and fear."

"And when the Teleks are out of the way—what's the next phase? Is history only a series of bloody phases? Where's the leveling-off point?"

She smiled wanly. "Perhaps when we're all Teleks."

Shorn gave her a strange look—calculation, curiosity, wonder. He returned to his tea as if to practical reality. "I suppose Geskamp has been trying to get hold of me all morning." He considered a moment, then rose to his feet. "I'll call the job and find out what's happened."

A moment later he returned. "Geskamp's nowhere around. A message just came in for me at the hotel, and it's to be delivered by hand only."

"Perhaps Geskamp went of his own accord."

"Perhaps."

"More likely—" she paused. "Anyway, the hotel is a good place to stay away from."

Shorn clenched and unclenched his hands. "It frightens me."

"What?" She seemed surprised.

"My own—vindictiveness. It's not right to hate anyone."

"You're too much the idealist, Will."

Shorn mused, talking in a monotone. "Our war is the war of ants against giants. They have the power—but they loom, we see them for miles. We're among the swarm. We move a hundred feet, into a new group of people, we're lost. Anonymity, that's our advantage. So we're safe—until Judas-ant identifies us, drags us forth from the swarm. Then we're lost; the giant foot comes down, there's no escape. We—"

The young woman raised her hand. "Listen."

A voice from the sound-line running under the ceiling molding, said, "The murder of a Telek, Forence Nollinrude, Liaison Lieutenant, by subversive conspiracy has been announced. The murderer, Ian Geskamp, superintendent of construction at the Swanscomb Valley Stadium, has disappeared. It is expected that he will implicate a number of confederates when captured."

Shorn sat quietly.

"What will they do if they catch him? Will they turn him over to the authorities?"

Shorn nodded. "They've announced the murder. If they want to maintain the fiction of their subservience to federal law, then they've got to submit to the regular courts. Once he's out of their direct custody, then no doubt he'll die— any one of a number of unpleasant deaths. And then there will be further acts of God. Another meteor into Geskamp's home town, something of the sort...."

"Why are you smiling?"

"It just occurred to me that Geskamp's home town was Cobent Village. That used to be in Swanscomb Valley; they've already wiped that one off the map. But they'll do something significant enough to point up the moral—that killing Teleks is a very expensive process."

"It's odd that they bother with legality at all."

"It means that they want no sudden showdown. Whatever revolution there is to be, they want it to come gradually, with as little dislocation as possible, no sudden flood of annoying administrative detail." He sat tapping his fingers nervously. "Geskamp was a good fellow. I'm wondering about this message at the hotel."

"If he were captured, drugged, your name and address would come out. You would be a valuable captive."

"Not while I can bite down on my back tooth. But I'm curious about that message. If it's from Geskamp he needs help, and we should help him. He knows about the mitrox under the stadium. The subject might arise during the course of questioning, especially under drugs, but we don't want to run the risk."

"Suppose it's a trick?"

"Well...we might learn something."

"I could get it," she said doubtfully.

Shorn frowned.

"No," she said, "I don't mean by walking in and asking for it; that would be foolish. You write a note authorizing delivery of the message to bearer."

The young woman said to the boy, "It's very important that you follow instructions exactly."

"Yes, miss."

The boy rode the slipway to the Marmion Tower, whose seventh and eighth floors were given over to the Cort Hotel. He rode the lift to the seventh floor, went quietly to the desk.

"Mr. Shorn sent me to pick up his mail." He passed the note across the desk.

The clerk hesitated, looked away in preoccupation, then without words handed the boy an envelope.

The boy returned to the ground floor, walked out on the street, where he paused, waited. Apparently no one followed him. He rode the slipway north, along the gray streets to the Tarrogat, stepped around the corner, jumped on the highspeed East Division slipway. Heavy commercial traffic growled through the street beside him, trucks and drays, a few surface cars. The boy spied a momentary gap, stepped to the outside band, jumped running into the street. He darted across, climbed on the slipway moving in the opposite direction, watching over his shoulder. No one followed. He rode a mile, past the Flatiron Y, turned into Grant Avenue, jumped to the stationary, crouched by the corner.

No one came hurrying after.

He crossed the street, entered the Grand Maison Cafe.

The food panel made an island down the center; to either side were tables. The boy walked around the food panel, ignoring a table where a young woman in a brown cloak sat by herself. He ducked out an entrance opposite to where he entered, rounded the building, entered once more.

The young woman rose to her feet, followed him out. At the exit they brushed together accidentally.

The boy went about his business, and the young woman turned, went back to the restroom. As she opened the door a black beetle buzzed through with her.

She ducked, looked around the ceiling, but the insect had disappeared. She went to a visiphone, tapped a code.

"Well?"

"I've got it."

"Anyone follow?"

"No. I watched him leave Marmion Tower. I watched behind him in—" her voice broke off.

"What's the matter?"

She said in a strained voice, "Get out of there fast. Hurry. Don't ask questions. Get away—*fast!*"

She hung up, pretending that she had not noticed the black bug pressed against the glass, crystal eyes staring at the visiphone dial.

She reached in her pouch, selected one of the four weapons she carried, drew it forth, closed her eyes, snapped the release.

White glare flooded the room, seared behind her closed lids. She ran out the door, picked up the dazed bug in her handkerchief, stuffed it into her pouch. It was strangely heavy, like a slug of lead.

She must hurry. She ran from the restroom, up through the cafe, out into the street.

Safe among the crowds she watched six emergency vans vomit Black and Golds who rushed to the exits of the Grand Maison Cafe.

Bitterly she rode the slipway north. The Teleks controlled the police; it was no secret.

She wondered about the beetle in her pouch. It evinced no movement, no sign of life. If her supposition were correct, it would remain quiet so long as she kept light from its eyes, so long as she denied it reference points.

For an hour she wandered the city, intent on evading not only men, but also little black beetle-things. At last she ducked into a narrow passageway in the hard industry quarter, ran up a flight of wooden steps, entered a drab sitting room.

She went to a closet, found a small canister with a screw top, gingerly pushed the handkerchief and the beetle-thing inside, screwed down the lid.

She removed her long brown cloak, drew a cup of coffee from the dispenser, waited.

Half an hour passed. The door opened. Shorn looked in. His face was haggard and pale as a dog-skull, his eyes glowed with an unhealthy yellow light.

She jumped to her feet. "What's happened?"

"Sit still, Laurie, I'm all right." He slumped into a seat. She drew another cup of coffee, passed it to him. "What happened?"

His eyes burnt brighter. "As soon as I heard from you, I left the tavern. Twenty seconds later—no more—the place exploded. Flame shooting out the door, out the windows...thirty or forty people inside; I can hear them yelling now...." His mouth sagged. He licked his lips. "I hear them—"

Laurie controlled her voice. "Just ants."

Shorn assented with a ghastly grin. "The giant steps on forty ants, but the guilty ant, the marked ant, the intended ant—he's gone."

She told him about the black bug. He groaned ironically. "It was bad enough dodging spies and Black and Golds. Now little bugs—can it hear?"

"I don't know. I suppose so. It's shut up tight in the can, but sound probably gets through."

"We'd better move it."

She wrapped the can in a towel, tucked it in a closet, shut the door. When she returned, Shorn was eyeing her with a new look in his eye. "You thought very swiftly, Laurie."

"I had to."

"You still have the message?"

She handed the envelope across the table.

He read, " 'Get in touch with Clybom at the Perendailia.' "

"Do you know him?"

"No. We'll make discreet inquiries. I don't imagine there'll be anything good come out of it."

"It's so much—work."

"Easy for the giants. One or two of them manage the entire project. I've heard that the one called Dominion is in charge, and the others don't even realize there's dissatisfaction. Just as we appoint a dog-catcher, then dismiss the problem of stray dogs from our minds."

After a moment she asked, "Do you think we'll win, Will?"

"I don't know. We have nothing to lose." He yawned, stretched. "Tonight I meet Circumbright; you remember him?"

"He's the chubby little biophysicist."

Shorn nodded. "If you'll excuse me, I think I'll take a nap."

IV

At eleven o'clock Shorn descended to the street. The sky was bright with glow from the lakeshore entertainment strip, the luxury towers of downtown Tran.

He walked along the dark street till he came to Bellman Boulevard, and stepped out on to the slipway.

There was a cold biting wind and few people were aboard; the hum of the rollers below was noticeable. He turned into Stockbridge Street, and as he approached the quarter-mile strip of night stores, the slipway became crowded and Shorn felt more secure. He undertook a few routine precautions, sliding quickly through doors, to break contact with any spy-beetles that might have fixed on him.

At midnight the fog blew in thick from the harbor, smelling of oil, mercaptan, ammonia. Pulling up his hood Shorn descended a flight of stairs, pushed into a basement recreation hall, sidled past the dull-eyed men at the mechanical games. He walked directly toward the men's room, turned at the last minute into a short side corridor, passed through a door marked "Employees" into a workshop littered with bits and parts from the amusement machines.

Shorn waited a moment, ears alert for sound, then went to the rear of the room, unlocked a steel door, and slipped through into a second workshop, much more elaborately fitted than the first. A short, stout man with a big head and mild blue eyes looked up. "Hello, Will."

Shorn waved his hand. "Hello, Gormān."

He stood with his back to the door, looking around the molding for a black, apparently innocent, beetle. Nothing in sight. He crossed the room, scribbled on a bit of paper. "*We've got to search the room. Look for a flying spy-cell, like this.*" He sketched the beetle he carried with him in the canister, then appended a postscript. "*I'll cover the ventilator.*"

An hour's search revealed nothing.

Shorn sighed, relaxed. "Ticklish. If there was one of the things here, and it saw us searching, the Telek at the other end would have known the jig was up. We'd have been in trouble. A fire, an explosion. They missed me once already today by about ten seconds." He set the canister on a bench. "I've got one of the things in here. Laurie caught it; rare presence of mind. Her premise is, that if its eyes and ears are made useless—in other words, if it loses its identity on a spatial frame of reference—then it ceases to exist for the Teleks, and they can no longer manipulate it. I think she's right; the idea seems intuitively sound."

Gorman Circumbright picked up the canister, jiggled it.

"Rather heavy. Why did you bring it down here?"

"We've got to figure out a counter to it. It must function like a miniature video transmitter. I suppose Alvac Corporation makes them. If we can identify the band it broadcasts on, we can build ourselves detectors, warning units.

Circumbright sat looking at the can. "If it's still in operation, if it's still broadcasting, I can find out very swiftly."

He set the can beside an all-wave tuner. Shorn unscrewed the lid, gingerly removed the bug, still wrapped the cloth, set it on the bench. Circumbright pointed to a scale, glowing at several points. He started to speak, but Shorn motioned for silence, pointed to the bug. Circumbright nodded, wrote, *"The lower lines are possibly static, from the power source. The sharp line at the top is the broadcast frequency—very sharp. Powerful."*

Shorn replaced the bug in the can. Circumbright turned away from the tuner. "If it's insensitive to infrared we can see to take it apart, disconnect the power."

Shorn frowned doubtfully. "How could we be sure?"

"Give it to me." Circumbright clipped leads from an oscillograph to the back of the tuner, dialed to the spy-beetle's carrier frequency.

The oscillograph showed a normal sine-curve.

"Now. Turn out the lights."

Shorn threw the switch. The room was dark except for the dancing light of the oscillograph and the dull, red murk from the infrared projector.

Circumbright's bulk cut off the glow from the projector. Shorn watched the oscillograph face. There was no change in the wave.

"Good," said Circumbright. "And I think that if I strain my eyes I can—or better, reach in the closet and hand me the conversion lenses. Top shelf."

He worked fifteen minutes, then suddenly the carrier wave on the face of the oscillograph vanished. "Ah," sighed Circumbright. "That's got it. You can turn the lights back on now."

Together they stood looking down at the bug—a little black torpedo two inches long with two crystalline eyes bulging at each side of the head.

"Nice job," said Circumbright. "It's an Alvac product all right. I'll say a word to Graythorne; maybe he can introduce a few disturbing factors."

"What about that detector unit?"

Circumbright pursed his lips. "For each of the bugs there's probably a different frequency; otherwise they'd get their signals mixed up. But the power-bank probably radiates about the same in all cases. I can fix up a jury-rig which you can use for a few days, the Graythorne can bring us down some tailor-made jobs from Alvac, using the design data."

He crossed the room, found a bottle of red wine which he set beside Shorn. "Relax a few minutes."

Half an hour passed. Shorn watched quietly while Circumbright soldered together stock circuits, humming in a continuous tuneless drone.

"There," said Circumbright finally. "If one of those bugs gets within a hundred yards, this will vibrate, thump."

"Good." Shorn tucked the device tenderly in his breast pocket, while Circumbright settled himself into an armchair, stuffed tobacco in a pipe. Shorn watched him curiously. Circumbright, placid and unemotional as a man could be, revealed himself to Shorn by various small signs, such as pressing the tobacco home with a thumb more vigorous than necessary.

"I hear another Telek was killed yesterday."

"Yes. I was there."

"Who is this Geskamp?"

"Big blond fellow. What's the latest on him?"

"He's dead."

"Hm-m-m." Shorn was silent a moment. "How?"

"The Teleks turned him over to the federal marshal at Knoll. He was shot trying to escape."

Shorn felt as if anger were being pumped inside him, as if he were swelling, as if the pressure against his taut muscles were too great to bear.

"Take it easy," said Circumbright mildly.

"I'll kill Teleks from a sense of duty," said Shorn. "I won't enjoy it. But—and I feel ashamed, I'll admit—I *want* to kill the federal marshal at Knoll."

"It wasn't the federal marshal himself," said Circumbright. "It was two of his deputies. And it's always possible that Geskamp actually did try to escape. We'll know for sure tomorrow."

"How so?"

"We're moving out a little bit. There'll be an example made of those two if they're guilty. We'll narcotize them tonight, find out the truth. If they're working for the Teleks—they'll go." Circumbright spat on the floor. "Although I dislike the label of a terrorist organization."

"What else can we do? If we got a confession, turned them over to the Section Attorney, they'd be reprimanded, turned loose."

"True enough." Circumbright puffed meditatively.

Shorn moved restlessly in his chair. "It frightens me, the imminence, the urgency of all this—and how few people are aware of it! Surely there's never been an emergency so ill-publicized before! In a week, a month, three months, there'll be more dead people on Earth than live ones, unless we get the entire shooting-match at once in the stadium."

Circumbright puffed at his pipe. "Will, sometimes I wonder whether we're not approaching the struggle from the wrong direction."

"How so?"

"Perhaps instead of attacking the Teleks, we should be learning more of the fundamental nature of telekinetics."

Shorn leaned back fretfully. "The Teleks don't know themselves."

"A bird can't tell you much about aerodynamics. The Teleks have a disadvantage that is not at all obvious—the fact that action comes too easy, that they are under no necessity to think. To build a dam, they look at a mountain, move it down into the valley. If the damn gives way, they move down another mountain, but they never look at a slide rule. In this respect, at least, they represent a retrogression rather than an advance."

Shorn slowly opened and closed his hands, watching as if it were the first time he had ever seen them. "They're caught in the stream of life, like the rest of us. It's part of the human tragedy that there can't be any compromise; it's them or us."

Circumbright heaved a deep sigh. "I've racked my brains....Compromise. Why can't two kinds of people live together? Our abilities complement each other."

"One time it was that way. The first generation. The Teleks were still common men, perhaps a little peculiar in that things always turned out lucky for them. Then Joffrey and his Telekinetic Congress, and the reinforcing, the catalysis, the forcing, whatever it was—and suddenly they're different."

"If there were no fools," said Circumbright, "either among us or among them, we could co-inhabit the earth. There's the flaw in any compromise negotiation—the fact that fools, both among the Teleks and the common men."

"I don't quite follow you."

Circumbright gestured with his pipe. "There will always be Telek fools to antagonize common-man fools; then the common-man fools will ambush the Teleks, and the Teleks will be very upset, especially since for every Telek, there are forty Earth fools eager to kill him. So they use force, terror. Inexorable, inevitable. But—they have a choice. They can leave Earth, find a home somewhere among the planets they claim they visit; they can impose this reign of power; or they can return to humanity, renounce telekinesis entirely. Those are the choices open to them."

"And our choices?"

"We submit or we challenge. In the first instance we become slaves. In the second we either kill the Teleks, drive them away, or we all become dead men."

Shorn sipped at his wine glass. "We might all become Teleks ourselves."

"Or we might find a scientific means to control or cancel our telekinesis." Circumbright poured a careful finger of wine for himself. "My own instinct is to explore the last possibility."

"There's nowhere to get a foothold in the subject."

"Oh, I don't know. We have a number of observations. Telekinesis and teleportation have been known for thousands of years. It took the concentration of telekinetics at Joffrey's Congress to develop the power fully. We know that Telek children are telekinetic—whether by contagion or by genetics we can't be sure."

"Probably both. A genetic predisposition; parental training."

Circumbright nodded. "Probably both. Although as you know, in rare instances they reward a common man by making a Telek out of him."

"Evidently telekinesis is latent in everyone."

"There's a large literature of early experiments and observations. The so-called spiritualist study of poltergeists and house-demons might be significant."

Shorn remained silent.

"I've tried to systematize the subject," Circumbright continued, "deal with it logically. The first question seems to be, does the Law of Conservation of Energy apply or not? When a Telek floats a ton of iron across the sky by looking at it, is he creating energy or is he directing the use of energy from an unseen source? There is no way of knowing offhand."

Shorn stretched, yawned, settled back in his chair. "I have heard a metaphysical opinion, to the effect that the Telek uses nothing more than confidence. The universe that he perceives has reality only to the backdrop of his own brain. He sees a chair; the image of a chair exists in his mind. He orders the chair to move across the room. His confidence is so great that, in his mind, he believes he sees the chair move, and he bases his future actions on the perception. Somehow he is not disappointed. In other words, the chair has moved because he believes he has moved it."

Circumbright puffed placidly on his pipe.

Shorn grinned. "Go on; I'm sorry I interrupted you."

"Where does the energy come from? Is the mind a source, a valve or a remote control? There are the three possibilities. Force is applied; the mind directs the force. But does the force *originate* in the mind, is the force *collected, channeled through* the mind, or does the mind act like a modulator?"

Shorn slowly shook his head. "So far we have not even defined the type of energy at work. If we knew that, we might recognize the function of the mind."

"Or vice versa. It works either way. But if you wish, consider the force at work. In all cases, an object moves in a single direction. That is to say, there has been no observed case of an explosion or a compression. The object moves as a unit. How? Why? To say the mind projects a force-field is ignoring the issue, redefining at an equal level of abstraction."

"Perhaps the mind is able to control poltergeists—creatures like the old Persian genii."

Circumbright tapped the ash from his pipe. "I've considered the possibility. Who are the poltergeists? Ghosts? Souls of the dead? A matter of speculation. Why are the Teleks able to control them, and ordinary people not?"

Shorn grinned. "I assume these are rhetorical questions—because I don't have the answers."

"Perhaps a form of gravity is at work. Imagine a cup-shaped gravity screen around the object, open on the side the Telek desires motion. I have not calculated the gravitational acceleration generated by matter at its average universal density, from here to infinity, but I assume it would be insignificant. A millimeter a day, perhaps. Count the cup-shaped gravity screen out; likewise a method for rendering the object opaque to the passage of neutrinos in a given direction."

"Poltergeists, gravity, neutrinos—all eliminated. What have we left?"

Circumbright chuckled. "I haven't eliminated the poltergeists. But I incline to the Organic Theory. That is, the concept that all the minds and all the matter of the universe are interconnected, much like brain cells and muscular tissue of the body. When certain of these brain cells achieve a sufficiently close vinculum, they are able to control certain twitchings of the corporeal frame of the universe. How? Why? I don't know. After all, it's only an idea, a sadly anthropomorphic idea."

Shorn looked thoughtfully up at the ceiling. Circumbright was a three-way scientist. He not only proposed theories, he not only devised critical experiments to validate them, but he was an expert laboratory technician. "Does your theory suggest any practical application?"

Circumbright scratched his ear.

"Not yet. I need to cross-fertilize it with a few other notions. Like the metaphysics you brought up a few moments ago. If I only had a Telek who would submit himself to experiments, we might get somewhere...and I think I hear Dr. Kurgill."

He rose to his feet, padded to the door. He opened it; Shorn saw him stiffen.

A deep voice said, "Hello, Circumbright; this is my son. Cluche, meet Gorman Circumbright, one of our foremost tacticians."

The two Kurgills came into the laboratory. The father was short, spare, with simian length to his arms. He had a comical simian face with a high forehead, long upper lip, flat nose. The son resembled his father not at all: a striking young man with noble features, a proud crest of auburn hair, an extreme mode of dress, reminiscent of Telek style. The elder was quick of movement, talkative, warm; the younger was careful of eye and movement.

Circumbright turned toward Shorn. "Will—" he stopped short. "Excuse me," he said to the Kurgills. "If you'll sit down I'll be with you at once."

He hurried into the adjoining storeroom. Shorn stood in the shadows.

"What's the trouble?"

Shorn took Circumbright's hand, held it against the warning unit in his pocket.

Circumbright jerked. "The thing's vibrating!"

Shorn looked warily into the room beyond. "How well do you know the Kurgills?"

Circumbright said. "The doctor's my lifelong friend, I'd go my life for him."

"And his son?"

"I can't say."

They stared at each other, then by common accord, looked through the crack of the door. Cluche Kurgill had seated himself in the chair Shorn had vacated, while his father stood in front of him, teetering comfortably on his toes, hands behind his back.

"I'd swear that no bug slipped past us while I stood in the doorway," muttered Circumbright.

"No, I don't think it did."

"That means it's on one or the other of their persons."

"It might be unintentional—a plant. But how would the Teleks know the Kurgills intended to come down here?"

Shorn shook his head.

Circumbright sighed. "I guess not."

"The bug will be where it can see, but where it can't be seen—or at least, not noticed."

Their glances went to the ornate headdress Cluche Kurgill wore on one side of his head: a soft roll of gray-green leather, bound by a strip across his hair, trailing a dangle of moon-opals past his ear.

Circumbright said in a tight voice, "We can expect destruction at any time. Explosion—."

Shorn said slowly, "I doubt if they'll send an explosion. If they feel they are unsuspected, they'll prefer to bide their time."

Circumbright said huskily, "Well, what do you propose, then?"

Shorn hesitated a moment before replying. "We're in a devil of a ticklish position. Do you have a narco-hypnotic stringer handy?"

Circumbright nodded.

"Perhaps then..."

Two minutes later Circumbright rejoined the Kurgills. The old doctor was in a fine humor. "Gorman," he said to Circumbright, "I'm very proud of Cluche here. He's been a scapegrace all his life—but now he wants to make something of himself."

"Good," said Circumbright with hollow heartiness. "If he were of our conviction, I could use him right now—but I wouldn't want him to do anything against his—"

"Oh, no, not at all," said Cluche. "What's your problem?"

"Well, Shorn just left for a very important meeting—the regional chiefs—and he's forgotten his code book. I couldn't trust an ordinary messenger, but if you will deliver the code book you'd be doing us a great service."

"Any little thing I can do to help," said Cluche. "I'll be delighted."

His father regarded him with fatuous pride. "Cluche has surprised me. He caught me out just the day before yesterday, and now nothing must do but that he plunges in after me. Needless to say, I'm very pleased; glad to see that he's a chip off the old block; nothing stands in his way."

Circumbright said, "I can count on you, then? You'll have to follow instructions exactly."

"Quite all right, sir, glad to help."

"Good," said Circumbright. "First thing then—you'll have to change your clothes. You'd be too conspicuous as you are."

"Oh, now!" protested Cluche. "Surely a cloak—"

"No!" snapped Circumbright. "You'll have to dress as a dock worker from the skin out. No cloak would hide that headgear. In the next room you'll find some clothes. Come with me, I'll make a light."

He held open the door; reluctantly Cluche stepped through.

The door closed. Shorn expertly seized Cluche's neck, digging strong fingers into the motor nerves. Cluche stiffened, trembling.

Circumbright slapped the front of his neck with a barbful of drug, then fumbled for Cluche's headdress. He felt a smooth little object bulging with two eyes like a tadpole. He said easily, "Can't seem to find the light...." He tucked the bug into his pouch. "Here it is. Now—that fancy headgear. I'll put it into this locker; it'll be safe till you get back." He winked at Shorn, shoved the pouch into a heavy metal tool chest.

They looked down at the sprawled body. "There's not much time," said Circumbright. "I'll send Kurgill home and we'll have to get out ourselves." He looked regretfully around the room. "There's a lot of fine equipment here....We can get more I suppose."

Shorn clicked his tongue. "What will you tell Kurgill?"

"Um-m-m. The truth would kill him."

"Cluche was killed by the Teleks. He died defending the code book. The Teleks have his name; he'll have to go underground himself."

"He'll have to go under tonight. I'll warn him to lay low, say in Capistrano's, until we call him, then we can give him the bad news. As soon as he's gone we'll take Cluche out the back way, to Laurie's."

Cluche Kurgill sat in a chair, staring into space. Circumbright leaned back smoking his pipe. Laurie, in white pajamas and a tan robe, lay sidewise on a couch in the corner watching; Shorn sat beside her.

"How long have you been spying for the Teleks, Cluche?"

"Three days."

"Tell us about it."

"I found some writings of my father's which led me to believe he was a member of a suborganization. I needed money. I reported to a police sergeant who I knew to be interested. He wanted me to furnish him the details; I refused. I demanded to speak to a Telek. I threatened the policeman—"

"What is his name?"

"Sergeant Henry Lewis, of the Moxenwohl Precinct."

"Go on."

"Finally he arranged an appointment with Adlari Dominion. I met Dominion at the Pequinade, out in Vireburg. He gave me a thousand crowns and a spy-cell which I was to carry with me at all times. When anything interesting occurred I was to press an attention button."

"What were your instructions?"

"I was to become a conspirator along with my father, accompanying him as much as possible. If my efforts resulted in the arrest of important figures, he hinted that I might be made a Telek myself."

"Did he intimate how this metamorphosis is accomplished?"

"No."

"When are you to report to Dominion again?"

"I am to contact him by visiphone at two p.m. tomorrow, at Glarietta Pavilion."

"Is there any password or identification code?"

"No."

Silence held the room for several minutes. Shorn stirred, rose to his feet. "Gorman—suppose I were to be metamorphosed, suppose I were to become a Telek."

Circumbright looked, grimaced, straightened up in his seat.

Shorn watched expectantly. "Could it be done?"

"Oh. I see. Give you more nose, a longer chin, fuller cheeks, a lot of red hair—."

"And Cluche's clothes."

"You'd pass."

"Especially if I come with information."

"That's what's puzzling me. What kind of information could you give Dominion that would please him but wouldn't hurt us?"

Shorn told him.

Circumbright puffed on his pipe. "It's a big decision. But it's a good exchange. Unless he's got the same thing already, from other sources."

"Such as Geskamp? In which case, we lose nothing."

"True." Circumbright went to the visiphone. "Tino? Bring your gear over to—" he looked at Laurie. "What's the address?"

"Two-nine two-four fourteen Martinvelt."

V

The red-haired man moved with a taut wiriness that had not been characteristic of Cluche Kurgill. Laurie inspected him critically.

"Walk slower, Will. Don't flail your arms so. Cluche was very languid."

"Check this." Shorn walked across the room.

"Better."

"Very well. I'm gone. Wish me luck. My first stop is the old workshop for Cluche's spy-cell. He'd hardly be likely to leave it there."

"But aren't you taking a chance, going back to the workshop?"

"I don't think so. I hope not. If the Teleks planned to destroy it, they would have done so last night." He waved his hand abruptly and was gone.

He rode the slipway, aping the languorous and lofty condescension he associated with Cluche. The morning had been overcast and blustery, with spatters of cold rain, but at noon the clouds broke. The sun surged through gaps in the hurrying wrack, and the great gray buildings of Tran stood forth like proud lords. Shorn tilted his head back; this was the grandeur of simple bulk, but nevertheless impressive. He himself preferred construction on a smaller scale, buildings to suit a lesser number of more highly individualized people. He thought of the antique Mediterranean temples, gaudy in their pinks and green and blues, although now the marble had bleached white. Such idiosyncrasy was possible, even enforced, in the ancient monarchies. Today every man, in theory his own master, was required to mesh with his fellows, like a part in a great gear cluster. The culture-colors and culture-tones came out at the common denominator, the melange of all colors: gray. Buildings grew taller and wider from motives of economy—the volume increased by the cube but the enclosing surface only by the square. The *motif* was utilitarianism, mass policy, each tenant relinquishing edges and fringes of his personality, until only the common basic core—a sound roof, hot and cold water, good light, air-conditioning, and good elevator service—remained.

People living in masses, thought Shorn, were like pebbles on a beach, each grinding and polishing his neighbor until all were absolutely uniform. Color and flair were to be found only in the wilderness and among the Teleks. Imagine a world populated by Teleks; imagine the four thousand expanded to four hundred million, four billion! First to go would be the cities. There would be no more concentrations, no more giant gray buildings, no directed rivers of men and women. Humanity would explode like a nova. The cities would corrode and crumble, great mournful hulks, the final monuments to medievalism. Earth would be too small, too limited. Out to the planets, where the Teleks claimed to roam at will. Flood Mars with blue oceans, filter the sky of Venus. Neptune, Uranus, Pluto—call them in, bestow warm new orbits upon them. Bring in even Saturn, so vast and yet with a surface gravity only a trifle more than Earth's....But these great works, suppose they exhausted the telekinetic energy, wherever it originated? Suppose some morning the Teleks awoke and found the power gone! Then—the crystal sky-castles falling! Food, shelter, warmth needed, and no secure gray cities, no ant-hill buildings, none of the pedestrian energies of metal and heat and electricity! Then what calamity! What wailing and cursing!

Shorn heaved a deep sigh. Speculation. Telekinetic energy might well be infinite. Or it might be at the point of exhaustion at this moment. Speculation, and not germane to his present goal.

He frowned. Perhaps it was important. Perhaps some quiet circuit in his mind was at work, aligning him into new opinions....

Ahead was the basement recreation hall. Shorn realized guiltily that he had been swinging along at his own gait, quite out of character with the personality of Cluche Kurgill. Best not forget these details; there would be opportunity for only one mistake.

He descended the stairs, strode through the hall, past the clicking, glowing, humming game machines, where men, rebelling at the predict-ability of their lives, came to buy synthetic surprise.

He walked unchallenged through the door marked "Employees"; at the next door he paused, wondering whether he had remembered to bring the key, wondering if a spy-cell might be hidden in the shadows, watching the door.

If so, would Cluche Kurgill be likely to possess a key? It was in the bounds of possibility, he decided, and in any event would not be interpre-ted as suspicious.

Shorn groped into his pouch. The key was there. He opened the door and assuming the furtive part of a spy entered the workshop.

It was as they had left it the night before. Shorn went quickly to the tool chest, found Circumbright's pouch, brought forth the bug, set it carefully into his headdress.

Now—get out as fast as possible. He looked at his watch. Twelve noon. At two, Cluche's appointment with Adlari Dominion, chief of the Telek Liaison Committee.

Shorn ate an uncomfortable lunch in one corner of the Mercantile Mart Foodairum, a low-ceilinged acreage dotted with tables precisely as a tile floor, and served by a three-tier display of food moving slowly under a transparent case. His head itched furiously under the red toupee, and he dared not scratch lest he disturb Tino's elaborate effort. Secondly, he decided that the Foodarium, the noon resort of hurried day-workers, was out of character for Cluche Kurgill. Among the grays and dull greens and browns, his magnificent Telek-style garments made him appear like a flamingo in a chicken-run. He felt glances of dull hostility; the Teleks were envied but respected; one of their own kind aping the Teleks was despised with the animosity that found no release elsewhere.

Shorn ate quickly and departed. He followed Zyke Alley into Multiflores Park, where he sauntered back and forth among the dusty sycamores.

At two he sat himself deliberately in a kiosk, coded Glarietta Pavilion on the visiphone. The connection clicked home; the screen glowed with a fanciful black and white drawing of Glarietta Pavilion, and a terse man's voice spoke. "Glarietta Pavilion."

"I want to speak to Adlari Dominion; Cluche Kurgill calling."

A thin face appeared, inquisitive, impertinent, with a lumpy nose, pale blue eyes set at a birdlike slant. "What do you want?"

Shorn frowned. He had neglected an important item of information; it would hardly do to ask the man in the visiphone if he were Adlari Dominion whom he was supposed to have met three days previously.

"I had an appointment for today at two," and cautiously he watched the man in the screen.

"You can report to me."

"No," said Shorn, now confident. The man was too pushing, too authoritative. "I want to speak to Adlari Dominion. What I have to say is not for your ears."

The thin man glared. "I'll be the judge of that; Dominion can't be bothered every five minutes."

"If Dominion learns that you are standing in my way, he will not be pleased."

The thin face flushed red. His hand swept up, the screen went pale green. Shorn waited.

The screen lit once more, showing a bright room with high white walls. Windows opened on sun-dazzled clouds. A man, thin as the first to answer the screen, but somber, with gray hair and oil-black eyes, looked quietly at him. Under the bore of the sharp eyes, Shorn suddenly felt uneasy. Would his disguise hold up?

"Well, Kurgill, what do you have to tell me?"

"It's a face-to-face matter."

"Hardly wise," Dominion commented. "Don't you trust the privacy of the visiphone? I assure you it's not tapped."

"No. I trust the visiphone. But—I stumbled on something big. I want to be sure I get what's coming to me."

"Oh." Dominion made no play at misunderstanding. "You've been working—how long?"

"Three days."

"And already you expect the great reward it's in our power to bestow?"

"It's worth it. If I'm a Telek, it's to my advantage to help you. If I'm not—it isn't. Simple as that."

Dominion frowned. "You're hardly qualified to estimate the value of your information."

"Suppose I knew of a brain disease which attacks only Teleks. Suppose I knew that inside of a year half or three-quarters of the Teleks would be dead?"

Dominion's face changed not a flicker. "Naturally I want to know about it."

Shorn made no reply.

Dominion said slowly, "If such is your information, and we authenticate it, you will be rewarded suitably."

Shorn shook his head. "I can't take the chance. This is my windfall. I've got to make sure I get what I'm after; I may not have another chance."

Dominion's mouth tightened, but he said mildly enough, "I understand your viewpoint."

"I want to come up to the Pavilion. But a word of warning to you; there's no harm in clear understanding between friends."

"None whatever."

"Don't try drugs on me. I've got a cyanide capsule in my mouth. I'll kill myself before you get something for nothing."

Dominion smiled grimly. "Very well, Kurgill. Don't execute yourself, swallow it by mistake."

Shorn smiled likewise. "Only as a gesture of protest. How shall I come up to Glarietta?"

"Hire a cab."

"Openly?"

"Why not?"

"You're not afraid of counterespionage?"

Dominion's eyes narrowed; his head tilted slightly. "I thought we discussed that at our previous meeting."

Shorn took care not to protest his recollection too vehemently. "Very well, I'll be right up."

Glarietta Pavilion floated high above the ocean, a fairy-book cloud-castle—shining white terraces, ranked towers with red and blue parasol roofs, gardens verdant with foliage and vines trailing down into the air.

The cab slid down on a landing flat. Shorn alighted. The driver looked at him without favor. "Want me to wait?"

"No, you can go." Shorn thought wryly, he'd either be leaving under his own power or not be leaving at all.

A door slid back before him; he entered a hall walled with russet, orange, purple, and green prisms, glowing in the brilliant upper-air light. In a raised alcove sat a young woman, a beautiful creature with glossy butter-colored hair, a cream-smooth face.

"Yes, sir?" she asked, impersonally courteous.

"I want to see Adlari Dominion. I'm Cluche Kurgill."

She touched a key below her. "To your right."

He climbed a glass staircase which spiraled up a green glass tube, came out in a waiting room walled with gold-shot red rock that had never been quarried on Earth. Dark-green ivy veiled one wall; white columns opposite made a graceful frame into an herbarium full of green light and lush green growth, white and scarlet flowers.

Shorn hesitated, looked around him. A golden light blinked in the wall, an aperture appeared. Adlari Dominion stood in the opening. "Come in, Kurgill."

Shorn stepped into the wash of light, and for a moment lost Dominion in the dazzle. When vision returned, Dominion was lounging in a hammock-chair supported by a glistening rod protruding horizontally from the wall. A red-leather ottoman was the only other article of furniture visible. Three of the walls were transparent glass, giving on a magnificent vista: clouds bathed in sunlight, blue sky, blue sea.

Dominion pointed to the ottoman. "Have a seat."

The ottoman was only a foot high; sitting in it Shorn would be forced to crane his neck to see Dominion.

"No, thanks. I prefer to stand." He put a foot on the ottoman, inspected Dominion coolly, eye to eye.

Dominion said evenly, "What do you have to tell me?"

Shorn started to speak, but found it impossible to look into the smoldering black eyes and think at the same time. He turned his eyes out the window to a pinnacle of white cloud. "I've naturally considered this situation carefully. If you've done the same—as I imagine you have—then there's no point in each of us trying to outwit the other. I have information that's important, critically important, to a great number of Teleks. I want to trade this information for Telek status." He glanced toward Dominion whose eyes had never faltered, looked away once more.

"I'm trying to arrange this statement with absolute clarity, so there'll be complete understanding between us. First, I want to remind you, I have poison in my mouth. I'll kill myself before I part with what I know, and I guarantee you'll never have another chance to learn what I can tell you." Shorn glanced earnestly sidewise at Dominion. "No hypnotic drug can act fast enough to prevent me from biting open my cyanide—well, enough of that.

"Second: I can't trust any verbal or written contract you make; if I accepted such a contract I'd have no means to enforce it. You are in a stronger position. If you deliver your part of the bargain, and I fail to deliver my part, you can still arrange that I be—well, penalized. Therefore, to demonstrate your good faith, you must make delivery before I do.

"In other words, make me a Telek. Then I'll tell you what I know."

Dominion sat staring at him a full thirty seconds. Then he said softly, "Three days ago Cluche Kurgill was not so rigorous."

"Three days ago, Cluche Kurgill did not know what he knows now."

Dominion said abruptly, "I cannot argue with your exposition. If I were you, in your position, I would make the same stipulation. However"—he looked Shorn keenly up and down—"three days ago I would have considered you an undesirable adjunct."

Shorn assumed a lofty expression. "Judging from the Teleks I have known, I would not have assumed you to be so critical."

"You talk past your understanding," said Dominion crisply. "Do you think that men like Nollinrude, for instance, who was just killed, are typical of the Teleks? Do you think that we are all careless of our destiny?" His mouth twisted contemptuously. "There are forces at work which you do not know of, tremendous patterns laid out for the future. But enough; these are high-level ideas."

He floated clear of his chair, lowered to the floor. "I agree to your stipulation. Come with me, we'll get it over with. You see, we are not inflexible; we can move swiftly and decisively when we wish."

He led Shorn back into the green glass tube, jerked himself to the upper landing, watched impatiently while Shorn circled up the steps.

"Come." He stepped out on a wide white terrace bathed in afternoon sunlight, went directly to a low table on which rested a cubical block of marble.

He reached into a cabinet under the table, pulled out a small speaker, spoke into the mesh. "The top two hundred to Glarietta Pavilion." He turned back to Shorn. "Naturally there'll be certain matters you must familiarize yourself with."

"In order to become a Telek, you mean?"

"No, no," snapped Dominion. "That's a simple mechanical matter. Your perspective must be adjusted; you'll be living with a new orientation toward life."

"I had no idea it was quite so involved."

"There's a great deal you don't understand." He motioned brusquely. "Now to business. Watch that marble block on the table. Think of it as part of yourself, controlled by your own nervous impulses. No, don't look around; fix on the marble block. I'll stand here." He took a place near the table. "When I point to the right, move it to the right. Mind now, the cube is part of your organism, part of your flesh, like your hands and feet."

There was murmuring and a rustle behind Shorn; obedient to Dominion he fastened his eyes on the cube.

"Now." Dominion pointed to the left.

Shorn willed the cube to the left.

"The cube is part of you," said Dominion. "Your own body."

Shorn felt a cool tremor at his skin. The cube moved to the left.

Dominion pointed to the right. Shorn willed the cube to the right. The tingling increased. It was as if he were gradually finding himself immersed in cool carbonated water.

Left. Right. Left. Right. The cube seemed to be nearer to him, though he had not moved. As near as his own hand. His mind seemed to break through a tough sphincter into a new medium, cool and wide; he saw the world in a sudden new identity, something part of himself.

Dominion stepped away from the table; Shorn was hardly conscious that he no longer made directive gestures. He moved the cube right, left, raised it six feet into the air, twenty feet, sent it circling high around the sky. As he followed it with his eyes, he became aware of Teleks standing silently behind him, watching expressionlessly.

He brought the cube back to the table. Now he knew how to do it. He lifted himself into the air, moved across the terrace, set himself down. When he looked around the Teleks had gone.

Dominion wore a cool smile. "You take hold with great ease."

"It seems natural enough. What is the function of the others, the Teleks behind on the terrace?"

Dominion shrugged. "We know little of the actual mechanism. At the beginning, of course, I helped you move the cube, as did the others. Gradually we let our minds rest, and you did it all."

Shorn stretched. "I feel myself the center, the hub, of everything—as far as I can see."

Dominion nodded without interest. "Now—come with me." He sped through the air. Shorn followed, exulting in his new power and freedom. Dominion paused by the corner of the terrace, glanced over his shoulder. Shorn saw his face in the fore-shortened angle: white, rather pinched features, eyes subtly tilted, brows drawn down, mouth subtly down-curving. Shorn's elation gave way to sudden wariness. Dominion had arranged the telekinetic indoctrination with a peculiar facility. The easiest way to get the desired information, certainly; but was Dominion sufficiently free from vindictiveness to accept defeat? Shorn considered the expression he had surprised on Dominion's face.

It was a mistake to assume that any man, Telek or not, would accept with good grace the terms dictated by a paid turncoat.

Dominion would restrain himself until he learned what Shorn could tell him; then—and then?

Shorn slowed his motion. How could Dominion arrange a moment of gloating before he finally administered the *coup de grace*? Poison seemed most likely. Shorn grinned. Dominion would consider it beautifully just if Shorn could be killed with his own poison. A sharp blow or pressure under the jaw would break the capsule in his tooth.

Somehow Dominion would manage.

They entered a great echoing hall, suffused with green-yellow light that entered through the panes in the high-vaulted dome. The floor was silvershot marble; dark-green foliage grew in formal raised boxes. The air was fresh and odorous with the scent of leaves.

Dominion crossed without pause. Shorn halted halfway across.

Dominion turned his head. "Come."

"Where?"

Dominion's mouth slowly bent into a grimace that was unmistakably dangerous. "Where we can talk."

"We can talk here. I can tell you what I want to tell you in ten seconds. Or if you like, I'll take you to the source of the danger."

"Very well," said Dominion. "Suppose you reveal the nature of the threat against the Teleks. A brain disease, you said?"

"No. I used the idea as a figure of speech. The danger I refer to is more cataclysmic than a disease. Let's go out in the open air. I feel constricted." He grinned at Dominion.

Dominion drew in a deep breath. It must infuriate him, thought Shorn, to be commanded and forced to obey a common man and a traitor to boot. Shorn made a careless gesture. "I intend to keep my part of the bargain; let's have no misunderstanding there. However—I want to escape with my winnings, if you understand me."

"I understand you," said Dominion. "I understand you very well." He made an internal adjustment, managed to appear almost genial. "However, perhaps you misjudge my motives. You are a Telek now; we conduct ourselves by a strict code of behavior which you must learn."

Shorn put on a face as gracious as Dominion's. "I suggest then that we hold our conference down on Earth."

Dominion pursed his lips. "You must acclimate yourself to Telek surroundings—think, act, like a Telek."

"In due time," said Shorn. "At the moment I'm rather confused; the sense of power comes as a great intoxication."

"It apparently has not affected your capacity for caution," Dominion observed dryly.

"I suggest that we at least go out into the open, where we can talk at leisure."

Dominion sighed. "Very well."

VI

Laurie went restlessly to the dispenser, drew tea for herself, coffee for Circumbright. "I just can't seem to sit still...."

Circumbright inspected the pale face with scientific objectivity. If Laurie condescended to even the slightest artifice or coquetry, he thought, she would become a creature of tremendous charm. He watched her appreciatively as she went to the window, looked up into the sky.

Nothing to see but reflected glow; nothing to hear but the hum of far traffic.

She returned to the couch. "Have you told Doctor Kurgill...of Cluche?"

Circumbright stirred his tea. "Naturally I couldn't tell him the truth."

"No." Laurie looked off into space. She shuddered. "I've never been so nervous before. Suppose—" her forebodings could find no words.

"You're very fond of Shorn, aren't you?"

The quick look, the upward flash of her eyes, was enough.

They sat in silence.

"Sh," said Laurie. "I think he's coming."

Circumbright said nothing.

Laurie rose to her feet. They both watched the door latch. It moved. The door slid back. The hall was empty.

Laurie gasped in something like terror. There came a tapping at the window.

They wheeled. Shorn was outside, floating in the air.

For a moment they stood paralyzed. Shorn rapped with his knuckles; they saw his mouth form the words, "Let me in."

Laurie walked stiffly to the window, swung it open. Shorn jumped down into the room.

"Why did you scare us like that?" she asked indignantly.

"I'm proud of myself. I wanted to demonstrate my new abilities." He drew himself a cup of coffee. "I guess you'll want to hear my adventures."

"Of course!"

He sat down at the table and described his visit to Glarietta Pavilion.

Circumbright listened placidly. "And now what?"

"And now—you've got a Telek to experiment on. Unless Dominion conceives a long-distance method of killing me. He's spending a restless night, I should imagine."

Circumbright grunted.

"First," said Shorn, "they put a bug on me. I expected it. They knew I expected it. I got rid of it in the Beaux-Arts Museum. Then I began thinking, since they would expect me to dodge the bug and feel secure after I'd done so, no doubt they had a way to locate me again. Tracker material sprayed on my clothes, fluorescent in a nonvisual frequency. I threw away Cluche's clothes, which I didn't like in the first place, washed in three changes of solvicine and water, disposed of the red wig. Cluche Kurgill has disappeared. By the way, where is Cluche's body?"

"Safe."

"We can let it be found tomorrow morning. With a sign on him reading. 'I am a Telek spy.' Dominion will certainly hear of it; he'll think I'm dead, and that will be one problem the less."

"Good idea."

"But poor old Doctor Kurgill," remonstrated Laurie.

"He'll never believe such a note."

"No...I suppose not." She looked Shorn over from head to feet. "Do you feel different from before?"

"I feel as if all of creation were part of me. Identification with the cosmos, I guess you'd call it."

"But how does it work?"

Shorn deliberated. "I'm really not sure. I can move the chair the same way I move my arm, with about the same effort."

"Evidently," said Circumbright, "Geskamp had told them nothing of the mitrox under the stadium."

"They never asked him. It was beyond their imagination that we could conceive such an atrocity." Shorn laughed. "Dominion was completely flabbergasted. Bowled over. For a few minutes I think he was grateful to me."

"And then?"

"And then, I suppose he remembered his resentment, and began plotting how best to kill me. But I told him nothing until we were in the open air; any weapon he held I could protect myself from. A bullet I could think aside, even back at him; a heat-gun I could deflect."

"Suppose his will on the gun and your will clashed?" Circumbright asked mildly.

"I don't know what would happen. Perhaps nothing. Like a man vacillating between two impulses. Or perhaps the clash and the subsequent lack of reaction would invalidate both our confidence, and down we'd fall into the ocean. Because now we were standing on nothing, a thousand feet over the ocean."

"Weren't you afraid, Will?" asked Laurie.

"At first—yes. But a person becomes accustomed to the sensation very quickly. It's a thing we've all experienced in our dreams. Perhaps it's only a trifling aberration that stands in the way of telekinesis for everyone."

Circumbright grunted, loaded his pipe. "Perhaps we'll find that out, along with the other things."

"Perhaps. Already I begin to look at life and existence from another viewpoint."

Laurie looked worried. "I thought things were just the same."

"Fundamentally, yes. But this feeling of power—of not being tied down—" Shorn laughed. "Don't look at each other like that. I'm not dangerous. I'm only a Telek by courtesy. And now, where can we get three pressure suits?"

"At this time of night? I don't know."

"No matter. I'm a Telek. We'll get them. Provided of course you'd like to visit the Moon. All-expense tour, courtesy of Adlari Dominion. Laurie, would you like to fly up, fast as light, fast as thought, stand in the Earthshine, on the lip of Erastosthenes, looking out over the Mare Imbrium?"

She laughed uneasily. "I'd love it, Will. But...I'm scared."

"What about you, Gorman?"

"No. You two go. There'll be other chances for me."

Laurie jumped to her feet. Her cheeks were pink, her mouth was red and half open in excitement. Shorn looked at her with a sudden new vision. "Very well, Gorman. Tomorrow you can start your experiments. Tonight—"

Laurie found herself picked up, carried out through the window.

"Tonight," said Shorn by her side, "we'll pretend that we're souls—happy souls—exploring the universe."

Circumbright lived in a near-abandoned suburb to the north of Tran. His house was a roomy old antique, rearing like a balky horse over the Meyne River. Big industrial plants blocked the sky in all directions; the air reeked with foundry fumes, sulfur, chlorine, tar, burnt-earth smells.

Within, the house was cheerful and untidy. Circumbright's wife was a tall, strange woman who worked ten hours a day in her studio, sculpturing dogs and horses. Shorn had met her only once; so far as he knew she had no interest or even awareness of Circumbright's anti-Telek activities.

He found Circumbright basking in the sun, watching the brown river water roll past. He sat on a little porch he had built apparently for no other purpose but this.

Shorn dropped a small cloth sack in his lap. "Souvenirs."

Circumbright opened the bag unhurriedly, pulled out a handful of stones, each tagged with a card label. He looked at the first, hefted it. "Agate." He read the label. " 'Mars.' Well, well." A bit of black rock was next. "Gabbro? From—let's see. 'Gannymede.' My word, you wandered far afield." He shot a bland blue glance up at Shorn. "Telekinesis seems to have agreed with you. You've lost that haggard, hunted expression. Perhaps I'll have to become a Telek myself."

"You don't look haggard and hunted. Quite the reverse."

Circumbright returned to the rocks. "Pumice. From the Moon, I suppose." He read the label. "No—Venus. You made quite a trip."

Shorn looked up into the sky. "Rather hard to describe. There's naturally a feeling of loneliness. Darkness. Something like a dream. Out on a Gannymede we were standing on a ridge, obsidian, sharp as a razor. Jupiter filled a third of the sky, the red spot right in the middle, looking at us. There was a pink and blue dimness. Peculiar. Black rock, the big bright planet. It was...weird. I thought, suppose the power fails me now, suppose we can't get home? It gave me quite a chill."

"You seem to have made it."

"Yes, we made it." Shorn seated himself, thrust out his legs. "I'm not hunted and haggard, but I'm confused. Two days ago I thought I had a good grasp on my convictions—."

"And now?"

"Now—I don't know."

"About what?"

"About our efforts. Their ultimate effect, assuming we're successful."

"Hm-m-m." Circumbright rubbed his chin. "Do you still want to submit to experiments?"

"Of course. I want to know why and how telekinesis works."

"When will you be ready?"

"Whenever you wish."

"Now?"

"Why not? Let's get started."

"As soon as you're ready, we'll try encephalographs as a starting point."

Circumbright was tired. His face, normally pink and cherubic, sagged; filling his pipe, his fingers trembled.

Shorn leaned back in the leather chaise lounge, regarded Circumbright with mild curiosity. "Why are you so upset?"

Circumbright gave the litter of paper on the workbench a contemptuous flick of the fingers. "It's the cursed inadequacy of the technique, the instruments. Trying to paint miniatures with a whisk broom, fix a watch with a pipe wrench. There"—he pointed—"encephalograms. Every lobe of your brain. Photographs—by x-ray, by planar section, by metabolism triggering. We've measured your energy flow so closely that if you tossed me a paper clip I'd find it on paper somewhere."

"And there's what?"

"Nothing suggestive. Wavy lines on the encephalograms. Increased oxygen absorption. Pineal tumescence. All gross by-products of whatever is happening."

Shorn yawned and stretched. "About as we expected."

Circumbright nodded heavily. "As we expected."

VII

In Laurie's apartment on upper Martinvelt, Shorn and Circumbright sat drinking coffee.

Circumbright was unaccustomedly nervous and consulted his watch at five-minute intervals.

Shorn watched quizzically. "Who are you expecting?"

Circumbright glanced quickly, guiltily, around the room. "I suppose there's no spy-beetle anywhere close."

"Not according to the detector cell."

"I'm waiting for the messenger. A man called Luby, from East Shore."

"I don't think I know him."

"You'd remember him if you did."

Laurie said, "I think I hear him now."

She went to the door, slid it back. Luby came into the room, quiet as a cat. He was a man of forty who looked no more than seventeen. His skin was clear gold, his features chiseled and handsome, his hair a close cap of tight bronze curls. Shorn thought of the Renaissance Italians—Cesare Borgia, Lorenzo Medici.

Circumbright made introductions which Luby acknowledged with a nod of the head and a lambent look; then he took Circumbright aside, muttered in a rapid flow of syllables.

Circumbright raised his eyebrows, asked a question; Luby shook his head, responded impatiently. Circumbright nodded, and without another word Luby left the room, as quietly as he had entered.

"There's a high-level meeting—policy-makers—out at Portinari Gate. We're wanted." He rose to his feet, stood indecisively a moment. "I suppose we had better be going."

Shorn went to the door, looked out into the corridor. "Luby moves quietly. Isn't it unusual to concentrate top minds in a single meeting?"

"Unprecedented. I suppose it's something important."

Shorn thought a moment. "Perhaps it would be better to say nothing of my new…achievements."

"Very well."

They flew north through the night, into the foothills, and Lake Paienza spread like a dark blot below, rimmed by the lights of Portinari.

Portinari Gate was a rambling inn six hundred years old, high on a hillside, overlooking lake and town. They dropped to the soft turf in the shadow of great pines, walked to the back entrance.

Circumbright knocked, and they felt a quiet scrutiny.

The door opened, an iron-faced woman with a halo of iron-gray hair stood facing them. "What do you want?"

Circumbright muttered a password; silently she stepped back. Shorn felt her wary scrutiny as he and Laurie entered the room.

A brown-skinned man with black eyes and gold rings in his ears flipped up a hand. "Hello, Circumbright."

"Hello…Thursby, this is Will Shorn, Laurita Chelmsford."

Shorn inspected the brown man with interest. The Great Thursby, rumored coordinator of the world-wide anti-Telek underground.

There were others in the room, sitting quietly, watchfully. Circumbright nodded to one or two, then took Shorn and Laurie to the side.

"I'm surprised," he said. "The brains of the entire movement are here." He shook his head. "Rather ticklish."

Shorn felt of the detector. "No spy-cells."

More people gathered, until possibly fifty men and women occupied the room. Among the last to enter was the young old Luby.

A stocky dark-skinned man rose to his feet. "This meeting is a departure from our previous methods, and I hope it won't be necessary again for a long time."

Circumbright whispered to Shorn, "That's Kasselbarg, European Post."

Kasselbarg swung a slow glance around the room. "We're starting a new phase of the campaign. Our first was organizational; we built a world-wide underground, a communication system, set up a ladder of command. Now—the second stage; preparation for our eventual action...which, of course, will constitute the third stage.

"We all know the difficulties under which we work; since we can't hold up a clear and present danger, our government is not sympathetic to us, and in many cases actively hostile—especially in the persons of suborned police officials. Furthermore, we're under the compulsion of striking an absolutely decisive blow on our first sally. There won't be a second chance for us. The Teleks must be"—he paused—"they must be killed. It's a course toward which we all feel an instinctive revulsion, but any other course bares us to the incalculable power of the Teleks. Now, any questions, any comments?"

Shorn, compelled by a sudden pressure he only dimly understood, rose to his feet. "I don't want to turn the movement into a debating society—but there's another course where killing is unnecessary. It erases the need of the decisive blow, it gives us a greater chance of success."

"Naturally," said Kasselbarg mildly, "I'd like to hear your plan."

"No operation, plan it as carefully as you will, can guarantee the death of every Telek. And those who aren't killed may go crazy in anger and fear; I can picture a hundred million deaths, five hundred million, a billion deaths in the first few seconds after the operation starts—but does not quite succeed."

Kasselbarg nodded. "The need for a hundred percent *coup* is emphatic. The formulation of such a plan will constitute Phase Two, of which I just now spoke. We certainly can't proceed on any basis other than a ninety-nine percent probability of fulfillment."

The iron-faced woman spoke. "There are four thousand Teleks, more or less. Here on Earth ten thousand people die every day. Killing the Teleks seems a small price to pay for security against absolute tyranny. It's either act now, while we have limited freedom of choice, or dedicate the human race to slavery for as long into the future as we can imagine."

Shorn looked around the faces in the room. Laurie was sympathetic; Circumbright looked away uncomfortably; Thursby frowned thoughtfully; Kasselbarg waited with courteous deference.

"Everything you say is true," Shorn said. "I would be the most ruthless of us all, if these four thousand deaths did not rob the human race of the most precious gift it possesses. Telekinesis to date has been misused; the Teleks have been remarkable for their selfishness and egotism. But in reacting to the Telek's mistakes, we should not make mistakes on our own."

Thursby said in a cool, clear voice, "What is your concrete proposal, Mr. Shorn?"

"I believe we should dedicate ourselves, not to killing Teleks, but to giving telekinesis to every sane man and woman."

A small red-haired man sneered. "The ancient fallacy, privilege for the chosen ones—in this case, the sane."

Shorn smiled. "Better than privilege—of this kind—for the insane. But let me return to my fundamental proposition: that taking telekinesis out of monopoly and broadcasting it is a better solution to the problem than killing Teleks. One way is up, the other down; building versus destruction. In one direction we put mankind at its highest potential for achievement; in the other we have four thousand dead Teleks, if our plan succeeds. Always latent is the possibility of a devastated world."

Thursby said, "You're convincing, Mr. Shorn. But aren't you operating on the unproved premise that universal telekinesis is a possibility? Killing the Teleks seems to be easier than persuading them to share their power; we've got to do one or the other."

Shorn shook his head. "There are at least two methods to create Teleks. The first is slow and a long-range job: that is, duplicating the conditions that produced the first Teleks. The second is much easier, quicker, and, I believe, safer. I have good reason for—" he stopped short. A faint buzzing, a vibration in his pocket.

The detector.

He turned to Luby, who stood by the door. "Turn out the lights! There's a Telek spy-cell nearby! Out with the lights, or we're all done for."

Luby hesitated. Shorn cursed under his breath. Thursby rose to his feet, startled and tense. "What's going on?"

There was a pounding at the door. "Open up, in the name of the law."

Shorn looked at the windows: the tough vitripane burst out; the windows were wide open. "Quick, out the window!"

Circumbright said in a voice of deadly passion, "Somewhere there's a traitor—."

A man in black and gold appeared at the window with a heat-gun. "Out the door," he bellowed. "You can't get away, the place is surrounded. Move out the door in an orderly fashion; move out the door. You're all under arrest. Don't try to break for it; our orders are to shoot to kill."

Circumbright sidled close to Shorn. "Can't you do something?"

"Not here. Wait till we're all outside; we don't want anyone shot."

Two burly troopers appeared in the doorway, gestured with pistols. "Outside, everybody. Keep your hands up."

Thursby led the way, his face thoughtful. Shorn followed; behind came the others. They marched into the parking area, now flooded with light from police lamps.

"Stop right there," barked a new voice.

Thursby halted. Shorn squinted against the searchlight; he saw a dozen men standing in a circle around them.

"This is a catch and no mistake," muttered Thursby.

"Quiet! No talking."

"Better search them for weapons," came another new voice. Shorn recognized the dry phrasing, the overtones of careless contempt. Adlari Dominion.

Two Black and Golds walked through the group, making a quick search.

A mocking voice came from behind the searchlights. "Isn't that Colonel Thursby, the people's hero? What's he doing in this nasty little conspiracy?"

Thursby stared ahead with an immobile face. The red-haired man who had challenged Shorn cried to the unseen voice: "You Telek boot-licker, may the money they pay rot the hands off your wrists!"

"Easy, Walter," said Circumbright.

Thursby spoke toward the lights. "Are we under arrest?"

There was no answer, only a contemptuous silence.

Thursby repeated in a sharper tone: "Are we under arrest? I want to see your warrant; I want to know what we're charged with."

"You're being taken to headquarters for questioning," came the reply. "Behave yourselves; if you've committed no crime, there'll be no charge."

"We'll never reach headquarters," Circumbright muttered to Shorn. Shorn nodded grimly, staring into the lights, seeking Dominion. Would he recognize the Cluche Kurgill whom he had invested with Telek power?

The voice called out, "Were you contemplating resistance to arrest? Go ahead. Make it easy on us."

There was motion in the group, a swaying as if from the wind that moved the tops of the dark pine trees.

The voice said, "Very well, then, march forward, one at a time. You first, Thursby."

Thursby turned slowly, like a bull, followed the trooper who walked ahead waving a flashlight.

Circumbright muttered to Shorn, "Can't you do something?"

"Not while Dominion is out there—."

"Silence!"

One by one the group followed Thursby. An air barge loomed ahead, the rear hatch gaping like the mouth of a cave.

"Up the ramp; inside."

The hold was a bare, metal-walled cargo space. The door clanged shut, and the fifty captives stood in sweating silence.

Thursby's voice came from near the wall. "A clean sweep. Did they get everybody?"

Circumbright answered in a carefully toneless voice. "So far as I know."

"This will set the movement back ten years," said another voice, controlled but tremulous.

"More likely destroy it entirely."

"But—what can they convict us of? We're guilty of nothing they can prove."

Thursby snorted. "We'll never get to Tran. My guess is gas."

"Gas?"—a horrified whisper.

"Poison gas pumped through the ventilator. Then out to sea, drop us, and no one's the wiser. Not even 'killed while escaping.' Nothing."

The aircraft vibrated, rose into the air; under their feet was the soft feeling of air-borne flight.

Shorn called out softly, "Circumbright?"

"Right here."

"Make a light."

A paper torch cast a yellow flicker around the hold; faces glowed pale and damp as toad-bellies; eyes glared and reflected in the flare of the torch.

The row of ports was well shuttered, the hand keys were replaced by bolts. Shorn turned his attention to the door. He should be able to break it open. But the problem was new; in a sense this bulging open of a door was a concept several times more advanced than movement of a single object, no matter how large. There was also a psychological deterrent in the fact that the door was locked. What would happen if he attempted to telekinecize and nothing happened? Would he retain his power?

Thursby was standing with his ear to the ventilator. He turned, nodded. "Here it comes, I can hear the hiss...."

The paper torch was guttering; in darkness Shorn was as helpless as the others. Desperately he plunged his mind at the door; the door burst open, out into the night. Shorn caught it before it fluttered away into the dark air, brought it edgewise back through the door opening.

The wind had blown out the torch; Shorn could only vaguely feel the black bulk of the door. He yelled, to be heard over the roar of the wind rushing past the door, "Stand back, stand back—" He could wait no longer; he felt reality slipping in the darkness; the door was only a vague blot. He concentrated on it, strained his eyes to see, hurled it against the metal hull, stove out a great rent. Air swept through the hold, whisked out any gas that might have entered.

Shorn took himself out the door, rose above the cabin, looked through the sky dome. A dozen Black and Golds sat in the forward compartment looking uneasily back toward the cargo hold whence had come the rending jar. Adlari Dominion was not visible. Luby, the bronze-haired courier with the medallion face, sat statue-quiet in a corner. Luby was to be preserved, thought Shorn. Luby was the traitor.

He had neither time nor inclination for half-measures. He tore a strip off the top of the ship; the troopers and Luby looked up in terror. If they saw him at all, he was a white-faced demon of the night, riding the wind above them. They were shucked out of the cabin like peas from a pod, flung out into the night, and their cries came thinly back to Shorn over the roar of the wind.

He jumped down into the cabin, cut off the motors, jerked the cylinder of gas away from the ventilation system, then whisked the craft east, toward the Monaghill Mountains.

Clouds fell away from the moon; he saw a field below. Here was as good a spot as any to land and reorganize.

The aircraft settled to the field. Dazed, trembling, buffeted, fifty men and women crept from the hold.

Shorn found Thursby leaning against the hull. Thursby looked at him through the moonlight as a child might watch a unicorn. Shorn grinned. "I know you must be puzzled; I'll tell you all about it as soon as we're settled. But now—."

Thursby squinted. "It's hardly practical our going home, acting as if nothing had happened. The Black and Golds took photographs; and there's a number of us that...are not unknown to them."

Circumbright appeared out of the darkness like a pink and brown owl. "There'll be a great deal of excitement at the Black and Golds' headquarters when there's no news of this hulk."

"There'll be a great deal of irritation at Glarietta Pavilion."

Shorn counted the days on his fingers. "Today is the twenty-third. Nine days to the first of the month."

"What happens on the first of the month?"

"The First Annual Telekinetic Olympiad, at the new stadium in Swanscomb Valley. In the meantime—there's an old mine back of Mount Mathias. The bunkhouses should hold two or three hundred."

"But there's only fifty of us—."

"We'll want others. Two hundred more. Two hundred good people. And to avoid any confusion"—he looked around to find the red-haired man who thought that sanity was no more than a function of individual outlook—"we will equate goodness to will to survive for self, the family group, human culture, and tradition."

"That's broad enough," said Thursby equably, "to suit almost anyone. As a practical standard—?" In the moonlight Shorn saw him cock his eyebrows humorously.

"Practically," said Shorn, "we'll pick out people we like."

VIII

Sunday morning, June 1, was dull and overcast. Mist hung along the banks of the Swanscomb River as it wound in its new looping course down the verdant valley; the trees dripped with clammy condensations.

At eight o'clock a man in rich garments of purple, black, and white dropped from the sky to the rim of the stadium. He glanced up at the overcast, the cloud-wrack broke open like a scum, slid across the sky.

Horizon to horizon the heavens showed pure and serene blue; the sun poured warmth into Swanscomb Valley.

The man looked carefully around the stadium, his black eyes keen, restless. At the far end stood a man in a black and gold police uniform; the Telek brought the man through the air to the rim of the stadium beside him.

"Good morning, Sergeant. Any disturbance?"

"None at all, Mr. Dominion."

"How about below?"

"I couldn't say, sir. I'm only responsible for the interior, and I've had the lights on all night. Not a fly has showed itself."

"Good." Dominion glanced around the great bowl. "If there are no trespassers now, there won't be any, since there's no ground level entrance."

He took himself and the trooper to the ground. Two other men in uniform appeared.

"Good morning," said Dominion.

"Any disturbance?"

"No sir. Not a sound."

"Curious." Dominion rubbed his pale, peaked chin. "Nothing below the stadium?"

"Nothing, sir. Not a nail. We've searched every nook and cranny, down to bedrock, inch by inch."

"Nothing on the detectors?"

"No, sir. If a gopher had tunneled under the stadium, we'd have known it."

Dominion nodded. "Perhaps there won't be any demonstration after all." He stroked his chin. "My intuition is seldom at fault. But never mind. Take all your men, station them at the upper and lower ends of the valley. Allow no one to enter. No one, on any pretext whatever. Understand me?"

"Yes, sir."

"Good."

Dominion returned to the rim of the stadium, gazed around the sunny bowl. The grass was green and well cropped; the colored upholstery of the chairs made circular bands of pastel around the stadium.

He took himself through the air to the director's cupola, an enclosed booth hanging in a vantage point over the field on a long transparent spar. He entered, seated himself at the table.

Other Teleks began to arrive, dropping little brilliant birds from the sky, settling to bask in the sunlight. Refreshment trays floated past; they sipped wine and ate spice cakes.

Dominion presently left the high cupola, drifted low over the stadium. There was no expectation of filling it; thirty thousand seats would allow room for future increase. Thirty thousand Teleks was the theoretical limit that the economy of Earth could maintain at the present standard of living. And after thirty thousand? Dominion shrugged aside the question; the problem had no contemporary meaning. The solution should prove simple enough; there had been talk of swinging Venus out into a cooler orbit, moving in Neptune, and creating two habitable worlds by transferring half of Neptune's mantle of ice to dusty Venus. A problem for tomorrow. Today's concern was the creation of the Telek Earth State, the inculcation of religious awe into the common folk of Earth—the only means, as it had been decided, to protect Teleks from witless assassination.

He dropped into a group of friends, seated himself. His work was done for the day; now, with security achieved, he could relax, enjoy himself.

Teleks came in greater numbers. Here was a large group—fifty together. They settled into a section rather high up on the shady side, somewhat apart from the others. A few minutes later another group of fifty joined them, and later there were other similar groups.

At nine o'clock the voice of Lemand De Troller, the program director, sounded from the speakers:

"Sixty years ago, at the original Telekinetic Congress, our race was born. Today is the first annual convention of the issue of these early giants, and I hope the custom will persist down the stream of history, down the million years that is our destined future, ten million times a million years...."

Circumbright and Shorn listened with dissatisfaction as De Troller announced the program. He finished with "—the final valediction by Graycham Gray, our chairman for the year."

Circumbright said to Shorn, "There's nothing there, no mass telekinesis in the entire program."

Shorn said nothing. He leaned back in his seat, looked up to the director's cupola.

"Ample opportunity for mass exercise," complained Circumbright, "and they overlook it entirely."

Shorn brought his attention back down from the cupola. "It's an obvious stunt—perhaps too obvious for such a sophisticated people."

Circumbright scanned the 265 men and women in radiant Telek costumes that Shorn had brought into the stadium. He looked over his shoulder to Thursby, in the seat behind him. "Any ideas?"

Thursby, in brown and yellow, said tentatively, "We can't very well force them to indoctrinate us."

Laurie, beside Shorn, laughed nervously. "Let's send Circumbright out to plead with them."

Shorn moved restlessly in his seat. Two hundred and sixty-five precious lives, dependent for continued existence on his skill and vigilance. "Maybe something will turn up."

A game of bumpball was underway. Five men lying prone in eight-foot red torpedoes competed against five men in blue torpedoes, each team trying to bump a floating three-foot ball into the opposition goal. The game was lightning swift, apparently dangerous. The ten little boats moved so fast as to be mere flickers; the ball slammed back and forth like a ping-pong ball.

Shorn began to notice curious glances cast up toward his group. There was no suspicion, only interest, somehow they were attracting attention. He looked around and saw his group sitting straight and tense as vestrymen at a funeral—obviously uneasy and uncomfortable. He rose to his feet, spoke in an angry undertone, "Show a little life; act as if you're enjoying yourselves!"

He turned back to the field, noticed a service wagon not in use, pulled it up, moved it past his charges. Gingerly they took tea, rum punch, cakes, fruit. Shorn set the case back on the turf.

The bumpball game ended; now began the water sculpture. Columns of water reared into the air: glistening, soft forms, catching the sunlight glowing deep from within.

There were other displays: the air over the stadium swam with colors, shapes, films, patterns, and so passed the morning. At noon buffet tables dropped from the sky to the stadium turf. And now Shorn found himself on the horns of a dilemma. By remaining aloof from the tables his group made themselves conspicuous; but they risked quick detection by mingling with the Teleks.

Thursby resolved the problem. He leaned forward. "Don't you think we'd better go down to lunch? Maybe a few at a time. We stick out like a sore thumb sitting up here hungry."

Shorn acquiesced. By ones and twos he set the members of his company down to the sward. Laurie nudged him. "Look. There's Dominion. He's talking to old Pool."

Circumbright in unusual agitation said, "I hope Poole keeps his wits about him."

Dominion turned away. A moment later Shorn brought Poole back to his seat. "What did Dominion want?"

Poole was a scholarly-looking man of middle age, mild and myopic. "Dominion? Oh, the gentleman who spoke to me. He was very pleasant. Asked if I were enjoying the spectacles, and said that he didn't think he recognized me."

"And what did you say?"

"I said I didn't get out very much, and that there were many here I hardly knew."

"And then?"

"He just moved away."

Shorn sighed. "Dominion is very sharp."

Thursby wore a worried frown. "Things haven't gone too well this morning."

"No. But there's still the afternoon."

IX

Three o'clock.

"There's not much more," said Circumbright.

Shorn sat hunched forward. "No."

Circumbright clenched the arms of his seat. "We've got to do something. Somehow, someway: mass telekinesis!"

Shorn looked up at the director's cupola. "It's got to come from there. And I've got to arrange it." He reached over, clasped Laurie's hand, nodded to Thursby, rose to his feet, took himself by an inconspicuous route along the back wall, up to the transparent spar supporting the cupola. Inside he glimpsed the shapes of two men.

He slid back the door, entered quietly, froze in his footprints. Adlari Dominion, lounging back in an elastic chair, smiled up at him, ominous as a cobra. "Come in. I've been expecting you."

Shorn looked quickly to Lemand De Troller, the program director, a bulky blond man with lines of self-indulgence clamping his mouth.

"How so?"

"I have a pretty fair idea of your intentions, and I admit their ingenuity. Unluckily for you, I inspected the body of Cluche Kurgill, assassinated a short time ago, and it occurred to me that this was not the man whom I entertained at Glarietta; I have since reprimanded myself for not scrutinizing the catch at Portinari Gate more carefully. In any event, today will be a complete debacle, from your standpoint. I have excised from the program any sort of business which might have helped you."

Shorn said thickly, "You showed a great deal of forbearance in allowing us to enjoy your program."

Dominion made a lazy gesture. "It's just as well not to bring our problems too sharply to the attention of the spectators; it might lay a macabre overtone upon the festival for them to observe at close hand two hundred and sixty-five condemned anarchists and provocateurs."

"You would have been made very uncomfortable if I had not come up here to the cupola."

Dominion shook his head. "I asked myself, what would I do in your position? I answered, I would proceed to the cupola and myself direct an event such as to suit my purposes. So—I preceded you." He smiled. "And now—the sorry rebellion is at its end. The entire nucleus of your gang is within reach, helpless; if you recall, there is no exit, they have no means to scale the walls."

Shorn felt the bile rising in his throat; his voice sounded strange to his ears. "It's not necessary to revenge yourself on all these people; they're merely decent individuals, trying to cope with—" He spoke on, pleading half-angrily for the 265. Meanwhile, his mind worked at a survival sublevel. Dominion, no matter how lazy-seeming and catlike, was keyed-up, on his guard, there would be no surprising him. In any struggle Lemand De Troller would supply the decisive force. Shorn might be able to parry the weapons of one man, but two cores of thought would be too much for him.

Decision and action came to him simultaneously. He gave the cupola a great shake; startled, De Troller seized the desk. Shorn threw a coffee mug at his head. Instantly, before the mug had even struck, Shorn flung himself to the floor. Dominion, seizing the instant of Shorn's distraction, aimed a gun at him, fired an explosive pellet. Shorn hit the floor, saw De Troller slump, snatched the weapon from Dominion's hand—all at once.

The gun clattered to the deck, and Shorn found himself looking into Dominion's pale glowing eyes.

Dominion spoke in a low voice, "You're very quick. You've effectively reduced the odds against yourself."

Shorn smiled. "What odds do you give me now?"

"Roughly, a thousand to one."

"Seems to me they're even. You against me."

"No. I can hold you helpless, at the very least, until the program property man returns."

Shorn slowly rose to his feet. Careful. Let no movement escape his eye. Without moving his eyes from Dominion's he lifted the coffee mug, hurled it at Dominion's head. Dominion diverted it, accelerated it toward Shorn. Shorn bounced it back, into Dominion's face. It stopped only an inch short, then sprang back at Shorn's head with tremendous speed. Shorn flicked it with a thought, he felt the breath of its passage and it shattered against the wall.

"You're fast," said Dominion. "Very fast, indeed. In theory, your reactions should have missed that."

"I've got a theory of my own," said Shorn.

"I'd like to hear it."

"What happens when two minds try to teleport an object in opposing directions?"

"An exhausting matter," said Dominion, "if carried to the limit. The mind with the greater certainty wins, the other mind...sometimes...lapses."

Shorn stared at Dominion. "I believe my mind to be stronger than yours."

"Suppose it is? What do I gain in proving otherwise?"

Shorn said, "If you want to save your life—you'll have to." With his eyes still on Dominion, he took a knife from his pocket, flicked open the blade.

It leaped from his hand at his eyes. He frantically diverted it, and in the instant his defense was distracted, the gun darted to Dominion's hand. Shorn twisted up the muzzle by a hair's-breadth; the pellet sang past his ear.

Fragments of the coffee mug pelted the back of his head, blinding him with pain. Dominion, smiling and easy, raised the gun. It was all over, Shorn thought. His mind, wilted and spent, stood naked and bare of defense—for the flash of an instant. Before Dominion could pull the trigger Shorn flung the knife at his throat. Dominion turned his attention away from the gun to divert the knife; Shorn reached out, grabbed the gun with his bare hands, tossed it under the table out of sight.

Dominion and Shorn glared eye to eye. Both of them thought of the knife. It lay on the table, and now under the impulse of both minds, slowly trembled, rose quivering into the air, hilt up, blade down, swinging as if hung by a short string. Gradually it drifted to a position midway between their eyes.

The issue was joined. Sweating, breathing hard, they glared at the knife, and it vibrated, sang to the induced quiver from the opposing efforts. Eye to eye stared Dominion and Shorn, faces red, mouths open, distorted. No opportunity now for diversionary tactics; relax an instant and the knife would stab; blunt force strained against force.

Dominion said slowly, "You can't win, you who have only known telekinesis a few days; your certainty is as nothing compared to mine. I've lived my lifetime in certainty; it's part of my living will, and now see—your reality is weakening, the knife is aiming at you, to slash your neck."

Shorn watched the knife in fascination, and indeed it slowly turned toward him like the clock-hand of Fate. Sweat streamed into his eyes; he was aware of Dominion's grimace of triumph.

No. Allow no words to district you; permit no suggestion; bend down

Dominion's own resolution. His vocal chords were like rust wire, his voice was a croak.

"My certainty is stronger than yours because"—as he said the words the knife halted its sinister motion toward his throat—"time has no effect upon telekinesis! Because I've got the will of all humanity behind me, and you've got only yourself!"

The knife trembled, twisted, as if it were a live thing, tortured by indecision.

"I'm stronger than you are, because...I've *got to be!*" He sank the words into Dominion's mind.

Dominion said quickly, "Your neck hurts, your mind hurts, you cannot see."

Shorn's neck hurt indeed, his head ached, sweat stung his eyes, and the knife made a sudden lurch toward him. this can't go on, thought Shorn. "I don't need tricks, Dominion; you need them only because your confidence is going and you're desperate." He took a deep breath, reached out, seized the knife, plunged it into Dominion's breast.

Shorn stood looking down at the body. "I won—and by a trick. He was so obsessed by the need for defeating me mentally that he forgot the knife had a handle."

Panting, he looked out over the stadium. Events had come to a halt. The spectators restively waited for word from the program director.

Shorn picked up the microphone.

"Men and women of the future..." as he spoke he watched the little huddle of 265. He saw Laurie stir, look up; he saw Circumbright turn, clap Thursby's knee. He felt the wave of thankfulness, of hero-worship, almost insane in its fervor that welled up from their minds. At that moment he could have commanded any of them to their death.

An intoxicated elation came to him; he fought to control his voice. "This is an event improvised to thank Lemand De Troller, our program director, for his work in arranging the events. All of us will join our telekinetic powers together; we will act as one mind. I will guide this little white ball"—he lifted a small ball used in the obstacle race—"through the words 'thank you, Lemand De Troller.' You, with your united wills, will follow with the large bumpball." He rolled it out into the center of the stadium. "With more preparation we would have achieved something more elaborate, but I know Lemand will be just as pleased if he feels all of us are concentrating on the big ball, putting our hearts into the thanks. So—now. Follow the little white ball."

Slowly he guided the white ball along imaginary block letters in the air; faithfully, the big bumpball followed.

It was finished.

Shorn looked anxiously toward Circumbright. No signal.

Once again.

"Now—there is one other whom we owe a vote of thanks: Adlari Dominion, the capable liaison officer. This time we will spell out, 'Thank you and good luck, Adlari Dominion.'"

The white ball moved. The big ball followed. Four thousand minds impelled, 265 minds sough to merge into the pattern: each a new Prometheus trying to steal a secret more precious than fire from a race more potent than the Titans.

Shorn finished the last N, glanced toward Circumbright. Still no signal. Anxiety beset him; was this the right indoctrination technique? Suppose it was effective only under special conditions, suppose he had been operating on a misapprehension the entire time?

"Well," said Shorn doggedly, "once again." But the spectators would be growing restless. Who to thank this time?

The ball was moving on its own volition. Shorn, fascinated, followed its path. It was spelling a word.

W-I-L-L—then a space—S-H-O-R-N—another space—T-H-A-N-K-S.

Shorn sank back into the elastic seat, his eyes brimming with tears of release and thankfulness. "Someone is thanking Will Shorn," he said into the microphone. "It's time for them to leave." He paused. And 265 new telekinetics lifted themselves from the stadium, flew west toward Tran, disappeared into the afternoon.

Shorn returned to the microphone. "There're a few more words I want to say; please be patient a moment or two longer.

"You have just been witnesses—unwitting witnesses—to an event as important as Joffrey's original congress. The future will consider the sixty-year interval only a transition, humanity's final separation from the beast.

"We have completely subdued the material world; we know the law governing all the phenomena that our senses can detect. Now we turn ourselves into a new direction; humanity enters a new stage, and wonderful things lie before us." He noticed a ripple of uneasiness running along the ranks of the Teleks. "This new world is on us, we can't evade it. For six years the Teleks have rejoiced in a state of special privilege, and this is the last shackle humanity throws off: the idea that one man may dominate or control another man."

He paused; the uneasiness was ever more marked.

"There are trying times to come—a period of severe readjustment. At the moment you are not quite certain to what I am referring, and that is just as well. Thank you for your attention and good-bye. I hope you enjoyed the program as much as I did."

He rose to his feet, stepped over Dominion's body, slid back the door, stepped out of the cupola.

Teleks leaving the stadium rose up past him like May flies, some turning him curious glances as they flew. Shorn, smiling, watched them flit past, toward their glittering pavilions, their cloud-castles, their sea-bubbles. The last one was gone; he waved an arm after them as if in valediction.

Then he himself rose, plunged westward toward the towers of Tran, where 265 men and women were already starting to spread telekinesis through all of mankind.

ULLWARD'S RETREAT

Bruham Ullward had invited three friends to lunch at his ranch: Ted and Ravelin Seehoe, and their adolescent daughter, Iugenae. After an eye-bulging feast, Ullward offered around a tray of the digestive pastilles which had won him his wealth.

"A wonderful meal," said Ted Seehoe reverently. "Too much, really. I'll need one of these. The algae was absolutely marvelous."

Ullward made a smiling, easy gesture. "It's the genuine stuff."

Ravelin Seehoe, a fresh-faced, rather positive young woman of eighty or ninety, reached for a pastille. "A shame there's not more of it. The synthetic we get is hardly recognizable as algae."

"It's a problem," Ullward admitted. "I clubbed up with some friends; we bought a little mat in the Ross Sea and grow all of our own."

"Think of that," exclaimed Ravelin. "Isn't it frightfully expensive?"

Ullward pursed his lips whimsically. "The good things in life come high. Luckily, I'm able to afford a bit extra."

"What I keep telling Ted—" began Ravelin, then stopped as Ted turned her a keen warning glance.

Ullward bridged the rift. "Money isn't everything. I have a flat of algae, my ranch; you have your daughter—and I'm sure you wouldn't trade."

Ted patted Iugenae's hand. "When do you have your own child, Lamster Ullward?" (*Lamster: Contraction of Landmaster—the polite form of address in current use.*)

159

"Still some time yet. I'm thirty-seven billion down the list."

"A pity," said Ravelin Seehoe brightly, "when you could give a child so many advantages."

"Some day, some day, before I'm too old."

"A shame," said Ravelin, "but it has to be. Another fifty billion people and we'd have no privacy whatever!" She looked admiringly around the room, which was used for the sole purpose of preparing food and dining.

Ullward put his hands on the arms of the chair, hitched forward a little. "Perhaps you'd like to look around the ranch?" He spoke in a casual voice, glancing from one to the other.

Iugenae clapped her hands; Revelin beamed. "If it wouldn't be too much trouble!"

"Oh, we'd love to, Lamster Ullward!" cried Iugenae.

"I've always wanted to see your ranch," said Ted. "I've heard so much about it."

"It's an opportunity for Iugenae I wouldn't want her to miss," said Ravelin. She shook her finger at Iugenae. "Remember, Miss Puss, notice everything very carefully—and don't *touch*!"

"May I take pictures, Mother?"

"You'll have to ask Lamster Ullward."

"Of course, of course," said Ullward. "Why in the world not?" He rose to his feet—a man of more than middle stature, more than middle pudginess, with straight sandy hair, round blue eyes, a prominent beak of a nose. Almost three hundred years old, he guarded his health with great zeal, and looked little more than two hundred.

He stepped to the door, checked the time, touched a dial on the wall. "Are you ready?"

"Yes, we're quite ready," said Ravelin.

Ullward snapped back the wall, to reveal a view over a sylvan glade. A fine oak tree shaded a pond growing with rushes. A path led through a field toward a wooden valley a mile in the distance.

"Magnificent," said Ted. "Simply magnificent!"

They stepped outdoors into the sunlight. Iugenae flung her arms out, twirled, danced in a circle. "Look! I'm all alone. I'm out here all by myself!"

"Iugenae!" called Ravelin sharply. "Be careful! Stay on the path! That's real grass and you mustn't damage it."

Iugenae ran ahead to the pond. "Mother!" she called back. "Look at these funny little jumpy things! And look at the flowers!"

"The animals are frogs," said Ullward. "They have a very interesting life history. You see the little fishlike things in the water?"

"Aren't they funny! Mother, do come here!"

"Those are called tadpoles and they will presently become frogs, indistinguishable from the ones you see."

Ravelin and Ted advanced with more dignity, but were as interested as Iugenae in the frogs.

"Smell the fresh air," Ted told Ravelin. "You'd think you were back in the early times."

"It's absolutely exquisite," said Ravelin. She looked around her. "One has the feeling of being able to wander on and on and on."

"Come around over here," called Ullward from beyond the pool. "This is the rock garden."

In awe, the guests stared at the ledge of rock, stained with red and yellow lichen, tufted with green moss. Ferns grew from a crevice; there were several fragile clusters of white flowers.

"Smell the flowers, if you wish," Ullward told Iugenae. "But please don't touch them; they stain rather easily."

Iugenae sniffed. "Mmmm!"

"Are they real?" asked Ted.

"The moss, yes. That clump of ferns and these little succulents are real. The flowers were designed for me by a horticulturist and are exact replicas of certain ancient species. We've actually improved on the odor."

"Wonderful, wonderful," said Ted.

"Now come this way—no, don't look back; I want you to get the total effect..." An expression of vexation crossed his face.

"What's the trouble?" asked Ted.

"It's a damned nuisance," said Ullward. "Hear that sound?"

Ted became aware of a faint rolling rumble, deep and almost unheard. "Yes. Sounds like some sort of factory."

"It is. On the floor below. A rug-works. One of the looms creates this terrible row. I've complained, but they pay no attention...Oh, well, ignore it. Now stand over here—and look around!"

His friends gasped in rapture. The view from this angle was of a rustic bungalow in an Alpine valley, the door being the opening into Ullward's dining room.

"What an illusion of distance!" exclaimed Ravelin. "A person would almost think he was alone."

"A beautiful piece of work," said Ted. "I'd swear I was looking into ten miles—at least five miles—of distance."

"I've got a lot of space here," said Ullward proudly. "Almost three-quarters of an acre. Would you like to see it by moonlight?"

"Oh, could we?"

Ullward went to a concealed switch-panel; the sun seemed to race across the sky. A fervent glow of sunset lit the valley; the sky burned peacock blue, gold, green, then came twilight—and the rising full moon came up behind the hill.

"This is absolutely marvelous," said Ravelin softly. "How can you bring yourself to leave it?"

"It's hard," admitted Ullward. "But I've got to look after business too. More money, more space."

He turned a knob; the moon floated across the sky, sank. Stars appeared, forming the age-old patterns. Ullward pointed out the constellations and the first-magnitude stars by name, using a penciltorch for a pointer. Then the sky flushed with lavender and lemon yellow and the sun appeared once more. Unseen ducts sent a current of cool air through the glade.

"Right now I'm negotiating for an area behind this wall here." He tapped at the depicted mountainside, an illusion given reality and three-dimensionality by laminations inside the pane. "It's quite a large area— over a hundred square feet. The owner wants a fortune, naturally."

"I'm surprised he wants to sell," said Ted. "A hundred square feet means real privacy."

"There's been a death in the family," explained Ullward. "The owner's four-great-grandfather passed on and the space is temporarily surplus."

Ted nodded. "I hope you're able to get it."

"I hope so too. I've got rather flamboyant ambitions—eventually I hope to own the entire quarterblock—but it takes time. People don't like to sell their space and everyone is anxious to buy."

"Not we," said Ravelin cheerfully. "We have our little home. We're snug and cozy and we're putting money aside for investment."

"Wise," agreed Ullward. "A great many people are space-poor. Then when a chance to make real money comes up, they're undercapitalized. Until I scored with the digestive pastilles, I lived in a single rented locker. I was cramped—but I don't regret it today."

They returned through the glade toward Ullward's house, stopping at the oak tree. "This is my special pride," said Ullward. "A genuine oak tree!"

"Genuine?" asked Ted in astonishment. "I assumed it was simulation."

"So many people do," said Ullward. "No, it's genuine."

"Take a picture of the tree, Iugenae, please. But don't touch it. You might damage the bark."

"Perfectly all right to touch the bark," assured Ullward.

He looked up into the branches, then scanned the ground. He stooped, picked up a fallen leaf. "This grew on the tree," he said. "Now, Iugenae, I want you to come with me." He went to the rock garden, pulled a simulated rock aside, to reveal a cabinet with washbasin. "Watch carefully." He showed her the leaf. "Notice? It's dry and brittle and brown."

"Yes, Lamster Ullward." Iugenae craned her neck.

"First I dip it in this solution." He took a beaker full of dark liquid from a shelf. "So. That restores the green color. We wash off the excess, then dry it. Now we rub this next fluid carefully into the surface. Notice, it's flexible and strong now. One more solution—a plastic coating—and there we are, a true oak leaf, perfectly genuine. It's yours."

"Oh, Lamster Ullward! Thank you ever so much!" She ran off to show her father and mother, who were standing by the pool, luxuriating in the feeling of space, watching the frogs. "See what Lamster Ullward gave me!"

"You be very careful with it," said Ravelin. "When we get home, we'll find a nice little frame and you can hang it in your locker."

The simulated sun hung in the western sky. Ullward led the group to a sundial. "An antique, countless years old. Pure marble, carved by hand. It works too—entirely functional. Notice. Three-fifteen by the shadow on the dial..." He peered at his beltwatch, squinted at the sun. "Excuse me one moment." He ran to the control board, made an adjustment. The sun lurched ten degrees across the sky. Ullward returned, checked the sundial. "That's better. Notice. Three-fifty by the sundial, three-fifty by my watch. Isn't that something now?"

"It's wonderful," said Ravelin earnestly.

"It's the loveliest thing I've ever seen," chirped Iugenae. Ravelin looked around the ranch, sighed wistfully. "We hate to leave, but I think we must be returning home."

"It's been a wonderful day, Lamster Ullward," said Ted. "A wonderful lunch, and we enjoyed seeing your ranch."

"You'll have to come out again," invited Ullward. "I always enjoy company."

He led them into the dining room, through the living room-bedroom to the door. The Seehoe family took a last look across the spacious interior, pulled on their mantles, stepped into their run-shoes, made their farewells. Ullward slid back the door. The Seehoes looked out, waited till a gap appeared in the traffic. They waved good-bye, pulled the hoods over their heads, stepped out into the corridor.

The run-shoes spun them toward their home, selecting the appropriate turnings, sliding automatically into the correct lift and drop-pits. Deflection fields twisted them through the throngs. Like the Seehoes, everyone wore mantle and hood of filmy reflective stuff to safeguard privacy. The illusion-pane along the ceiling of the corridor presented a view of towers dwindling up into a cheerful blue sky, as if the pedestrian were moving along one of the windy upper passages.

The Seehoes approached their home. Two hundred yards away, they angled over to the wall. If the flow of traffic carried them past, they would be forced to circle the block and make another attempt to enter. Their door slid open as they spun near; they ducked into the opening, swinging around on a metal grab-bar.

They removed their mantles and run-shoes, sliding skillfully past each other. Iugenae pivoted into the bathroom and there was room for both Ted and Ravelin to sit down. The house was rather small for the three of them; they could well have used another twelve square feet, but rather than pay exorbitant rent, they preferred to save the money with an eye toward Iugenae's future.

Ted sighed in satisfaction, stretching his legs luxuriously under Ravelin's chair. "Ullward's ranch notwithstanding, it's nice to be home."

Iugenae backed out of the bathroom.

Ravelin looked up. "It's time for your pill, dear."

Iugenae sullenly took a pill from the dispenser. "Runy says you make us take pills to keep us from growing up."

Ted and Ravelin exchanged glances.

"Just take your pill," said Ravelin, "and never mind what Runy says."

"But how is it that I'm 38 and Ermara Burk's only 32 and she's got a figure and I'm like a slat?"

"No arguments, dear. Take your pill."

Ted jumped to his feet. "Here, Babykin, sit down."

Iugenae protested, but Ted held up his hand. "I'll sit in the niche. I've got a few calls that I have to make."

He sidled past Ravelin, seated himself in the niche in front of the communication screen. The illusion-pane behind him was custom-built— Ravelin, in fact, had designed it herself. It simulated a merry little bandit's den, the walls draped in red and yellow silk, a bowl of fruit on the rustic table, a guitar on the bench, a copper teakettle simmering on the countertop stove. The pane had been rather expensive, but when anyone communicated with the Seehoes, it was the first thing they saw, and here the house-proud Ravelin had refused to stint.

Before Ted could make his call, the signal light flashed. He answered; the screen opened to display his friend Loren Aigle, apparently sitting in an airy arched rotunda, against a background of fleecy clouds— an illusion which Ravelin had instantly recognized as an inexpensive stock effect.

Loren and Elme, his wife, were anxious to hear of the Seehoes' visit to the Ullward ranch. Ted described the afternoon in detail. "Space, space, and more space! Isolation pure and simple! Absolute privacy! You can hardly imagine it! A fortune in illusion-panes."

"Nice," said Loren Aigle. "I'll tell you and you'll find it hard to believe. Today I registered a whole planet to a man." Loren worked in the Certification Bureau of the Extraterrestrial Properties Agency.

Ted was puzzled and uncomprehending. "A whole planet? How so?"

Loren explained. "He's a free-lance spaceman. Still a few left."

"But what's he planning to do with an entire planet?"

"Live there, he claims."

"Alone?"

Loren nodded. "I had quite a chat with him. Earth is all very well, he says, he prefers the privacy of his own planet. Can you imagine that?"

"Frankly, no! I can't imagine the fourth dimension either. What a marvel, though!"

The conversation ended and the screen faded. Ted swung around to his wife. "Did you hear that?"

Ravelin nodded; she had heard but not heeded. She was reading the menu supplied by the catering firm to which they subscribed. "We won't want anything heavy after that lunch. They've got simulated synthetic algae again."

Ted grunted. "It's never as good as the genuine synthetic."

"But it's cheaper and we've all had an enormous lunch."

"Don't worry about me, Mom!" sang Iugenae. "I'm going out with Runy."

"Oh, you are, are you? And where are you going, may I ask?"

"A ride around the world. We're catching the seven o'clock shuttle, so I've got to hurry."

"Come right home afterward," said Ravelin severely. "Don't go anywhere else."

"For heaven's sake, Mother, you'd think I was going to elope or something."

"Mind what I say, Miss Puss. I was a girl once myself. Have you taken your medicine?"

"Yes, I've taken my medicine."

Iugenae departed; Ted slipped back into the niche. "Who are you calling now?" asked Ravelin.

"Lamster Ullward. I want to thank him for going to so much trouble for us."

Ravelin agreed that an algae-and-margarine call was no more than polite.

Ted called, expressed his thanks, then—almost as an afterthought—chanced to mention the man who owned a planet.

"An entire planet?" inquired Ullward. "It must be inhabited."

"No, I understand not, Lamster Ullward. Think of it! Think of the privacy!"

"Privacy!" exclaimed Ullward bluffly. "My dear fellow, what do you call this?"

"Oh, naturally, Lamster Ullward—you have a real showplace."

"The planet must be very primitive," Ullward reflected. "An engaging idea, of course—if you like that kind of thing. Who is this man?"

"I don't know, Lamster Ullward. I could find out, if you like."

"No, no, don't bother. I'm not particularly interested. Just an idle thought." Ullward laughed his hearty laugh. "Poor man. Probably lives in a dome."

"That's possible, of course, Lamster Ullward. Well, thanks again, and good night."

The spaceman's name was Kennes Mail. He was short and thin, tough as synthetic herring, brown as toasted yeast. He had a close-cropped pad of gray hair, a keen, if ingenuous, blue gaze. He showed a courteous interest in Ullward's ranch, but Ullward thought this recurrent use of the world "clever" rather tactless.

As they returned to the house, Ullward paused to admire his oak tree.

"It's absolutely genuine, Lamster Mail! A living tree, survival of past ages! Do you have trees as fine as that on your planet?"

Kennes Mail smiled. "Lamster Ullward, that's just a shrub. Let's sit somewhere and I'll show you photographs."

Ullward had already mentioned his interest in acquiring extraterrestrial property; Mail, admitting that he needed money, had given him to understand that some sort of deal might be arranged. They sat at a table; Mail opened his case. Ullward switched on the wallscreen.

"First I'll show you a map," said Mail. He selected a rod, dropped it into the table socket. On the wall appeared a world projection: oceans, an enormous equatorial landmass named Gaea; the smaller sub-continents Atalanta, Persephone, Alcyone. A box of descriptive information read:

MAIL'S PLANET
Claim registered and endorsed at Extraterrestrial
Properties Agency

Surface area:	.87 Earth normal
Gravity:	.93 Earth normal
Diurnal rotation:	22.15 Earth hours
Annual revolution:	2.97 Earth years
Atmosphere:	Invigorating
Climate:	Salubrious
Noxious conditions and influences:	None
Population:	1

Mail pointed to a spot on the eastern shore of Gaea. "I live here. Just got a rough camp at present. I need money to do a bit better for myself. I'm willing to lease off one of the smaller continents, or, if you prefer, a section of Gaea, say from Murky Mountains west to the ocean."

Ullward, with a cheerful smile, shook his head. "No sections for me,

Lamster Mail. I want to buy the world outright. You set your price; if it's within reason, I'll write a check."

Mail glanced at him sideways.

"You haven't even seen the photographs."

"True." In a businesslike voice, Ullward said, "By all means, the photographs."

Mail touched the projection button. Landscapes of an unfamiliar wild beauty appeared on the screen. There were mountain crags and roaring rivers, snow-powdered forests, ocean dawns and prairie sunsets, green hillsides, meadows spattered with blossoms, beaches white as milk.

"Very pleasant," said Ullward. "Quite nice." He pulled out his check-book. "What's your price?"

Mail chuckled and shook his head. "I won't tell. I'm willing to lease off a section—providing my price is met and my rules are agreed to."

Ullward sat with compressed lips. He gave his head a quick little jerk. Mail started to rise to his feet.

"No, no," said Ullward hastily. "I was merely thinking...Let's look at the map again."

Mail returned the map to the screen. Ullward made careful inspection of the various continents, inquired as to physiography, climate, flora, and fauna.

Finally he made his decision. "I'll lease Gaea."

"No, Lamster Ullward!" declared Mail. "I'm reserving this entire area—from Murky Mountain and the Calliope River east. This western section is open. It's maybe a little smaller than Atalanta or Persephone, but the climate is warmer."

"There aren't any mountains on the western section," Ullward protested. "Only these insignificant Rock Castle Crags."

"They're not so insignificant," said Mail. "You've also got the Purple Bird Hills, and down here in the south is Mount Cariasco—a live volcano. What more do you need?"

Ullward glanced across his ranch. "I'm in the habit of thinking big."

"West Gaea is a pretty big chunk of property."

"Very well," said Ullward. "What are your terms?"

"So far as money goes, I'm not greedy," Mail said. "For a twenty-year lease: two hundred thousand a year, the first five years in advance."

Ullward made a startled protest. "Great guns, Lamster Mail! That's almost half my income!"

Mail shrugged. "I'm not trying to get rich. I want to build a lodge myself. It costs money. If you can't afford it, I'll have to speak to someone who can."

Ullward said in a nettled voice, "I can afford it, certainly—but my entire ranch here costs less than a million."

"Well, either you want it or you don't," said Mail. "I'll tell you my rules, then you can make up your mind."

"What rules?" demanded Ullward, his face growing red.

"They're simple and their only purpose is to maintain privacy for both of us. First, you have to stay on your own property. No excursions hither and yon on your own property. Second, no subleasing. Third, no residents except yourself, your family, and your servants. I don't want any artists' colony springing up, nor any wild noisy resort atmosphere. Naturally you're entitled to bring out your guests, but they've got to keep to your property just like yourself."

He looked sideways at Ullward's glum face. "I'm not trying to be tough, Lamster Ullward. Good fences make good neighbors, and it's better that we have the understanding than hard words and beam-gun evictions later."

"Let me see the photographs again," said Ullward. "Show me West Gaea."

He looked, heaved a deep sigh. "Very well. I agree."

The construction crew had departed. Ullward was alone on West Gaea. He walked around the new lodge, taking deep breaths of pure quiet air, thrilling to the absolute solitude and privacy. The lodge had cost a fortune, but how many other people of Earth owned—leased, rather—anything to compare with this?

He walked out on the front terrace, gazed proudly across miles—genuine unsimulated miles—of landscape. For his home site, he had selected a shelf in the foothills of the Ullward Range (as he had renamed the Purple Bird Hills). In front spread a great golden savannah dotted with blue-green trees; behind rose a tall gray cliff.

A stream rushed down a cleft in the rock, leaping, splashing, cooling the air, finally flowing into a beautiful clear pool, beside which Ullward had erected a cabana of red, green and brown plastic. At the base of the cliff and in crevices grew clumps of spiky blue cactus, lush green bushes covered with red trumpet-flowers, a thick-leafed white plant holding up a stalk clustered with white bubbles.

Solitude! The real thing! No thumping of factories, no roar of traffic two feet from one's bed. One arm outstretched, the other pressed to his chest, Ullward performed a stately little jig of triumph on the terrace. Had he been able, he might have turned a cartwheel. When a person has complete privacy, absolutely nothing is forbidden!

Ullward took a final turn up and down the terrace, made a last appreciative survey of the horizon. The sun was sinking through banks of fire-fringed clouds. Marvelous depth of color, a tonal brilliance to be matched only in the very best illusion-panes!

He entered the lodge, made a selection from the nutrition locker. After a leisurely meal, he returned to the lounge. He stood thinking for a moment, then went out upon the terrace, strolled up and down. Wonderful! The night was full of stars, hanging like blurred white lamps, almost as he had always imagined them.

After ten minutes of admiring the stars, he returned into the lodge. Now what? The wall-screen, with its assortment of recorded programs. Snug and comfortable, Ullward watched the performance of a recent musical comedy.

Real luxury, he told himself. Pity he couldn't invite his friends out to spend the evening. Unfortunately impossible, considering the inconvenient duration of the trip between Mail's Planet and Earth. However—only three days until the arrival of his first guest. She was Elf Intry, a young woman who had been more than friendly with Ullward on Earth. When Elf arrived, Ullward would broach a subject which he had been mulling over for several months—indeed, ever since he had first learned of Mail's Planet.

Elf Intry arrived early in the afternoon, coming down to Mail's Planet in a capsule discharged from the weekly Outer Ring Express packet. A woman of normally good disposition, she greeted Ullward in a seethe of indignation. "Just who is that brute around the other side of the planet? I thought you had absolute privacy here!"

"That's just old Mail," said Ullward evasively. "What's wrong?"

"The fool on the packet set me the wrong coordinates and the capsule came down on a beach. I noticed a house and then I saw a naked man jumping rope behind some bushes. I thought it was you, of course. I went over and said 'Boo!' You should have *heard* the language he used!" She shook her head. "I don't see why you allow such a boor on your planet."

The buzzer on the communication screen sounded. "That's Mail now," said Ullward. "You wait here. I'll tell him how to speak to *my* guests!"

He presently returned to the terrace. Elf came over to him, kissed his nose. "Ully, you're pale with rage! I hope you didn't lose your temper."

"No," said Ullward. "We merely—well, we had an understanding. Come along, look over the property."

He took Elf around to the back, pointing out the swimming pool, the waterfall, the mass of rock above. "You won't see that effect on any illusion-pane! That's genuine rock!"

"Lovely, Ully. Very nice. The color might be just a trifle darker, though. Rock doesn't look like that."

"No?" Ullward inspected the cliff more critically. "Well, I can't do anything about it. How about the privacy?"

"Wonderful! It's so quiet, it's almost eerie!"

"Eerie?" Ullward looked around the landscape. "It hadn't occurred to me."

"You're not sensitive to these things, Ully. Still, it's very nice, if you can tolerate that unpleasant creature Mail so close."

"Close?" protested Ullward. "He's on the other side of the continent!"

"True," said Elf. "It's all relative, I suppose. How long do you expect to stay out here?"

"That depends. Come along inside. I want to talk with you."

He seated her in a comfortable chair, brought her a globe of Gluco-Fructoid Nectar. For himself, he mixed ethyl alcohol, water, a few drops of Haig's Oldtime Esters.

"Elf, where do you stand in the reproduction list?"

She raised her fine eyebrows, shook her head. "So far down, I've lost count. Fifty or sixty billion."

"I'm down thirty-seven billion. It's one reason I bought this place. Waiting list, piffle! Nobody stops Bruham Ullward's breeding on his own planet!"

Elf pursed her lips, shook her head sadly. "It won't work, Ully."

"And why not?"

"You can't take the children back to Earth. The list would keep them out."

"True, but think of living here, surrounded by children. All the children you wanted ! And utter privacy to boot! What more could you ask for?"

Elf sighed. "You fabricate a beautiful illusion-pane, Ully. But I think not. I love the privacy and solitude—but I thought there'd be more people to be private from."

The Outer Ring Express packet came past four days later. Elf kissed Ullward good-bye. "It's simply exquisite here, Ully. The solitude is so magnificent it gives me gooseflesh. I've had a wonderful visit." She climbed into the capsule. "See you on Earth."

"Just a minute," said Ullward suddenly. "I want you to post a letter or two for me."

"Hurry. I've only got twenty minutes."

Ullward was back in ten minutes. "Invitations," he told her breathlessly. "Friends."

"Right." She kissed his nose. "Good-bye, Ully." She slammed the port; the capsule rushed away, whirling up to meet the packet.

The new guests arrived three weeks later: Frobisher Worbeck, Liornetta Stobard, Harris and Hyla Cabe, Ted and Ravelin and Iugenae Seehoe, Juvenal Aquister and his son, Runy.

Ullward, brown from long days of lazing in the sun, greeted them with great enthusiasm. "Welcome to my little retreat! Wonderful to see you all! Frobisher, you pink-cheeked rascal! And Iugenae! Prettier than ever! Be careful, Ravelin—I've got my eye on your daughter! But Runy's here, guess I'm out of the picture! Liornetta, damned glad you could make it! And Ted! Great to see you, old chap! This is all your doing, you know! Harris, Hyla, Juvenal—come on up! We'll have a drink, a drink, a drink!"

Running from one to the other, patting arms, herding the slow-moving Frobisher Worbeck, he conducted his guests up the slope to the terrace. Here they turned to survey the panorama. Ullward listened to their remarks, mouth pursed against a grin of gratification.

"Magnificent!"

"Grand!"

"Absolutely genuine!"

"The sky is so far way, it frightens me!"

"The sunlight's so pure!"

"The genuine thing's always best, isn't it?"

Runy said a trifle wistfully, "I thought you were on a beach, Lamster Ullward."

"Beach? This is mountain country, Runy. Land of the wide open spaces! Look out over that plain!"

Liornetta Stobart patted Runy's shoulder. "Not every planet has beaches, Runy. The secret of happiness is to be content with what one has."

Ullward laughed gaily. "Oh, I've got beaches, never fear for that! There's a fine beach—ha, ha—five hundred miles due west. Every step Ullward domain!"

"Can we go?" asked Iugenae excitedly. "Can we go, Lamster Ullward?"

"We certainly can! That shed down the slope is headquarters for the Ullward Airlines. We'll fly to the beach, swim in Ullward Ocean! But now refreshment! After that crowded capsule, your throats must be like paper!"

"It wasn't too crowded," said Ravelin Seehoe. "There were only nine of us." She looked critically up at the cliff. "If that were an illusion-pane, I'd consider it grotesque."

"My dear Ravelin!" cried Ullward. "It's impressive! Magnificent!"

"All of that," agreed Frobisher Worbeck, a tall, sturdy man, white-haired, red-jowled, with a blue benevolent gaze. "And now, Bruham, what about those drinks?"

"Of course! Ted, I know you of old. Will you tend bar? Here's the alcohol, here's water, here are the esters. Now, you two," Ullward called to Runy and Iugenae. "How about some nice cold soda pop?"

"What kind is there?" asked Runy.

"All kinds, all flavors. This is Ullward's Retreat! We've got methylamyl glutamine, cycloprodacterol phosphate, metathiobromine-r-glycocitrose..."

Runy and Iugenae expressed their preferences; Ullward brought the globes, then hurried to arrange tables and chairs for the adults. Presently everyone was comfortable and relaxed.

Iugenae whispered to Ravelin, who smiled and nodded indulgently. "Lamster Ullward, you remember the beautiful oak leaf you gave Iugenae?"

"Of course I do."

"It's still as fresh and green as ever. I wonder if Iugenae might have a leaf or two from some of these other trees?"

"My dear Ravelin!" Ullward roared with laughter. "She can have an entire tree!"

"Oh Mother! Can—"

"Iugenae, don't be ridiculous!" snapped Ted. "How could we get it home? Where would we plant the thing? In the bathroom?"

Ravelin said, "You and Runy find some nice leaves, but don't wander too far."

"No, Mother." She beckoned to Runy. "Come along, dope. Bring a basket."

The others of the party gazed out over the plain. "A beautiful view, Ullward," said Frobisher Worbeck. "How far does your property extend?"

"Five hundred miles west to the ocean, six hundred miles east to the mountains, eleven hundred miles north and two hundred miles south."

Worbeck shook his head solemnly. "Nice. A pity you couldn't get the whole planet. Then you'd have real privacy!"

"I tried, of course," said Ullward. "The owner refused to consider the idea."

"A pity."

Ullward brought out a map. "However, as you see, I have a fine volcano, a number of excellent rivers, a mountain range, and down here on the delta of Cinnamon River an absolutely miasmic swamp."

Ravelin pointed to the ocean. "Why, it's Lonesome Ocean! I thought the name was Ullward Ocean."

Ullward laughed uncomfortably. "Just a figure of speech—so to speak. My rights extend ten miles. More than enough for swimming purpose."

"No freedom of the seas here, eh, Lamster Ullward?" laughed Harris Cabe.

"Not exactly," confessed Ullward.

"A pity," said Frobisher Worbeck.

Hyla Cabe pointed to the map. "Look at these wonderful mountain ranges! The Magnificent Mountains! And over here—the Elysian Gardens! I'd love to see them, Lamster Ullward."

Ullward shook his head in embarrassment. "Impossible, I'm afraid. They're not on my property. I haven't even seen them myself."

His guests stared at him in astonishment. "But surely—"

"It's an atom-welded contract with Lamster Mail," Ullward explained. "He stays on his property, I stay on mine. In this way, our privacy is secure."

"Look," Hyla Cabe said aside to Ravelin, "the Unimaginable Caverns! Doesn't it make you simply wild not to be able to see them?"

Aquister said hurriedly, "It's a pleasure to sit here and just breathe this wonderful fresh air. No noise, no crowds, no bustle or hurry."

The party drank and chatted and basked in the sunlight until late afternoon. Enlisting the aid of Ravelin Seehoe and Hyla Cabe, Ullward set out a simple meal of yeast pellets, processed protein, thick slices of algae crunch.

"No animal flesh, cooked vegetation?" questioned Worbeck curiously.

"Tried them the first day," said Ullward. "Revolting. Sick for a week."

After dinner, the guests watched a comic melodrama on the wallscreen. Then Ullward showed them to their various cubicles, and after a few minutes of badinage and calling back and forth, the lodge became quiet.

Next day, Ullward ordered his guests into their bathing suits. "We're off to the beach, we'll gambol on the sand, we'll frolic in the surf of Lonesome Ullward Ocean!"

The guests piled happily into the air-car. Ullward counted heads. "All aboard! We're off!"

They rose and flew west, first low over the plain, then high into the air, to obtain a panoramic view of the Rock Castle Crags.

"The tallest peak—there to the north—is almost ten thousand feet high. Notice how it juts up, just imagine the mass! Solid rock! How'd you like that dropped on your toe, Runy? Not so good, eh? In a moment, we'll see a precipice over a thousand feet straight up and down. There—now! Isn't that remarkable?"

"Certainly impressive," agreed Ted.

"What those Magnificent Mountains must be like!" said Harris Cabe with a wry laugh.

"How tall are they, Lamster Ullward?" inquired Liornetta Stobart.

"What? Which?"

"The Magnificent Mountains."

"I don't know for sure. Thirty or forty thousand feet, I suppose."

"What a marvelous sight they must be!" said Frobisher Worbeck. "Probably make these look like foothills."

"These are beautiful too," Hyla Cabe put in hastily.

"Oh, naturally," said Frobisher Worbeck. "A damned fine sight! You're a lucky man, Bruham!"

Ullward laughed shortly, turned the air-car west. They flew across a rolling forested plain and presently Lonesome Ocean gleamed in the distance. Ullward slanted down, landed the air-car on the beach, and the party alighted.

The day was warm, the sun hot. A fresh wind blew in from the ocean. The surf broke upon the sand in massive roaring billows.

The party stood appraising the scene. Ullward swung his arms. "Well, who's for it? Don't wait to be invited! We've got the whole ocean to ourselves!"

Ravelin said, "It's so rough! Look how that water crashes down!"

Liornetta Stobart turned away with a shake of her head. "Illusion-pane surf is always so gentle. This could lift you right up and give you a good shaking!"

"I expected nothing quite so vehement," Harris Cabe admitted.

Ravelin beckoned to Iugenae. "You keep well away, Miss Puss. I don't want you swept out to sea. You'd find it Lonesome Ocean indeed!"

Runy approached the water, waded gingerly into a sheet of retreating foam. A comber thrashed down at him and he danced quickly back to the shore.

"The water's cold," he reported.

Ullward poised himself. "Well, here goes! I'll show you how it's done!" He trotted forward, stopped short, then flung himself into the face of a great white comber.

The party on the beach watched.

"Where is he?" asked Hyla Cabe.

Iugenae pointed. "I saw part of him out there. A leg, or an arm."

"There he is!" cried Ted. "Woof! Another one's caught him. I suppose some people might consider it sport..."

Ullward staggered to his feet, lurched through the retreating wash to shore. "Hah! Great! Invigorating! Ted! Harris! Juvenal! Take a go at it!"

Harris shook his head. "I don't think I'll try it today, Bruham."

"The next time for me too," said Juvenal Aquister. "Perhaps it won't be so rough."

"But don't let us stop you!" urged Ted. "You swim as long as you like. We'll wait here for you."

"Oh, I've had enough for now," said Ullward. "Excuse me while I change."

When Ullward returned, he found his guests seated in the air-car. "Hello! Everyone ready to go?"

"It's hot in the sun," explained Liornetta, "and we thought we'd enjoy the view better from inside."

"When you look through the glass, it's almost like an illusion-pane," said Iugenae.

"Oh, I see. Well, perhaps you're ready to visit other parts of the Ullward domain?"

The proposal met with approval; Ullward took the air-car into the air. "We can fly north over the pine woods, south over Mount Cairasco, which unfortunately isn't erupting just now."

"Anywhere you like, Lamster Ullward," said Frobisher Worbeck. "No doubt it's all beautiful."

Ullward considered the varied attractions of his leasehold. "Well, first to the Cinnamon Swamp."

For two hours they flew, over the swamp, across the smoking crater of Mount Cairasco, east to the edge of Murky Mountains, along Calliope River to its source in Goldenleaf Lake. Ullward pointed out noteworthy views, interesting aspects. Behind him, the murmurs of admiration dwindled and finally died.

"Had enough?" Ullward called back gaily. "Can't see half a continent in one day! Shall we save some for tomorrow?"

There was a moment's stillness. Then Liornetta Stobart said, "Lamster Ullward, we're simply dying for a peek at the Magnificent Mountains. I wonder—do you think we could slip over for a quick look? I'm sure Lamster Mail wouldn't really mind."

Ullward shook his head with a rather stiff smile. "He's made me agree to a very definite set of rules. I've already had one brush with him."

"How could he possibly find out?" asked Juvenal Aquister.

"He probably wouldn't find out," said Ullward, "but—"

"It's a damned shame for him to lock you off into this drab little peninsula!" Frobisher Worbeck said indignantly.

"Please, Lamster Ullward," Iugenae wheedled.

"Oh, very well," Ullward said recklessly.

He turned the air-car east. The Murky Mountains passed below. The party peered from the windows, exclaiming at the marvels of the forbidden landscape.

"How far are the Magnificent Mountains?" asked Ted.

"Not far. Another thousand miles."

"Why are you hugging the ground?" asked Frobisher Worbeck. "Up in the air, man! Let's see the countryside!"

Ullward hesitated. Mail was probably asleep. And, in the last analysis, he really had no right to forbid an innocent little—

"Lamster Ullward," called Runy, "there's an air-car right behind us."

The air-car drew up level. Kennes Mail's blue eyes met Ullward's across the gap. He motioned Ullward down.

Ullward compressed his mouth, swung the air-car down. From behind him came murmurs of sympathy and outrage.

Below as a dark pine forest; Ullward set down in a pretty little glade. Mail landed nearby, jumped to the ground, signaled to Ullward. The two men walked to the side. The guests murmured together and shook their heads.

Ullward presently returned to the air-car. "Everybody please get in," he said crisply.

They rose into the air and flew west. "What did the chap have to say for himself?" queried Worbeck.

Ullward chewed at his lips. "Not too much. Wanted to know if I'd lost the way. I told him one or two things. Reached an understanding..." His voice dwindled, then rose in a burst of cheerfulness. "We'll have a party back at the lodge. What do we care for Mail and his confounded mountains?"

"That's the spirit, Bruham!" cried Frobisher Worbeck.

Both Ted and Ullward tended bar during the evening. Either one or the other mingled rather more alcohol to rather less esters into the drinks than standard practice recommended. As a result, the party became quite loud and gay. Ullward damned Mail's interfering habits; Worbeck explored six thousand years of common law in an effort to prove Mail a domineering tyrant; the women giggled; Iugenae and Runy watched cynically, then presently went off to attend to their own affairs.

In the morning, the group slept late. Ullward finally tottered out on the terrace, to be joined one at a time by the others. Runy and Iugenae were missing.

"Young rascals," groaned Worbeck. "If they're lost, they'll have to find their own way back. No search parties for me."

At noon, Runy and Iugenae returned in Ullward's air-car.

"Good heavens," shrieked Ravelin. "Iugenae, come here this instant! Where have you been?"

Juvenal Aquister surveyed Runy sternly. "Have you lost your mind, taking Lamster Ullward's air-car without his permission?"

"I asked him last night," Runy declared indignantly. "He said yes, take anything except the volcano because that's where he slept when his feet got cold, and the swamp because that's where he dropped his empty containers."

"Regardless," said Juvenal in disgust, "you should have had better sense. Where have you been?"

Runy fidgeted. Iugenae said, "Well, we went south for a while, then turned and went east—I think it was east. We thought if we flew low,

Lamster Mail wouldn't see us. So we flew low, through the mountains, and pretty soon we came to an ocean. We went along the beach and came to a house. We landed to see who lived there, but nobody was home."

Ullward stifled a groan.

"What would anyone want with a pen of birds?" asked Runy.

"Birds? What birds? Where?"

"At the house. There was a pen with a lot of big birds, but they kind of got loose while we were looking at them and all flew away."

"Anyway," Iugenae continued briskly, "we decided it was Lamster Mail's house, so we wrote a note, telling what everybody thinks of him and pinned it to his door."

Ullward rubbed his forehead. "Is that all?"

"Well, practically all." Iugenae became diffident. She looked at Runy and the two of them giggled nervously.

"There's more?" yelled Ullward. "What, in heaven's name?"

"Nothing very much," said Iugenae, following a crack in the terrace with her toe. "We put a booby-trap over the door—just a bucket of water. Then we came home."

The screen buzzer sounded from inside the lodge. Everybody looked at Ullward. Ullward heaved a deep sigh, rose to his feet, went inside.

That very afternoon, the Outer Ring Express packet was due to pass the junction point. Frobisher Worbeck felt sudden and acute qualms of conscience for the neglect his business suffered while he dawdled away hours in idle enjoyment.

"But my dear old chap!" exclaimed Ullward. "Relaxation is good for you!"

True, agreed Frobisher Worbeck, if one could make himself oblivious to the possibility of fiasco through the carelessness of underlings. Much as he deplored the necessity, in spite of his inclination to loiter for weeks, he felt impelled to leave—and not a minute later than that very afternoon.

Others of the group likewise remembered important business which they had to see to, and those remaining felt it would be a shame and an imposition to send up the capsule half-empty and likewise decided to return.

Ullward's arguments met unyielding walls of obstinacy. Rather glumly, he went down to the capsule to bid his guests farewell. As they climbed through the port, they expressed their parting thanks:

"Bruham, it's been absolutely marvelous!"

"You'll never know how we've enjoyed this outing, Lamster Ullward!"

"The air, the space, the privacy—I'll never forget!"

"It was the most, to say the least."

The port thumped into its socket. Ullward stood back, waving rather uncertainly.

Ted Seehoe reached to press the Active button. Ullward sprang forward, pounded on the port.

"Wait!" he bellowed. "A few things's I've got to attend to! I'm coming with you!"

"Come in, come in," said Ullward heartily, opening the door to three of his friends: Coble and his wife, Heulia Sansom, and Coble's young, pretty cousin Landine. "Glad to see you!"

"Oh, come now! It's not so marvelous as all that!"

"Not to you, perhaps—you live here!"

Ullward smiled. "Well, I must say I live here and still like it. Would you like to have lunch, or perhaps you'd prefer to walk around for a few minutes? I've just finished making a few changes, but I'm happy to say everything is in order."

"Can we just take a look?"

"Of course. Come over here. Stand just so. Now—are you ready?"

"Ready."

Ullward snapped the wall back.

"Oooh!" breathed Landine. "Isn't it beautiful!"

"The space, the open feeling!"

"Look, a tree! What a wonderful simulation!"

"That's no simulation," said Ullward. "That's a genuine tree!"

"Lamster Ullward, are you telling the truth?"

"I certainly am. I never tell lies to a lovely young lady. Come along, over this way."

"Lamster Ullward, that cliff is so convincing, it frightens me."

Ullward grinned. "It's a good job." He signaled a halt. "Now—turn around."

The group turned. They looked out across a great golden savannah, dotted with groves of blue-green trees. A rustic lodge commanded the view, the door being the opening into Ullward's living room.

The group stood in silent admiration. Then Heulia sighed. "Space. Pure space."

Ullward smiled, a trifle wistfully. "Glad you like my little retreat. Now what about lunch? Genuine algae!"

DODKIN'S JOB

The Theory of Organized Society (as developed by Kinch, Kolbig, Penton, and others) yields such a wealth of significant information, revealing manifold intricacies and portentous projections, that occasionally it is well to consider its deceptively simple major premise (here stated by Kolbig):

When self-willed microunits combine to form and sustain a durable macrounit, certain freedoms of action are curtailed.

This is the basic process of Organization.

The more numerous and erratic the microunits, the more complex must be the structure and function of the macrounit—hence the more pervasive and restricting the details of Organization.

—from Leslie Penton, *First Principles of Organization*

The general population of the city had become forgetful of curtailed freedoms, as a snake no longer remembers the legs of its forebears. Somewhere someone has stated, "When the discrepancy between the theory and practice of a culture is very great, this indicates that the culture is undergoing rapid change." By such a test the culture of the city was stable, if not static. The population ordered their lives by schedule, classification, and precedent, satisfied with the bland rewards of Organization.

But in the healthiest tissue bacteria exist, and the most negligible impurity flaws a critical crystallization.

Luke Grogatch was forty, thin and angular, dour of forehead, with a sardonic cast to his mouth and eyebrows and a sideways twist to his head as if he suffered from an earache. He was too astute to profess Nonconformity; too perverse to strive for improved status; too pessimistic, captious, sarcastic, and outspoken to keep the jobs to which he found himself assigned. Each new reclassification depressed his status; he disliked each new job with increasing fervor.

Finally, rated as *Flunky/Class D/Unskilled*, Luke was dispatched to the District 8892 Sewer Maintenance Department and from there ordered out as night-shift swamper on Tunnel Gang Number 3's rotary drilling machine.

Reporting for work, Luke presented himself to the gang foreman, Fedor Miskitman, a big, buffalo-faced man with flaxen hair and placid blue eyes. Miskitman produced a shovel and took Luke to a position close up behind the drilling machine's cutting head. Here, said Miskitman, was Luke's station. Luke would be required to keep the tunnel floor clean of loose rock and gravel. When the tunnel broke through into an old sewer, there would be scale and that detritus known as "wet waste" to remove. Luke was to keep the dust trap clean and in optimum adjustment. During the breaks he would lubricate those bearings isolated from the automatic lubrication system, and he was to replace broken teeth on the cutting head whenever necessary.

Luke inquired if this was the extent of his duties, his voice strong with an irony the guileless Fedor Miskitman failed to notice.

"That is all," said Miskitman. He handed Luke the shovel. "Mostly it is the trash. The floor must be clean."

Luke suggested to the foreman a modification of the hopper jaws which would tend to eliminate the spill of broken rock; in fact, went Luke's argument, why bother it all? Let the rock lie where it fell. The concrete lining of the tunnel would mask so trivial a scatter of gravel.

Miskitman dismissed the suggestion out of hand: the rock must be removed. When Luke asked why, Miskitman told him, "That is the way the job is done."

Luke made a rude noise under his breath. He tested the shovel and shook his head in dissatisfaction. The handle was too long, the blade too short. He reported this fact to Miskitman, who merely glanced at his watch and signaled to the drill operator. The machine whined into revolution and with an ear-splitting roar made contact with the rock. Miskitman departed, and Luke went back to work.

During the shift he found that if he worked in a half-crouch most of the hot, dust-laden exhaust from the machine would pass over his head. Changing a cutting tooth during the first rest period he burned a blister on his left thumb. At the end of the shift a single consideration deterred Luke from declaring himself unqualified: he would be declassified from *Flunky/Class D/Unskilled* to *Junior Executive*, with a corresponding cut in expense account. Such a declassification would take him to the very bottom of the Status List, and so could not be countenanced; his present expense account was barely adequate, covering nutrition at a Type RP Victualing Service, sleeping space in a Sublevel 22 dormitory, and sixteen Special Coupons per month. He took Class 14 Erotic Processing, and was allowed twelve hours per month at his recreation club, with optional use of barbells, table-tennis equipment, two miniature bowling alleys, and any of the six telescreens tuned permanently to Band H. Luke often daydreamed of a more sumptuous life: AAA nutrition, a suite of rooms for his exclusive use, Special Coupons by the bale, Class 7 Erotic Processing, or even Class 6, or 5: despite Luke's contempt for the High Echelon he had no quarrel with High Echelon perquisites. And always as a bitter coda to the daydreams came the conviction that he might have been enjoying these good things in all reality. He had watched his fellows jockeying; he knew all the tricks and techniques: the beavering, the gregariousness, the smutting, knuckling....Why not make use of this knowledge?

"I'd rather be Class D Flunky," sneered Luke to himself.

Occasionally a measure of doubt would seep into Luke's mind. Perhaps he merely lacked the courage to compete, to come to grips with the world! And the seep of doubt would become a trickle of self-contempt. A Non-conformist, that's what he was—and he lacked the courage to admit it!

Then Luke's obstinacy would reassert itself. Why admit to Nonconformity when it meant a trip to the Disorganized House? A fool's trick— and Luke was no fool. Perhaps he was a Nonconformist in all reality; again, perhaps not—he had never really made up his mind. He presumed that he was suspected; occasionally he intercepted queer side glances and significant jerks of the head among his fellow workers. Let them leer. They could prove nothing.

But now...he was Luke Grogatch, Class D Flunky, separated by a single status from the nonclassified sediment of criminals, idiots, children, and proved Nonconformists. Luke Grogatch, who had dreamed such dreams of the High Echelon, of pride and independence! Instead—Luke Grogatch, Class D Flunky. Taking orders from a hay-headed lunk, working with semi-skilled laborers with status almost as low as his own: Luke Grogatch, flunky.

Seven weeks passed. Luke's dislike for his job became a mordant passion. The work was arduous, hot, repellent. Fedor Miskitman turned an uncomprehending gaze on Luke's most rancorous grimaces, grunted and shrugged at Luke's suggestions and arguments. This was the way things were done—his manner implied—always had been done, and always would be done.

Fedor Miskitman received a daily policy directive from the works superintendent which he read to the crew during the first rest break of the shift. These directives generally dealt with such matters as work norms, team spirit, and cooperation; pleas for a finer polish on the concrete; warnings against off-shift indulgence which might dull enthusiasm and decrease work efficiency. Luke usually paid small heed, until one day Fedor Miskitman, pulling out the familiar yellow sheet, read in his stolid voice:

PUBLIC WORKS DEPARTMENT, PUBLIC UTILITIES DIVISION
AGENCY OF SANITARY WORKS, DISTRICT 8892
SEWAGE DISPOSAL SECTION
Bureau of Sewer Construction and Maintenance
Office of Procurement

Policy Directive:	6511 Series BV96
Order Code:	GZP—AAR—REG
Reference:	G98—7542
Date Code:	BT—EQ—LLT
Authorized:	LL8—P—SC 8892
Checked:	48
Counterchecked:	92C

From:	Lavester Limon, Manager, Office of Procurement
Through:	All construction and maintenance offices
To:	All construction and maintenance superintendents
Attention:	All job foremen

Subject: Tool longevity, the promotion thereof
Instant of Application: Immediate
Duration of Relevance: Permanent
Substance: At beginning of each shift all hand tools shall be checked out of District 8892 Sewer Maintenance Warehouse. At close of each shift all hand tools shall be carefully cleaned and returned to District 8892 Sewer Maintenance Warehouse.
Directives reviewed and transmitted: Butry Keghorn, General Superintendent of Construction, Bureau of Sewer Construction. Clyde Kaddo, Superintendent of Sewer Maintenance

As Fedor Miskitman read the "Substance" section, Luke expelled his breath in an incredulous snort. Miskitman finished, folded the sheet with careful movements of his thick fingers, looked at his watch. "That is the directive. We are twenty-five seconds over time; we must get back to work."

"Just a minute," said Luke. "One or two things about that directive I want explained."

Miskitman turned his mild gaze upon Luke. "You did not understand it?"

"Not altogether. Who does it apply to?"

"It is an order for the entire gang."

"What do they mean, 'hand tools'?"

"These are tools which are held in the hands."

"Does that mean a shovel?"

"A shovel?" Miskitman shrugged his burly shoulders. "A shovel is a hand tool."

Luke asked in a voice of hushed wonder: "They want me to polish my shovel, carry it four miles to the warehouse, then pick it up tomorrow and carry it back here?"

Miskitman unfolded the directive, held it at arm's length, and read with moving lips. "That is the order." He refolded the paper and returned it to his pocket.

Luke again feigned astonishment. "Certainly there's a mistake."

"A mistake?" Miskitman was puzzled. "Why should there be a mistake?"

"They can't be serious," said Luke. "It's not only ridiculous, it's peculiar."

"I do not know," said Miskitman incuriously. "To work. We are late one minute and a half."

"I assume that all this cleaning and transportation is done on Organization time," Luke suggested.

Miskitman unfolded the directive, held it at arm's length, read. "It does not say so. Our quota is not different." He folded the directive and put it in his pocket.

Luke spat on the rock floor. "I'll bring my own shovel. Let 'em carry around their own precious hand tools."

Miskitman scratched his chin and once more reread the directive. He shook his head dubiously. "The order says that all hand tools must be cleaned and taken to the warehouse. It does not say who owns the tools."

Luke could hardly speak for exasperation. "You know what I think of that directive?"

Fedor Miskitman paid him no heed. "To work. We are overtime."

"If I were general superintendent—" Luke began, but Miskitman rumbled roughly.

"We do not earn perquisites by talking. To work. We are late."

The rotary cutter started up; seventy-two teeth snarled into gray-brown sandstone. Hopper jaws swallowed the chunks, passing them down an epiglottis into a feeder gut which evacuated far down the tunnel into life-buckets. Stray chips rained upon the tunnel floor, which Luke

Grogatch must scrape up and return into the hopper. Behind Luke two reinforcement men flung steel hoops into place, flash-welding them to longitudinal bars with quick pinches of the fingers, contact-plates in their gauntlets discharging the requisite gout of energy. Behind came the concrete-spray man, mix hissing out of his revolving spider, followed by two finishers, nervous men working with furious energy, stroking the concrete into a glossy polish. Fedor Miskitman marched back and forth, testing the reinforcement, gauging the thickness of the concrete, making frequent progress checks on the chart to the rear of the rotary cutter, where an electronic device traced the course of the tunnel, guiding it through the system of conduits, ducts, passages, pipes, and tubes for water, air, gas, steam, transportation, freight, and communication which knit the city into an organized unit.

The night shift ended at four o'clock in the morning. Miskitman made careful entries in his log; the concrete-spray man blew out his nozzles; the reinforcement workers removed their gauntlets, power packs, and insulating garments. Luke Grogatch straightened, rubbed his sore back, and stood glowering at the shovel. He felt Miskitman's ox-calm scrutiny. If he threw the shovel to the side of the tunnel as usual and marched off about his business, he would be guilty of disorganized conduct. The penalty, as Luke knew well, was declassification. Luke stared at the shovel, fuming with humiliation. Conform or be declassified. Submit—or become a Junior Executive.

Luke heaved a deep sigh. The shovel was clean enough; one or two swipes with a rag would remove the dust. But there was the ride by crowded man-belt to the warehouse, the queue at the window, the check-in, the added distance to his dormitory. Tomorrow the process must be repeated. Why the necessity for this added effort? Luke knew well enough. An obscure functionary somewhere along the chain of bureaus and commissions had been at a loss for a means to display his diligence. What better method than concern for valuable city property? Consequently the absurd directive, filtering down to Fedor Miskitman and ultimately to Luke Grogatch, the victim. What joy to meet this obscure functionary face to face, to tweak his sniveling nose, to kick his craven rump along the corridors of this own office....

Fedor Miskitman's voice disturbed his reverie. "Clean your shovel. It is the end of the shift."

Luke made token resistance. "The shovel is clean," he growled. "This is the most absurd antic I've ever been coerced into. If only I—"

Fedor Miskitman, in a voice as calm and unhurried as a deep river, said, "If you do not like the policy, you should put a petition in the suggestion box. That is the privilege of all. Until the policy is changed you must conform. That is the way we live. That is Organization, and we are Organized men."

"Let me see that directive," Luke barked. "I'll get it changed. I'll cram it down somebody's throat. I'll—"

"You must wait until it is logged. Then you may have it; it is useless to me."

"I'll wait," said Luke between clenched teeth.

With method and deliberation Fedor Miskitman made a final check of the job, inspecting machinery, the teeth of a cutter head, the nozzles of the spider, the discharge belt. He went to his little desk at the rear of the rotary drill, noted progress, signed expense-account vouchers, finally registered the policy directive on minifilm. Then with a ponderous sweep of his arm he tendered the yellow sheet to Luke. "What will you do with it?"

"I'll find who formed the idiotic policy. I'll tell him what I think of it and what I think of him, to boot."

Miskitman shook his head in disapproval. "That is not the way such things should be done."

"How would you do it?" asked Luke with a wolfish grin.

Miskitman considered, pursing his lips, jerking his bristling eyebrows. At last with great simplicity of manner he said, "I would not do it."

Luke threw up his hands and set off down the tunnel. Miskitman's voice boomed against his back. "You must take the shovel."

Luke halted. Slowly he faced about, glared back at the hulking figure of the foreman. Obey the policy directive or be declassified. With slow steps, with hanging head and averted eyes, he retraced his path. Snatching the shovel, he stalked back down the tunnel. His bony shoulder blades were exposed and sensitive; Fedor Miskitman's mild blue gaze, following him, seemed to scrape the nerves of his back.

Ahead the tunnel extended, a glossy pale sinus, dwindling back along the distance they had bored. Through some odd trick of refraction alternate bright and dark rings circled the tube, confusing the eye, creating a hypnotic semblance of two-dimensionality. Luke shuffled drearily into this illusory bull's-eye, dazed with shame and helplessness, the shovel a load of despair. Had he come to this—Luke Grogatch, previously so arrogant in his cynicism and barely concealed Nonconformity? Must he cringe at last, submit slavishly to witless regulations?... If only he were a few places further up the list! Drearily he pictured the fine incredulous shock with which he would have greeted the policy directive, the sardonic nonchalance with which he would have let the shovel fall from his limp hands....Too late, too late! Now he must toe the mark, must carry his shovel dutifully to the warehouse. In a spasm of rage he flung the blameless implement clattering down the tunnel ahead of him. Nothing he could do! Nowhere to turn! No way to strike back! Organization: smooth and relentless; Organization: massive and inert, tolerant of the submissive, serenely cruel to the unbeliever...Luke came to his shovel and, whispering an obscenity, snatched it up and half-ran down the pallid tunnel.

He climbed through a manhole and emerged upon the deck of the 1123rd Avenue Hub, where he instantly absorbed the crowds trampling between the man-belts, which radiated like spokes, and the various escalators. Clasping the shovel to his chest, Luke struggled aboard the Fontego man-belt and rushed south, in a direction opposite to that of his dormitory. He rode ten minutes to Astoria Hub, dropped a dozen levels of the Grimesby College Escalator, and crossed a gloomy dank area smelling of old rock to a local feeder-belt which carried him to the District 8892 Sewer Maintenance Warehouse.

Luke found the warehouse brightly lit, the center of considerable activity, with several hundred men coming and going. Those coming, like Luke, carried tools; those going were empty-handed.

Luke joined the line which formed in front of the tool storeroom. Fifty or sixty men preceded him, a drab centipede of arms, shoulders, heads, legs, the tools projecting to either side. The centipede moved slowly, the men exchanging badinage and quips.

Observing their patience, Luke's normal irascibility asserted itself. Look at them, he thought, standing like sheep, jumping to attention at the rustle of an unfolding directive. Did they inquire about the reason for the order? Did they question the necessity for their inconvenience? No! The louts stood chuckling and chatting, accepting the directive as one of life's incalculable vicissitudes, something elemental and arbitrary, like the changing of the seasons....And he, Luke Grogatch, was he better or worse? The question burned in Luke's throat like the aftertaste of vomit.

Still, better or worse, where was his choice? Conform or declassify. A poor choice. There was always the recourse of the suggestion box, as Fedor Miskitman, perhaps in bland jest, had pointed out. Luke growled in disgust. Weeks later he might receive a printed form with one statement of a multiple-choice list checked off by some clerical flunky or junior executive: "The situation described by your petition is already under study by responsible officials. Thank you for your interest." Or, "The situation described by your petition is the product of established policy and is not subject to change. Thank you for your interest."

A novel thought occurred to Luke: he might exert himself and reclassify *up* the list....As soon as the idea arrived he dismissed it. In the first place he was close to middle age; too many young men were pushing up past him. Even if he could goad himself into the competition....

The line moved slowly forward. Behind Luke a plump little man sagged under the weight of a Velstro inchskip. A forelock of light brown floss dangled over his moony face; his mouth was puckered into a rosebud of concentration; his eyes were absurdly serious. He wore a rather dapper pink and brown coverall with orange ankle-boots and a blue beret with the three orange pompoms affected by the Velstro technicians.

Between shabby, sour-mouthed Luke and this short moony man in the dandy's overalls existed so basic a difference that an immediate mutual dislike was inevitable.

The short man's prominent hazel eyes rested on Luke's shovel, traveled thoughtfully over Luke's dirt-stained trousers and jacket. He turned his eyes to the side.

"Come a long way?" Luke asked maliciously.

"Not far," said the moon-faced man.

"Worked overtime, eh?" Luke winked. "A bit of quiet beavering, nothing like it—or so I'm told."

"We finished the job," said the plump man, with dignity. "Beavering doesn't enter into it. Why spend half tomorrow's shift on five minutes' work we could do tonight?"

"I know a reason," said Luke wisely. "To do your fellow man a good one in the eye."

The moon-faced man twisted his mouth in a quick uncertain smile, then decided that the remark was not humorous. "That's not my way of working," he said stiffly.

"That thing must be heavy," said Luke, noting how the plump little arms struggled and readjusted to the irregular contours of the tool.

"Yes," came the reply. "It is heavy."

"An hour and a half," intoned Luke. "That's how long it's taking me to park this shovel. Just because somebody up the list has a nightmare. And we poor hoodlums at the bottom suffer."

"I'm not at the bottom of the list. I'm a Technical Tool Operator."

"No difference," said Luke. "The hour and a half is the same. Just for somebody's silly notion."

"It's not really so silly," said the moon-faced man. "I fancy there is a good reason for the policy."

Luke shook the shovel by its handle. "And so I have to carry this back and forth along the man-belt three hours a day?"

The little man pursed his lips. "The author of the directive undoubtedly knows his business very well. Otherwise he'd not hold his classification."

"Just who is this unsung hero?" sneered Luke. "I'd like to meet him. I'd like to learn why he wants me to waste three hours a day."

The short man now regarded Luke as he might an insect in his victual ration. "You talk like a Nonconformist. Excuse me if I seem offensive."

"Why apologize for something you can't help?" asked Luke and turned his back.

He flung his shovel to the clerk behind the wicket and received a check. Elaborately Luke turned to the moon-faced man and tucked the check into the breast pocket of the pink and brown coveralls. "You keep this; you'll be using that shovel before I will."

He stalked proudly out of the warehouse. A grand gesture, but—he hesitated before stepping on the man-belt—was it sensible? The technical tool operator in the pink and brown coveralls came out of the warehouse behind him, giving him a queer glance, and hurried away.

Luke looked back into the warehouse. If he returned now he could set things right, and tomorrow there'd be no trouble. If he stormed off to his dormitory, it meant another declassification. Luke Grogatch, Junior Executive. Luke reached into his jumper and took out the policy directive he had acquired from Fedor Miskitman: a bit of yellow paper, printed with a few lines of type, a trivial thing in itself—but it symbolized the Organization: massive force in irresistible operation. Nervously Luke plucked the paper and looked back into the warehouse. The tool operator had called him a Nonconformist; Luke's mouth squirmed in a brief, weary grimace. It wasn't true. Luke was not a Nonconformist; Luke was nothing in particular. And he needed his bed, his nutrition ticket, his meager expense account. Luke groaned quietly—almost a whisper. The end of the road. He had gone as far as he could go; had he ever thought he could defeat the Organization? Maybe he was wrong and everyone else was right. Possible, thought Luke without conviction. Miskitman seemed content enough; the technical tool operator seemed not only content but complacent. Luke leaned against the warehouse wall, eyes burning and moist with self-pity. Nonconformist. Misfit. What was he going to do?

He curled his lip spitefully, stepped forward onto the man-belt. Devil take them all! They could declassify him; he'd become a junior executive and laugh!

In subdued spirits Luke rode back to the Grimesby Hub. Here, about to board the escalator, he stopped short, blinking and rubbing his long sallow chin, considering still another aspect to the matter. It seemed to offer the chance of—but no. Hardly likely...and yet, why not? Once again he examined the directive. Lavester Limon, Manager of the District Office of Procurement, presumably had issued the policy; Lavester Limon could rescind it. If Luke could so persuade Limon, his troubles, while not dissipated, at least would be lessened. He could report shovel-less to his job; he could return sardonic grin for bland hidden grin with Fedor Miskitman. He might even go to the trouble of locating the moon-faced little technical tool operator with the inchskip....

Luke sighed. Why continue this futile daydream? First Lavester Limon must be induced to rescind the directive—and what were the odds of this?....Perhaps not astronomical, after all, mused Luke as he rode the man-belt back to his dormitory. The directive clearly was impractical. It worked an inconvenience on many people, while accomplishing very little. If Lavester Limon could be persuaded of this, if he could be shown that his own prestige and reputation were suffering, he might agree to recall the ridiculous directive.

Luke arrived at his dormitory shortly after seven. He went immediately to the communication booth, called the District 8892 Office of Procurement. Lavester Limon, he was told, would be arriving at eight-thirty.

Luke made a careful toilet, and after due consideration invested four Special Coupons in a fresh set of fibers: a tight black jacket and blue trousers of somewhat martial cut, of considerably better quality than his usual costume. Surveying himself in the washroom mirror, Luke felt that he cut not so poor a figure.

He took his morning quota of nutrition at a nearby Type RP Victualing Service, then ascended to the Sublevel 14 and rode the man-belt to District 8892 Bureau of Sewer Construction and Maintenance.

A pert office girl, dark hair pulled forward over her face in the modish "robber baron" style, conducted Luke into Lavester Limon's office. At the door she glanced demurely backward, and Luke was glad that he had invested in new clothes. Responding to the stimulus, he threw back his shoulders and marched confidently into Lavester Limon's office.

Lavester Limon, sitting at his desk, bumped briefly to his feet in courteous acknowledgement—an amiable-seeming man of middle stature, golden-brown hair brushed carefully across a freckled and suntanned bald spot; golden-brown eyes, round and easy; a golden-brown lounge jacket and trousers of fine golden-brown corduroy. He waved his arm at a chair. "Won't you sit down, Mr. Grogatch?"

In the presence of so much cordiality Luke relaxed his truculence, and even felt a burgeoning of hope. Limon seemed a decent sort; perhaps the directive was, after all, an administrative error.

Limon raised his golden-brown eyebrows inquiringly.

Luke wasted no time on preliminaries. He brought forth the directive. "My business concerns this, Mr. Limon: a policy which you seem to have formulated."

Limon took the directive, read, nodded. "Yes, that's my policy. Something wrong?"

Luke felt surprise and a pang of premonition: surely so reasonable a man must instantly perceive the folly of the directive!

"It's simply not a workable policy," said Luke earnestly. "In fact, Mr. Limon, it's completely unreasonable!"

Lavester Limon seemed not at all offended. "Well, well! And why do you say that? Incidentally, Mr. Grogatch, you're...." Again the golden-brown eyebrows arched inquiringly.

"I'm a flunky, Class D, on a tunnel gang," said Luke. "Today it took me an hour and a half to check my shovel. Tomorrow, there'll be another hour and a half checking the shovel out. All on my own time. I don't think that's reasonable."

Lavester Limon reread the directive, pursed his lips, nodded his head once or twice. He spoke into his desk phone. "Miss Rab, I'd like to see—" he consulted the directive's reference number—"Item seven-five-four-two, File G ninety-eight." To Luke he said in rather an absent voice: "Sometimes these things become a trifle complicated."

"But can you change the policy?" Luke burst out. "Do you agree that it's unreasonable?"

Limon cocked his head to the side, made a doubtful grimace. "We'll see what's on the reference. If my memory serves me...." His voice faded away.

Twenty seconds passed. Limon tapped his fingers on his desk. A soft chime sounded. Limon touched a button and his desk-screen exhibited the item he had requested: another policy directive similar in form to the first.

PUBLIC WORKS DEPARTMENT, PUBLIC UTILITIES DIVISION
AGENCY OF SANITARY WORKS, DISTRICT 8892
SEWAGE DISPOSAL SECTION
Director's Office

Policy Directive:	2888 Series BQ008
Order Code:	GZP—AAR—REF
Reference:	OP9 123
Date Code:	BR—EQ—LLT
Authorized:	JR D-SDS
Checked:	AC
Counterchecked:	CX McD

From:	Judiath Ripp, Director
To:	Lavester Limon, Manager, Office of Procurement
Attention:	
Subject:	Economies of operation
Instant of Application:	Immediate
Duration of Relevance:	Permanent
Substance:	Your monthly quota of supplies for

disbursement Type A, B, D, F, H is hereby reduced 2.2%. It is suggested that you advise affected personnel of this reduction, and take steps to insure most stringent economies. It has been noticed that department use of supplies Type D in particular is in excess of calculated norm.

Suggestion: Greater care by individual users of tools, including warehouse storage at night.

"Type D supplies," said Lavester Limon wryly, "are hand tools. Old Ripp wants stringent economies. I merely pass along the word. That's the story behind six-five-one-one." He returned the directive in question to Luke and leaned back in his seat. "I can see how you're exercised, but—" he raised his hands in a careless, almost flippant gesture—"that's the way the Organization works."

Luke sat rigid with disappointment. "Then you won't revoke the directive?"

"My dear fellow! How can I?"

Luke made an attempt at reckless nonchalance. "Well, there's always room for me among the junior executives. I told them where to put their shovel."

"Mmmf. Rash. Sorry I can't help." Limon surveyed Luke curiously, and his lips curved in a faint grin. "Why don't you tackle old Ripp?"

Luke squinted sideways in suspicion. "What good will that do?"

"You never know," said Limon breezily. "Suppose lightning strikes—suppose he rescinds his directive? I can't agitate with him myself; I'd get in trouble—but there's no reason why you can't." He turned Luke a quick, knowing smile, and Luke understood that Lavester Limon's amiability, while genuine, served as a useful camouflage for self-interest and artful playing of the angles.

Luke rose abruptly to his feet. He played cat's paw for no one, and he opened his mouth to tell Lavester Limon as much. In that instant a recollection crossed his mind: the scene in the warehouse, where he had contemptuously tossed the check for his shovel to the technical tool operator. Always Luke had been prone to the grand gesture, the reckless commitment which left him no scope for retreat. When would he learn self-control? In a subdued voice Luke asked, "Who is this Ripp again?"

"Judiath Ripp, Director of the Sewage Disposal Section. You may have difficulty getting in to see him; he's a troublesome old brute. Wait, I'll find out if he's at his office."

He made inquiries into his desk phone. Information returned to the effect that Judiath Ripp had just arrived at the Section office on Sublevel 3, under Bramblebury Park.

Limon gave Luke tactical advice. "He's choleric—something of a barker. Here's the secret: pay no attention to him. He respects firmness. Pound the table. Roar back at him. If you pussyfoot he'll sling you out. Give him tit for tat and he'll listen."

Luke looked hard at Lavester Limon, well aware that the twinkle in the golden-brown eyes was malicious glee. He said, "I'd like a copy of that directive, so he'll know what I'm talking about."

Limon sobered instantly. Luke could read his mind: *Will Ripp hold it against me if I send up this crackpot? It's worth the chance.* "Sure," said Limon. "Pick it up from the girl."

Luke ascended to Sublevel 3 and walked through the pleasant trilevel arcade below Bramblebury Park. He passed the tall, glass-walled fishtank open to the sky and illuminated by sunlight, boarded the local man-belt, and after a ride of two or three minutes alighted in front of the District 8892 Agency of Sanitary Works.

The Sewage Disposal Section occupied a rather pretentious suite off a small courtyard garden. Luke walked along a passage tiled with blue, gray, and green mosaic and entered a white room furnished in pale gray and pink. A long mural of cleverly twisted gold, black, and white tubing decorated one wall; another was swathed in heavy green leaves growing from a chest-high planter. At a desk sat the receptionist, a plump pouty blonde girl with a simulated bone through her nose and a shark's-tooth necklace dangling around her neck. She wore her hair tied up over her head like a sheaf of wheat, and an amusing black and brown primitive symbol decorated her forehead.

Luke explained that he wished a few words with Mr. Judiath Ripp, Director of the Section.

Perhaps from uneasiness, Luke spoke brusquely. The girl, blinking in surprise, examined him curiously. After a moment's hesitation she shook her head doubtfully. "Won't someone else do? Mr. Ripp's day is tightly scheduled. What did you want to see him about?"

Luke, attempting a persuasive smile, achieved instead a leer of sinister significance. The girl was frankly startled.

"Perhaps you'll tell Mr. Ripp I'm here," said Luke. "One of his policy directives—well, there have been irregularities, or rather a misapplication—"

"Irregularities?" The girl seemed to hear only the single word. She gazed at Luke with new eyes, observing the crisp new black and blue garments with their quasi-military cut. Some sort of inspector? "I'll call Mr. Ripp," she said nervously. "Your name, sir, and status?"

"Luke Grogatch. My status—" Luke smiled once more, and the girl averted her eyes. "It's not important."

"I'll call Mr. Ripp, sir. One moment, if you please." She swung around, murmured anxiously into her screen, looked at Luke, and spoke again. A thin voice rasped a reply. The girl swung back around and nodded at Luke. "Mr. Ripp can spare a few minutes. The first door, please."

Luke walked with stiff shoulders into a tall, wood-paneled room, one wall of which displayed green-glowing tanks of darting red and yellow fish. At the desk sat Judiath Ripp, a tall, heavy man, himself resembling a large fish. His head was narrow, pale as mackerel, and rested backward-tilting on his shoulders. He had no perceptible chin; the neck ran up to his carplike mouth. Pale eyes stared at Luke over small round nostrils; a low brush of hair thrust up from the rear of his head like dry grass over a sand dune. Luke remembered Lavester Limon's verbal depiction of Ripp: "choleric." Hardly appropriate. Had Limon a grudge against Ripp? Was he using Luke as an instrument of mischievous revenge? Suspecting as much, Luke felt uncomfortable and awkward.

Judiath Ripp surveyed him with cold unblinking eyes. "What can I do for you, Mr. Grogatch? My secretary tells me you are an investigator of some sort."

Luke considered the situation, his narrow black eyes fixed on Ripp's face. He told the exact truth. "For several weeks I have been working in the capacity of a Class D Flunky on a tunnel gang."

"What the devil do you investigate on a tunnel gang?" Ripp asked in chilly amusement.

Luke made a slight gesture, one signifying much of nothing, as the other might choose to take it. "Last night the foreman of this gang received a policy directive issued by Lavester Limon of the Office of Procurement. For sheer imbecility this policy caps any of my experience."

"If it's Limon's doings, I can well believe it," said Ripp between his teeth.

"I sought him out in his office. He refused to accept the responsibility and referred me to you."

Ripp sat a trifle straighter in his chair. "What policy is this?"

Luke passed the two directives across the desk. Ripp read slowly, then reluctantly returned the directives. "I fail to see exactly—" He paused. "I should say, these directives merely reflect instructions received by me which I have implemented. Where is the difficulty?"

"Let me cite my personal experience," said Luke. "This morning—as I say, in my temporary capacity as a flunky—I carried a shovel from tunnel head to warehouse and checked it. The operation required an hour and a half. If I were working steadily on a job of this sort, I'd be quite demoralized."

Ripp appeared untroubled. "I can only refer you to my superiors." He spoke aside into his desk phone. "Please transmit File OR nine, Item one-two-three." He turned back to Luke. "I can't take responsibility, either for the directive or for revoking it. May I ask what sort of investigation takes you down into the tunnels? And to whom you report?"

At a loss for words at once evasive and convincing, Luke conveyed an attitude of contemptuous silence.

Judiath Ripp contracted the skin around his blank round eyes in a frown. "As I consider this matter I become increasingly puzzled. Why is this subject a matter for investigation? Just who—"

From a slot appeared the directive Ripp had requested. He glanced at it, then tossed it to Luke. "You'll see that this relieves me totally of responsibility," he said curtly.

The directive was the standard form:

Office of
The Commissioner of Public Utilities

Policy Directive:	449 Series UA-14-G2
Order Code:	GZP—AAR—REF
Reference:	TQ9—1422
Date Code:	BP—EQ—LLT
Authorized:	PU-PUD-Org.
Checked:	G. Evan
Counterchecked:	Hernon Klanech

From:	Parris de Vicker, Commissioner of Public Utilities
Through:	All District Agencies of Sanitary Works
To:	All Department Heads
Attention:	
Subject:	The urgent need for sharp and immediate

economies in the use of equipment and consumption of supplies.

Instant of Application:	Immediate
Duration of Relevance:	Permanent
Substance:	All department heads are instructed to

initiate, effect, and enforce rigid economies in the employment of supplies and equipment, especially those items comprised of or manufac-
tured from alloy metals or requiring the functional consumption of
same, in those areas in which official authority is exercised. A decre-
ment of 2% will be considered minimal. Status augmentation will in
some measure be affected by economies achieved.

Directive reviewed and transmitted: Lee Jon Smith, District Agent
of Sanitary Works 8892.

Luke rose to his feet, concerned now only to depart from the office
as quickly as possible. He indicated the directive. "This is a copy?"

"Yes."

"I'll take it, if I may." He included it with the previous two.

Judiath Ripp watched with a faint but definite suspicion. "I fail to
understand whom you represent."

"Sometimes the less one knows the better," said Luke.

The suspicion faded from Judiath Ripp's piscine face. Only a person
secure in his status could afford to use language of this sort to a member
of the low High Echelon. He nodded slightly. "Is that all you require?"

"No," said Luke, "but it's all I can get here."

He turned toward the door, feeling the rake of Ripp's eyes on his
back.

Ripp's voice cut at him suddenly and sharply. "Just a moment."

Luke slowly turned.

"Who are you? Let me see your credentials?"

Luke laughed coarsely. "I don't have any."

Judiath Ripp rose to his feet, stood towering with knuckles pressed on the desk. Suddenly Luke saw that, after all, Judiath Ripp *was* choleric. His face, mackerel-pale, became suffused with salmon-pink. "Identify yourself," he said throatily, "before I call the watchman."

"Certainly," said Luke. "I have nothing to hide. I am Luke Grogatch. I work as Class D Flunky on Tunnel Gang Number Three, out of the Bureau of Sewer Construction and Maintenance."

"What are you doing here, misrepresenting yourself, wasting my time?"

"Where did I misrepresent myself?" demanded Luke in a contentious voice. "I came here to find out why I had to carry my shovel to the warehouse this morning. It cost me an hour and a half. It doesn't make sense. You've been ordered to economize two percent, so I spend three hours a day carrying a shovel back and forth."

Judiath Ripp stared at Luke for a few seconds, then abruptly sat down. "You're a Class D Flunky?"

"That's right."

"Hmm. You've been to the Office of Procurement. The manager sent you here?"

"No. He gave me a copy of his directive, just as you did."

The salmon-pink flush had died from Ripp's flat cheeks. The carplike mouth twitched in infinitesimal amusement. "No harm in that, certainly. What do you hope to achieve?"

"I don't want to carry that blasted shovel back and forth. I'd like you to issue orders to that effect."

Judiath Ripp spread his pale mouth in a cold, drooping smile. "Bring me a policy directive to that effect from Parris deVicker and I'll be glad to oblige you. Now—"

"Will you make an appointment for me?"

"An appointment?" Ripp was puzzled. "With whom?"

"With the Commissioner of Public Utilities."

"Pffah!" Ripp waved his hand in cold dismissal. "Get out."

Luke stood in the blue mosaic entry seething with hate for Ripp, Limon, Miskitman, and every intervening functionary. If he were only chairman of the board for a brief two hours (went the oft-repeated daydream), how they'd quickstep! In his mind's eye he saw Judiath Ripp shoveling wads of wet waste with a leaden shovel while a rotary driller, twice as noisy and twice as violent, blew back gales of hot dust and rock chips across his neck. Lavester Limon would be forced to change the smoking teeth of the drill with a small and rusty monkey wrench, while Fedor Miskitman, before and after the shift, carried shovel, monkey wrench, and all the worn teeth to and from the warehouse.

Luke stood moping in the passage for five minutes, then escalated to the surface, which at this point, by virtue of Bramblebury Park, could clearly be distinguishable as the surface and not just another level among coequal levels. He walked slowly along the gravel paths, ignoring the open sky for the immediacy of his problems. He faced a dead end. There was no further scope of action. Judiath Ripp had mockingly suggested that he consult the Commissioner of Public Utilities. Even if by some improbable circumstance he secured an appointment with the Commissioner, what good would ensue? Why should the Commissioner revoke a policy direc-tive of such evident importance? Unless he could be persuaded—by some instrumentality Luke was unable to define or even imagine—to issue a special directive exempting Luke from the provision of the policy...Luke chuckled hollowly, a noise which alarmed the pigeons strutting along the walk. Now what? Back to the dormitory. His dormitory privileges included twelve hours' use of his cot per day, and he was not extracting full value from his expense account unless he made use of it. But Luke had no desire for sleep. As he glanced up at the perspective of the towers surrounding the park he felt a melancholy exhilaration. The sky, the wonderful clear open sky, blue and brilliant! Luke shivered, for the sun here was hidden by the Morgenthau Moonspike, and the air was brisk.

Luke crossed the park, thinking to sit where a band of hazy sunlight slashed down between the towers. The benches were crowded with blink-ing old men and women, but Luke presently found a seat. He sat looking up into the sky, enjoying the mild natural sun warmth. How seldom did he see the sun! In his youth he had frequently set forth on long cross-city hikes, rambling high along the skyways, with space to right and left, the clouds near enough for intimate inspection, the sunlight sparkling and stinging his skin. Gradually the hikes had spread apart, coming at ever longer intervals, and now he could hardly remember when last he'd tramped the wind-lanes. What dreams he had had in those early days, what exuberant visions! Obstacles seemed trivial; he had seen himself clawing up the list, winning a good expense account, the choicest of perquisites, unnumbered Special Coupons! He had planned to have a private air-car, unrestricted nutrition, an apartment far above the surface, high and remote....Dreams. Luke had been victimized by his tongue, his quick temper, his obstinacy. At heart, he was no Nonconformist—no, cried Luke, never! Luke has been born of tycoon stock, and through influence, a word here, a hint there, had been launched into the Organi-zation of a high status. But circumstances and Luke's chronic truculence had driven him into opposition with established ways, and down the Status List he had gone: through professional scholarships, technical trainee appointments, craft apprenticeships, all the varieties of semiskills and machine operation. Now he was Luke Grogatch, flunky, unskilled, Class D, facing the final declassification. But still too vain to carry a shovel. No: Luke corrected himself. His vanity was not at stake. Vanity he had discarded long ago, along with his youthful dreams. All he had left was pride, his right to use the word "I" in connection with himself. If he submitted to Policy Directive 6511 he would relinquish this right; he would be absorbed into the masses of the Organization as a spatter of foam falls back and is absorbed into the ocean....Luke jerked nervously to his feet. He wasted time sitting here. Judiath Ripp, with conger-like malice, had suggested a directive from the Commissioner of Public Utilities. Very well, Luke would obtain that directive and fling it down under Ripp's pale round nostrils.

How?

Luke rubbed his chin dubiously. He walked to a communication booth and checked the directory. As he had surmised, the Commission of Public Utilities was housed in the Organization Central Tower, in Silverado, District 3666, ninety miles to the north.

Luke stood in the watery sunlight, hoping for inspiration. The aged idlers, huddling on the benches like winterbound sparrows, watched him incuriously. Once again Luke was obscurely pleased with his purchase of new clothes. A fine figure he cut, he assured himself.

How? wondered Luke. How to gain an appointment with the Commissioner? How to persuade him to change his views?

No inkling of a solution presented itself.

He looked at his watch: it was still only midmorning. Ample time to visit Organization Central and return in time to report for duty....Luke grimaced wanly. Was his resolution so feeble, then? Was he, after all, to slink back into the tunnel tonight carrying the hated shovel? Luke shook his head slowly. He did not know.

At the Bramblebury Interchange Luke boarded an express highline northbound for Silverado Station. With a hiss and a whine, the shining metal worm darted forward, sliding up to the 13th Level, flashing north at great speed in and out of the sunlight, through tunnels, across chasms between towers, with far below the nervous seethe of the city. Four times the express sighed to a halt: at IBM University, at Braemar, at Great Northern Junction, and finally, thirty minutes out of Bramblebury, at Silverado Central, Luke disembarked; the express slid away through the towers, lithe as an eel through waterweed.

Luke entered the tenth-level foyer of the Central Tower, a vast cave of marble and bronze. Throngs of men and women thrust past him: grim, striding tycoons, stamped with the look of destiny, High Echelon personnel, their assistants, the assistants to their assistants, functionaries on down the list, all dutifully wearing high-status garments, the lesser folk hoping to be mistaken for their superiors. All hurried, tense-faced and abrupt, partly from habit, partly because only a person of low status had no need to hurry. Luke thrust and elbowed with the best of them, and made his way to the central kiosk where he consulted a directory.

Parris de Vicker, Commissioner of Public Utilities, had his office on the 59th Level. Luke passed him by and located the Secretary of Public Affairs, Mr. Sewell Sepp, on the 81st Level. No more underlings, thought Luke. This time I'm going to the top. If anyone can resolve this matter, it's Sewell Sepp.

He put himself aboard the lift and emerged into the lobby of the Department of Public Affairs—a splendid place, glittering with disciplined color and ornament after the mock-antique decor known as Second Institutional. The walls were of polished milk glass inset with medallions of shifting kaleidoscopic flashes. The floor was diapered in blue and white sparklestone. A dozen bronze statues dominated the room, massive figures symbolizing the basic public services: communication, transport, education, water, energy, and sanitation. Luke skirted the pedestals and crossed to the reception counter, where ten young women in handsome brown and black uniforms stood with military precision, each to her six feet of counter top. Luke selected one of these girls, who curved her lips in an automatic empty smile.

"Yes, sir?"

"I want to see Mr. Sepp," said Luke brazenly.

The girl's smile remained frozen while she looked at him with startled eyes. "Mr. who?"

"Sewell Sepp, the Secretary of Public Affairs."

The girl asked gently, "Do you have an appointment, sir?"

"No."

"It's impossible, sir."

Luke nodded sourly. "Then I'll see Commissioner Parris de Vicker."

"Do you have an appointment to see Mr. de Vicker?"

"No, I'm afraid not."

The girl shook her head with a trace of amusement. "Sir, you can't just walk in on these people. They're extremely busy. Everyone must have an appointment."

"Oh, come now," said Luke. "Surely it's conceivable that—"

"Definitely not, sir."

"Then," said Luke, "I'll make an appointment. I'd like to see Mr. Sepp some time today, if possible."

The girl lost interest in Luke. She resumed her manner of impersonal courtesy. "I'll call the office of Mr. Sepp's appointment secretary."

She spoke into a mesh, then turned back to Luke. "No appointments are open this month, sir. Will you speak to someone else? Some under-official?"

"No," said Luke. He gripped the edge of the counter for a moment, started to turn away, then asked, "Who authorizes these appointments?"

"The secretary's first aide, who screens the list of applications."

"I'll speak to the first aide, then."

The girl sighed. "You need an appointment, sir."

"I need an appointment to make an appointment?"

"Yes, sir."

"Do I need an appointment to make an appointment for an appointment?"

"No, sir. Just walk right in."

"Where?"

"Suite Forty-two, inside the rotunda, sir."

Luke passed through twelve-foot crystal doors and walked down a short hall. Scurrying patterns of color followed him like shadows along both the walls, grotesque cubistic shapes parodying the motion of his body: a whimsy which surprised Luke and which might have pleased him under less critical circumstances.

He passed through another pair of crystal portals into the rotunda. Six levels above, a domed ceiling depicted scenes of legend in stained glass. Behind a ring of leather couches doors gave into surrounding offices; one of these doors, directly across from the entrance, bore the words:

OFFICES OF THE SECRETARY
DEPARTMENT OF PUBLIC AFFAIRS

On the couches, half a hundred men and women waited with varying degrees of patience. The careful disdain with which they surveyed each other suggested that their status was high; the frequency with which they consulted their watches conveyed the impression that they were momentarily on the point of departure.

A mellow voice sounded over a loudspeaker: "Mr. Artur Coff, please, to the Office of the Secretary." A plump gentleman threw down the periodical he had fretfully been examining and jumped to his feet. He crossed to the bronze and black glass door and passed through.

Luke watched him enviously, then turned aside through an arch marked *Suite 42*. An usher in a brown and black uniform stepped forward: Luke stated his business and was conducted into a small cubicle.

A young man behind a metal desk peered intently at him. "Sit down, please." He motioned to a chair. "Your name?"

"Luke Grogatch."

"Ah, Mr. Grogatch. May I inquire your business?"

"I have something to say to the Secretary of Public Affairs."

"Regarding what subject?"

"A personal matter."

"I'm sorry, Mr. Grogatch. The Secretary is more than busy. He's swamped with important Organization business. But if you'll explain the situation to me, I'll recommend you to an appropriate member of the staff."

"That won't help," said Luke. "I want to consult the Secretary in relation to a recently issued policy directive."

"Issued by the Secretary?"

"Yes."

"You wish to object to this directive?"

Luke grudgingly admitted as much.

"There are appropriate channels for this process," said the aide decisively. "If you will fill out this form—not here, but in the rotunda—drop it into the suggestion box to the right of the door as you go out—"

In sudden fury Luke wadded up the form and flung it down on the desk. "Surely he has five minutes free—"

"I'm afraid not, Mr. Grogatch," the aide said in a voice of ice. "If you will look through the rotunda you will see a number of very important people who have waited, some of them for months, for five minutes with the Secretary. If you wish to fill out an application, stating your business in detail, I will see that it receives due consideration."

Luke stalked out of the cubicle. The aide watched him go with a bleak smile of dislike. The man obviously had Nonconformist tendencies, he thought...probably should be watched.

Luke stood in the rotunda, muttering, "What now? What now? What now?" in a half-mesmerized undertone. He stared around the rotunda, at the pompous High Echelon folk, arrogantly consulting their watches, and tapping their feet. "Mr. Jepper Prinn!" called the mellow voice over the loudspeaker. "The Office of the Secretary, if you please." Luke watched Jepper Prinn walk to the bronze and black glass portal.

Luke slumped into a chair, scratched his long nose, looked cautiously around the rotunda. Nearby sat a big, bull-necked man with a red face, protruding lips, a shock of rank blond hair—a tycoon, judging from his air of absolute authority.

Luke rose and went to a desk placed for the convenience of those waiting. He took several sheets of paper with the Tower letterhead and unobtrusively circled the rotunda to the entrance into Suite 42. The bull-necked tycoon paid him no heed.

Luke girded himself, closing his collar, adjusting the set of his jacket. He took a deep breath, then, when the florid man glanced in his direction, came forward officiously. He looked briskly around the circle of couches, consulting his papers; then catching the eye of the tycoon, frowned, squinted, walked forward.

"Your name, sir?" asked Luke in a official voice.

"I'm Hardin Arthur," rasped the tycoon. "Why?"

Luke nodded, consulted his paper. "The time of your appointment?"

"Eleven-ten. What of it?"

"The Secretary would like to know if you can conveniently lunch with him at one-thirty?"

Arthur considered. "I suppose it's possible," he grumbled. "I'll have to rearrange some other business....An inconvenience—but I can do it, yes."

"Excellent," said Luke. "At lunch the Secretary feels that he can discuss your business more informally and at greater length than at eleven-ten, when he can only allow you seven minutes."

"Seven minutes!" rumbled Arthur indignantly. "I can hardly spread my plans out in seven minutes."

"Yes, sir," said Luke. "The Secretary realized this, and suggests that you lunch with him."

Arthur petulantly hauled himself to his feet. "Very well. Lunch at one-thirty, correct?"

"Correct, sir. If you will walk directly into the Secretary's office at that time."

Arthur departed the rotunda, and Luke settled into the seat Arthur had vacated.

Time passed very slowly. At ten minutes after eleven the mellow voice called out, "Mr. Hardin Arthur, please. To the Office of the Secretary."

Luke rose to his feet, stalked with great dignity across the rotunda, and went through the bronze and black glass door.

Behind a long black desk sat the Secretary, a rather undistinguished man with gray hair and snapping gray eyes. He raised his eyebrows as Luke came forward: Luke evidently did not fit his preconception of Hardin Arthur.

The Secretary spoke. "Sit down, Mr. Arthur. I may as well tell you bluntly and frankly that we think your scheme is impractical. By 'we' I mean myself and the Board of Policy Evaluation—who of course have referred to the Files. First, the costs are excessive. Second, there's no guarantee that you can phase your program into that of our other tycoons. Third, the Board of Policy Evaluation tells me that Files doubts whether we'll need that much new capacity."

"Ah," Luke nodded wisely. "I see. Well, no matter. It's not important."

"Not important?" The Secretary sat up in his chair, stared at Luke in wonder. "I'm surprised to hear you say so."

Luke made an airy gesture. "Forget it. Life's too short to worry about these things. Actually there's another matter I want to discuss with you."

"Ah?"

"It may seem trivial, but the implications are large. A former employee called the matter to my attention. He's now a flunky on one of the sewer maintenance tunnel gangs, an excellent chap. Here's the situation. Some idiotic jack-in-office has issued a directive which forces this man to carry a shovel back and forth to the warehouse every day, before and after work. I've taken the trouble to follow up the matter and the chain leads here." He displayed his three policy directives.

Frowning, the Secretary glanced through them. "These all seem perfectly regular. What do you want me to do?"

"Issue a directive clarifying the policy. After all, we can't have these poor devils working three hours overtime for tomfoolishness."

"Tomfoolishness?" The Secretary was displeased. "Hardly that, Mr. Arthur. The economy directive came to me from the Board of Directors, from the Chairman himself, and if—"

"Don't mistake me," said Luke hastily. "I've no quarrel with economy; I merely want the policy applied sensibly. Checking a shovel into the warehouse—where's the economy in that?"

"Multiply that shovel by a million, Mr. Arthur," said the Secretary coldly.

"Very well, multiply it," argued Luke. "We have a million shovels. How many of these million shovels are conserved by this order? Two or three a year?"

The Secretary shrugged. "Obviously in a general directive of this sort, inequalities occur. So far as I'm concerned, I issued the directive because I was instructed to do so. If you want it changed you'll have to consult the Chairman of the Board."

"Very well. Can you arrange an appointment for me?"

"Let's settle the matter even sooner," said the Secretary. "Right now. We'll talk to him across the screen, although, as you say, it seems a trivial matter...."

"Demoralization of the working force isn't trivial, Secretary Sepp."

The Secretary shrugged, touched a button, spoke into a mesh. "The Chairman of the Board, if he's not occupied."

The screen glowed. The Chairman of the Board of Directors looked out at them. He sat in a lounge chair on the deck of his penthouse at the pinnacle of the tower. In one hand he held a glass of pale effervescent liquid; beyond him opened sunlight and blue air and a wide glimpse of the miraculous city.

"Good morning, Sepp," said the Chairman cordially, and nodded toward Luke. "Good morning to you, sir."

"Chairman, Mr. Arthur here is protesting the economy directive you sent down a few days ago. He claims that strict application is causing hardship among the labor force: demoralization, actually. Something to do with shovels."

The Chairman considered. "Economy directive? I hardly recall the exact case."

Secretary Sepp described the directive, citing code and reference numbers, explaining the provisions, and the Chairman nodded in recollection. "Yes, the metal shortage thing. Afraid I can't help you, Sepp, or you, Mr. Arthur. Policy Evaluation sent it up. Apparently we're running short of minerals; what else can we do? Cinch in the old belts, eh? Hard on all of us. What's this about shovels?"

"It's the whole matter," cried Luke in sudden shrillness, evoking startled glances from Secretary and Chairman. "Carrying a shovel back and forth to the warehouse—three hours a day! It's not economy, it's a disorganized farce!"

"Come now, Mr. Arthur," the Chairman chided humorously. "So long as you're not carrying the shovel yourself, why the excitement? It works the very devil with one's digestion. Until Policy Evaluation changes its collective mind—as it often does—then we've got to string along. Can't go counter to Policy Evaluation, you know. They're the people with the facts and figures."

"Neither here nor there," mumbled Luke. "Carrying a shovel three hours—"

"Perhaps a bit of bother for the men concerned," said the Chairman with a hint of impatience, "but they've got to see the thing from the long view. Sepp, perhaps you'll lunch with me? A marvelous day, lazy weather."

"Thank you, Mr. Chairman. I'll be pleased indeed."

"Excellent. At one or one-thirty, whenever it's convenient for you."

The screen went blank. Secretary Sepp rose to his feet. "There it is, Mr. Arthur. I can't do any more."

"Very well, Mr. Secretary," said Luke in a hollow voice.

"Sorry I can't be of more help in that other matter, but as I say—"

"It's inconsequential."

Luke turned, left the elegant office, passed through the bronze and black glass doors into the rotunda. Through the arch into Suite 42 he saw a large, bull-necked man, tomato-red in the face, hunched forward across a counter. Luke stepped forward smartly, leaving the rotunda just as the authentic Mr. Arthur and the aide came forth, deep in agitated conversation.

Luke stopped by the information desk. "Where is the Policy Evaluation Board?"

"Twenty-ninth Level, sir, this building."

In Policy Evaluation on the 29th Level Luke talked with a silk-mustached young man, courtly and elegant, with the status classification Plan Coordinator. "Certainly!" exclaimed the young man in response to Luke's question. "Authoritative information is the basis of authoritative organization. Material from Files is collated and digested in the Bureau of Abstracts, and sent up to us. We shape it and present it to the Board of Directors in the form of a daily precis."

Luke expressed interest in the Bureau of Abstracts, and the young man quickly became bored. "Grubbers among the statistics, barely able to compose an intelligible sentence. If it weren't for us...." His eyebrows, silken as his mustache, hinted of the disasters which in the absence of Policy Evaluation would overtake the Organization. "They work in a suite down on the Sixth Level."

Luke descended to the Bureau of Abstracts, and found no difficulty gaining admission to the general office. In contrast to the rather nebulous intellectualism of Policy Evaluation, the Bureau of Abstracts seemed workaday and matter-of-fact. A middle-aged woman, cheerfully fat, inquired Luke's business, and when Luke professed himself a journalist, conducted him about the premises. They went from the main lobby, walled in antique cream-colored plaster with gold scrollwork, past the fusty cubicles, where clerks sat at projection-desks, scanning ribbons of words. Extracting idea-sequence, amending, excising, condensing, cross-referring, finally producing the abstract to be submitted to Policy Evaluation. Luke's fat and cheerful guide brewed them a pot of tea; she asked questions which Luke answered in general terms, straining his voice and pursing his mouth in the effort to seem agreeable and hearty. He himself asked questions.

"I'm interested in a set of statistics on the scarcity of metals, or ores, or something similar, which recently went up to Policy Evaluation. Would you know anything about this?"

"Heavens, no!" the woman responded. "There's just too much material coming in—the business of the entire Organization.

"Where does this material come from? Who sends it to you?"

The woman made a humorous little grimace of distaste. "From Files, down on Sublevel Twelve. I can't tell you much, because we don't associate with the personnel. They're low status: clerks and the like. Sheer automatons."

Luke expressed an interest in the source of the Bureau of Abstract's information. The woman shrugged, as if to say, everyone to his own taste. "I'll call down to the Chief File Clerk; I know him, very slightly."

The Chief File Clerk, Mr. Sidd Boatridge, was self-important and brusque, as if aware of the low esteem in which he was held by the Bureau of Abstracts. He dismissed Luke's questions with a stony face of indifference. "I really have no idea, sir. We file, index, and cross-index material into the Information Bank, but we concern ourselves very little with outgoing data. My duties in fact are mainly administrative. I'll call in one of the under-clerks; he can tell you more than I can."

The under-clerk who answered Boatridge's summons was a short, turnip-faced man with matted red hair. "Take Mr. Grogatch into the outer office," said the Chief File Clerk testily. "He wants to ask you a few questions."

In the outer office, out of the Chief File Clerk's hearing, the under-clerk became rather surly and pompous, as if he had divined the level of Luke's status. He referred to himself as a "line-tender" rather than as a file clerk, the latter apparently being a classification of lesser prestige. His "line-tending" consisted of sitting beside a panel which glowed and blinked with a thousand orange and green lights. "The orange lights indicate information going down into the Bank," said the file clerk. "The green lights show where somebody up-level is drawing information out—generally at the Bureau of Abstracts."

Luke observed the orange and green flickers for a moment. "What information is being transmitted now?"

"Couldn't say," the file clerk grunted. "It's all coded. Down in the old office we had a monitoring machine and never used it. Too much else to do."

Luke considered. The file clerk showed signs of restiveness. Luke's mind worked hurriedly. He asked, "So—as I understand it—you file information, but have nothing further to do with it?"

"We file it and code it. Whoever wants information puts a program into the works and the information goes out to him. We never see it, unless we go and look in the old monitoring machine."

"Which is still down at your old office?"

The file clerk nodded. "They call it the staging chamber now. Nothing there but input and output pipes, the monitor, and the custodian."

"Where is the staging chamber?"

"Way down the levels, behind the Bank. Too low for me to work. I got more ambition." For emphasis he spat on the floor.

"A custodian is there, you say?"

"An old junior executive named Dodkin. He's been there a hundred years."

Luke dropped thirty levels aboard an express lift, then rode the down escalator another six levels to Sublevel 46. He emerged on a dingy landing with a low-perquisite nutrition hall to one side, a life attendant's dormi-tory to the other. The air carried the familiar reek of the deep under-ground, a compound of dank concrete, phenol, mercaptans, and a discreet but pervasive human smell. Luke realized with bitter amusement that he had returned to familiar territory.

Following instructions grudgingly detailed by the under-file clerk, Luke stepped aboard a chattering man-belt labeled 902—Tanks. Pres-ently he came to a brightly lit landing marked by a black and yellow sign:

INFORMATION TANKS. TECHNICAL STATION.

Inside the door a number of mechanics sat on stools, dangling their legs, lounging, chaffering.

Luke changed to a side-belt, even more dilapidated, almost in a state of disrepair. At the second junction—this one unmarked—he left the man-belt and turned down a narrow passage toward a far yellow bulb. The passage was silent, almost sinister in its dissociation from the life of the city.

Below the single yellow bulb a dented metal door was daubed with a sign:

INFORMATION TANKS—STAGING CHAMBER
NO ADMITTANCE

Luke tested the door and found it locked. He rapped and waited.

Silence shrouded the passage, broken only by a faint sound from the distant man-belt.

Luke rapped again, and now from within came a shuffle of movement. The door slid back and a pale placid eye looked forth. A rather weak voice inquired, "Yes, sir?"

Luke attempted a manner of easy authority. "You're Dodkin the custodian?"

"Yes, sir, I'm Dodkin."

"Open up, please. I'd like to come in."

The pale eye blinked in mild wonder. "This is only the staging room, sir. There's nothing here to see. The storage complexes are around to the front; if you'll go back to the junction—"

Luke broke into the flow of words. "I've just come down from the Files; it's you I want to see."

The pale eye blinked once more; the door slid open. Luke entered the long, narrow, concrete-floored staging room. Conduits dropped from the ceiling by the thousands, bent, twisted, and looped, and entered the wall, each conduit labeled with a dangling metal tag. At one end of the room was a grimy cot where Dodkin apparently slept; at the other end was a long black desk: the monitoring machine? Dodkin himself was small and stooped, but moved nimbly in spite of his evident age. His white hair was stained but well brushed; his gaze, weak and watery, was without guile, and fixed on Luke with an astronomer's detachment. He opened his mouth, and words quavered forth in spate, with Luke vainly seeking to interrupt.

"Not often do visitors come from above. Is something wrong?"

"No, nothing wrong."

"They should tell me if aught isn't correct, or perhaps there's been new policies of which I haven't been notified."

"Nothing like that, Mr. Dodkin. I'm just a visitor—"

"I don't move out as much as I used to, but last week I—"

Luke pretended to listen while Dodkin maundered on in obbligato to Luke's bitter thoughts. The continuity of directives leading from Fedor Miskitman to Lavester Limon to Judiath Ripp, bypassing Parris deVicker to Sewell Sepp and the Chairman of the Board, then returning down the classifications, down the levels, through the Policy Evaluation Board, the Bureau of Abstracts, the File Clerk's Office—the continuity had finally ended; the thread he had traced with such forlorn hope seemed about to lose itself. Well, Luke told himself, he had accepted Miskitman's challenge; he had failed, and now was faced with his original choice. Submit, carry the wretched shovel back and forth to the warehouse, or defy the order, throw down his shovel, assert himself as a free-willed man, and be declassified, to become a junior executive like old Dodkin—who, sucking and wheezing, still rambled on in compulsive loquacity.

"...Something incorrect, I'd never know, because who ever tells me? From year end to year end I'm quiet down here, and there's no one to relieve me, and I only get to the up-side rarely, once a fortnight or so, but then once you've seen the sky, does it every change? And the sun, the marvel of it, but once you've seen a marvel—"

Luke drew a deep breath. "I'm investigating an item of information which reached the File Clerk's Office. I wonder if you can help me."

Dodkin blinked his pale eyes. "What item is this, sir? Naturally I'll be glad to help in any way, even though—"

"The item dealt with economy in the use of metals and metal tools."

Dodkin nodded. "I remember them perfectly."

It was Luke's turn to stare. "You *remember* this item?"

"Certainly. It was, if I may say so, one of my little interpolations. A personal observation which I included among the other material."

"Would you be kind enough to explain?"

Dodkin would be only too pleased to explain. "Last week I had occasion to visit an old friend over by Claxton Abbey, a fine conformist, well adapted and cooperative, even if, alas, like myself, a junior executive. Of course, I mean no disrespect to good Davy Evans, like myself about ready for the pension—though little enough they allow nowadays—"

"The interpolation?"

"Yes, indeed. On my way home along the man-belt—on Sublevel Thirty-two, as I recall—I saw a workman of some sort—perhaps an electrical technician—toss several tools into a crevice on his way off-shift. I thought, now there's a slovenly act—disgraceful! Suppose the man forgot where he had hidden his tools? They'd be lost! Our reserves of raw metallic ore are very low—that's common knowledge—and every year the ocean water becomes weaker and more dilute. That man had no regard for the future of Organization. We should cherish our natural resources, do you not agree, sir?"

"I agree, naturally. But—"

"In any event, I returned here and added a memorandum to that effect into the material which goes up to the Assistant File Clerk. I thought that perhaps he'd be impressed and say a word to someone with influence—perhaps the Head File Clerk. In any event, there's the tale of my interpolation. Naturally I attempted to give it weight by citing the inevitable diminution of our natural resources."

"I see," said Luke. "And do you frequently include interpolations into the day's information?"

"Occasionally," said Dodkin, "and sometimes, I'm glad to say, people more important than I share my views. Only three weeks ago I was delayed several minutes on my way between Claxton Abbey and Kittsville on Sublevel Thirty. I made a note of it, and last week I noticed that construction has commenced on a new eight-lane man-belt between the two points, a really magnificent and modern undertaking. A month ago I noticed a shameless group of girls daubed like savages with cosmetic. What a waste, I told myself; what vanity and folly! I hinted as much in a little message to the Under-File Clerk. I seem to be just one of the many with these views, for two days later a general order discouraging these petty vanities was issued by the Secretary of Education."

"Interesting," Luke muttered. "Interesting indeed. How do you include these—interpolations—into the information?"

Dodkin hobbled nimbly to the monitoring machine. "The output from the tanks comes through here. I print a bit on the typewriter and tuck it where the Under-Clerk will see it."

"Admirable," sighed Luke. "A man with your intelligence should have ranked higher in the Status List."

Dodkin shook his placid old head. "I don't have the ambition nor the ability. I'm fit for just this simple job, and that only barely. I'd take my pension tomorrow, only the Chief File Clerk asked me to stay on a bit until he could find a man to take my place. No one seems to like the quiet down here."

"Perhaps you'll have your pension sooner than you think," said Luke.

Luke strolled along the glossy tube, ringed with alternate pale and dark refractions like a bull's eye. Ahead was motion, the glint of metal, the mutter of voices. The entire crew of Tunnel Gang Number 3 stood idle and restless.

Fedor Miskitman waved his arm with uncharacteristic vehemence. "Grogatch! At your post! You've held up the entire crew!" His heavy face was suffused with pink. "Four minutes already we're behind schedule."

Luke strolled closer.

"Hurry!" bellowed Miskitman. "What do you think this is, a blasted promenade?"

If anything, Luke slackened his pace. Fedor Miskitman lowered his big head, staring balefully. Luke halted in front of him.

"Where's your shovel?" Fedor Miskitman asked.

"I don't know," said Luke. "I'm here on the job. It's up to you to provide tools."

Fedor Miskitman stared unbelievingly. "Didn't you take it to the warehouse?"

"Yes," said Luke. "I took it there. If you want it go get it—"

Fedor Miskitman opened his mouth. He roared, "Get off the job!"

"Just as you like," said Luke. "You're the foreman."

"Don't come back!" bellowed Miskitman. "I'll report you before the day is out. You won't gain status from me, I tell you that!"

"Status?" Luke laughed. "Go ahead. Cut me down to junior executive. Do you think I care? No. And I'll tell you why. There's going to be a change or two made. When things seem different to you, think of me."

Luke Grogatch, Junior Executive, said good-bye to the retiring custodian of the staging chamber. "Don't thank me, not at all," said Luke. "I'm here by my own doing. In fact—well, never mind all that. Go up-side, sit in the sun, enjoy the air."

Finally Dodkin, in mingled joy and sorrow, hobbled for the last time down the musty passageway to the chattering man-belt.

Luke was alone in the staging chamber. Around him hummed the near-inaudible rush of information. From behind the wall came the sense of a million relays clicking, twitching, meshing; of cylinders and trace-tubes and memory-lakes whirring with activity. At the monitoring machine the output streamed forth on a reel of yellow tape. Nearby rested the typewriter.

Luke seated himself. His first interpolation: what should it be? Freedom for the Nonconformists? Tunnel gang foreman to carry tools for the entire crew? A higher expense account for junior executives?

Luke rose to his feet and scratched his chin. Power...to be subtly applied. How should he use it? To secure rich perquisites for himself? Yes, of course, this he would accomplish, by devious means. And then—what? Luke thought of the billions of men and women living, and working in the Organization. He looked at the typewriter. He could shape their lives, change their thoughts, disorganize the Organization. Was this wise? Or right? Or even amusing?

Luke sighed. In his mind's eye he saw himself standing on a high terrace overlooking the city. Luke Grogatch, Chairman of the Board. Not impossible, quite feasible. A little at a time, the correct interpolations...Luke Grogatch, Chairman of the Board. Yes. This for a starter. But it was necessary to move cautiously, with great delicacy.

Luke seated himself at the typewriter and began to pick out his first interpolation.

THE DEVIL ON SALVATION BLUFF

A few minutes before noon the sun took a lurch south and set.

Sister Mary tore the solar helmet from her fair head and threw it at the settee—a display that surprised and troubled her husband, Brother Raymond.

He clasped her quivering shoulders. "Now, dear, easy does it. A blow-up can't help us at all."

Tears were rolling down Sister Mary's cheeks. "As soon as we start from the house the sun drops out of sight! It happens every time!"

"Well—we know what patience is. There'll be another soon."

"It may be an hour! Or ten hours! And we've got our jobs to do!"

Brother Raymond went to the window, pulled aside the starched lace curtains, peered into the dusk. "We could start now, and get up the hill before night."

"Night?" cried Sister Mary. "What do you call this?"

Brother Raymond said stiffly, "I mean night by the Clock. *Real* night."

"The Clock...." Sister Mary sighed, sank into a chair. "If it weren't for the Clock we'd all be lunatics."

Brother Raymond, at the window, looked up toward Salvation Bluff, where the great clock bulked unseen. Mary joined him; they stood gazing through the dark. Presently Mary sighed. "I'm sorry, dear. But I get so upset."

211

Raymond patted her shoulder. "It's no joke living on Glory."

Mary shook her head decisively. "I shouldn't let myself go. There's the Colony to think of. Pioneers can't be weaklings."

They stood close, drawing comfort from each other.

"Look!" said Raymond. He pointed. "A fire, and up in Old Fleetville!"

In perplexity they watched the far spark.

"They're all supposed to be down in New Town," muttered Sister Mary. "Unless it's some kind of ceremony....The salt we gave them...."

Raymond, smiling sourly, spoke a fundamental postulate of life on Glory. "You can't tell anything about the Flits. They're liable to do most anything."

Mary uttered a truth even more fundamental. "*Anything* is liable to do anything."

"The Flits most liable of all.... They've even taken to dying without our comfort and help!"

"We've done our best," said Mary. "It's not our fault!"—almost as if she feared that it was.

"No one could possibly blame us."

"Except the Inspector....The Flits were thriving before the Colony came."

"We haven't bothered them; we haven't encroached, or molested, or interfered. In fact we've knocked ourselves out to help them. And for thanks they tear down our fences and break open the canal and throw mud on our fresh paint!"

Sister Mary said in a low voice, "Sometimes I hate the Flits.... Sometimes I hate Glory. Sometimes I hate the whole Colony."

Brother Raymond drew her close, patted the fair hair that she kept in a neat bun. "You'll feel better when one of the suns comes up. Shall we start?"

"It's dark," said Mary dubiously. "Glory is bad enough in the daytime."

Raymond shot his jaw forward, glanced up toward the Clock. "It *is* daytime. The Clock says it's daytime. That's Reality; we've got to cling to it! It's our link with truth and sanity!"

"Very well," said Mary, "we'll go."

Raymond kissed her cheek. "You're very brave, dear. You're a credit to the Colony."

Mary shook her head. "No, dear. I'm no better or braver than any of the others. We came out here to found homes and live the Truth. We knew there'd be hard work. So much depends on everybody; there's no room for weakness."

Raymond kissed her again, although she laughingly protested and turned her head. "I still think you're brave—and very sweet."

"Get the light," said Mary. "Get several lights. One never knows how long these—these insufferable darknesses will last."

They set off up the road, walking because in the Colony private power vehicles were considered a social evil. Ahead, unseen in the darkness, rose the Grand Montagne, the preserve of the Flits. They could feel the harsh bulk of the crags, just as behind them they could feel the neat fields, the fences, the roads of the Colony. They crossed the canal, which led the meandering river into a mesh of irrigation ditches. Raymond shone his light into the concrete bed. They stood looking in a silence more eloquent than curses.

"It's dry! They've broken the banks again."

"Why?" asked Mary. "*Why?* They don't use the river water!"

Raymond shrugged. "I guess they just don't like canals. Well," he sighed, "all we can do is the best we know how."

The road wound back and forth up the slope. They passed the lichen-covered hulk of a star-ship which five hundred years ago had crashed on Glory. "It seems impossible," said Mary. "The Flits were once men and women just like us."

"Not like *us*, dear," Raymond corrected gently.

Sister Mary shuddered. "The Flits and their goats! Sometimes it's hard to tell them apart."

A few minutes later Raymond fell into a mudhole, a bed of slime, with enough water-seep to make it suckling and dangerous. Floundering, panting, with Mary's desperate help, he regained solid ground, and stood shivering—angry, cold, wet.

"That blasted thing wasn't there yesterday!" He scraped slime from his face, his clothes. "It's these miserable things that make life so trying."

"We'll get the better of it, dear." And she said fiercely: "We'll fight it, subdue it! Somehow we'll bring order to Glory!"

While they debated whether or not to proceed, Red Robundus belled up over the northwest horizon, and they were able to take stock of the situation. Brother Raymond's khaki puttees and his white shirt of course were filthy. Sister Mary's outfit was hardly cleaner.

Raymond said dejectedly, "I ought to go back to the bungalow for a change."

"Raymond—do we have time?"

"I'll look like a fool going up to the Flits like this."

"They'll never notice."

"How can they help?" snapped Raymond.

"We haven't time," said Mary decisively. "The Inspector's due any day, and the Flits are dying like flies. They'll say it's our fault—and that's the end of Gospel Colony." After a puase she said carefully, "Not that we wouldn't help the Flits in any event."

"I still think I'd make a better impression in clean clothes," said Raymond dubiously.

"Pooh! A fig they care for clean clothes, the ridiculous way they scamper around."

"I suppose you're right."

A small, yellow-green sun appeared over the southwest horizon. "Here comes Urban.... If it isn't dark as pitch we get three or four suns at once!"

"Sunlight makes the crops grow," Mary told him sweetly.

They climbed half an hour, then stopped to catch their breath, turned to look across the valley to the colony they loved so well. Seventy-two thousand souls on a checkerboard green plain, rows of neat white houses, painted and scrubbed, with snowy curtains behind glistening glass; laws and flower gardens full of tulips; vegetable gardens full of cabbages, kale and squash.

Raymond looked up at the sky. "It's going to rain."

Mary asked, "How do you know?"

"Remember the drenching we had last time Urban and Robundus were both in the west?"

Mary shook her head. "That doesn't mean anything."

"Something's got to mean something. That's the law of our universe—the basis for all our thinking!"

A gust of wind howled down from the ridges, carrying great curls and feathers of dust. They swirled with complicated colors, films, shades, in the opposing lights of yellow-green Urban and Red Robundus.

"There's your rain," shouted Mary over the roar of the wind. Raymond pressed on up the road. Presently the wind died.

Mary said, "I believe in rain or anything else on Glory when I see it."

"We don't have enough facts," insisted Raymond. "There's nothing magic in unpredictability."

"It's just—unpredictable." She looked back along the face of the Grand Montagne. "Thank God for the Clock—something that's dependable."

The road wandered up the hill, through stands of horny spile, banks of gray scrub and purple thorn. Sometimes there was no road; then they had to cast ahead like surveyors; sometimes the road stopped at a bank or at a blank wall, continuing on a level ten feet above or below. These were minor inconveniences which they overcame as a matter of course. Only when Robundus drifted south and Urban ducked north did they become anxious.

"It wouldn't be conceivable that a sun should set at seven in the evening," said Mary. "That would be too normal, too matter-of-fact."

At seven-fifteen both suns set. There would be ten minutes of magnificent sunset, another fifteen minutes of twilight, then night of indeterminate extent.

They missed the sunset because of an earthquake. A tumble of stones came pelting across the road; they took refuge under a jut of granite while boulders clattered into the road and spun on down the mountainside.

The shower of rocks passed, except for pebbles bouncing down as an afterthought. "Is that all?" Mary asked in a husky whisper.

"Sounds like it."

"I'm thirsty."

Raymond handed her the canteen; she drank.

"How much further to Fleetville?"

"Old Fleetville or New Town?"

"I don't care," she said wearily. "Either one."

Raymond hesitated. "As a matter of fact, I don't know the distance to either."

"Well, we can't stay here all night."

"It's day coming up," said Raymond as the white dwarf Maude began to silver the sky to the northeast.

"It's night," Mary declared in quiet desperation. "The Clock says it's night; I don't care if every sun in the galaxy is shining, including Home Sun. As long as the Clock says it's night, it's night!"

"We can see the road anyway....New Town is just over the ridge; I recognize that big spile. It was here last time I came."

Of the two, Raymond was the more surprised to find New Town where he placed it. They trudged into the village. "Things are awful quiet."

There were three dozen huts, built of concrete and good clear glass, each with filtered water, a shower, wash-tub and toilet. To suit Flit prejudices the roofs were thatched with thorn, and there were no interior partitions. The huts were all empty.

Mary looked into a hut. "Mmmph—horrid!" She puckered her nose at Raymond. "The smell!"

The windows of the second hut were innocent of glass. Raymond's face was grim and angry. "I packed that glass up here on my blistered back! And that's how they thank us."

"I don't care whether they thank us or not," said Mary. "I'm worried about the Inspector. He'll blame us for—" she gestured—"this filth. After all it's supposed to be our responsibility."

Seething with indignation Raymond surveyed the village. He recalled the day New Town had been completed—a model village, thirty-six spotless huts, hardly inferior to the bungalows of the Colony. Arch-Deacon Burnette had voiced the blessing; the volunteer workers knelt to pray in the central compound. Fifty or sixty Flits had come down from the ridges to watch—a wide-eyed ragged bunch: the men all gristle and unkempt hair; the women sly, plump and disposed to promiscuity, or so the colonists believed.

After the invocation Arch-Deacon Burnette had presented the chief of the tribe a large key of gilded plywood. "In your custody, Chief—the future and welfare of your people! Guard it—cherish it!"

The chief stood almost seven feet tall; he was lean as a pike, his profile cut in and out, sharp and hard as a turtle's. He wore greasy black rags and carried a long staff, upholstered with goat-hide. Alone in the tribe he spoke the language of the colonists, with a good accent that always came as a shock. "They are no concern of mine," he said in a casual hoarse voice. "They do as they like. That's the best way."

Arch-Deacon Burnette had encountered this attitude before. A large-minded man, he felt no indignation, but rather sought to argue away what he considered an irrational attitude. "Don't you want to be civilized? Don't you want to worship God, to live clean, healthy lives?"

"No."

The Arch-Deacon grinned. "Well, we'll help anyway, as much as we can. We can teach you to read, to cipher; we can cure your disease. Of course you must keep clean and you must adopt regular habits—because that's what civilization means."

The chief grunted. "You don't even know how to herd goats."

"We are not missionaries," Arch-Deacon Burnette continued, "but when you choose to learn the Truth, we'll be ready to help you."

"Mmph-mmph—where do you profit by this?"

Arch-Deacon smiled. "We don't. You are fellow-humans; we are bound to help you."

The chief turned, called to the tribe; they fled up the rocks pell-mell, climbing like desperate wraiths, hair waving, goat-skins flapping.

"What's this? What's this?" cried the Arch-Deacon. "Come back here," he called to the chief, who was on his way to join the tribe.

The chief called down from a crag. "You are all crazy people."

"No, no," exclaimed the Arch-Deacon, and it was a magnificent scene, stark as a stage-set: the white-haired Arch-Deacon calling up to the wild chief with his wild tribe behind him; a saint commanding satrys, all in the shifting light of three suns.

Somehow he coaxed the chief back down to New Town. Old Fleet-ville lay half a mile farther up, in a saddle funnelling all the winds and clouds of the Grand Montagne, until even the goats clung with difficulty to the rocks. It was cold, dank, dreary. The Arch-Deacon hammered home each of Old Fleetville's drawbacks. The chief insisted he preferred it to New Town.

Fifty pounds of salt made the difference, with the Arch-Deacon compromising his principles over the use of bribes. About sixty of the tribe moved into the new huts with an air of amused detachment, as if the Arch-Deacon had asked them to play a foolish game.

The Arch-Deacon called another blessing upon the village; the colonists knelt; the Flits watched curiously from the doors and windows of their new homes. Another twenty or thirty bounded down from the crags with a herd of goats which they quartered in the little chapel. Arch-Deacon Burnette's smile became fixed and painful, but to his credit he did nothing to interfere.

After a while the colonists filed back down into the valley. They had done the best they could, but they were not sure exactly what it was they had done.

Two months later New Town was deserted. Brother Raymond and Sister Mary Dunton walked through the village; and the huts showed dark windows and gaping doorways.

"Where have they gone?" asked Mary in a hushed voice.

"They're all mad," said Raymond. "Stark staring mad." He went to the chapel, pushed his head through the door. His knuckles shone suddenly white where they gripped the door frame.

"What's the trouble?" Mary asked anxiously.

Raymond held her back. "Corpses....There's—ten, twelve, maybe fifteen bodies in there."

"Raymond!" They looked at each other. "How? Why?"

Raymond shook his head. With one mind they turned, looked up the hill toward Old Fleetville.

"I guess it's up to us to find out."

"But this is—is such a nice place," Mary burst out. "They're...they're *beasts*! They should *love* it here!" She turned away, looked out over the valley, so that Raymond wouldn't see her tears. New Town had meant so much to her; with her own hands she had white-washed rocks and laid neat borders around each of the huts. The borders had been kicked askew, and her feelings were hurt. "Let the Flits live as they like, dirty, shiftless creatures. They're irresponsible," she told Raymond, "just completely *irresponsible!*"

Raymond nodded. "Let's go on up, Mary; we have our duty."

Mary wiped her eyes. "I suppose they're God's creatures but I can't see why they should be." She glanced at Raymond. "And don't tell me about God moving in a mysterious way."

"Okay," said Raymond. They started to clamber up over the rocks, up toward Old Fleetville. The valley became smaller and smaller below. Maude swung up to the zenith and seemed to hang there.

They paused for breath. Mary mopped her brow. "Am I crazy, or is Maude getting larger?"

Raymond looked. "Maybe it is swelling a little."

"It's either a nova or we're falling into it!"

"I suppose anything could happen in this system," sighed Raymond. "If there's any regularity in Glory's orbit it's defied analysis."

"We might very easily fall into one of the suns," said Mary thoughtfully.

Raymond shrugged. "The System's been milling around for quite a few million years. That's our best guarantee."

"Our only guarantee." She clenched her fists. "If there were only some certainty somewhere—something you could look at and say, this is immutable, this is changeless, this is something you can count on. But there's nothing! It's enough to drive a person crazy!"

Raymond put on a glassy smile. "Don't, dear. The Colony's got too much trouble like that already."

Mary sobered instantly. "Sorry....I'm sorry, Raymond. Truly."

"It's got me worried," said Raymond. "I was talking to Director Birch at the Rest Home yesterday."

"How many now?"

"Almost three thousand. More coming in every day." He sighed. "There's something about Glory that grinds at a person's nerves—no question about it."

Mary took a deep breath, pressed Raymond's hand. "We'll fight it, darling, and beat it! Things will fall into routine; we'll straighten everything out."

Raymond bowed his head. "With the Lord's help."

"There goes Maude," said Mary. "We'd better get up to Old Fleetville while there's still light."

A few minutes later they met a dozen goats, herded by as many scraggly children. Some wore rags; some wore goat-skin clothes; others ran around naked, and the wind blew on their washboard ribs.

On the other side of the trail they met another herd of goats—perhaps a hundred, with one urchin in attendance.

"That's the Flit way," said Raymond, "twelve kids herd twelve goats and one kid herds a hundred."

"They're surely victims of some mental disease....Is insanity hereditary?"

"That's a moot point....I can smell Old Fleetville."

Maude left the sky at an angle which promised a long twilight. With aching legs Raymond and Mary plodded up into the village. Behind them came the goats and the children, mingled without discrimination.

Mary said in a disgusted voice, "They leave New Town—pretty, clean New Town—to move up into this filth."

"Don't step on that goat!" Raymond guided her past the gnawed carcass which lay on the trail. Mary bit her lip.

They found the chief sitting on a rock, staring into the air. He greeted them with neither surprise nor pleasure. A group of children were building a pyre of brush and dry spile.

"What's going on?" asked Raymond with forced cheer. "A feast? A dance?"

"Four men, two women. They go crazy, they die. We burn them."

Mary looked at the pyre. "I didn't know you cremated your dead."

"This time we burn them." He reached out, touched Mary's glossy golden hair. "You be my wife for a while."

Mary stepped back, and said in a quivering voice. "No, thanks. I'm married to Raymond."

"All the time?"

"All the time."

The chief shook his head. "You are crazy. Pretty soon you die."

Raymond said sternly, "Why did you break the canal? Ten times we've fixed it; ten times the Flits come down in the dark and pulled down the banks."

The chief deliberated. "The canal is crazy."

"It's not crazy. It helps irrigate, helps the farmers."

"It goes too much the same."

"You mean, it's straight?"

"Straight? Straight? What word is that?"

"In *one* line—in one direction."

The chief rocked back and forth. "Look—mountain. Straight?"

"No, of course not."

"Sun—straight?"

"Look here—"

"My leg." The chief extended his left leg, knobby and covered with hair. "Straight?"

"No," sighed Raymond. "Your leg is not straight."

"Then why make canal straight? Crazy." He sat back. The topic was disposed of. "Why do you come?"

"Well," said Raymond. "Too many Flits die. We want to help you."

"That's all right. It's not me, not you."

"We don't want you to die. Why don't you live in New Town?"

"Flits get crazy, jump off the rocks." He rose to his feet. "Come along, there's food."

Mastering their repugnance, Raymond and Mary nibbled on bits of grilled goat. Without ceremony, four bodies were tossed into the fire. Some of the Flits began to dance.

Mary nudged Raymond. "You can understand a culture by the pattern of its dances. Watch."

Raymond watched. "I don't see any pattern. Some take a couple hops, sit down; others run in circles; some just flap their arms."

Mary whispered, "They're all crazy. Crazy as sandpipers."

Raymond nodded. "I believe you."

Rain began to fall. Red Robundus burnt the eastern sky but never troubled to come up. The rain became hail. Mary and Raymond went into a hut. Several men and women joined them, and with nothing better to do, noisily began loveplay.

Mary whispered in agony. "They're going to do it right in front of us! They don't have any shame!"

Mary cuffed one of the men who sought to remove her shirt; he jumped back. "Just like dogs!" she gasped.

"No repressions there," said Raymond apathetically. "Repressions means psychoses."

"Then I'm psychotic," sniffed Mary, "because I have repressions!"

"I have too."

The hail stopped; the wind blew the clouds through the notch; the sky was clear. Raymond and Mary left the hut with relief.

The pyre was drenched; four charred bodies lay in the ashes; no one heeded them.

Raymond said thoughtfully, "It's on the tip of my tongue—the verge of my mind...."

"What?"

"The solution to this whole Flit mess."

"Well?"

"It's something like this: The Flits are crazy, irrational, irresponsible."

"Agreed."

"The Inspector's coming. We've got to demonstrate that the Colony poses no threat to the aborigines—the Flits, in this case."

"We can't force the Flits to improve their living standards."

"No. But if we could make them sane; if we could even make a start against their mass psychosis...."

Mary looked rather numb. "It sounds like a terrible job."

Raymond shook his head. "Use rigorous thinking, dear. It's a real problem: a group of aborigines too psychotic to keep themselves alive. But we've *got* to keep them alive. The solution: remove the psychoses."

"You make it sound sensible, but how in heaven's name shall we begin?"

The chief came spindle-legged down from the rocks, chewing at a bit of goat-intestine. "We've got to begin with the chief," said Raymond.

"That's like belling the cat."

"Salt," said Raymond. "He'd skin his grandmother for salt."

Raymond approached the chief, who seemed surprised to find him still in the village. Mary watched from the background.

Raymond argued; the chief looked first shocked, then sullen. Raymond expounded, expostulated. He made his telling point: salt—as much as the chief could carry back up the hill. The chief stared down at Raymond from his seven feet, threw up his hands, walked away, sat down on a rock, chewed at the length of gut.

Raymond rejoined Mary. "He's coming."

Director Birch used his heartiest manner toward the chief. "We're honored! It's not often we have visitors so distinguished. We'll have you right in no time!"

The chief had been scratching aimless curves in the ground with his staff. He asked Raymond mildly, "When do I get the salt?"

"Pretty soon now. First you've got to go with Director Birch."

"Come along," said Director Birch. "We'll have a nice ride."

The chief turned and strode off toward the Grand Montagne. "No, no!" cried Raymond. "Come back here!" The chief lenghtened his stride.

Raymond ran forward, tackled the knobby knees. The chief fell like a loose sack of garden tools. Director Birch administered a shot of sedative, and presently the shambling, dull-eyed chief was secure inside the ambulance.

Brother Raymond and Sister Mary watched the ambulance trundle down the road. Thick dust rolled up, hung in the green sunlight. The shadows seemed tinged with bluish-purple.

Mary said in a trembling voice, "I do so hope we're doing the right thing....The poor chief looked so—*pathetic*. Like one of his own goats trussed up for slaughter."

Raymond said, "We can only do what we think best, dear."

"But *is* it the best?"

The ambulance had disappeared; the dust had settled. Over the Grand Montagne lightning flickered from a black-and-green thunderhead. Faro shone like a cat's-eye at the zenith. The Clock—the staunch Clock, the good, sane Clock—said twelve noon.

"The best," said Mary thoughtfully. "A relative word...."

Raymond said, "If we clear up the Flit psychoses—if we can teach them clean, orderly lives—surely it's for the best." And he added after a moment, "Certainly it's best for the Colony."

Mary sighed. "I suppose so. But the chief looked so stricken."

"We'll go see him tomorrow," said Raymond. "Right now, sleep!"

When Raymond and Mary awoke, a pink glow seeped through the drawn shades: Robundus, possibly with Maude. "Look at the clock," yawned Mary. "Is it day or night?"

Raymond raised up on his elbow. Their clock was built into the wall, a replica of the Clock on Salvation Bluff, and guided by radio pulses from the central movement. "It's six in the afternoon—ten after."

They rose and dressed in their neat puttees and white shirts. They ate in the meticulous kitchenette, then Raymond telephoned the Rest Home.

Director Birch's voice came crisp from the sound box. "God help you, Brother Raymond."

"God help you, Director. How's the chief?"

Director Birch hesitated. "We've had to keep him under sedation. He's got pretty deap-seated troubles."

"Can you help him? It's important."

"All we can do is try. We'll have a go at him tonight."

"Perhaps we'd better be there," said Mary.

"If you like....Eight o'clock?"

"Good."

The Rest Home was a long, low building on the outskirts of Glory City. New wings had recently been added; a set of temporary barracks could also be seen to the rear.

Director Birch greeted them with a harassed expression.

"We're so pressed for room and time; is this Flit so terribly important?"

Raymond gave him assurance that the chief's sanity was a matter of grave concern for everyone.

Director Birch threw up his hands. "Colonists are clamoring for therapy. They'll have to wait, I suppose."

"The Home was built with five hundred beds," said Director Birch. "We've got thirty-six hundred patients now; not to mention the eighteen hundred colonists we've evacuated back to Earth."

"Surely things are getting better?" asked Raymond. "The Colony's over the hump; there's no need for anxiety."

"Anxiety doesn't seem to be the trouble."

"What *is* the trouble?"

"New environment, I suppose. We're Earth-type people; the surroundings are strange."

"But they're not really!" argued Mary. "We've made this place the exact replica of an Earth community. One of the nicer sort. There are Earth houses and Earth flowers and Earth trees."

"Where is the chief?" asked Brother Raymond.

"Well—right now, in the maximum-security ward."

"Is he violent?"

"Not unfriendly. He just wants to get out. Destructive! I've never seen anything like it!"

"Have you any ideas—even preliminary?"

Director Birch shook his head grimly. "We're still trying to classify him. Look." He handed Raymond a report. "That's his zone survey."

"Intelligence zero." Raymond looked up. "I *know* he's not that stupid."

"You'd hardly think so. It's a vague referent, actually. We can't use the usual tests on him—thematic perception and the like; they're weighted for our own cultural background. But these tests here—" he tapped the report "—they're basic; we use them on animals—fitting pegs into holes; matching up colors; detecting discordant patterns; threading mazes."

"And the chief?"

Director Birch sadly shook his head. "If it were possible to have a negative score, he'd have it."

"How so?"

"Well, for instance, instead of matching a small round peg into a small round hole, first he broke the star-shaped peg and forced it in sideways, and then he broke the board."

"But why?"

Mary said, "Let's go see him."

"He's safe, isn't he?" Raymond asked Birch.

"Oh, entirely."

The chief was confined in a pleasant room exactly ten feet on a side. He had a white bed, white sheets, gray coverlet. The ceiling was restful green, the floor was quiet gray.

"My!" said Mary brightly, "you've been busy!"

"Yes," said Doctor Birch between clenched teeth. "He's been busy."

The bedclothes were shredded, the bed lay on its side in the middle of the room, the walls were befouled. The chief sat on the doubled mattress.

Director Birch said sternly, "Why do you make this mess? It's really not clever, you know!"

"You keep me here," spat the chief. "I fix the way I like it. In your house you fix the way *you* like." He looked at Raymond and Mary. "How much longer?"

"In just a little while," said Mary. "We're trying to help you."

"Crazy talk, everybody crazy." The chief was losing his good accent; his words rasped with fricatives and glottals. "Why you bring me here?"

"It'll be just for a day or two," said Mary soothingly, "then you get salt—lots of it."

"Day—that's while the sun is up."

"No," said Brother Raymond. "See this thing?" He pointed to the clock in the wall. "When this hand goes around twice—that's a day."

The chief smiled cynically.

"We guide our lives by this," said Raymond. "It helps us."

"Just like the big Clock on Salvation Bluff," said Mary.

"Big devil," the chief said earnestly. "You good people; you all crazy. Come to Fleetville. I help you; lots of good goat. We throw rocks down at Big Devil."

"No," said Mary quietly, "that would never do. Now you try your best to do what the doctor says. This mess for instance—it's very bad."

The chief took his head in his hands. "You let me go. You keep salt; I go home."

"Come," said Director Birch kindly. "We won't hurt you." He looked at the clock. "It's time for your first therapy."

Two orderlies were required to conduct the chief to the laboratory. He was placed in a padded chair, and his arms and legs were constricted so that he might not harm himself. He set up a terribly, hoarse cry. "The Devil, the Big Devil—it comes down to look at my life...."

Director Birch said to the orderly, "Cover over the wall clock; it disturbs the patient."

"Just lie still," said Mary. "We're trying to help you—you and your whole tribe."

The orderly administered a shot of D-beta hypnidine. The chief relaxed, his eyes open, vacant, his skinny chest heaving.

Director Birch said in a low tone to Mary and Raymond, "He's not entirely suggestible—so be very quiet; don't make a sound."

Mary and Raymond eased themselves into chairs at the side of the room.

"Hello, Chief," said Director Birch.

"Hello."

"Are you comfortable?"

"Too much shine—too much white."

The orderly dimmed the lights.

"Better?"

"That's better."

"Do you have any troubles?"

"Goats hurt their feet, stay up in the hills. Crazy people down the valley; they won't go away."

"How do you mean 'crazy?'"

The chief was silent. Director Birch said in a whisper to Mary and Raymond, "By analyzing his concept of sanity we get a clue to his own derangement.."

The chief lay quiet. Director Birch said in his soothing voice, "Suppose you tell us about your own life."

The chief spoke readily. "Ah, that's good. I'm chief. I understand all talks; nobody else knows about things."

"A good life, eh?"

"Sure, everything good." He spoke on, in disjointed phrases, in words sometimes unintelligible, but the picture of his life came clear. "Everything go easy—no bother, no trouble—everything good. When it rain, fire feels good. When sun shines hot, then wind blow, feels good. Lots of goats, everybody eat."

"Don't you have troubles, worries?"

"Sure. Crazy people live in valley. They make town: New Town. No good. Straight—straight—straight. No good. Crazy. That's bad. We get lots of salt, but we leave New Town, run up hill to old place."

"You don't like the people in the valley?"

"They good people, they all crazy. Big Devil brings them to valley. Big Devil watch all time. Pretty soon all go tick-tick-tick—like Big Devil."

Director Birch turned to Raymond and Mary, his face in a puzzled frown. "This isn't going so good. He's too assured, too forthright."

Raymond said guardedly, "Can you cure him?"

"Before I can cure a psychosis," said Director Birch, "I have to locate it. So far I don't seem to be even warm."

"It's not sane to die off like flies," whispered Mary. "And that's what the Flits are doing."

The Director returned to the chief. "Why do your people die, Chief? Why do they die in New Town?"

The chief said in a hoarse voice, "They look down. No pretty scenery. Crazy cut-up. No river. Straight water. It hurts the eyes; we open canal, make good river....Huts all same. Go crazy looking at all same. People go crazy; we kill 'em."

Director Birch said, "I think that's all we'd better do just now till we study the case a little more closely."

"Yes," said Brother Raymond in a troubled voice. "We've got to think this over."

They left the Rest Home through the main reception hall. The benches bulged with applicants for admission and their relatives, with custodian officers and persons in their care. Outside the sky was wadded with overcast. Sallow light indicated Urban somewhere in the sky. Rain spattered in the dust, big, syrupy drops.

Brother Raymond and Sister Mary waited for the bus at the curve of the traffic circle.

"There's something wrong," said Brother Raymond in a bleak voice, "Something very very wrong."

"And I'm not so sure it isn't in us," Sister Mary looked around the landscape, across the young orchards, up Sarah Gulvin Avenue into the center of Glory City.

"A strange planet is always a battle," said Brother Raymond. "We've got to bear faith, trust in God—and fight!"

Mary clutched his arm. He turned. "What's the trouble?"

"I saw—or thought I saw—someone running through the bushes."

Raymond craned his neck. "I don't see anybody."

"I thought it looked like the chief."

"Your imagination dear."

They boarded the bus, and presently were secure in their white-walled, flower-gardened home.

The communicator sounded. It was Director Birch. His voice was troubled. "I don't want to worry you, but the chief got loose. He's off the premises—where we don't know."

Mary said under her breath, "I knew, I knew!"

Raymond said soberly, "You don't think there's any danger?"

"No. His pattern isn't violent. But I'd lock my door anyway."

"Thanks for calling, Director."

"Not at all, Brother Raymond."

There was a moment's silence. "What now?" asked Mary.

"I'll lock the doors, and then we'll get a good night's sleep."

Sometime in the night Mary woke up with a start. Brother Raymond rolled over on his side. "What's the trouble?"

"I don't know," said Mary. "What time is it?"

Raymond consulted the wall clock. "Five minutes to one."

Sister Mary lay still.

"Did you hear something?" Raymond asked.

"No. I just had a—twinge. Something's wrong, Raymond!"

He pulled her close, cradled her fair head in the hollow of his neck. "All we can do is our best, dear, and pray that it's God's will."

They fell into a fitful doze, tossing and turning. Raymond got up to go to the bathroom. Outside was night—a dark sky except for a rosy glow at the north horizon. Red Robundus wandered somewhere below.

Raymond shuffled sleepily back to bed.

"What's the time dear?" came Mary's voice.

Raymond peered at the clock. "Five minutes to one."

He got into bed. Mary's body was rigid. "Did you say—five minutes to one?"

"Why yes," said Raymond. A few seconds later he climbed out of bed, went into the kitchen. "It says five minutes to one in here, too. I'll call the Clock and have them send out a pulse."

He went to the Communicator, pressed buttons. No response.

"They don't answer."

Mary was at his elbow. "Try again."

Raymond pressed out the number. "That's strange."

"Call Information," said Mary.

Raymond pressed for Information. Before he could frame a question, a crisp voice said, "The Great Clock is momentarily out of order. Please have patience. The Great Clock is out of order."

Raymond thought he recognized the voice. He punched the visual button. The voice said, "God keep you, Brother Raymond."

"God keep you, Brother Ramsdell...What in the world has gone wrong?"

"It's one of your proteges, Raymond. One of the Flits—raving mad. He rolled boulders down on the Clock."

"Did he—did he—"

"He started a landslide. We don't have any more Clock."

Inspector Coble found no one to meet him at the Glory City spaceport. He peered up and down the tarmac; he was alone. A scrap of paper blew across the far end of the field; nothing else moved.

Odd, thought Inspector Coble. A committee had always been on hand to welcome him, with a program that was flattering but rather wearing. First to the Arch-Deacon's bungalow for a banquet, cheerful speeches and progress reports, then services in the central chapel, and finally a punctilious escort to the foot of the Grand Montagne.

Excellent people, by Inspector Coble's lights, but too painfully honest and fanatical to be interesting.

He left instructions with the two men who crewed the official ship, and set off on foot toward Glory City. Red Robundus was high, but sinking toward the east; he looked toward Salvation Bluff to check local time. A clump of smoky lace-veils blocked his view.

Inspector Coble, striding briskly along the road, suddenly jerked to a halt. He raised his head as if testing the air, looked about him in a complete circle. He frowned, moved slowly on.

The colonists had been making changes, he thought. Exactly what and how, he could not instantly determine: The fence there—a section had been torn out. Weeds were prospering in the ditch beside the road. Examining the ditch, he sensed movement in the harp-grass behind, the sound of young voices. Curiosity aroused, Coble jumped the ditch, parted the harp-grass.

A boy and girl of sixteen or so were wading in a shallow pond; the girl held three limp water-flowers, the boy was kissing her. They turned up startled faces; Inspector Coble withdrew.

Back on the road he looked up and down. Where in thunder was everybody? The fields—empty. Nobody working. Inspector Coble shrugged, continued.

He passed the Rest Home, and looked at it curiously. It seemed considerably larger than he remembered it: a pair of wings, some temporary barracks had been added. He noticed that the gravel of the driveway was hardly as neat as it might be. The ambulance drawn up to the side was dusty. The place looked vaguely run down. The inspector for the second time stopped dead in his tracks. Music? From the Rest Home?

He turned down the driveway, approached. The music grew louder. Inspector Coble slowly pushed through the front door. In the reception hall were eight or ten people—they wore bizarre costumes: feathers, fronds of dyed grass, fantastic necklaces of glass and metal. The music sounded loud from the auditorium, a kind of wild jig.

"Inspector!" cried a pretty woman with fair hair. "Inspector Coble! You've arrived!"

Inspector Coble peered into her face. She wore a kind of patchwork jacket sewn with small iron bells. "It's—it's Sister Mary Dunton, isn't it?"

"Of course! You've arrived at a wonderful time! We're having a carnival ball—costumes and everything!"

Brother Raymond clapped the inspector heartily on the back. "Glad to see you, old man! Have some cider—it's the early press."

Inspector Coble backed away. "No, no thanks." He cleared his throat. "I'll be off on my rounds...and perhaps drop in on you later."

Inspector Coble proceeded to the Grand Montagne. He noted that a number of the bungalows had been painted bright shades of green, blue, yellow; that fences in many cases had been pulled down, that gardens looked rather rank and wild.

He climbed the road to Old Fleetville, where he interviewed the chief. The Flits apparently were not being exploited, suborned, cheated, sickened, enslaved, forcibly proselyted or systematically irritated. The chief seemed in a good humor.

"I kill the Big Devil," he told Inspector Coble. "Things go better now."

Inspector Coble planned to slip quietly to the space-port and depart, but Brother Raymond Dunton hailed him as he passed their bungalow.

"Had you breakfast, Inspector?"

"Dinner, darling!" came Sister Mary's voice from within. "Urban just went down."

"But Maude just came up."

"Bacon and eggs anyway, Inspector!"

The inspector was tired; he smelled hot coffee. "Thanks," he said, "don't mind if I do."

After the bacon and eggs, over the second cup of coffee, the inspector said cautiously, "You're looking well, you two."

Sister Mary looked especially pretty with her fair hair loose.

"Never felt better," said Brother Raymond. "It's a matter of rhythm, Inspector."

The Inspector blinked. "Rhythm, eh?"

"More precisely," said Sister Mary, "a lack of rhythm."

"It all started," said Brother Raymond, "when we lost our Clock."

Inspector Coble gradually pieced out the story. Three weeks later, back at Surge City he put it in his own words to Inspector Keefer.

"They'd been wasting half their energies holding onto—well, call it a false reality. They were all afraid of the new planet. They pretended it was Earth—tried to whip it, beat it, and just plain hypnotize it into being Earth. Naturally they were licked before they started. Glory is about as completely random a world as you could find. The poor devils were trying to impose Earth rhythm and Earth routine upon this magnificent disorder; this monumental chaos!"

"No wonder they all went nuts."

Inspector Coble nodded. "At first, after the Clock went out, they thought they were goners. Committed their souls to God and just about gave up. A couple of days passed, I guess—and to their surprise they found they were still alive. In fact even enjoying life. Sleeping when it got dark, working when the sun shone."

"Sounds like a good place to retire," said Inspector Keefer. "How's the fishing out there on Glory?"

"Not so good. But the goat-herding is great!"

ECOLOGICAL ONSLAUGHT

Aboard the exploration-cruiser *Blauelm* an ugly variety of psycho-neural ailments was developing. There was no profit in extending the expedition, already in space three months overlong; Explorator Bernisty ordered a return to Blue Star.

But there was no rise of spirits, no lift of morale; the damage had been done. Reacting from hypertension, the keen-tuned technicians fell into glum apathy, and sat staring like andromorphs. They ate little, they spoke less. Bernisty attempted various ruses; competition, subtle music, pungent food, but without effect.

Bernisty went further; at his orders the play-women locked themselves in their quarters, and sang erotic chants into the ship's address-system. These protean measures failing, Bernisty had a dilemma on his hands. At stake was the identity of his team, so craftily put together—such a meteorologist to work with such a chemist; such a botanist for such a virus analyst. To return to Blue Star thus demoralized—Bernisty shook his craggy head. There would be no further ventures in *Blauelm*.

"Then let's stay out longer," suggested Berel, his own favorite among the play-women.

Bernisty shook his head, thinking that Berel's usual intelligence had failed her. "We'd make bad matters worse."

"Then what will you do?"

Bernisty admitted he had no idea, and went away to think. Later in the day, he decided on a course of immense consequence; he swerved aside to make a survey of the Kay System. If anything would rouse the spirits of his men, this was it.

There was danger to the detour, but none of great note; spice to the venture came from the fascination of the alien, the oddness of the Kay cities with their taboo against regular form, the bizarre Kay social system.

The star Kay glowed and waxed, and Bernisty saw that his scheme was succeeding. There was once more talk, animation, argument along the gray steel corridors.

The *Blauelm* slid above the Kay ecliptic; the various worlds fell astern, passing so close that the minute movement, the throb of the cities, the dynamic pulse of the workshops were plain in the viewplates. Kith and Kelmet—these two warted over with domes—Karnfray, Koblenz, Kavanaf, then the central sun-star Kay; then Kool, too hot for life; then Kerrykirk, the capitol world; then Kobald and Kinsle, the ammonia giants frozen and dead—and the Kay System was astern.

Now Bernisty waited on tenterhooks; would there be a relapse toward inanition, or would the intellectual impetus suffice for the remainder of the voyage? Blue Star lay ahead, another week's journey. Between lay a yellow star of no particular note....It was while passing the yellow star that the consequences of Bernisty's ruse revealed themselves.

"Planet!" sang out the cartographer.

This was a cry to arouse no excitement; during the last eight months it had sounded many times through the *Blauelm.* Always the planet had proved so hot as to melt iron; or so cold as to freeze gas; or so poisonous as to corrode skin; or so empty of air as to suck out a man's lungs. The call was no longer a stimulus.

"Atmosphere!" cried the cartographer. The meteorologist looked up in interest. "Mean temperature—twenty-four degrees!"

Bernisty came to look, and measured the gravity himself. "One and one-tenth normal..." He motioned to the navigator, who needed no more to compute for a landing.

Bernisty stood watching the disk of the planet in the viewplate. "There must be something wrong with it. Either the Kay or ourselves must have checked a hundred times; it's directly between us."

"No record of the planet, Bernisty," reported the librarian, burrowing eagerly among his tapes and pivots. "No record of exploration; no record of anything."

"Surely it's known the star exists?" demanded Bernisty with a hint of sarcasm.

"Oh, indeed—we call if Maraplexa, the Kay call it Melliflo. But there is no mention of either system exploring or developing."

"Atmosphere," called the meteorologist, "methane, carbon dioxide, ammonia, water vapor. Unbreathable, but Type 6-D—potential."

"No chlorophyll, haemaphyll, blusk, or petradine absorption," muttered the botanist, an eye to the spectrograph. "In short—no native vegetation."

"Let me understand all this," said Bernisty. "Temperature, gravity, pressure okay?"

"Okay."

"No corrosive gas?"

"None."

"No native life?"

"No sign."

"And no record of exploration, claim or development?"

"None."

"Then," said Bernisty triumphantly, "we're moving in." To the radioman: "Issue notice of intent. Broadcast to all quarters, the Archive Station. From this hour, Maraplexa is a Blue Star development!"

The *Blauelm* slowed, and swung down to land. Bernisty sat watching with Berel the play-girl.

"Why—why—*why!*" Blandwick the navigator argued with the cartographer. "Why have not the Kay started development?"

"The same reason, evidently, that we haven't; we look too far afield."

"We comb the fringes of the galaxy," said Berel with a sly side-glance at Bernisty. "We sift the globular clusters."

"And here," said Bernisty, ruefully, "a near-neighbor to our own star—a world that merely needs an atmosphere modification—a world we can mold into a garden!"

"But will the Kay allow?" Blandwick put forth.

"What may they do?"

"This will come hard to them."

"So much the worse for the Kay!"

"They will claim a prior right."

"There are no records to demonstrate."

"And then—"

Bernisty interrupted. "Blandwick, go croak your calamity to the play-girls. With the men at work, they will be bored and so will listen to your woe."

"I know the Kay," maintained Blandwick. "They will never submit to what they will consider a humiliation—a stride ahead by Blue Star."

"They have no choice; they must submit," declared Berel, with the laughing recklessness that originally had called her to Bernisty's eye.

"You are wrong," cried Blandwick excitedly, and Bernisty held up his hand for peace.

"We shall see, we shall see."

Presently, Bufco—the radioman—brought three messages. The first, from Blue Star Central, conveyed congratulations; the second, from the Archive Station, corroborated the discovery; the third, from Kerrykirk, was clearly a hasty improvisation. It declared that the Kay System had long regarded Maraplexa as neutral, a no-man's-land between the two Systems; that a Blue Star development would be unfavorably received.

Bernisty chuckled at each of the three messages, most of all at the last. "The ears of their explorers are singing; they need new lands even more desperately than we do, what with their fecund breeding."

"Like farrowing pigs, rather than true men," sniffed Berel.

"They're true men if legend can be believed. We're said to be all stock of the same planet—all from the same lone world."

"The legend is pretty, but—where is this world—this old Earth of the fable?"

Bernisty shrugged. "I hold no brief for the myth; and now—here is our world below us."

"What will you name it?"

Bernisty considered. "In due course we'll find a name. Perhaps 'New Earth,' to honor our primeval home."

The unsophisticated eye might have found New Earth harsh, bleak, savage. The windy atmosphere roared across plains and mountains; sunlight glared on deserts and seas of white alkali. Bernisty, however, saw the world as a diamond in the rough—the classic example of a world right for modification. The radiation was right; the gravity was right; the atmosphere held no halogens or corrosive fractions; the soil was free of alien life, and alien proteins, which poisoned even more effectively than the halogens.

Sauntering out on the windy surface, he discussed all this with Berel. "Of such ground are gardens built," indicating a plain of loess which spread away from the base of the ship. "And of such hills—" he pointed to the range of hills behind "—do rivers come."

"When aerial water exists to form rain," remarked Berel.

"A detail, a detail; could we call ourselves ecologists and be deterred by so small a matter?"

"I am a play-girl, no ecologist—"

"Except in the largest possible sense."

"—I can not consider a thousand billion tons of water a detail."

Bernisty laughed. "We go by easy stages. First the carbon dioxide is sucked down and reduced; for this reason we sowed standard 6-D Basic vetch along the loess today."

"But how will it breathe? Don't plants need oxygen?"

From the *Blauelm*, a cloud of brown-green smoke erupted, rose in a greasy plume to be carried off downwind. "Spores of symbiotic lichens: Type Z forms oxygen-pods on the vetch. Type RS is non-photosynthetic—it combines methane with oxygen to make water, which the vetch uses for its growth. The three plants are the standard primary unit for worlds like this one."

Berel looked around the dusty horizon. "I suppose it will develop as you predict—and I will never cease to marvel."

"In three weeks, the plain will be green; in six weeks, the sporing and seeding will be in full swing; in six months, the entire planet will be forty feet deep in vegetation, and in a year, we'll start establishing the ultimate ecology of the planet."

"If the Kay allow."

"The Kay cannot prevent; the planet is ours."

Berel inspected the burly shoulders, the hard profile. "You speak with masculine profile. "You speak with masculine positivity, where everything depends and stipulates from the traditions of the Archive Station. I have no such certainty; my universe is more dubious."

"You are intuitive, I am rational."

"Reason," mused Berel, "tells you the Kay will abide by the Archive laws; my intuition tells me they will not."

"But what can they do? Attack us? Drive us off?"

"Who knows?"

Bernisty snorted. "They'll never dare."

"How long do we wait here?"

"Only to verify the germination of the vetch, then back to Blue Star."

"And then?"

"And then—we return to develop the full scale ecology."

II

On the thirteenth day, Bartenbrock, the botanist, trudged back from a day on the windy loess to announce the first shoots of vegetation. He showed samples to Bernisty—small pale sprigs with varnished leaves at the tip.

Bernisty critically examined the stem. Fastened like tiny galls were sacs in two colors—pale green and white. He pointed these out to Berel. "The green pods store oxygen, the white collect water."

"So," said Berel, "already New Earth begins to shift its atmosphere."

"Before your life runs out, you will see Blue Star cities along that plain."

"Somehow, my Bernisty, I doubt that."

The head-set sounded. "X. Bernisty; Radioman Bufco here. Three ships circling the planet; they refuse to acknowledge signals."

Bernisty cast the sprig of vetch to the ground. "That'll be the Kay."

Berel looked after him. "Where are the Blue Star cities now?"

Bernisty hastening away made no answer. Berel came after, followed to the control room of the *Blauelm*, where Bernisty tuned the viewplate. "Where are they?" she asked.

"They're around the planet just now—scouting."

"What kind of ships are they?"

"Patrol-attack vessels. Kay design. Here they come now."

Three dark shapes showed on the screen. Bernisty snapped to Bufco, "Send out the Universal Greeting Code."

"Yes, Bernisty."

Bernisty watched, while Bufco spoke in the archaic Universal language.

The ships paused, swerved, settled.

"It looks," said Berel softly, "as if they are landing."

"Yes."

"They are armed; they can destroy us."

"They can—but they'll never dare."

"I don't think you quite understand the Kay psyche."

"Do you?" snapped Bernisty.

She nodded. "Before I entered my girl-hood, I studied; now that I near its end, I plan to continue."

"You are more productive as a girl; while you study and cram your pretty head, I must find a new companion for my cruising."

She nodded at the settling black ships. "If there is to be more cruising for any of us."

Bufco leaned over his instrument, as a voice spoke from the mesh. Bernisty listened to syllables he could not understand, though the peremptory tones told their own story.

"What's he say?"

"He demands that we vacate this planet; he says it is claimed by the Kay."

"Tell him to vacate himself; tell him he's crazy....No, better, tell him to communicate with Archive Station."

Bufco spoke in the archaic tongue, the response crackled forth.

"He is landing. He sounds pretty firm."

"Let him land; let him be firm! Our claim is guaranteed by the Archive Station!" But Bernisty nevertheless pulled on his head-dome, and went outside to watch the Kay ships settle upon the loess, and he winced at the energy singeing the tender young vetch he had planted.

There was movement at his back; it was Berel. "What do you do here?" he asked brusquely. "This is no place for play-girls."

"I come now as a student."

Bernisty laughed shortly; the concept of Berel as a serious worker seemed somehow ridiculous.

"You laugh," said Berel. "Very well, let me talk to the Kay."

"You!"

"I know both Kay and Universal."

Bernisty glared, then shrugged. "You may interpret."

The ports of the black ship opened; eight Kay men came forward. This was the first time Bernisty had ever met one of the alien system face-to-face, and at first sight he found them fully as bizarre as he had expected. They were tall spare men, on the whole. They wore flowing black cloaks; the hair had been shorn smooth from their heads, and their scalps were decorated with heavy layers of scarlet and black enamel.

"No doubt," whispered Berel, "they find us just as unique."

Bernisty made no answer, having never before considered himself unique.

The eight men halted, twenty feet distant, stared at Bernisty with curious, cold, unfriendly eyes. Bernisty noted that all were armed.

Berel spoke; the dark eyes swung to her in surprise. The foremost responded.

"What's he say?" demanded Bernisty.

Berel grinned. "They want to know if I, a woman, lead the expedition."

Bernisty quivered and flushed. "You tell them that I, Explorator Bernisty, am in full command."

Berel spoke, at rather greater length than seemed necessary to convey his message. The Kay answered.

"Well?"

"He says we'll have to go; that he bears authorization from Kerrykirk to clear the planet, by force if necessary."

Bernisty sized up the man. "Get his name," he said, to win a moment or two.

Berel spoke, received a cool reply.

"He's some kind of a commodore," she told Bernisty. "I can't quite get it clear. His name is Kallish or Kallis...."

"Well, ask Kallish if he's planning to start a war. Ask him which side the Archive Station will stand behind."

Berel translated. Kallish responded at length.

Berel told Bernisty, "He maintains that we are on Kay ground, that Kay colonizers explored this world, but never recorded the exploration. He claims that if war comes it is our responsibility."

"He wants to bluff us," muttered Bernisty from the corner of his mouth. "Well, two can play that game." He drew his needle-beam, scratched a smoking line in the dust two paces in front of Kallish.

Kallish reacted sharply, jerking his hand to his own weapon; the others in his party did likewise.

Bernisty said from the side of his mouth, "Tell 'em to leave—take off back to Kerrykirk, if they don't want the beam along their legs...."

Berel translated, trying to keep the nervousness out of her voice. For answer, Kallish snapped on his own beam, burned a flaring orange mark in front of Bernisty.

Berel shakily translated his message. "He says for us to leave."

Bernisty slowly burned another line into the dust, closer to the black-shod feet. "He's asking for it."

Berel said in a worried voice, "Bernisty, you underestimate the Kay! They're rock-hard—stubborn—"

"And they underestimate Bernisty!"

There was quick staccato talk among the Kay; then Kallish, moving with a jerky flamboyance, snapped down another flickering trench almost at Bernisty's toes.

Bernisty swayed a trifle, then setting his teeth, leaned forward.

"This is a dangerous game," cried Berel.

Bernisty aimed, spattered hot dust over Kallish's sandals. Kallish stepped back; the Kay behind him roared. Kallish, his face a saturnine grinning mask; slowly started burning a line that would cut across Bernisty's ankles. Bernisty could move back—or Kallish could curve aside his beam...

Berel sighed. The beam spat straight, Bernisty stood rock-still. The beam cut the ground, cut over Bernisty's feet, cut on.

Bernisty stood still grinning. He raised his needle-beam.

Kallish turned on his heel, strode away, the black cape flapping in the ammoniacal wine.

Bernisty stood watching; a taut shape, frozen between triumph, pain and fury. Berel waited, not daring to speak. A minute passed. The Kay ships rose up from the dusty soil of New Earth, and the energy burnt down more shoots of the tender young vetch....

Berel turned to Bernisty; he was stumbling; his face was drawn and ghastly. She caught him under the armpits. From the *Blauelm* came Blandwick and a medic. They placed Bernisty in a litter, and conveyed him to the sick-ward.

As the medic cut cloth and leather away from the charred bones, Bernisty croaked to Berel, "I won today. They're not done....But today—I won!"

"It cost you your feet!"

"I can grow new feet—" Bernisty gasped and sweat as the medic touched a live nerve "—I can't grow a new planet..."

Contrary to Bernisty's expectations, the Kay made no further landing on New Earth. Indeed, the days passed with deceptive calm. The sun rose, glared a while over the ocher, yellow and gray landscape, sank in a western puddle of greens and reds. The winds slowed; a peculiar calm fell over the loess plain. The medic, by judicious hormones, grafts and calcium transplants, set Bernisty's feet to growing again. Temporarily he hobbled around in special shoes, staying close to *Blauelm.*

Six days after the Kay had come and gone, the *Beaudry* arrived from Blue Star. It brought a complete ecological laboratory, with stocks of seeds, spores, eggs, sperm; spawn, bulbs, grafts; frozen fingerlings, copepods, experimental cells and embryos; grubs, larva, pupae; amoeba, bacteria, viruses; as well as nutritive cultures and solutions. There were also tools for manipulating or mutating established species; even a supply of raw nuclein, unpatterned tissue, clear protoplasm from which simple forms of life could be designed and constructed. It was now Bernisty's option either to return to Blue Star with the *Blauelm*, or remain to direct the development of New Earth. Without conscious thought he made his choice; he elected to stay. Almost two-thirds his technical crew made the same choice. And the day after the arrival of the *Beaudry*, the *Blauelm* took off for Blue Star.

This day was notable in several respects. It signalized the complete changeover in Bernisty's life; from Explorator, pure and simple, to the more highly-specialized Master Ecologist, with the corresponding rise in prestige. It was on this day that New Earth took on the semblance of a habitable world, rather than a barren mass of rock and gas to be molded. The vetch over the loess plain had grown to a mottled green-brown sea, beaded and wadded with lichen pods. Already it was coming to its first seed. The lichens had already spored three or four times. There was yet no detectable change in the New Earth atmosphere; it was still CO_2, methane, ammonia, with traces of water vapor and inert gases, but the effect of the vetch was geometrically progressive, and as yet the total amount of vegetation was small compared to what it would be.

The third event of importance upon this day was the appearance of Kathryn.

She came down in a small spaceboat, and landed with a roughness that indicated either lack of skill or great physical weakness. Bernisty watched the boat's arrival from the dorsal promenade of the *Beaudry*, with Berel standing at his elbow.

"A Kay boat," said Berel huskily.

Bernisty looked at her in quick surprise. "Why do you say that? It might be a boat from Alvan or Canopus—or the Graemer System, or a Dannic vessel from Copenhag."

"No. It is Kay."

"How do you know?"

Out of the boat stumbled the form of a young woman. Even at this distance it could be seen she was very beautiful—something in the confidence of movement, the easy grace....She wore a head-dome, but little else. Bernisty felt Berel stiffening. Jealousy? She felt none when he amused himself with other play-girls; did she sense here a deeper threat?

Berel said in a throaty voice, "She's a spy—a Kay spy. Send her away!"

Bernisty was pulling on his own dome; a few minutes later, he walked across the dusty plain to meet the young woman, who was pushing her way slowly against the wind.

Bernisty paused, sized her up. She was slight, more delicate in build than most of the Blue Star women; she had a thick cap of black elf-locks; pale skin with the luminous look of old vellum; wide dark eyes.

Bernisty felt a peculiar lump rising in his throat; a feeling of awe and protectiveness such as Berel nor any other woman had ever aroused. Berel was behind him. Berel was antagonistic; both Bernisty and the strange woman felt it.

Berel said, "She's a spy—clearly! Send her away!"

Bernisty said, "Ask her what she wants."

The woman said, "I speak your Blue Star language, Bernisty; you can ask me yourself."

"Very well. Who are you? What do you do here?"

"My name is Kathryn—"

"She is a Kay!" said Berel.

"—I am a criminal. I escaped my punishment, and fled in this direction."

"Come," said Bernisty. "I would examine you more closely."

In the *Beaudry* wardroom, crowded with interested watchers, she told her story. She claimed to be the daughter of a Kirkassian freeholder—

"What is that?" asked Berel in a skeptical voice.

Kathryn responded mildly. "A few of the Kirkassians still keep their strongholds in the Keviot Mountains—a tribe descended from ancient brigands."

"So you are the daughter of a brigand?"

"I am more; I am a criminal in my own right," replied Kathryn mildly.

Bernisty could contain his curiosity no more. "What did you do, girl; what did you do?"

"I committed the act of—" here she used a Kay word which Bernisty was unable to understand. Berel's knitted brows indicated that she likewise was puzzled. "After that," went on Kathryn, "I upset a brazier of incense on the head of priest. Had I felt remorse, I would have remained to be punished; since I did not I fled here in the space-boat."

"Incredible!" said Berel in disgust.

Bernisty sat watching in amusement. "Apparently, girl, you are believed to be a Kay spy. What do you say to that?"

"If I were or if I were not—in either case I would deny it."

"You deny it then?"

Kathryn's face creased; she broke out into a laugh of sheer delight. "No. I admit it. I am a Kay spy."

"I knew it, I knew it—"

"Hush, woman," said Bernisty. He turned to Kathryn, his brow creased in puzzlement. "You admit you are a spy?"

"Do you believe me?"

"By the Bulls of Bashan—I hardly know what I believe!"

"She's a clever trickster—cunning!" stormed Berel. "She's pulling her artful silk around your eyes."

"*Quiet!*" roared Bernisty. "Give me some credit for normal perceptiveness!" He turned to Kathryn. "Only a madwoman would admit to being a spy."

"Perhaps I am a madwoman," she said with grave simplicity.

Bernisty threw up his hands. "Very well, what is the difference? There are no secrets here in the first place. If you wish to spy, do so—as overtly or as stealthily as you please, whichever suits you. If you merely seek refuge, that is yours too, for you are on Blue Star soil."

"My thanks to you, Bernisty."

III

Bernisty flew out with Broderick, the cartographer, mapping, photographing, exploring and generally inspecting New Earth. The landscape was everywhere similar—a bleak scarred surface like the inside of a burned out kiln. Everywhere loess plains of wind-spread dust abutted harsh crags.

Broderick nudged Bernisty. "Observe."

Bernisty, following the gesture, saw three faintly-marked but unmistakable squares on the desert below—vast areas of crumbled stone, strewed over by wind-driven sand.

"Those are either the most gigantic crystals the universe has ever known," said Bernisty, "or—we are not the first intelligent race to set foot on this planet."

"Shall we land?"

Bernisty surveyed the squares through his telescope. "There is little to see....Leave it for the archaeologists; I'll call some out from Blue Star."

Returning toward the *Beaudry*, Bernisty suddenly called, "Stop!"

They set down the survey-boat; Bernisty alighted, and with vast satisfaction inspected a patch of green-brown vegetation: Basic 6-D vetch, podded over with the symbiotic lichens which fed it oxygen and water.

"Another six weeks," said Bernisty, "the world will froth with this stuff."

Broderick peered closely at a leaf. "What is that red blotch?"

"Red blotch?" Bernisty peered, frowned. "It looks like a rust, a fungus."

"Is that good?"

"No—of course not! It's—bad!...I can't quite understand it. This planet was sterile when we arrived."

"Spores drop in from space," suggested Broderick.

Bernisty nodded. "And space-boats likewise. Come, let's get back to the *Beaudry*. You have the position of this spot?"

"To the centimeter."

"Never mind. I'll kill this colony." And Bernisty seared the ground clean of the patch of vetch he had been so proud of. They returned to the *Beaudry* in silence, flying in over the plain which now grew thick with mottled foliage. Alighting from the boat, Bernisty ran not to the *Beaudry* but to the nearest shrub, and inspected the leaves. "None here...None here—nor here..."

"Bernisty!"

Bernisty looked around. Baron the botanist approached, his face stern. Bernisty's heart sank. "Yes?"

"There has been inexcusable negligence."

"Rust?"

"Rust. It's destroying the vetch."

Bernisty swung on is heel. "You've got a sample?"

"We're already working out a counter-agent in the lab."

"Good...."

But the rust was a hardy growth; finding an agency to destroy the rust and still leave the vetch and the lichens unharmed proved a task of enormous difficulty. Sample after sample of virus, germ, blot, wort and fungus failed to satisfy the conditions and were destroyed in the furnace. Meanwhile, the color of the vetch changed from brown-green to red-green to iodine-color; and the proud growth began to slump and rot.

Bernisty walked sleeplessly, exhorting, cursing his technicians. "You call yourselves ecologists? A simple affair of separating a rust from the vetch—you fail, you flounder! Here—give me that culture!" And Bernisty seized the culture-disk from Baron, himself red-eyed and irritable.

The desired agent was at last found in a culture of slime-molds; and another two days passed before the pure strain was isolated and set out in a culture. Now the vetch was rotting, and the lichens lay scattered like autumn leaves.

Aboard the *Beaudry* there was feverish activity. Cauldrons full of culture crowded the laboratory, the corridors; trays of spores dried in the saloon, in the engine-room, in the library.

Here Bernisty once more became aware of Kathryn, when he found her scraping dry spores into distribution boxes. He paused to watch her; he felt the shift of her attention from the task to himself, but he was too tired to speak. He merely nodded, turned and returned to the laboratory.

The slime-molds were broadcast, but clearly it was too late. "Very well," said Bernisty, "we broadcast another setting of seed—Basic 6-D vetch. This time we know our danger and we already have the means to protect ourselves."

The new vetch grew; much of the old vetch revived. The slime-mold, when it found no more rust, perished—except for one or two mutant varieties which attacked the lichen. For a time, it appeared as if these spores would prove as dangerous as the rust; but the *Beaudry* catalogue listed a virus selectively attacking slime-molds; this was broadcast, and the molds disappeared.

Bernisty was yet disgruntled. At an assembly of the entire crew he said, "Instead of three agencies—the vetch and the two lichens—there is now extant six, counting the rust, the slime-mold, the virus. The more life—the harder to control. I emphasize most strongly the need for care and absolute antisepsis."

In spite of the precautions, rust appeared again—this time a black variety. But Bernisty was ready; inside of two days, he disseminated counter-agent. The rust disappeared; the vetch flourished. Everywhere, now, across the planet lay the brown-green carpet. In spots it rioted forty feet thick, climbing and wrestling, stalk against stalk, leaf lapping leaf. It climbed up the granite crags; it hung festooned over precipices. And each day, countless tons of CO_2 became oxygen, methane became water and more CO_2.

Bernisty watched the atmospheric-analyses closely; and one day the percentage of oxygen in the air rose from the 'imperceptible' to the 'minute trace' category. On this day, he ordered a general holiday and banquet. It was Blue Star formal custom for men and women to eat separately, the sight of open mouths being deemed as immodest as the act of elimination. The occasion however was one of high comradeship and festivity, and Bernisty, who was neither modest nor sensitive, ordered the custom ignored; so it was in an atmosphere of gay abandon that the banquet began.

As the banquet progressed, as the ichors and alcohols took effect, the hilarity and abandon became more pronounced. At Bernisty's side sat Berel, and though she had shared his couch during the feverish weeks previously she had felt that his attentions were completely impersonal; that she was no more than play-girl. When she noticed his eyes almost of themselves on Kathryn's wine-flushed face, she felt emotions rising inside her that almost brought tears to her eyes.

"This must not be," she muttered to herself. "In a few months I am play-girl no more; I am student. I mate whom I choose; I do not choose this bushy egotistical brute, this philandering Bernisty!"

In Bernisty's mind there were strange stirrings, too. "Berel is pleasant and kind," he thought. "But Kathryn! The flair! The spirit!" And feeling her eyes on him he thrilled like a schoolboy.

Broderick the cartographer, his head spinning and fuzzy, at this moment seized Kathryn's shoulders and drew her back to kiss her. She pulled aside, cast a whimsical glance at Bernisty. It was enough. Bernisty was by her side; he lifted her, carried her back to his chair, still hobbling on his burnt feet. Her perfume intoxicated him as much as the wine; he hardly noticed Berel's furious face.

This must not be, thought Berel desperately. And now inspiration came to her. "Bernisty! Bernisty!" She tugged at his arm.

Bernisty turned his head. "Yes?"

"The rusts—I know how they appeared on the vetch!"

"They drifted down as spores—from space."

"They drifted down in Kathryn's space-boat! She's not a spy—she's a saboteur!" Even in her fury Berel had to admire the limpid innocence of Kathryn's face. "She's a Kay agent—an enemy."

"Oh, bah," muttered Bernisty, sheepishly. "This is woman-talk."

"Woman-talk, is it?" screamed Berel. "What do you think is happening now, while you feast and fondle?—" she pointed a finger on which the metal foil flower blossom quivered—"that—that *besom*!"

"Why—I don't understand you," said Bernisty, looking in puzzlement from girl to girl.

"While you sit lording it, the Kay spread blight and ruin!"

"Eh? What's this?" Bernisty continued to look from Berel to Kathryn, feeling suddenly clumsy and rather foolish. Kathryn moved on his lap. Her voice was easy, but now her body was stiff. "If you believe so, check on your radars and viewscopes."

Bernisty relaxed. "Oh—nonsense."

"No, no no!" shrilled Berel. "She tries to seduce your reason!"

Bernisty growled to Bufco, "Check the radar." Then he, too, rose to his feet. "I'll come with you."

"Surely you don't *believe*—" began Kathryn.

"I believe nothing till I see the radar tapes."

Bufco flung switches, focussed his viewer. A small pip of light appeared. "A ship!"

"Coming or going?"

"Right now it's going!"

"Where are the tapes?"

Bufco reeled out the records. Bernisty bent over them, his eyebrows bristling. "Humph."

Bufco looked at him questioningly.

"This is very strange."

"How so?"

"The ship had only just arrived—almost at once it turned aside, fled out, away from New Earth."

Bufco studied the tapes. "This occurred precisely four minutes and thirty seconds ago."

"Precisely when we left the saloon."

"Do you think—"

"I don't know what to think."

"It's almost as if they received a message—a warning...."

"But how? From where?" Bernisty hesitated. "The natural object of suspicion," he said slowly, "is Kathryn."

Bufco looked up with a curious glint in his eyes. "What will you do with her?"

"I didn't say she was guilty; I remarked that she was the logical object of suspicion...." He pushed the tape magazine back under the scanner. "Let's go see what's been done.... What new mischief...."

No mischief was apparent. The skies were clear and yellowish-green; the vetch grew well.

Bernisty returned inside the *Beaudry*, gave certain instructions to Blandwick, who took off in the survey-boat and returned an hour later with a small silk bag held carefully. "I don't know what they are," said Blandwick.

"They're bound to be bad." Bernisty took the small silk bag to the laboratory and watched while the two botanists, the two mycologists, the four entomologists studied the contents of the bag.

The entomologists identified the material. "These are eggs of some small insect—from the gene-count and diffraction-pattern one or another of the mites."

Bernisty nodded. He looked sourly at the waiting men. "Need I tell you what to do?"

"No."

Bernisty returned to his private office and presently sent for Berel. He asked, without preliminary, "How did you know a Kay ship was in the sky?"

Berel stood staring defiantly down at him. "I did not know; I guessed."

Bernisty studied for a moment. "Yes—you spoke of your intuitive abilities."

"This was not intuition," said Berel scornfully. "This was plain common sense."

"I don't follow you."

"It's perfectly clear. A Kay woman-spy appears. The ecology went bad right away; red rust and black rust. You beat the rust, you celebrate; you're keyed to a sense of relief. What better time to start a new plague?"

Bernisty nodded slowly. "What better time, indeed...."

"Incidentally—what kind of plague is it going to be?"

"Plant-lice—mites. I think we can beat it before it gets started."

"Then what?"

"I don't know...."

"It looks as if the Kay can't scare us off, they mean to work us to death."

"That's what it looks like."

"Can they do it?"

"I don't see how we can stop them from trying. It's easy to breed pests; hard to kill them."

Banta, the head entomologist, came in with a glass tube. "Here's some of them—hatched."

"Already?"

"We hurried it up a little."

"Can they live in this atmosphere? There's not much oxygen—lots of ammonia."

"They thrive on it; it's what they're breathing now."

Bernisty ruefully inspected the bottle. "And that's our good vetch they're eating, too."

Berel looked over his shoulder. "What can we do about them?"

Banta looked properly dubious. "The natural enemies are certain parasites, viruses, dragonflies, and a kind of a small armored gnat that breeds very quickly; and which I think we'd do best to concentrate on. In fact we're already engaging in large-scale selective breeding, trying to find a strain to live in this atmosphere."

"Good work, Banta." Bernisty rose to his feet.

"Where are you going?" asked Berel.

"Out to check on the vetch."

"I'll come with you."

Out on the plain, Bernisty seemed intent not so much on the vetch as on the sky.

"What are you looking for?" Berel asked.

Bernisty pointed. "See that wisp up there?"

"A cloud?"

"Just a bit of frost—a few sprinkles of ice crystals....But it's a start! Our first rainstorm—that'll be an event!"

"Provided the methane and oxygen don't explode—and send us all to kingdom come!"

"Yes, yes," muttered Bernisty. "We'll have to set out some new methanophiles."

"And how will you get rid of all this ammonia?"

"There's a marsh-plant from Salsiberry that under proper conditions performs the equation: $12 NH_3 + 9 O_2 = 18 H_2O + 6 N_2$."

"Rather a waste of time for it, I should say," remarked Berel. "What does it gain?"

"A freak, only a freak. What do we gain by laughing? Another freak."

"A pleasant uselessness."

Bernisty was examining the vetch. "There, here. Look. Under this leaf." He displayed the mites; slow yellow aphid-creatures.

"When will your gnats be ready?"

"Banta is letting half his stock free; maybe they'll feed faster on their own than in the laboratory."

"Does—does Kathryn know about the gnats?"

"You're still gunning for her, eh?"

Bernisty said mildly, "I can't think of a way that either one of you could have communicated with that Kay ship."

"*Either one of us!*"

"Someone warned him away. Kathryn is the logical suspect; but you knew he was there."

Berel swung on her heel, stalked back to the *Beaudry*.

IV

The gnats were countering the mites, apparently; the population of both first increased, then dwindled. After which the vetch grew taller and stronger. There was now oxygen in the air, and the botanists broadcast a dozen new species—broad-leaves, producers of oxygen; nitrogen-fixers, absorbing the ammonia; the methanophiles from the young methane-rich worlds, combining oxygen with methane, and growing in magnificent white towers like carved ivory.

Bernisty's feet were whole again, a size larger than his first ones and he was forced to discard his worn and comfortable boots for a new pair cut from stiff blue leather.

Kathryn was playfully helping him cram his feet into the hard vacancies. Casually, Bernisty said, "It's been bothering me, Kathryn: tell me, how did you call to the Kay?"

She started, gave him an instant piteous wide-eyed stare, like a trapped rabbit, then she laughed. "The same way you do—with my mouth."

"When?"

"Oh, every day about this time."

"I'd be glad to watch you."

"Very well." She looked up at the window, spoke in the ringing Kay tongue.

"What did you say?" asked Bernisty politely.

"I said that the mites were a failure; that there was good morale here aboard the *Beaudry*; that you were a great leader, a wonderful man."

"But you recommended no further steps."

She smiled demurely. "I am ecologist—neither constructive, nor destructive."

"Very well," said Bernisty, standing into his boots. "We shall see."

Next day the radar-tapes showed the presence of two ships; they had made fleeting visits—"long enough to dump their villainous cargo," so Bufco reported to Bernisty.

The cargo proved to be eggs of a ferocious blue wasp, which preyed on the gnats. The gnats perished; the mites prospered; the vetch began to wilt under the countless sucking tubes. To counter the wasp, Bernisty released a swarm of feathery blue flying-ribbons. The wasps bred inside a peculiar, small brown puff-ball fungus (the spores for which had been released with the wasp larva). The flying-ribbons ate these puff-balls. With no shelter for their larva, the wasps died; the gnats revived in numbers, gorging on mites till their thoraxes split.

The Kay assaulted on a grander scale. Three large ships passed by night, disgorging a witches-cauldron of reptiles, insects, arachnids, land crabs, a dozen phyla without formal classification. The human resources of the *Beaudry* were inadequate to the challenge; they began to fail, from insect stings; another botanist took a pulsing white-blue gangrene from the prick of a poisonous thorn.

New Earth was no longer a mild region of vetch, lichen, and dusty wind; New Earth was a fantastic jungle. Insects stalked each other through the leafy wildernesses; there were local specializations and improbable adaptations. There were spiders, and lizards the size of cats; scorpions which rang like bells when they walked; long-legged lobsters; poisonous butterflies; a species of giant moth, which, finding the environment congenial, grew ever more gigantic.

Within the *Beaudry* they was everywhere a sense of defeat. Bernisty walked limping along the promenade, the limp more of an unconscious attitude than a physical necessity. The problem was too complex for a single brain, he thought—or for a single team of human brains. The various life-forms on the planet, each evolving, mutating, expanding into vacant niches, selecting the range of their eventual destinies—they made a pattern too haphazard for an electronic computer, for a team of computers.

Blandwick, the meteorologist, came along the promenade with his daily atmospheric-report. Bernisty derived a certain melancholy pleasure to find that while there had been no great increase in oxygen and water-vapor, neither had there been any decrease. "In fact," said

Blandwick, "there's a tremendous amount of water tied up in all those bugs and parasites."

Bernisty shook his head. "Nothing appreciable....And they're eating away the vetch faster than we can kill 'em off. New varieties appear faster than we can find them."

Blandwick frowned. "The Kay are following no clear pattern."

"No, they're just dumping anything they hope might be destructive."

"Why don't we use the same technique? Instead of selective counter-action, we turn loose our entire biological program. Shotgun tactics."

Bernisty limped on a few paces. "Well, why not? The total effect might be beneficial....Certainly less destructive than what's going on out there now." He paused. "We deal in unpredictables of course—and this is contrary to my essential logic."

Blandwick sniffed. "None of our gains to date have been the predict-able ones."

Bernisty grinned, after a momentary irritation, since Blandwick's remark was inaccurate; had Blandwick been driving home a truth, then there would have been cause for irritation.

"Very well, Blandwick," he said jovially. "We shoot the works. If it succeeds we'll name the first settlement Blandwick."

"Humph," said the pessimistic Blandwick, and Bernisty went to give the necessary orders.

Now every vat, tub, culture tank, incubator, tray and rack in the laboratory was full; as soon as the contents achieved even a measure of acclimatization to the still nitrogenous atmosphere, they were discharged: pods, plants, molds, bacteria, crawling things, insects, annelids, crusta-ceans, land ganoids, even a few elementary mammals—life-forms from well over three dozen different worlds. Where New Earth had previously been a battleground, now it was a madhouse.

One variety of palms achieved instant success; inside of two months they towered everywhere over the landscape. Between them hung veils of a peculiar air-floating web, subsisting on flying things. Under the branches, the brambles, there was much killing; much breeding; much eating; growing; fighting; fluttering; dying. Aboard the *Beaudry*, Bernisty was well-pleased and once more jovial.

He clapped Blandwick on the back. "Not only do we call the city after you, we prefix your name to an entire system of philosophy, the Blandwick method."

Blandwick was unmoved by the tribute. "Regardless of the success of 'the Blandwick method,' as you call it, the Kay still have a word to say."

"What can they do?" argued Bernisty. "They can liberate creatures no more unique or ravenous than those we ourselves have loosed. Any-thing the Kay send to New Earth now is in the nature of anti-climax."

Blandwick smiled sourly. "Do you think they'll give up quite so easily?"

Bernisty became uneasy, and went off in search of Berel. "Well, play-girl," he demanded, "what does your intuition tell you now?"

"It tells me," she snapped, "that whenever you are the most optimistic, the Kay are on the verge of their most devastating attacks."

Bernisty put on a facetious front. "And when will these attacks take place?"

"Ask your spy-woman; she communicates secrets freely to anyone."

"Very well," said Bernisty. "Find her, if you please, and send her to me."

Kathryn appeared, "Yes, Bernisty?"

"I am curious," said Bernisty, "as to what you communicate to the Kay."

Kathryn said, "I tell them that Bernisty is defeating them, that he has countered their worst threats."

"And what do they tell you?"

"They tell me nothing."

"And what do you recommend?"

"I recommend that they either win at a massive single stroke, or give up."

"How do you tell them this?"

Kathryn laughed, showing her pretty white teeth. "I talk to them just as now I talk to you."

"And when do you think they will strike?"

"I don't know....It seems that certainly they are long overdue. Would you not think so?"

"Yes," admitted Bernisty, and turned his head to find Bufco the radioman approaching.

"Kay ships," said Bufco. "A round dozen—mountainous barrels! They made one circuit—departed!"

"Well," said Bernisty, "this is it." He turned upon Kathryn the level look of cold speculation, and she returned the expression of smiling demureness which both of them had come to find familiar.

V

In three days, every living thing on New Earth was dead. Not merely died, but dissolved into a viscous gray syrup which sank into the plain, trickled like sputum down the crags, evaporated into the wind. The effect was miraculous. Where the jungle had thronged the plain—now only plain existed, and already the wind was blowing up dust-devils.

There was one exception to the universal dissolution—the monstrous moths, which by some unknown method, or chemical make-up, had managed to survive. Across the wind they soared; frail fluttering shapes, seeking their former sustenance and finding nothing now but desert.

Aboard the *Beaudry* there was bewilderment; then dejection; then dull rage which could find no overt outlet, until at last Bernisty fell into a sleep.

He awoke with a sense of vague uneasiness, of trouble: the collapse of the New Earth ecology? No. Something deeper, more immediate. He jumped into his clothes, hastened to the saloon. It was nearly full, and gave off a sense of grim malice.

Kathryn sat pale, tense in a chair; behind her stood Banta with a garrote. He was clearly preparing to strangle her, with the rest of the crew as collaborators.

Bernisty stepped across the saloon, broke Banta's jaw and broke the fingers of his clenched fist. Kathryn sat looking up silently.

"Well, you miserable renegades," Bernisty began; but looking around the wardroom, he found no sheepishness, only growing anger, defiance. "What goes on here?" roared Bernisty.

"She is a traitor," said Berel; "we execute her."

"How can she be a traitor? She never promised us faith!"

"She is certainly a spy!"

Bernisty laughed. "She has never dissembled the fact that she communicates with the Kay. How can she then be a spy?"

No one made reply, there was uneasy shifting of eyes.

Bernisty kicked Banta who was rising to his feet. "Get away, you cur....I'll have no murderers, no lynchers in my crew!"

Berel cried, "She betrayed us!"

"How could she betray us? She never asked us to give her trust. Quite the reverse; she came to us frankly as a Kay; frankly she tells me she reports to the Kay."

"But how?" sneered Berel. "She claims to talk to them—to make you believe she jokes!"

Bernisty regarded Kathryn with the speculative glance. "If I read her character right, Kathryn tells no untruths. It is her single defense. If she says she talks to the Kay, so she does...." He turned to the medic, "Bring an infrascope."

The infrascope revealed strange black shadows inside Kathryn's body. A small button beside her larynx; two slim boxes flat against her diaphragm; wires running down under the skin of each leg.

"What is this?" gasped the medic.

"Internal radio," said Bufco. "The button takes her voice, the antenna are the leg-wires. What better equipment for a spy?"

"She is no spy, I tell you!" Bernisty bellowed. "The fault lies not with her—it lies with me! She *told* me! If I had asked her how her voice got to the Kay, she would have told me—candidly, frankly. I never asked her; I chose to regard the entire affair as a game! If you must garrote someone— garrote me! I am the betrayer—not she!"

Berel turned, walked from the wardroom, others followed. Bernisty turned to Kathryn. "Now—now what will you do? Your venture is a success."

"Yes," said Kathryn, "a success." She likewise left the wardroom. Bernisty followed curiously. She went to the outdoor locker, put on her head-dome, opened the double-lock, stepped out upon the dead plain.

Bernisty watched her from a window. Where would she walk to? Nowhere....She walked to death, like one walking into the surf and swimming straight out to sea. Overhead the giant moths fluttered, flick- ered down on the wind. Kathryn looked up; Bernisty saw her cringe. A moth flapped close, strove to seize her. She ducked; the wind caught the frail wings, and the moth wheeled away.

Bernisty chewed his lip; then laughed. "Devil take all; devil take the Kay; devil take all...." He jammed on his own head-dome.

Bufco caught his arm. "Bernisty, where do you go?"

"She is brave, she is steadfast; why should she die?"

"She is our enemy!"

"I prefer a brave enemy to cowardly friends." He ran from the ship, across the soft loess now crusted with dried slime.

The moths fluttered, plunged. One clung to Kathryn's shoulders with barbed legs; she struggled, beat with futile hands at the great soft shape.

Shadows fell over Bernisty; he saw the purple-red glinting of big eyes, the impersonal visage. He swung a fist, felt the chitin crunch. Sick pangs of pain reminded him that the hand had already been broken on Banta's jaw. With the moth flapping on the ground he ran off down the wind. Kathryn lay supine, a moth probing her with a tube ill-adapted to cutting plastics and cloth.

Bernisty called out encouragement; a shape swooped on his back, bore him to the ground. He rolled over, kicked; arose, jumped to his feet, tackled the moth on Kathryn, tore off the wings, snapped the head up.

He turned to fight the other swooping shapes but now from the ship came Bufco, with a needle-beam puncturing moths from the sky, and others behind him.

Bernisty carried Kathryn back to the ship. He took her to the surgery, laid her on the pallet. "Cut that radio out of her," he told the medic. "Make her normal, and then if she gets information to the Kay, they'll deserve it."

He found Berel in his quarters, lounging in garments of seductive diaphane. He swept her with an indifferent glance.

Conquering her perturbation she asked, "Well, what now, Bernisty?"

"We start again!"

"Again? When the Kay can sweep the world of life so easy?"

"This time we work differently."

"So?"

"Do you know the ecology of Kerrykirk, the Kay capitol world?"

"No."

"In six months—you will find New Earth as close a duplicate as we are able."

"But that is foolhardy! What other pests will the Kay know so well as those of their own world?"

"Those are my own views."

Bernisty presently went to the surgery. The medic handed him the international radio. Bernisty stared. "What are these—these little spores?"

"They are persuaders," said the medic. "They can be easily triggered to red-heat...."

Bernisty said abruptly, "Is she awake?"

"Yes."

Bernisty looked down into the pale face. "You have no more radio."

"I know."

"Will you spy any longer?"

"No. I give you my loyalty, my love."

Bernisty nodded, touched her face, turned, left the room, went to give his orders for a new planet.

Bernisty ordered stocks from Blue Star: Kerrykirk flora and fauna exclusively and set them out as conditions justified. Three months passed uneventfully. The plants of Kerrykirk throve; the air became rich; New Earth felt its first rains.

Kerrykirk trees and cycads sprouted, grew high, forced by growth hormones; the plains grew knee-deep with Kerrykirk grasses.

Then once again came the Kay ships; and now it was as if they played a sly game, conscious of power. The first infestations were only mild harassments.

Bernisty grinned, and released Kerrykirk amphibians into the new puddles. Now the Kay ships came at almost regular intervals, and each vessel brought pests more virulent or voracious; and the *Beaudry* technicians worked incessantly countering the successive invasions.

There was grumbling; Bernisty sent those who wished to go home to Blue Star. Berel departed; her time as a play-girl was finished. Bernisty felt a trace of guilt as she bade him dignified farewell. When he returned to his quarters and found Kathryn there, the guilt disappeared.

The Kay ships came; a new horde of hungry creatures to devastate the land.

Some of the crew cried defeat, "Where will it end? It is incessant; let us give up this thankless task!"

Others spoke of war. "Is not New Earth already a battleground?"

Bernisty waved a careless hand. "Patience, patience; just one more month."

"Why one more month?"

"Do you not understand? The Kay ecologists are straining their laboratories breeding these pests!"

"Ah!"

One more month, one more Kay visitation, a new rain of violent life, eager to combat the life of New Earth.

"Now!" said Bernisty.

The *Beaudry* technicians collected the latest arrivals, the most effective of the previous cargoes; they were bred; the seeds, spores, eggs, prepared carefully stored, packed.

One day a ship left New Earth and flew to Kerrykirk, the holds bulging with the most desperately violent enemies of Kerrykirk life that Kerrykirk scientists could find. The ship returned to New Earth with its holds empty. Not till six months later did news of the greatest plagues in history seep out past Kay censorship.

During this time there were no Kay visits to New Earth. "And if they are discreet," Bernisty told the serious man from Blue Star who had come to replace him, "they will never come again. They are too vulnerable to their own pests—so long as we maintain a Kerrykirk ecology."

"Protective coloration, you might say," remarked the new governor of New Earth with a thin-lipped smile.

"Yes, you might say so."

"And what do you do, Bernisty?"

Bernisty listened. A far-off hum came to their ears. "That," said Bernisty, "is the *Blauelm*, arriving from Blue Star. And it's mine for another flight, another exploration."

"You seek another New Earth?" And the thin-lipped smile became broader, with the unconscious superiority the settled man feels for the wanderer.

"Perhaps I'll even find Old Earth....Hm...." He kicked up a bit of chrome stamped with the letters FORD. "Curious bit, this...."